YEHUDI MERCA[DO]

CHUNKY

GOES TO CAMP

YAY

HUDI

KATHERINE TEGEN BOOKS
Imprints of HarperCollins Publishers

HARPER
alley

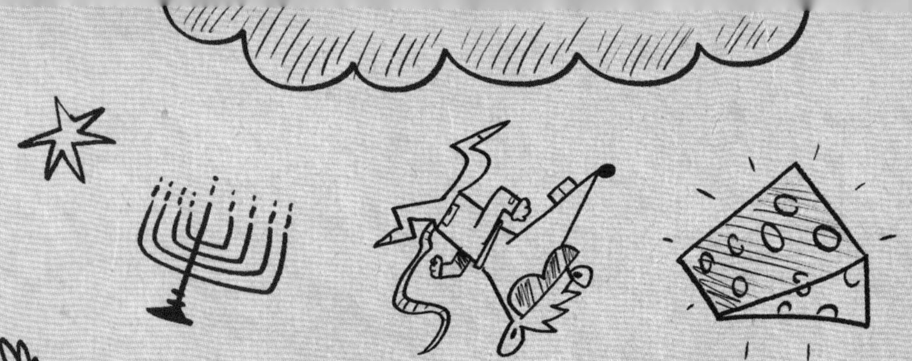

Dedicated to Pepe and Lonnie

Katherine Tegen Books is an imprint of HarperCollins Publishers.
HarperAlley is an imprint of HarperCollins Publishers.

Chunky Goes to Camp
Copyright © 2022 by SuperMercado Comics, Inc.
All rights reserved. Manufactured in Italy.

Library of Congress Control Number: 2021953134
ISBN 978-0-06-297282-8 – ISBN 978-0-06-297281-1 (pbk.)

The artist used Adobe Photoshop to create the digital illustrations
for this book.
Typography by Yehudi Mercado and Laura Mock
22 23 24 25 26   RTLO   10 9 8 7 6 5 4 3 2 1

❖

First Edition

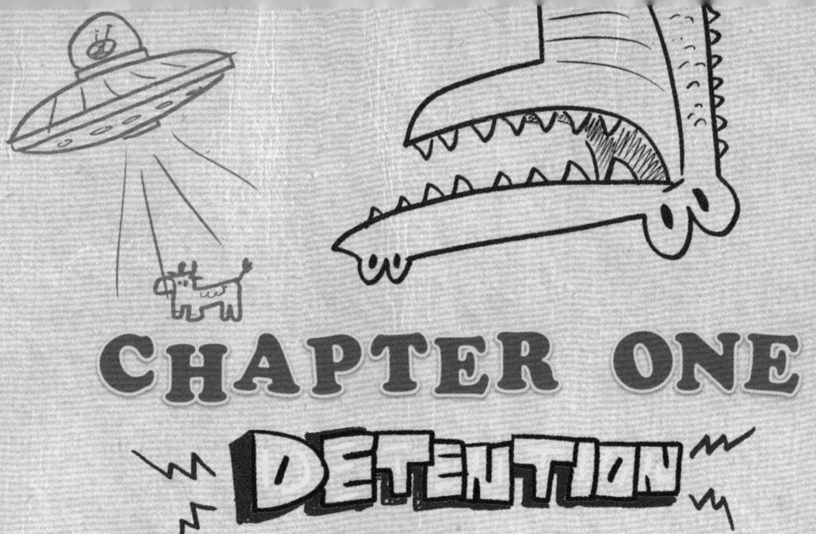

CHAPTER ONE

DETENTION

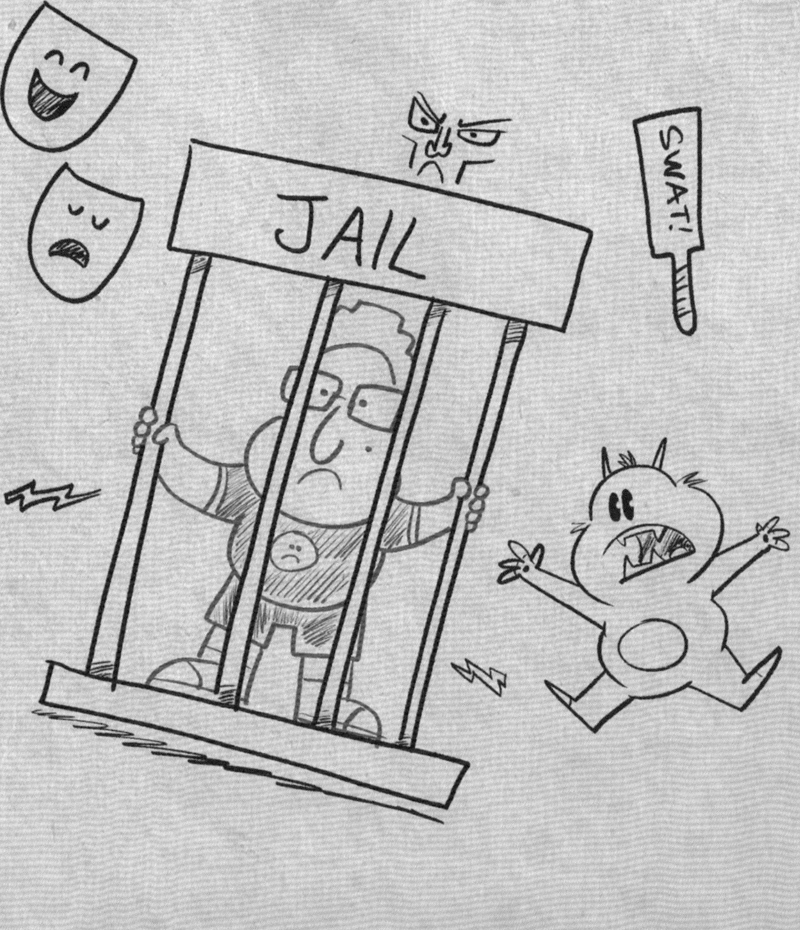
JAIL
SWAT!

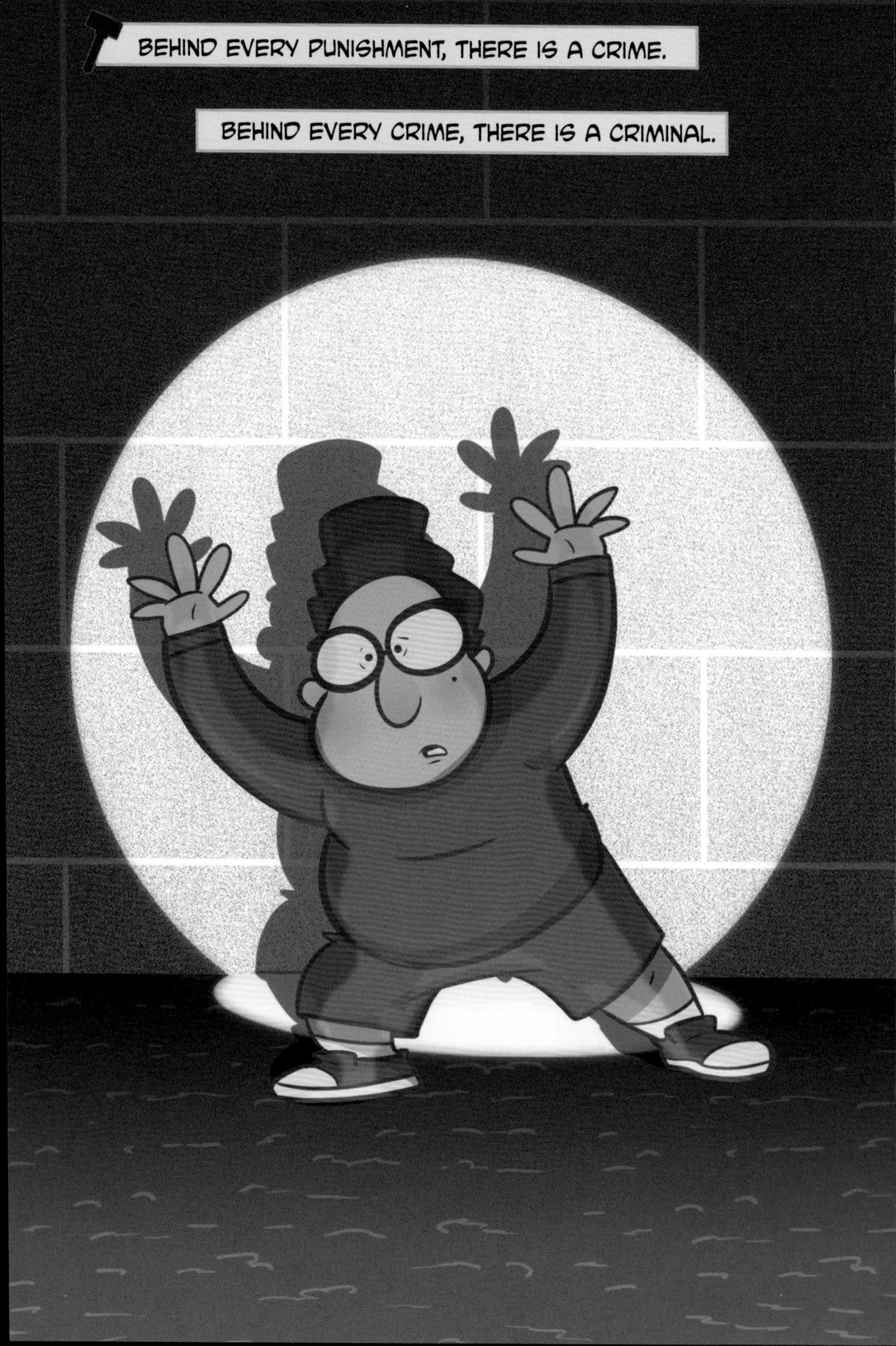
BEHIND EVERY PUNISHMENT, THERE IS A CRIME.
BEHIND EVERY CRIME, THERE IS A CRIMINAL.

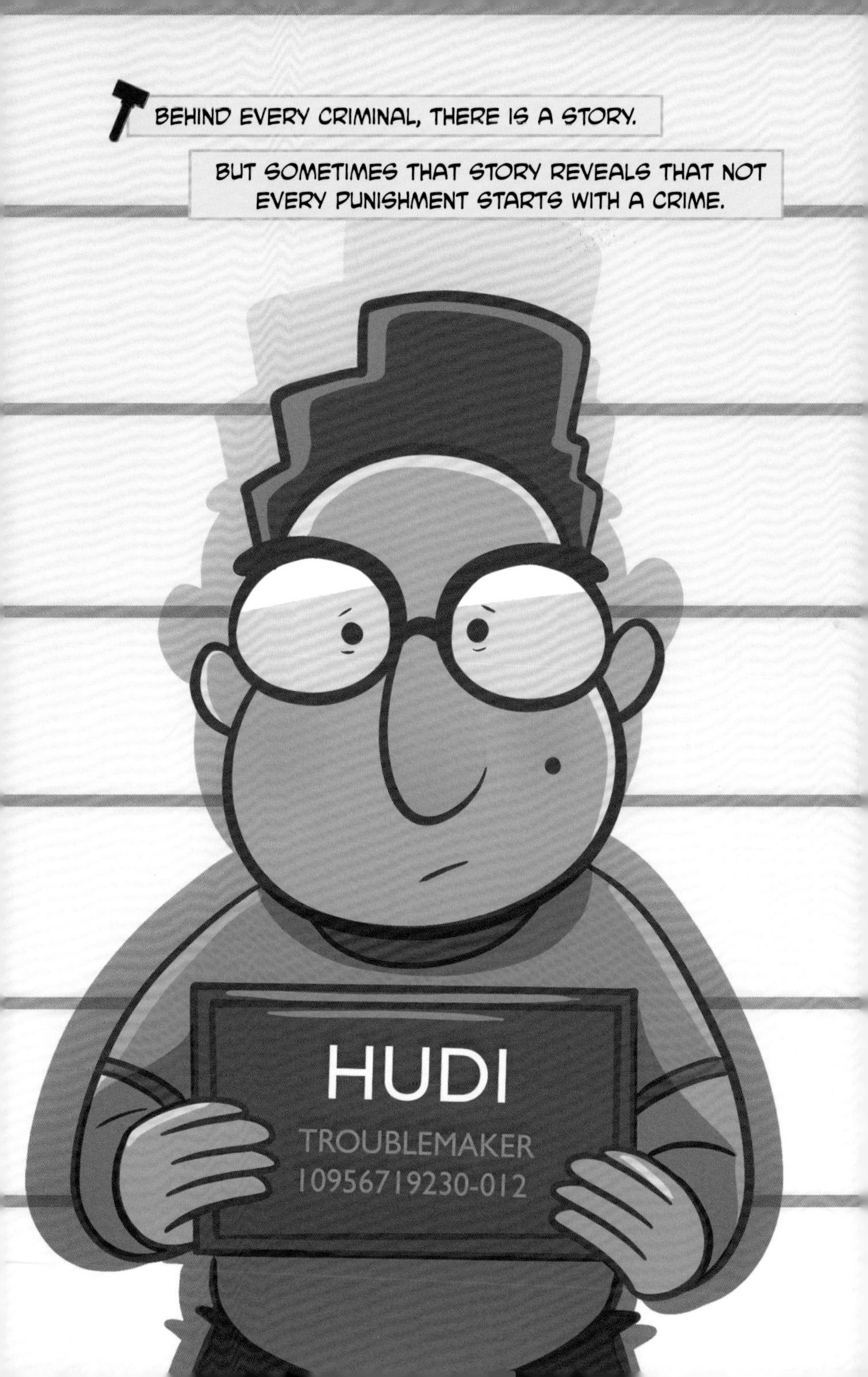
BEHIND EVERY CRIMINAL, THERE IS A STORY.
BUT SOMETIMES THAT STORY REVEALS THAT NOT EVERY PUNISHMENT STARTS WITH A CRIME.
HUDI
TROUBLEMAKER
10956719230-012

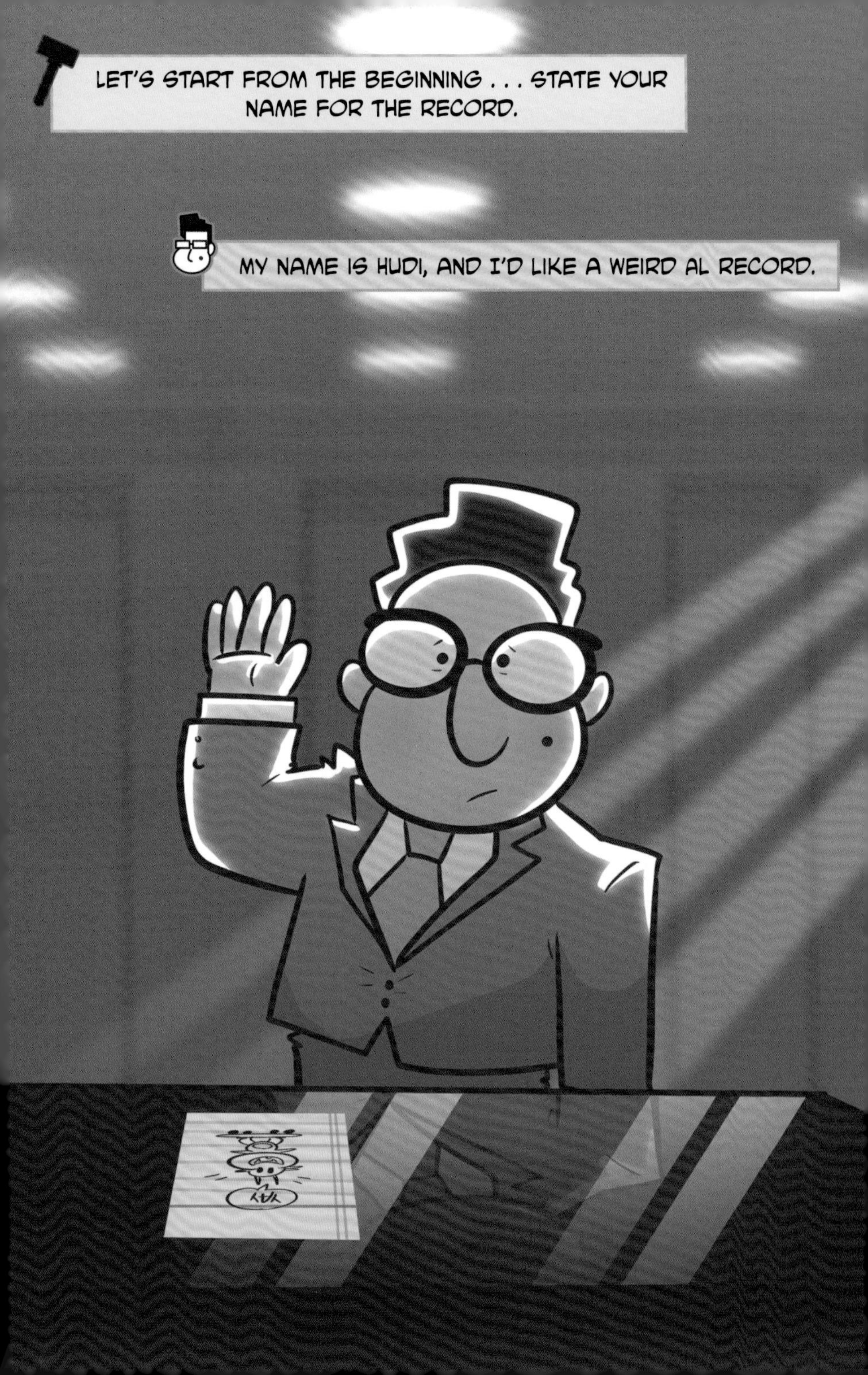
LET'S START FROM THE BEGINNING . . . STATE YOUR NAME FOR THE RECORD.
MY NAME IS HUDI, AND I'D LIKE A WEIRD AL RECORD.

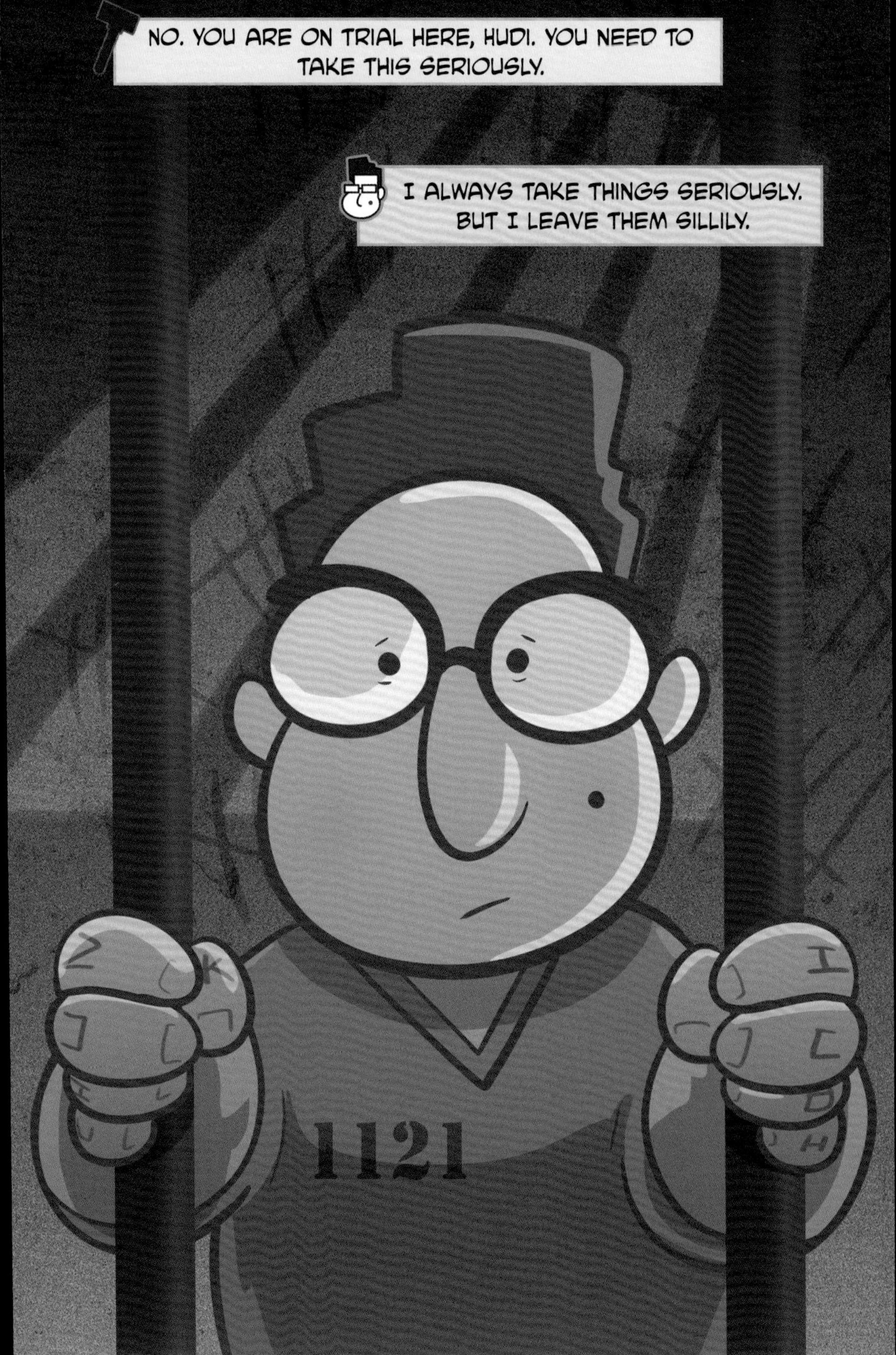
NO. YOU ARE ON TRIAL HERE, HUDI. YOU NEED TO TAKE THIS SERIOUSLY.
I ALWAYS TAKE THINGS SERIOUSLY. BUT I LEAVE THEM SILLILY.
1121

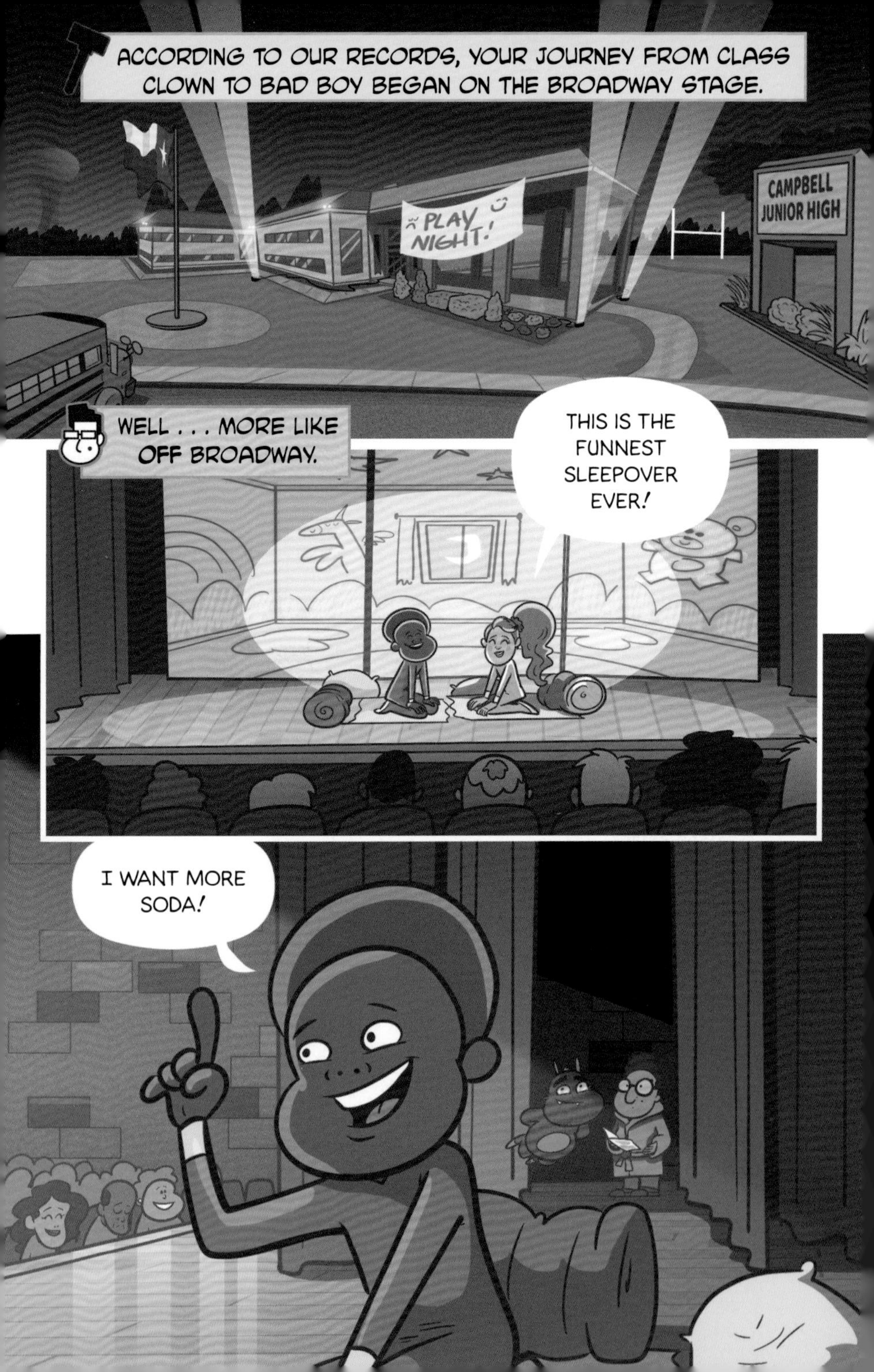
ACCORDING TO OUR RECORDS, YOUR JOURNEY FROM CLASS CLOWN TO BAD BOY BEGAN ON THE BROADWAY STAGE.
PLAY NIGHT!
CAMPBELL JUNIOR HIGH
WELL . . . MORE LIKE OFF BROADWAY.
THIS IS THE FUNNEST SLEEPOVER EVER!
I WANT MORE SODA!

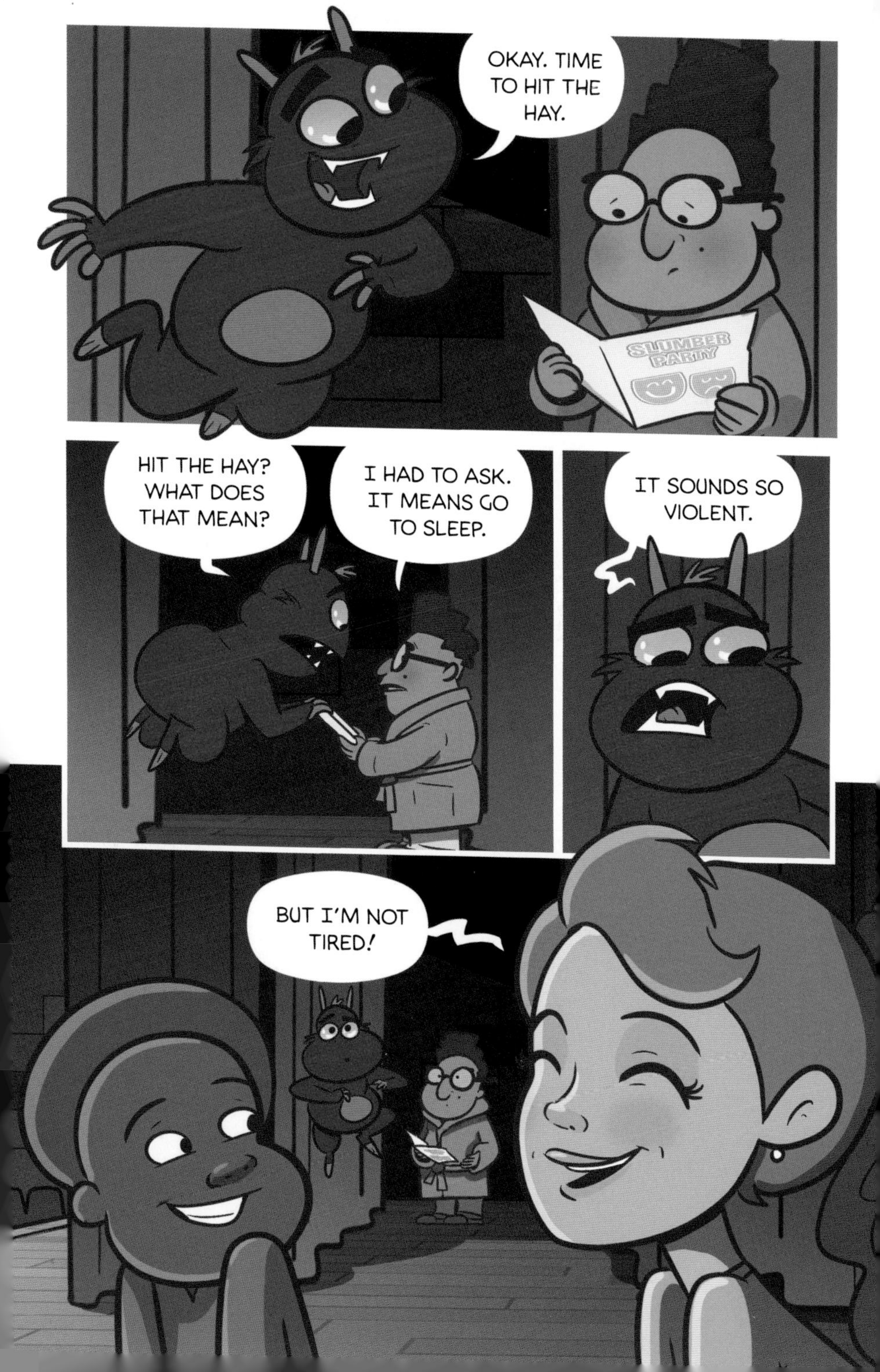
OKAY. TIME TO HIT THE HAY.
SLUMBER PARTY
HIT THE HAY? WHAT DOES THAT MEAN?
I HAD TO ASK. IT MEANS GO TO SLEEP.
IT SOUNDS SO VIOLENT.
BUT I'M NOT TIRED!

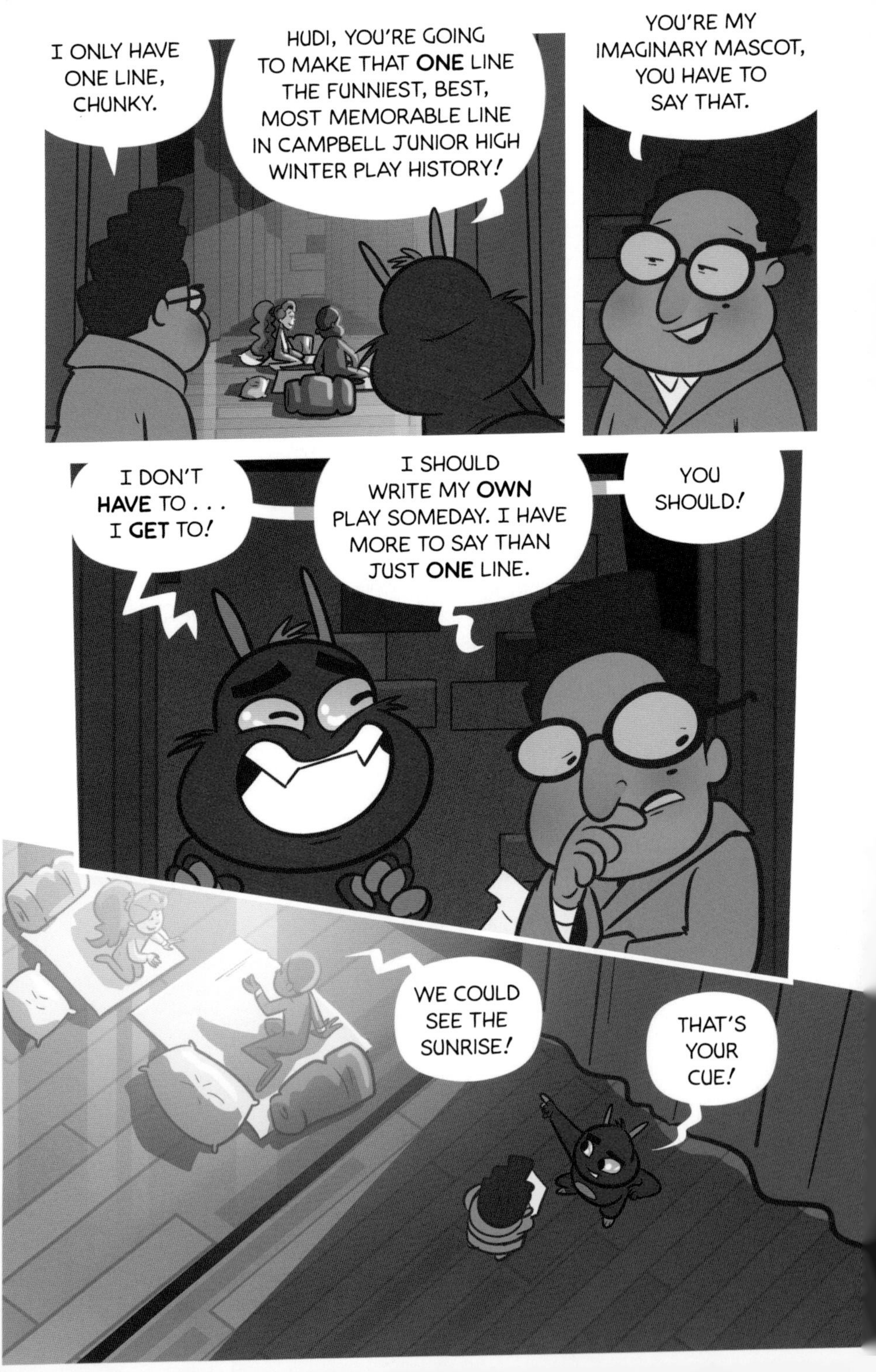
I ONLY HAVE ONE LINE, CHUNKY.
HUDI, YOU'RE GOING TO MAKE THAT **ONE** LINE THE FUNNIEST, BEST, MOST MEMORABLE LINE IN CAMPBELL JUNIOR HIGH WINTER PLAY HISTORY!
YOU'RE MY IMAGINARY MASCOT, YOU HAVE TO SAY THAT.
I DON'T **HAVE** TO . . . I **GET** TO!
I SHOULD WRITE MY **OWN** PLAY SOMEDAY. I HAVE MORE TO SAY THAN JUST **ONE** LINE.
YOU SHOULD!
WE COULD SEE THE SUNRISE!
THAT'S YOUR CUE!

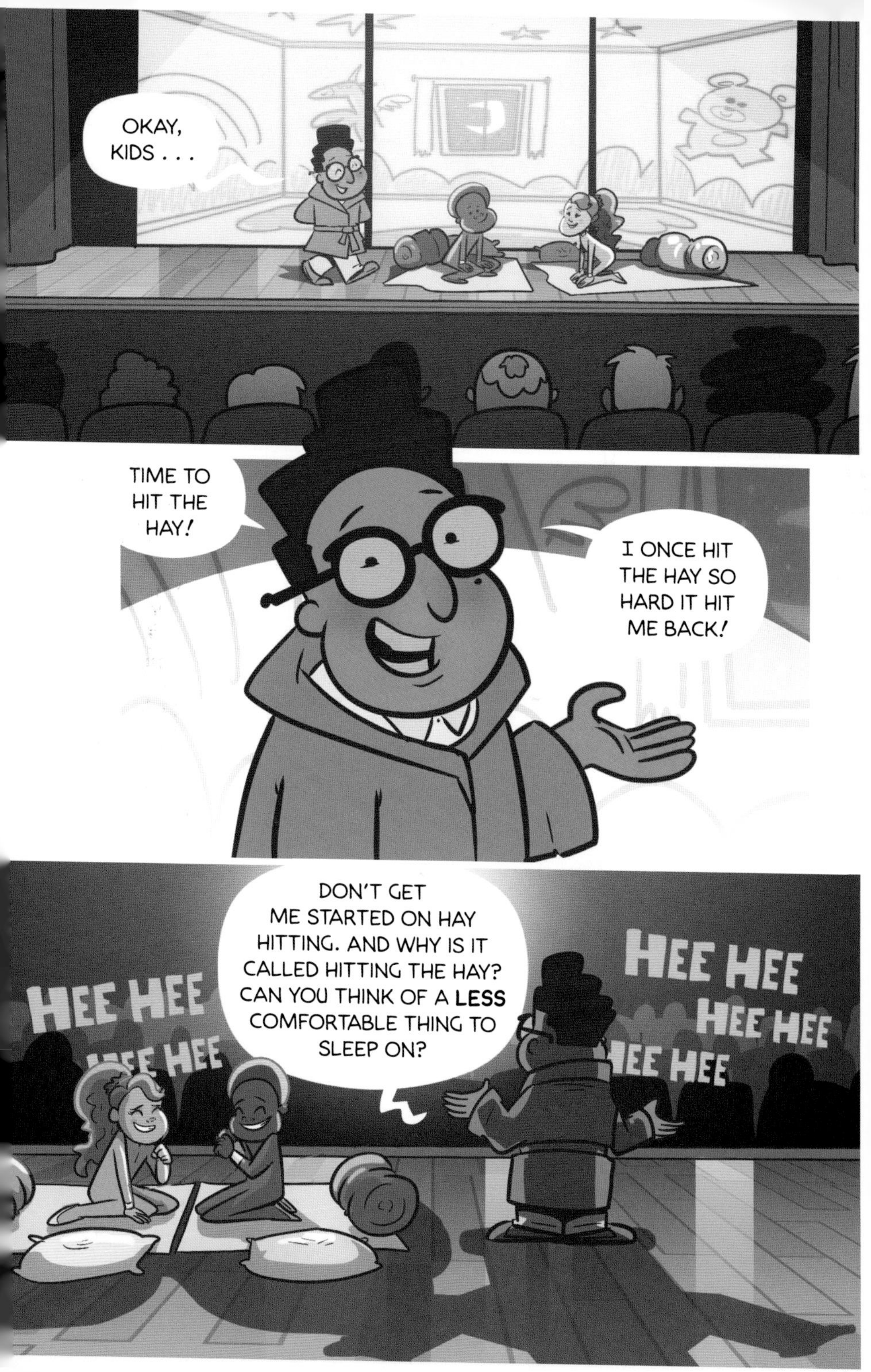
OKAY, KIDS . . .
TIME TO HIT THE HAY!
I ONCE HIT THE HAY SO HARD IT HIT ME BACK!
DON'T GET ME STARTED ON HAY HITTING. AND WHY IS IT CALLED HITTING THE HAY? CAN YOU THINK OF A **LESS** COMFORTABLE THING TO SLEEP ON?
HEE HEE
HEE HEE
HEE HEE
HEE HEE
HEE HEE

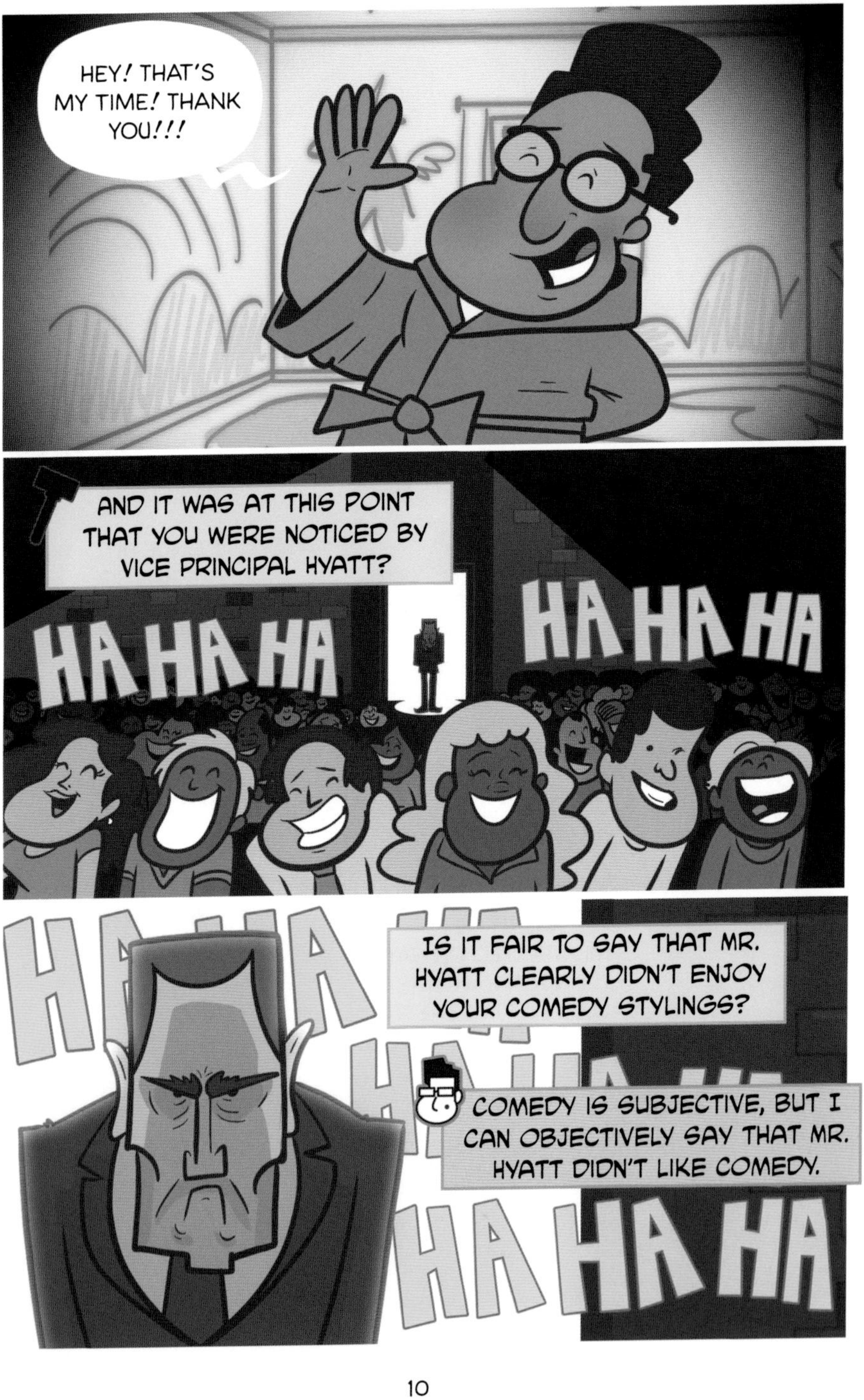
HEY! THAT'S MY TIME! THANK YOU!!!
AND IT WAS AT THIS POINT THAT YOU WERE NOTICED BY VICE PRINCIPAL HYATT?
HA HA HA
HA HA HA
IS IT FAIR TO SAY THAT MR. HYATT CLEARLY DIDN'T ENJOY YOUR COMEDY STYLINGS?
COMEDY IS SUBJECTIVE, BUT I CAN OBJECTIVELY SAY THAT MR. HYATT DIDN'T LIKE COMEDY.
HA HA HA

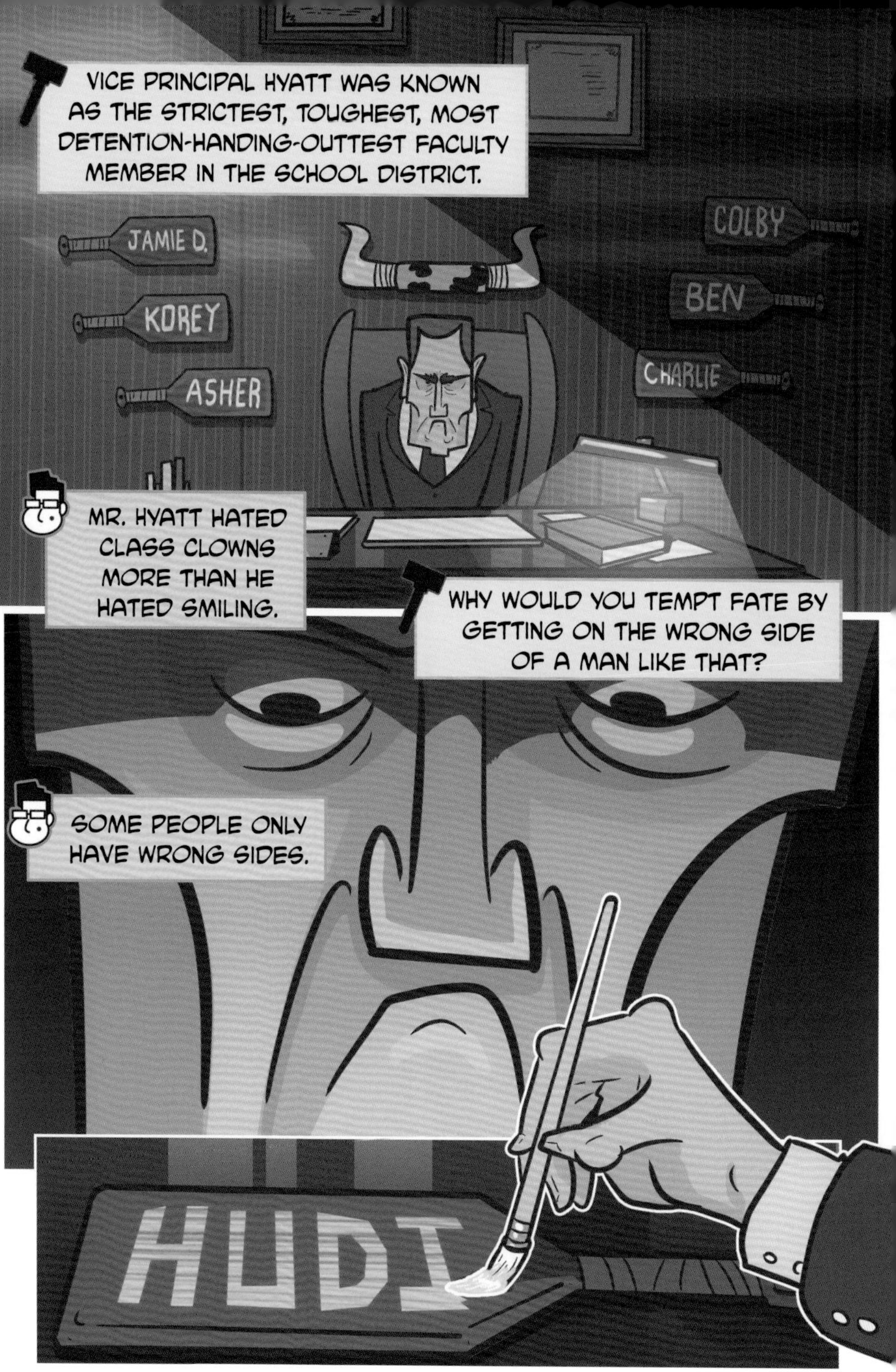
VICE PRINCIPAL HYATT WAS KNOWN AS THE STRICTEST, TOUGHEST, MOST DETENTION-HANDING-OUTTEST FACULTY MEMBER IN THE SCHOOL DISTRICT.
JAMIE D.
KOREY
ASHER
COLBY
BEN
CHARLIE
MR. HYATT HATED CLASS CLOWNS MORE THAN HE HATED SMILING.
WHY WOULD YOU TEMPT FATE BY GETTING ON THE WRONG SIDE OF A MAN LIKE THAT?
SOME PEOPLE ONLY HAVE WRONG SIDES.
HUDI

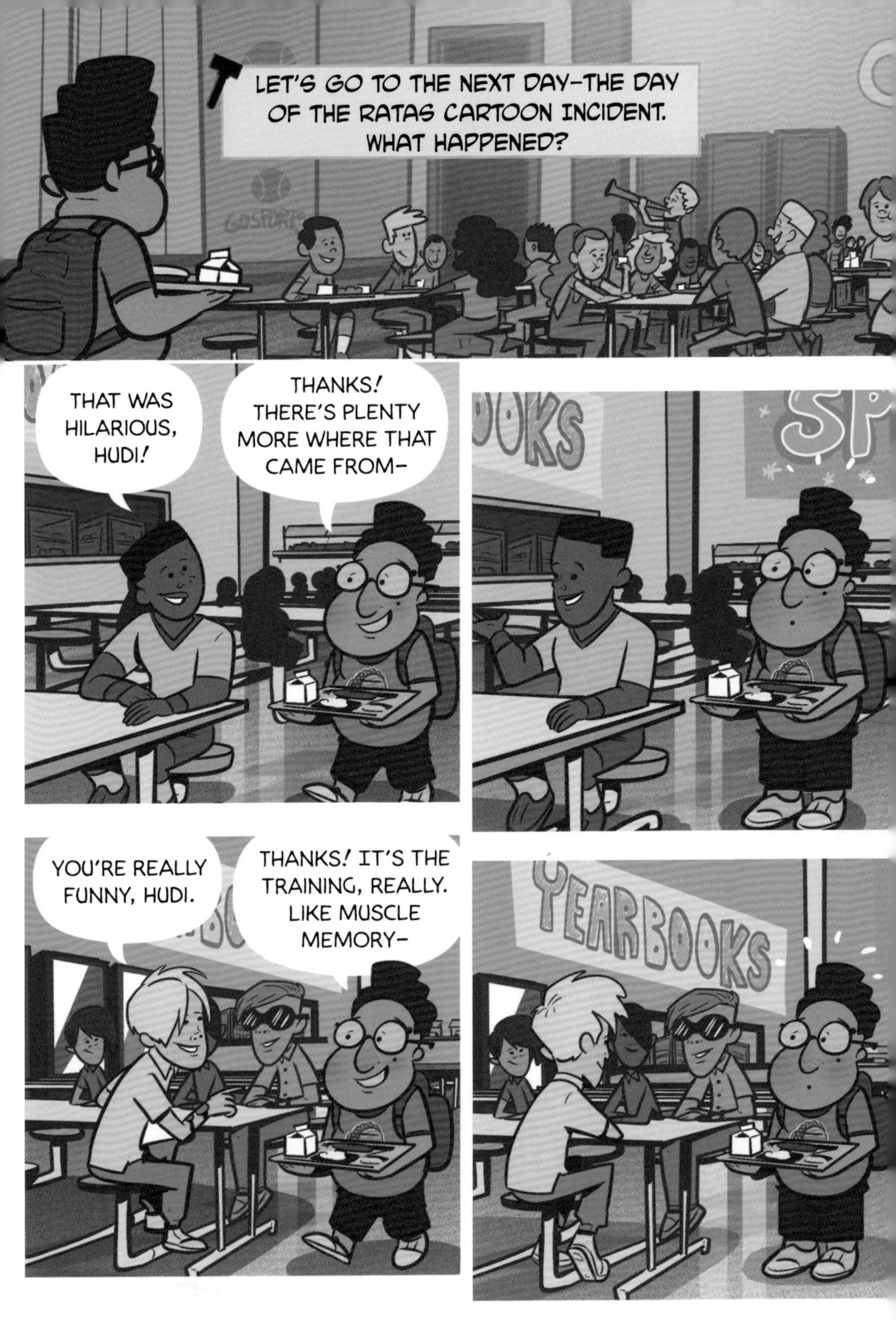
LET'S GO TO THE NEXT DAY—THE DAY OF THE RATAS CARTOON INCIDENT. WHAT HAPPENED?
THAT WAS HILARIOUS, HUDI!
THANKS! THERE'S PLENTY MORE WHERE THAT CAME FROM—
YEARBOOKS
YOU'RE REALLY FUNNY, HUDI.
THANKS! IT'S THE TRAINING, REALLY. LIKE MUSCLE MEMORY—
YEARBOOKS

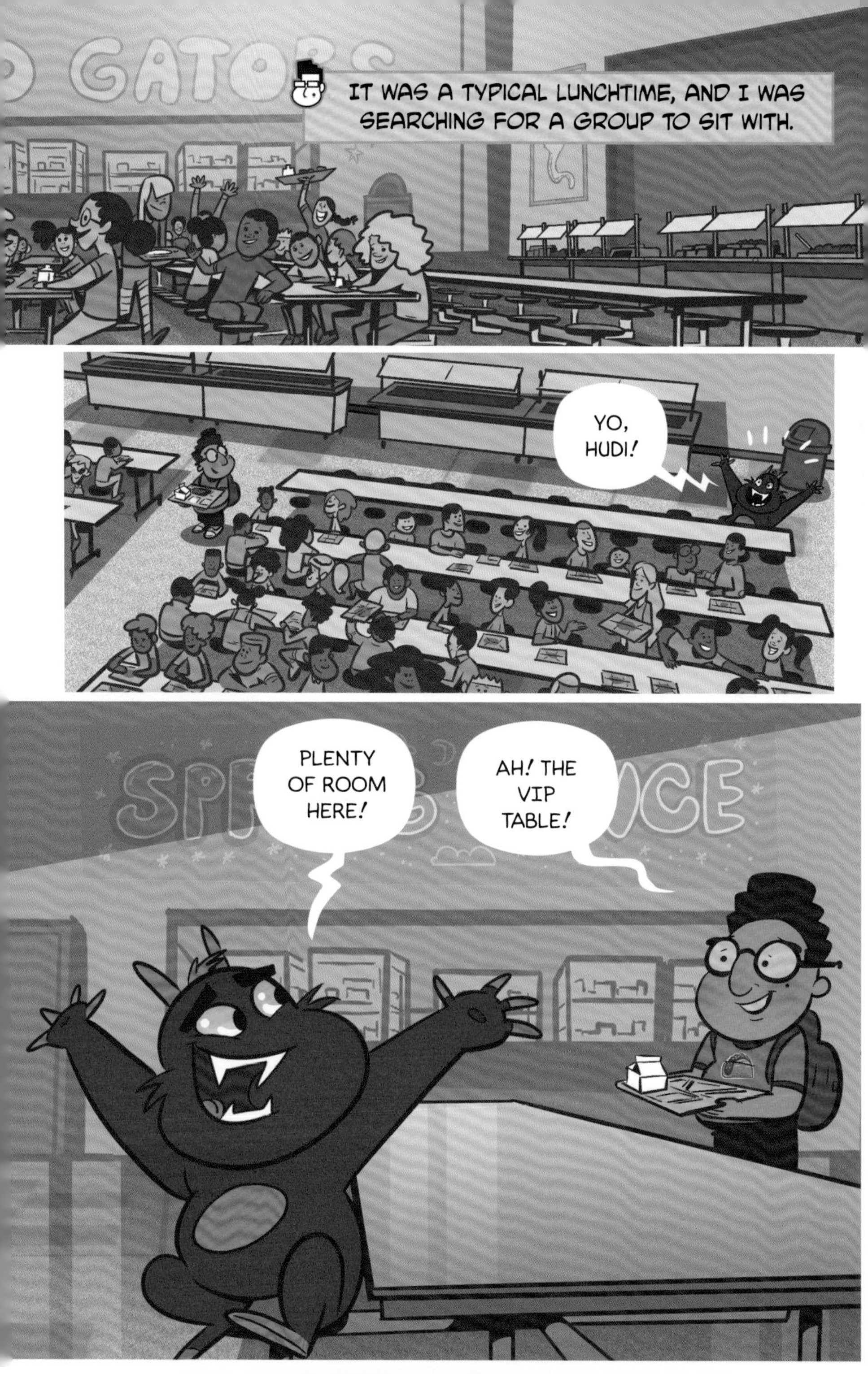
GATORS
IT WAS A TYPICAL LUNCHTIME, AND I WAS SEARCHING FOR A GROUP TO SIT WITH.
YO, HUDI!
PLENTY OF ROOM HERE!
AH! THE VIP TABLE!

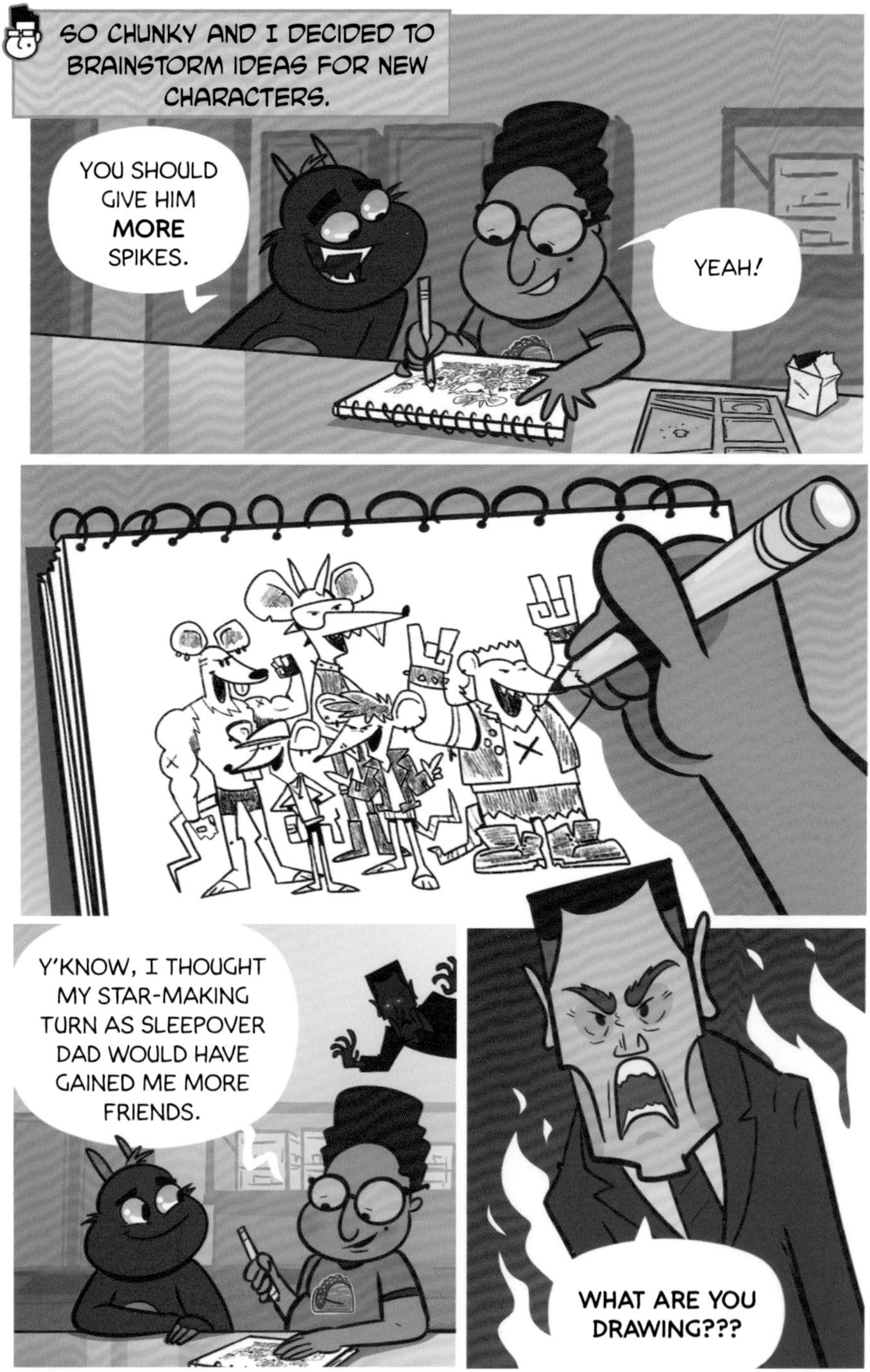
SO CHUNKY AND I DECIDED TO BRAINSTORM IDEAS FOR NEW CHARACTERS.
YOU SHOULD GIVE HIM **MORE** SPIKES.
YEAH!
Y'KNOW, I THOUGHT MY STAR-MAKING TURN AS SLEEPOVER DAD WOULD HAVE GAINED ME MORE FRIENDS.
WHAT ARE YOU DRAWING???

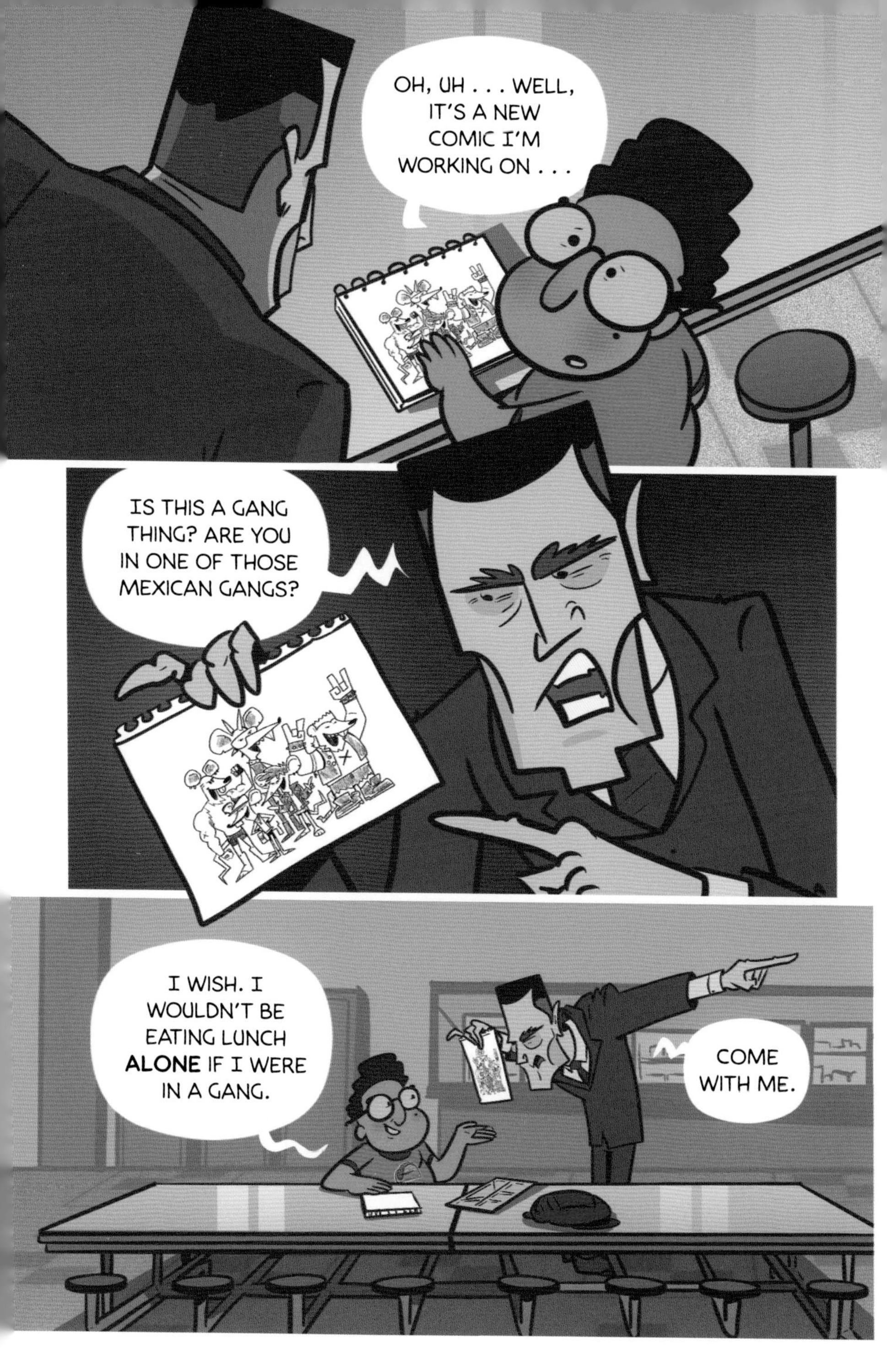
OH, UH . . . WELL, IT'S A NEW COMIC I'M WORKING ON . . .
IS THIS A GANG THING? ARE YOU IN ONE OF THOSE MEXICAN GANGS?
I WISH. I WOULDN'T BE EATING LUNCH **ALONE** IF I WERE IN A GANG.
COME WITH ME.

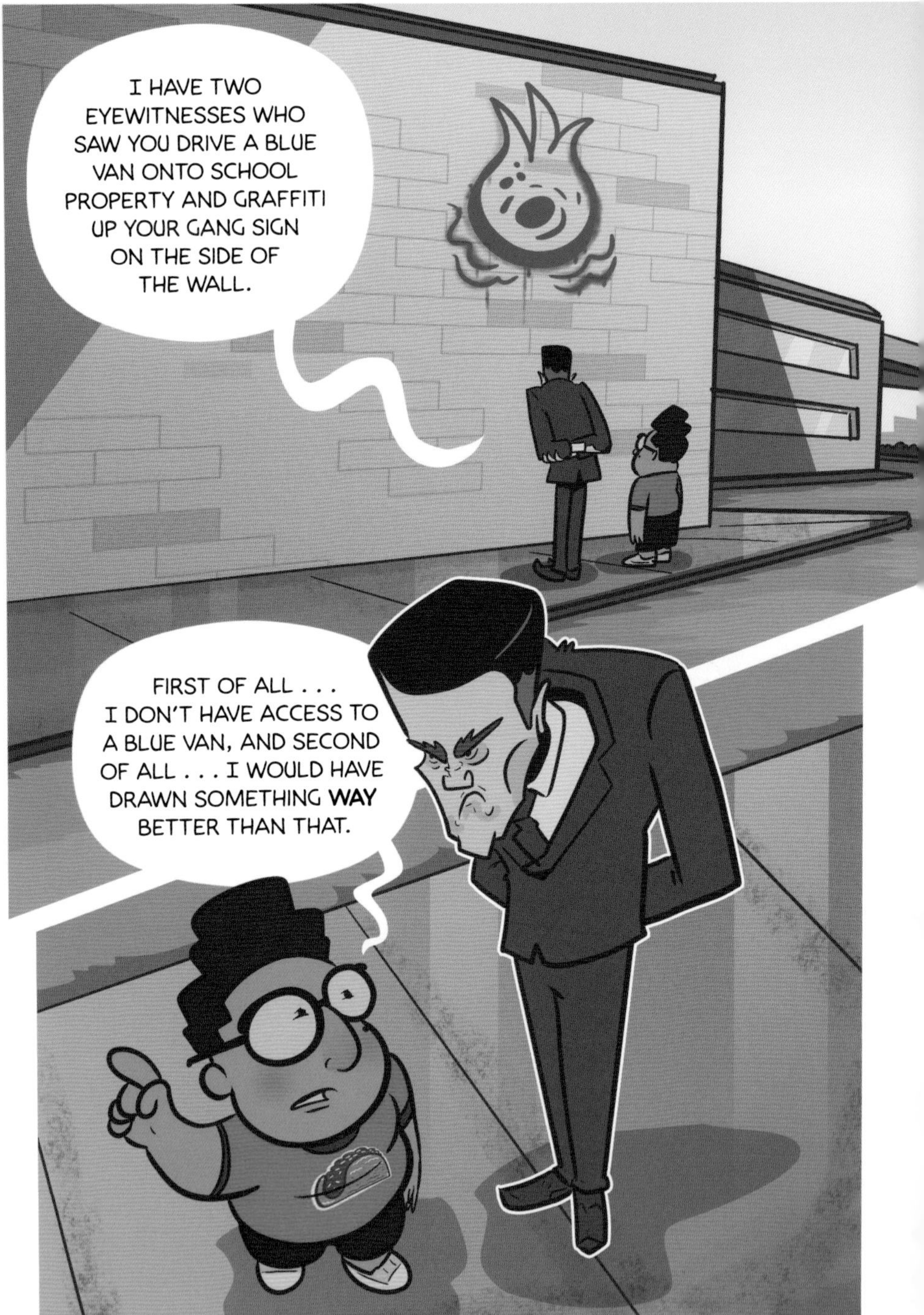
I HAVE TWO EYEWITNESSES WHO SAW YOU DRIVE A BLUE VAN ONTO SCHOOL PROPERTY AND GRAFFITI UP YOUR GANG SIGN ON THE SIDE OF THE WALL.
FIRST OF ALL . . . I DON'T HAVE ACCESS TO A BLUE VAN, AND SECOND OF ALL . . . I WOULD HAVE DRAWN SOMETHING **WAY** BETTER THAN THAT.

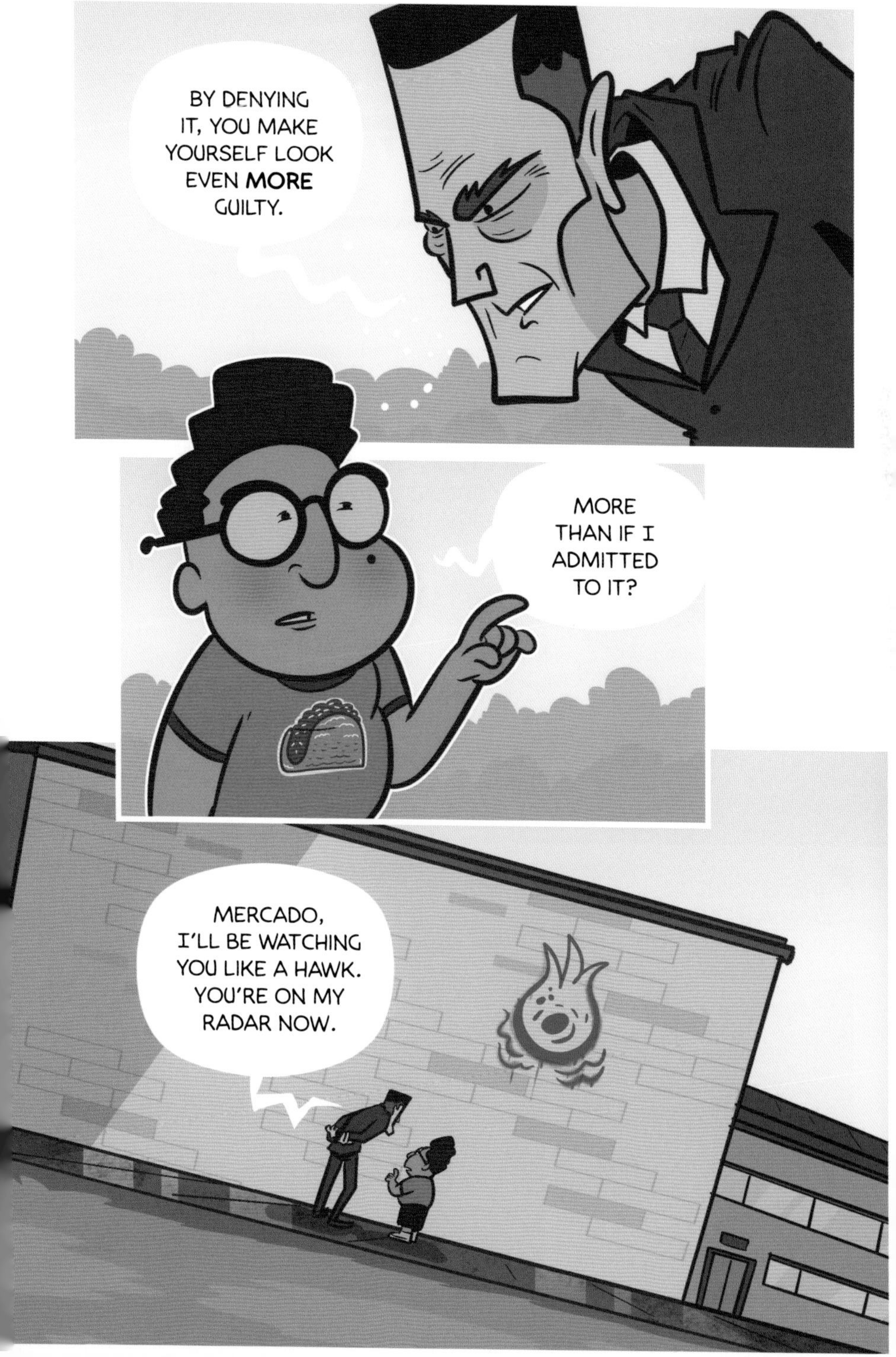
BY DENYING IT, YOU MAKE YOURSELF LOOK EVEN **MORE** GUILTY.
MORE THAN IF I ADMITTED TO IT?
MERCADO, I'LL BE WATCHING YOU LIKE A HAWK. YOU'RE ON MY RADAR NOW.

IT SEEMS AS THOUGH OLD MAN HYATT WAS KEEN ON PUNISHING YOU NO MATTER WHAT. HE HAD FINALLY FOUND HIS DISCIPLINARY WHITE WHALE.

DETENTION

WHILE I RESENT THE INSINUATION, I APPRECIATE THE LITERARY REFERENCE.

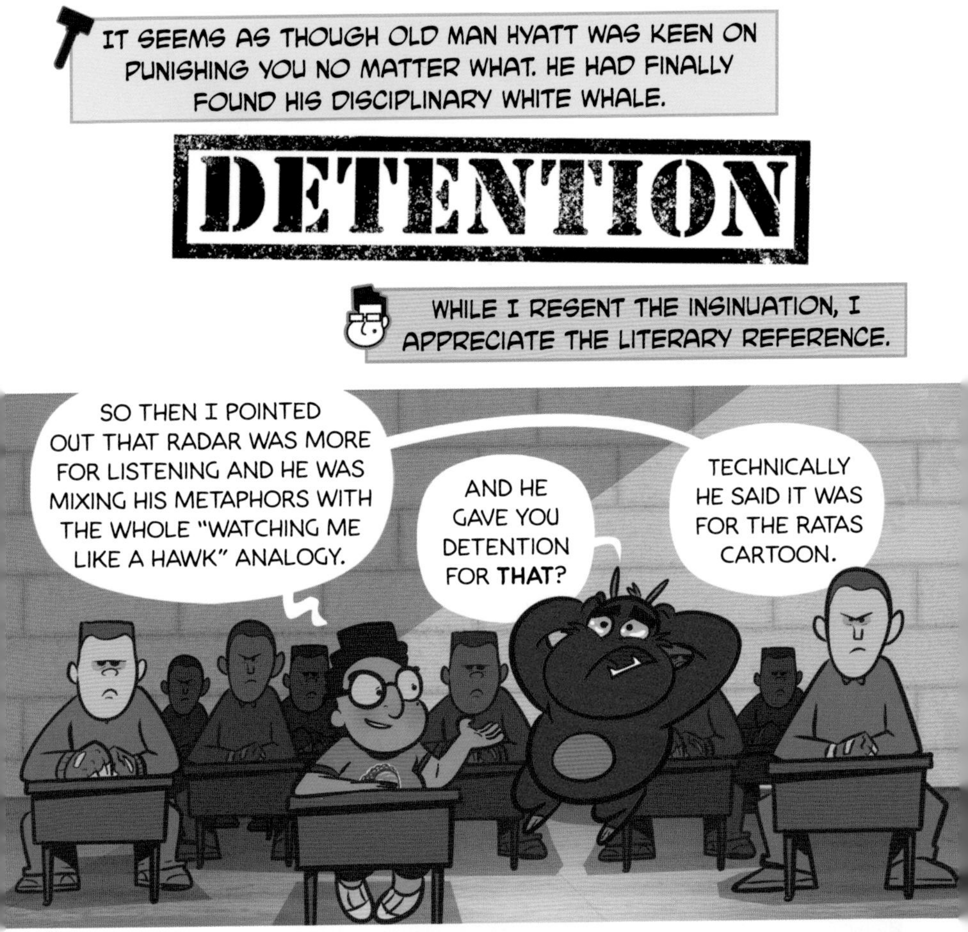
SO THEN I POINTED OUT THAT RADAR WAS MORE FOR LISTENING AND HE WAS MIXING HIS METAPHORS WITH THE WHOLE "WATCHING ME LIKE A HAWK" ANALOGY.
AND HE GAVE YOU DETENTION FOR **THAT**?
TECHNICALLY HE SAID IT WAS FOR THE RATAS CARTOON.

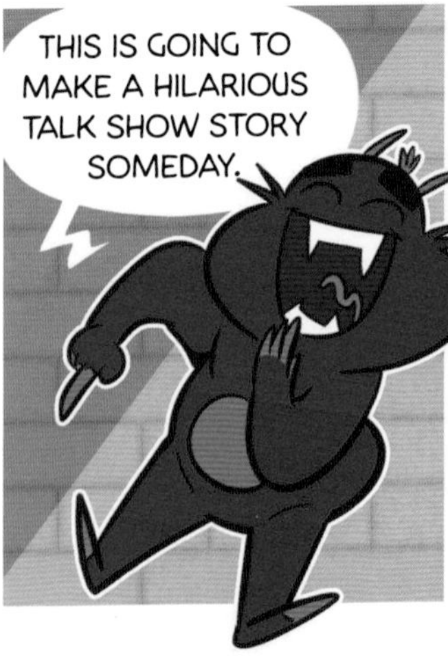
THIS IS GOING TO MAKE A HILARIOUS TALK SHOW STORY SOMEDAY.

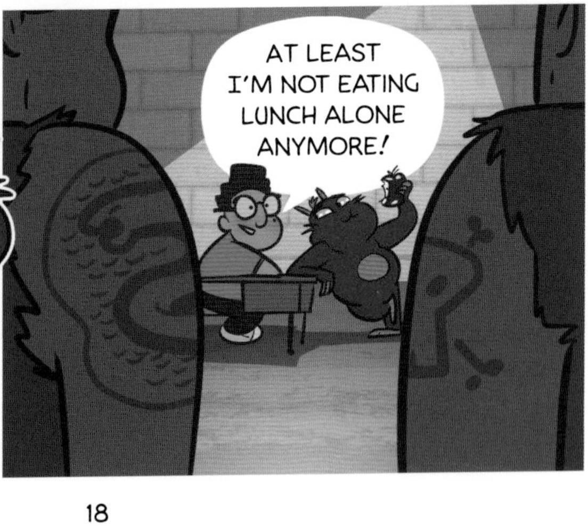
AT LEAST I'M NOT EATING LUNCH ALONE ANYMORE!

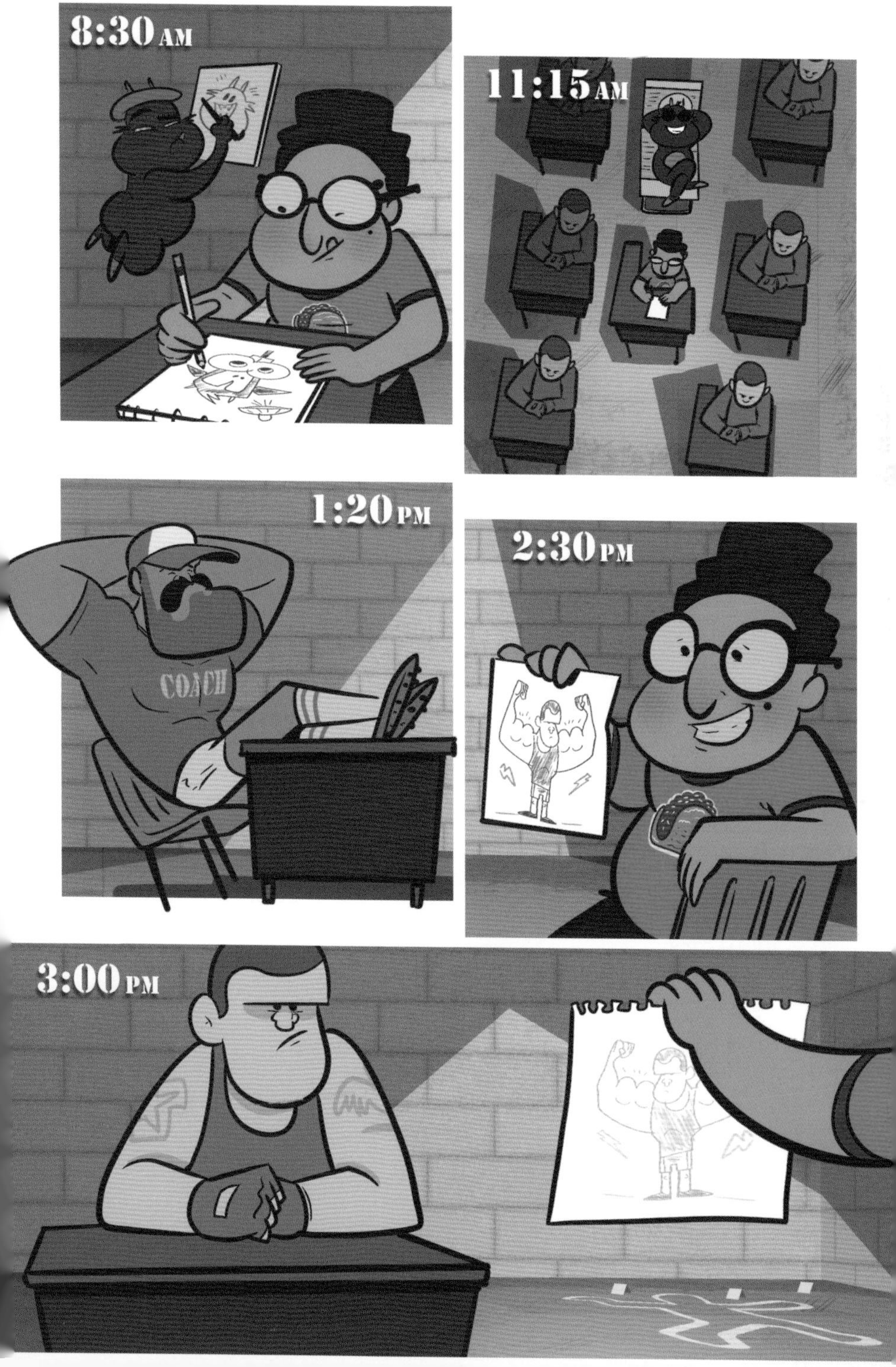
8:30 AM
11:15 AM
1:20 PM
COACH
2:30 PM
3:00 PM

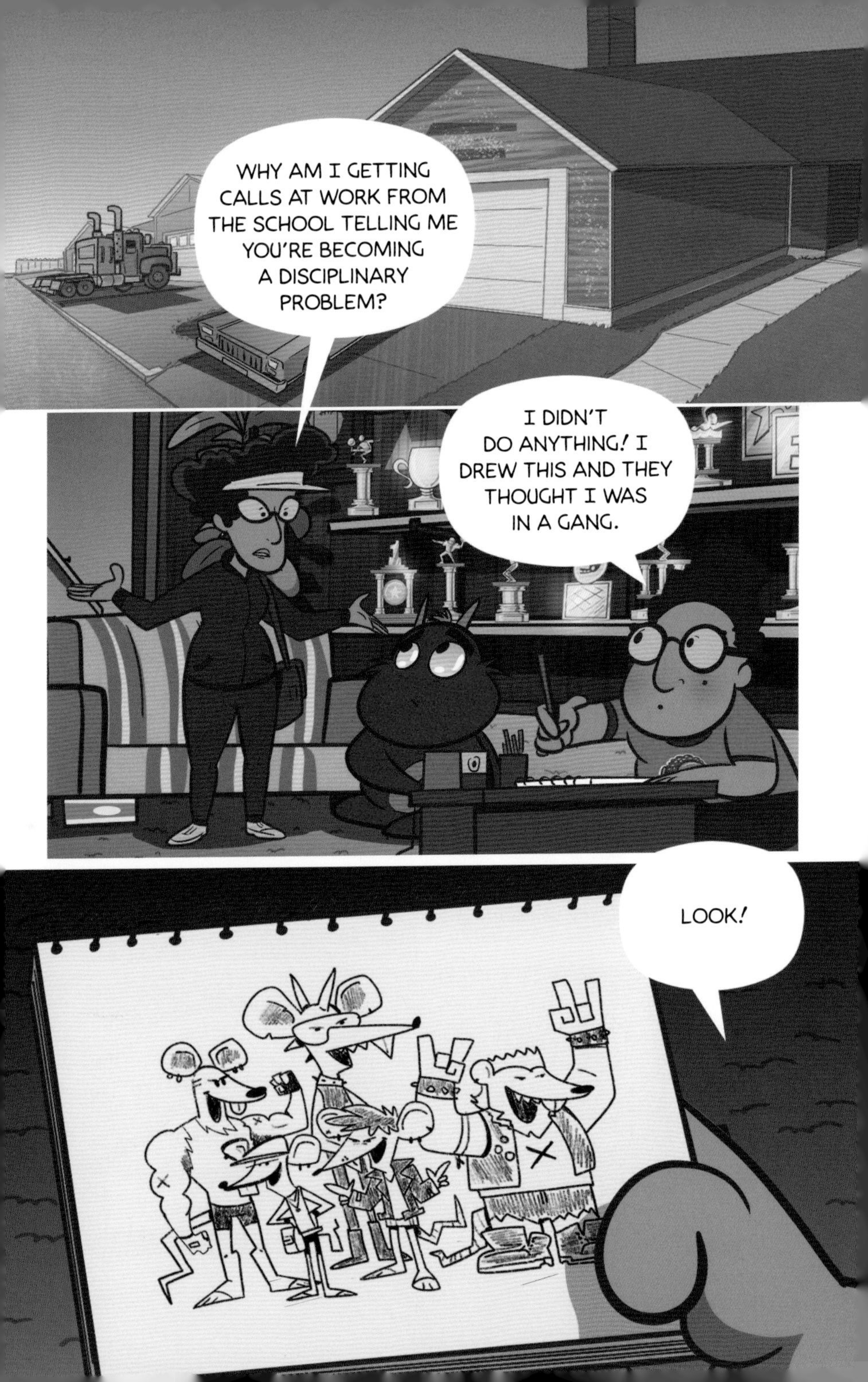
WHY AM I GETTING CALLS AT WORK FROM THE SCHOOL TELLING ME YOU'RE BECOMING A DISCIPLINARY PROBLEM?
I DIDN'T DO ANYTHING! I DREW THIS AND THEY THOUGHT I WAS IN A GANG.
LOOK!

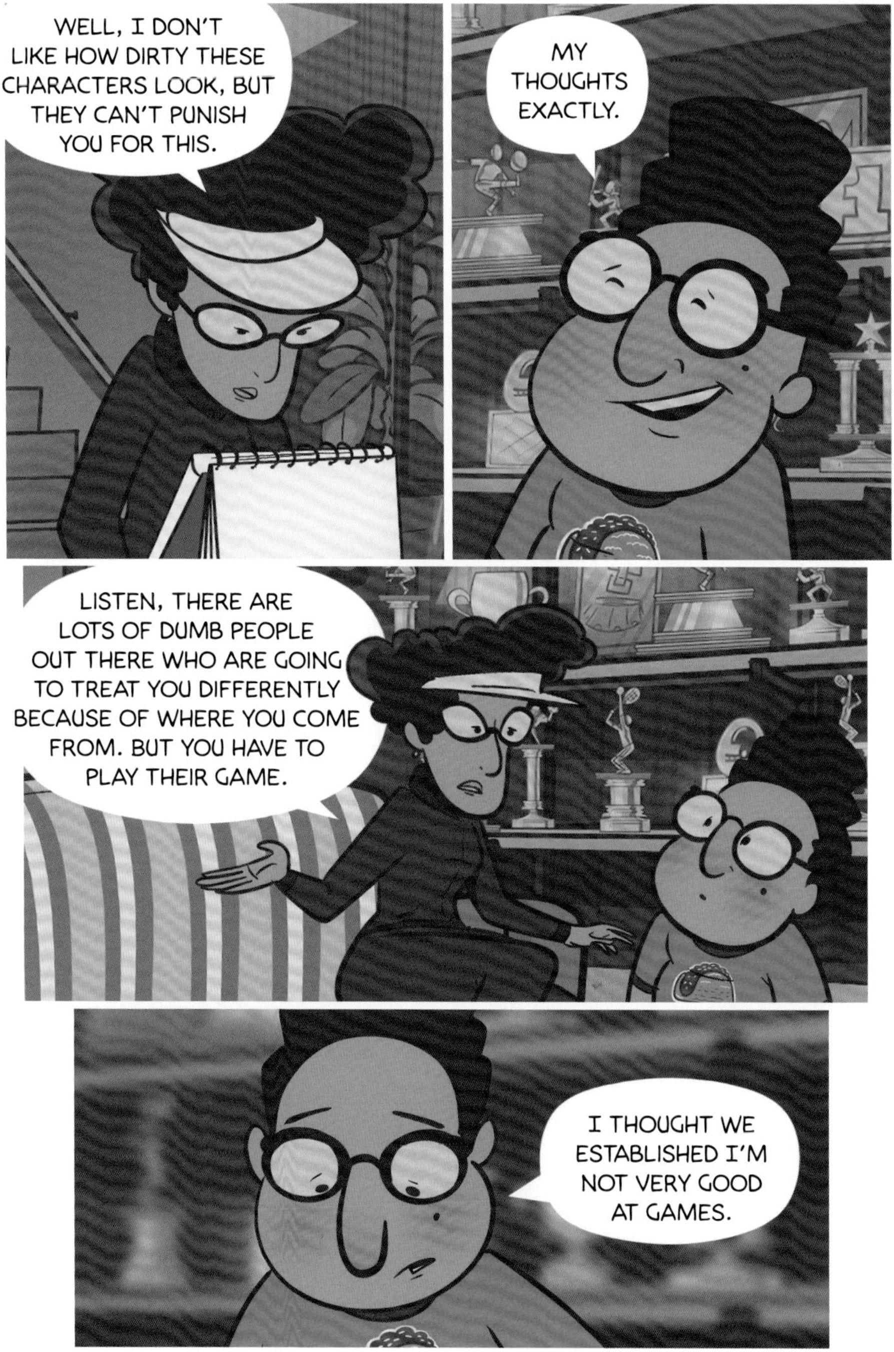
WELL, I DON'T LIKE HOW DIRTY THESE CHARACTERS LOOK, BUT THEY CAN'T PUNISH YOU FOR THIS.
MY THOUGHTS EXACTLY.
LISTEN, THERE ARE LOTS OF DUMB PEOPLE OUT THERE WHO ARE GOING TO TREAT YOU DIFFERENTLY BECAUSE OF WHERE YOU COME FROM. BUT YOU HAVE TO PLAY THEIR GAME.
I THOUGHT WE ESTABLISHED I'M NOT VERY GOOD AT GAMES.

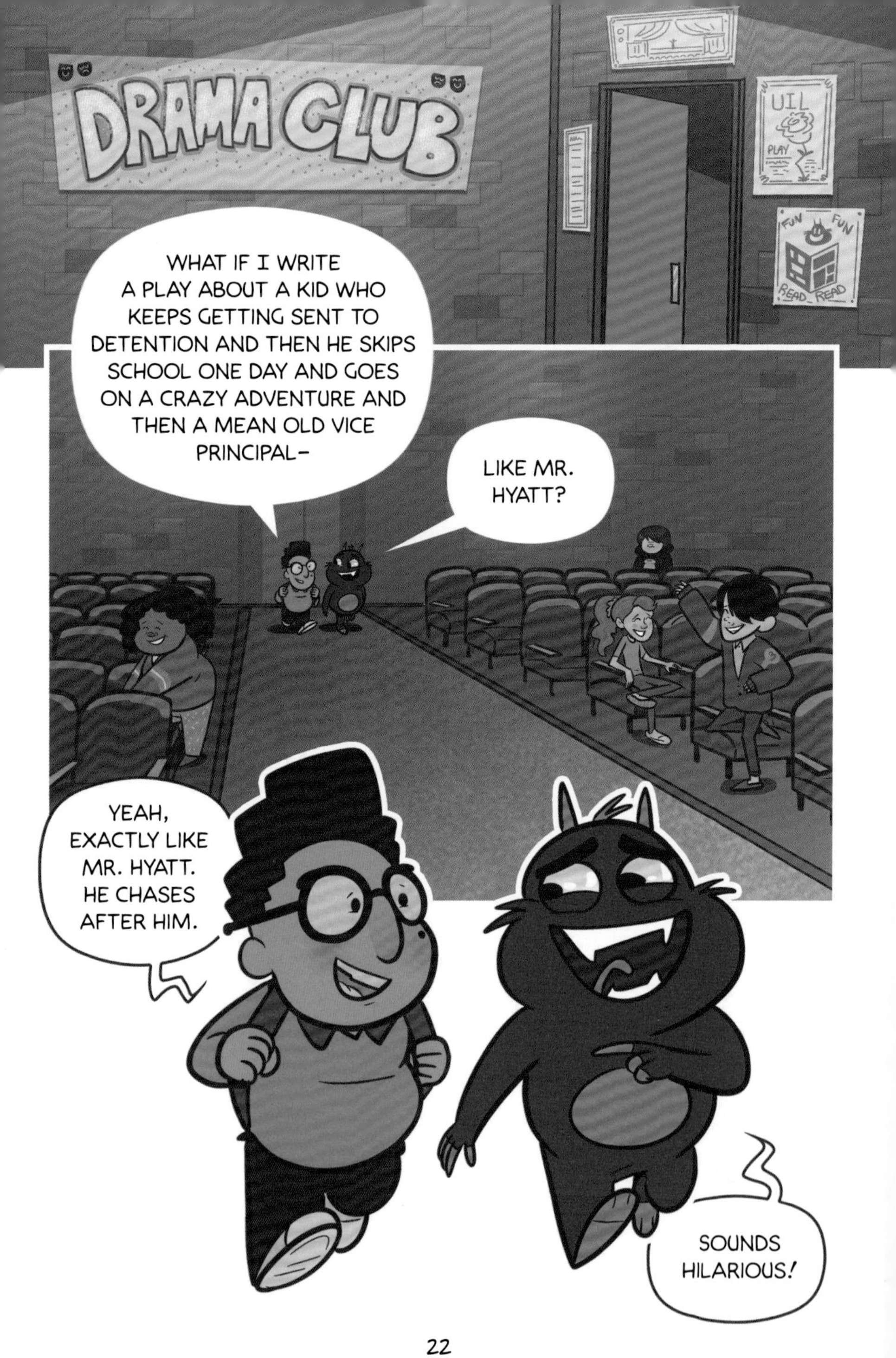
DRAMA CLUB
UIL PLAY
FUN FUN READ READ
WHAT IF I WRITE A PLAY ABOUT A KID WHO KEEPS GETTING SENT TO DETENTION AND THEN HE SKIPS SCHOOL ONE DAY AND GOES ON A CRAZY ADVENTURE AND THEN A MEAN OLD VICE PRINCIPAL–
LIKE MR. HYATT?
YEAH, EXACTLY LIKE MR. HYATT. HE CHASES AFTER HIM.
SOUNDS HILARIOUS!

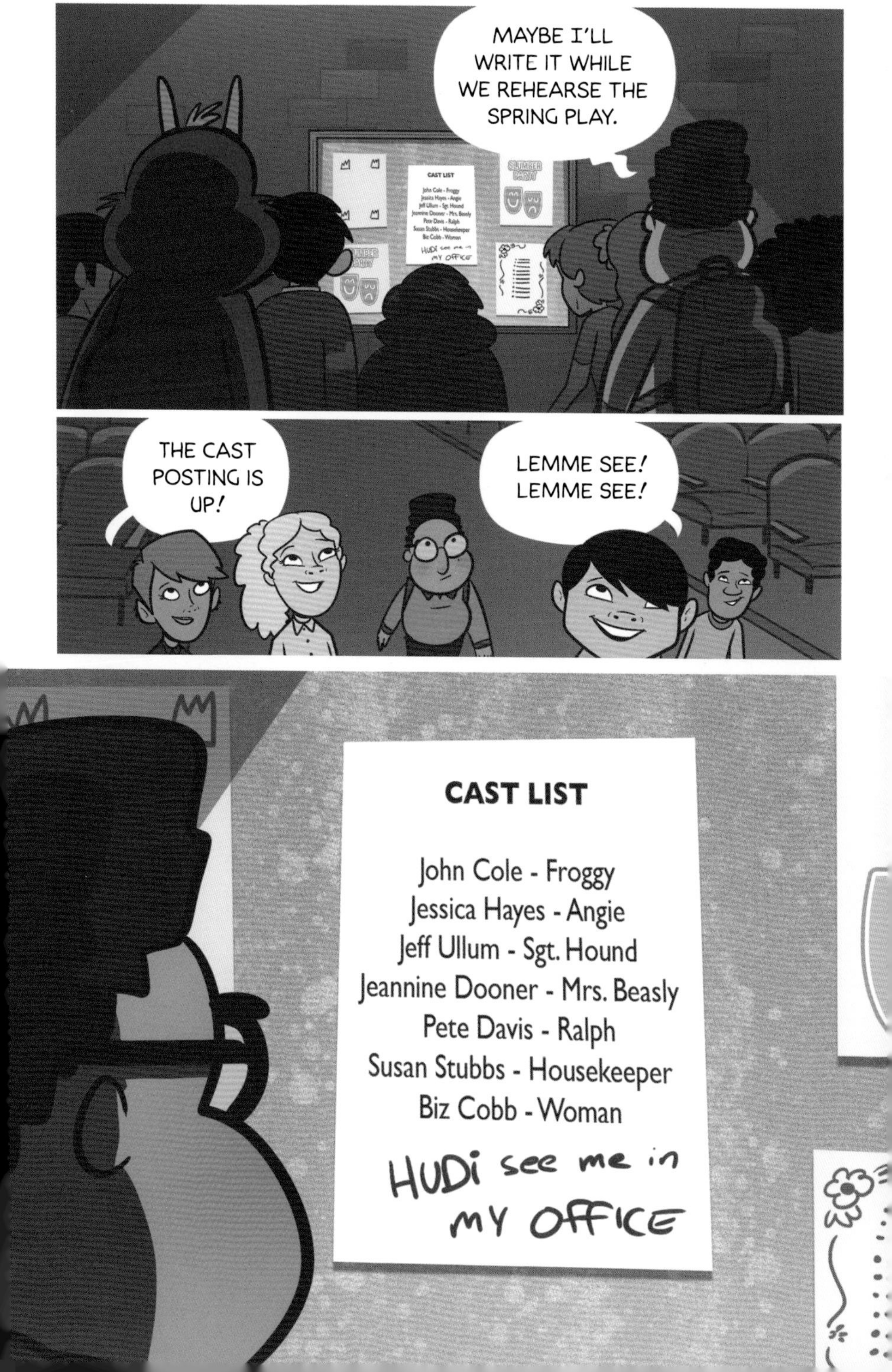
MAYBE I'LL WRITE IT WHILE WE REHEARSE THE SPRING PLAY.
THE CAST POSTING IS UP!
LEMME SEE! LEMME SEE!
CAST LIST
John Cole - Froggy
Jessica Hayes - Angie
Jeff Ullum - Sgt. Hound
Jeannine Dooner - Mrs. Beasly
Pete Davis - Ralph
Susan Stubbs - Housekeeper
Biz Cobb - Woman
HUDI see me in MY OFFICE

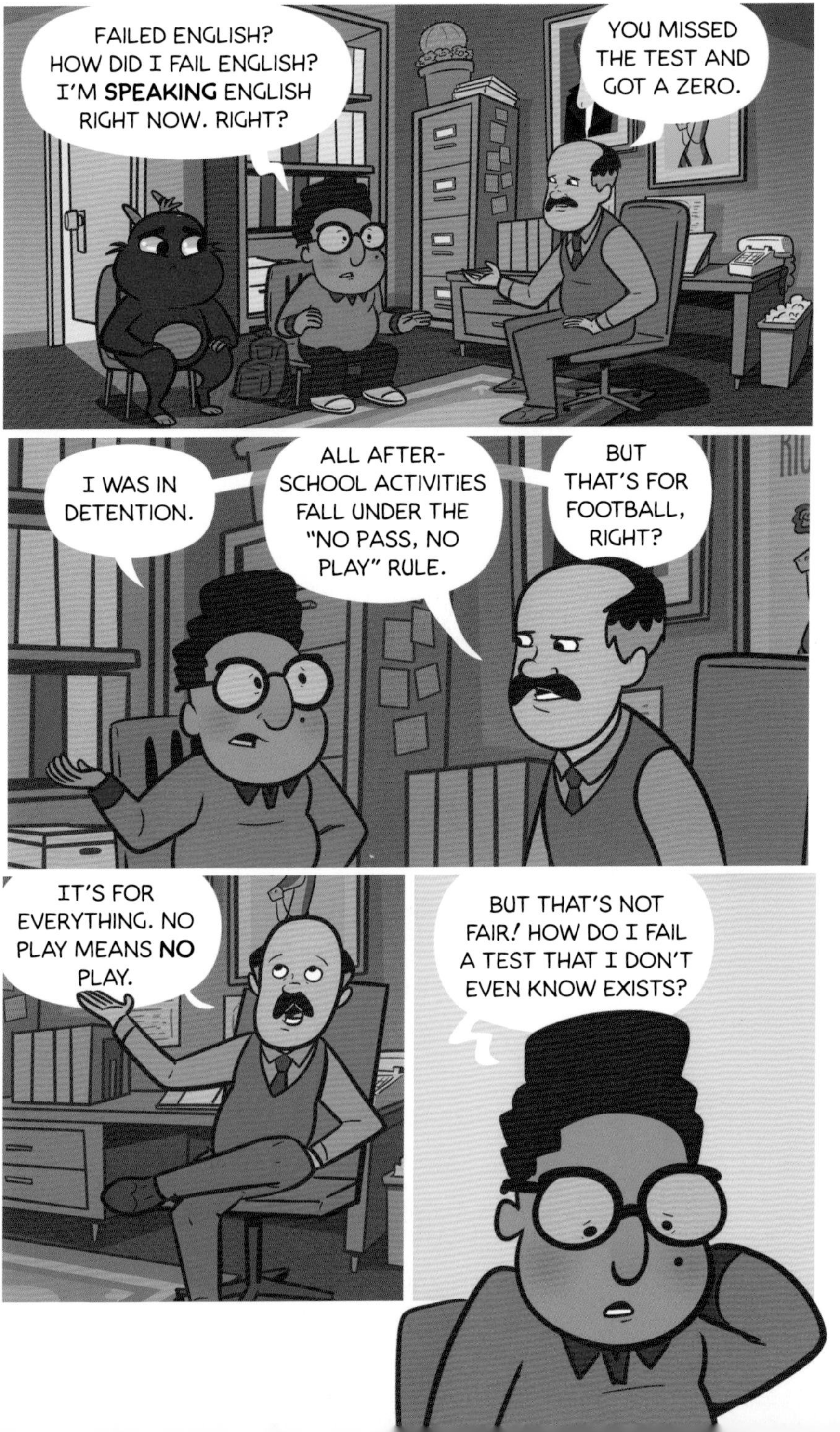
FAILED ENGLISH? HOW DID I FAIL ENGLISH? I'M **SPEAKING** ENGLISH RIGHT NOW. RIGHT?
YOU MISSED THE TEST AND GOT A ZERO.
I WAS IN DETENTION.
ALL AFTER-SCHOOL ACTIVITIES FALL UNDER THE "NO PASS, NO PLAY" RULE.
BUT THAT'S FOR FOOTBALL, RIGHT?
IT'S FOR EVERYTHING. NO PLAY MEANS **NO** PLAY.
BUT THAT'S NOT FAIR! HOW DO I FAIL A TEST THAT I DON'T EVEN KNOW EXISTS?

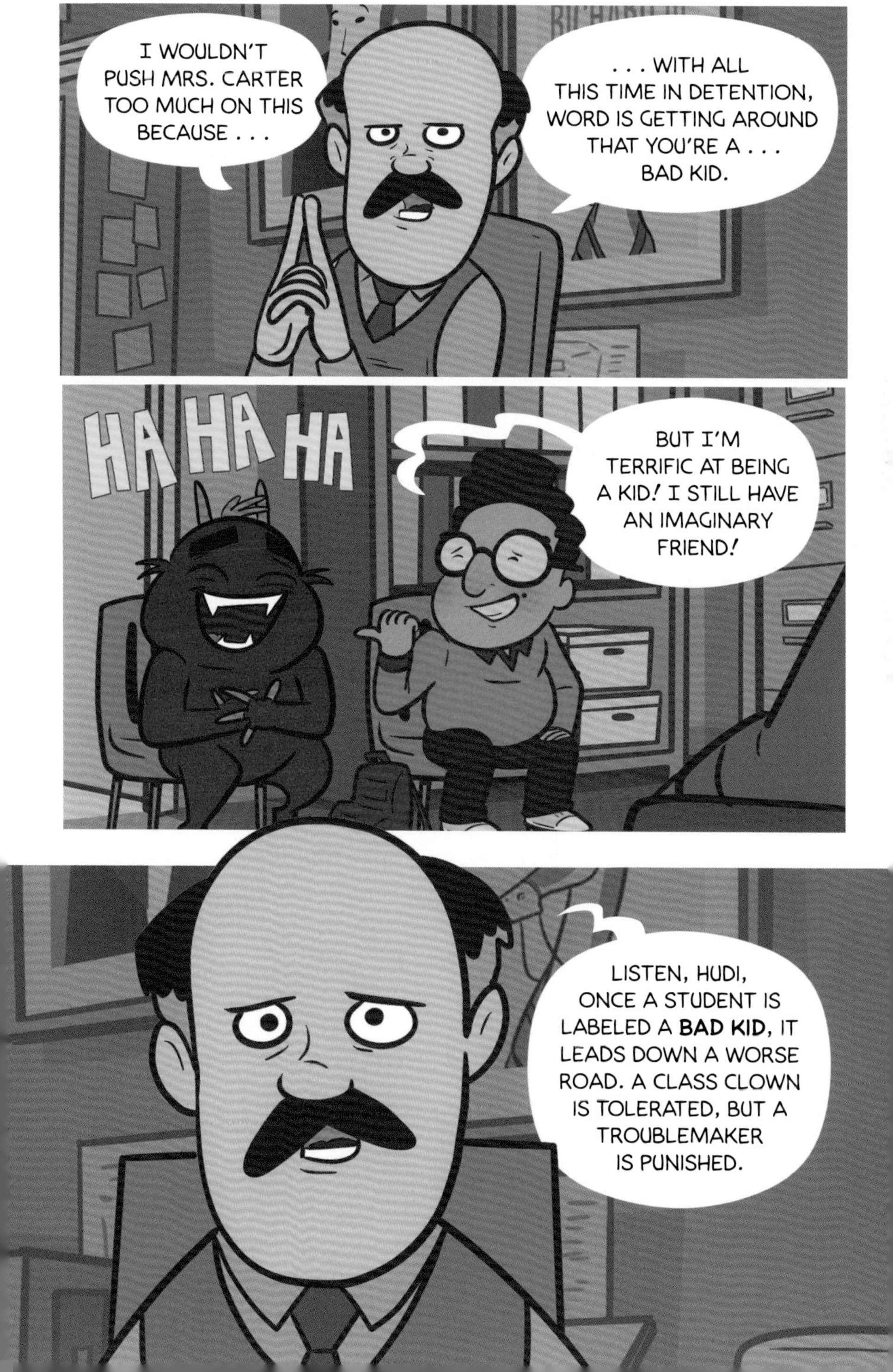
I WOULDN'T PUSH MRS. CARTER TOO MUCH ON THIS BECAUSE . . .
. . . WITH ALL THIS TIME IN DETENTION, WORD IS GETTING AROUND THAT YOU'RE A . . . BAD KID.
HA HA HA HA
BUT I'M TERRIFIC AT BEING A KID! I STILL HAVE AN IMAGINARY FRIEND!
LISTEN, HUDI, ONCE A STUDENT IS LABELED A **BAD KID**, IT LEADS DOWN A WORSE ROAD. A CLASS CLOWN IS TOLERATED, BUT A TROUBLEMAKER IS PUNISHED.

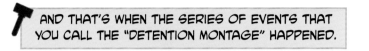

AND THAT'S WHEN THE SERIES OF EVENTS THAT YOU CALL THE "DETENTION MONTAGE" HAPPENED.

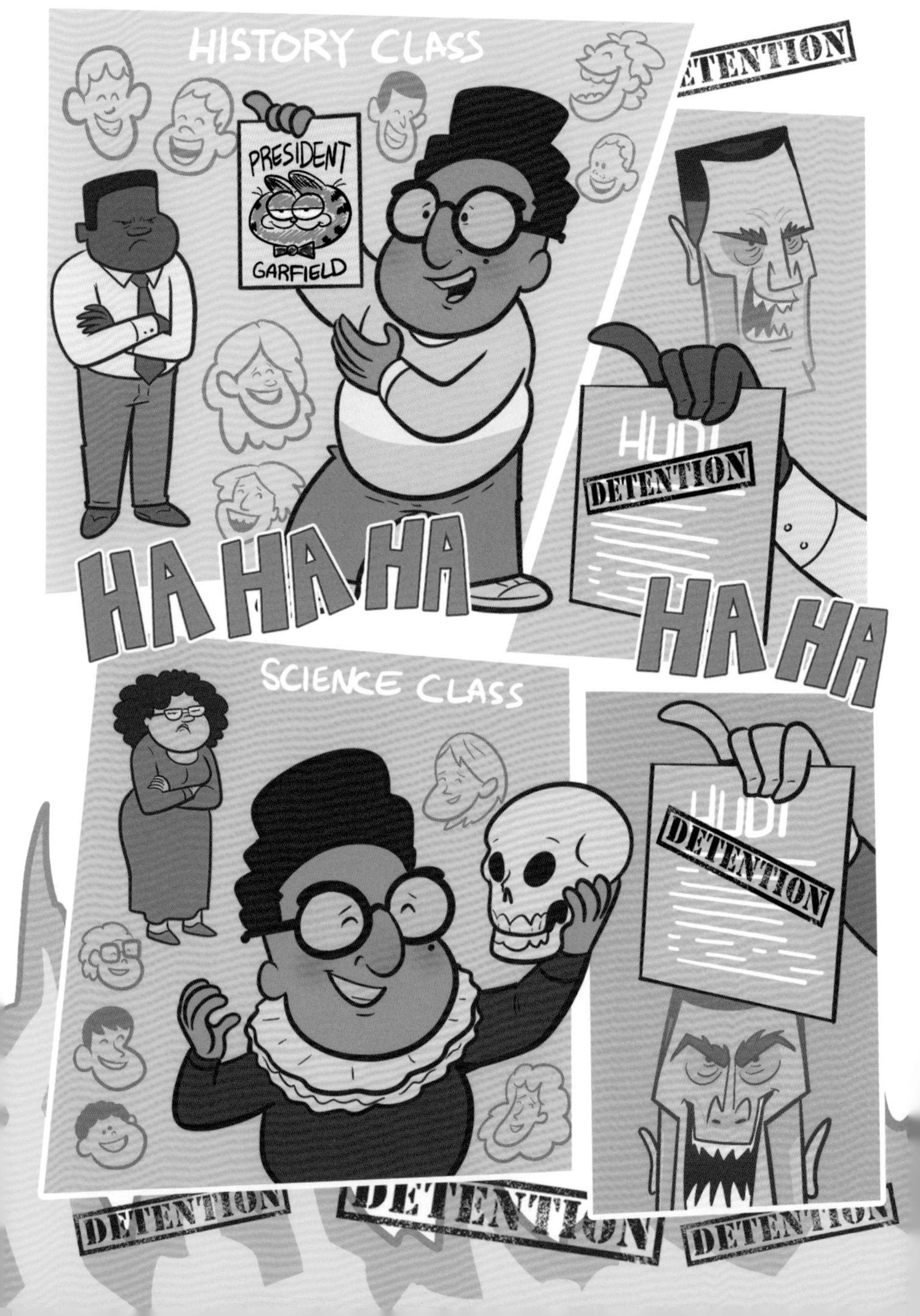
HISTORY CLASS
PRESIDENT
GARFIELD
DETENTION
DETENTION
HA HA HA
HA HA
SCIENCE CLASS
DETENTION
DETENTION
DETENTION
DETENTION

THAT'S RIGHT. IMAGINE LISTENING TO "BAD TO THE BONE" BY GEORGE THOROGOOD AND THE DESTROYERS.

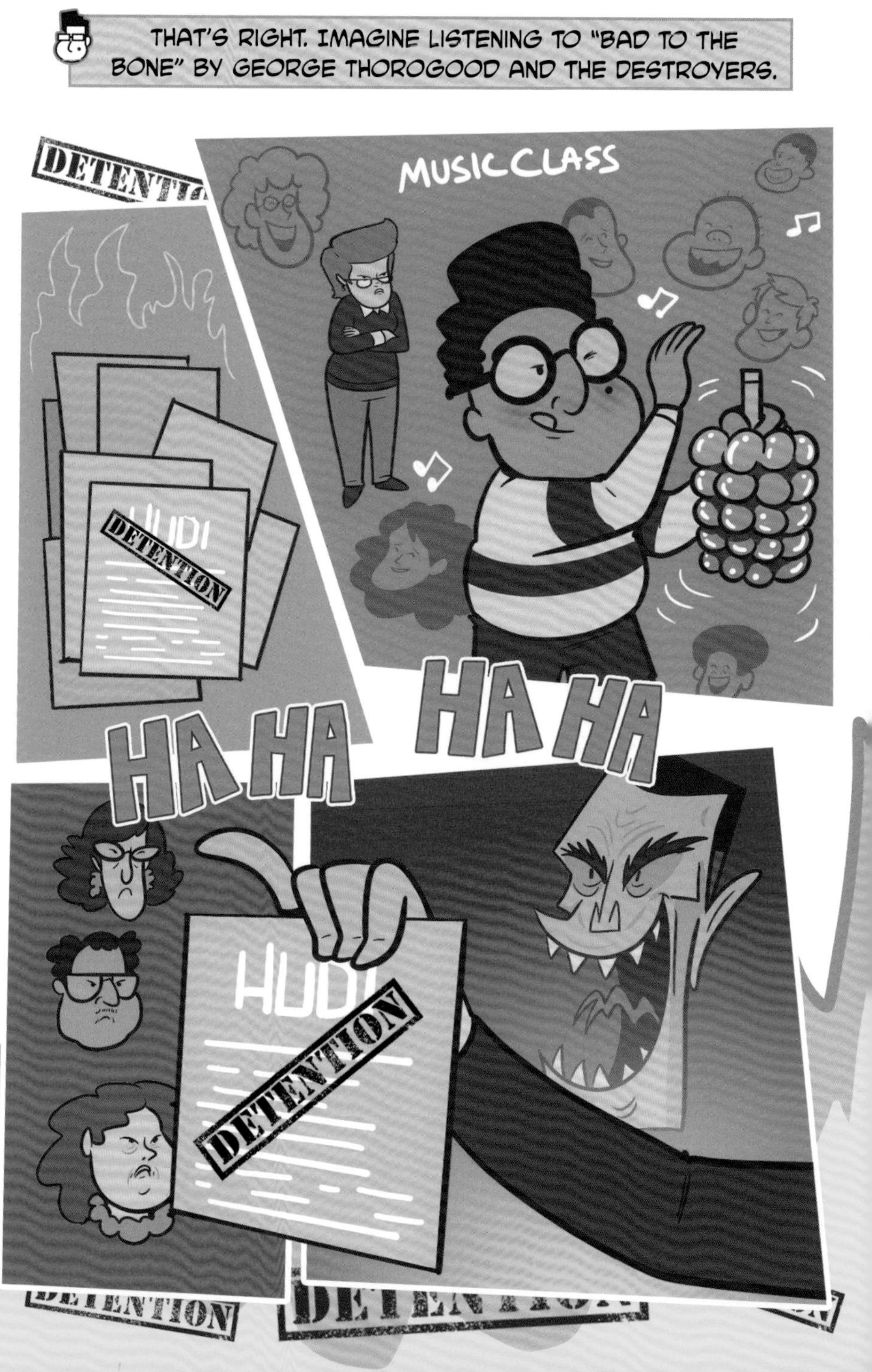

DETENTION
MUSIC CLASS
HUDI
DETENTION
HA HA
HA HA
HUDI
DETENTION
DETENTION

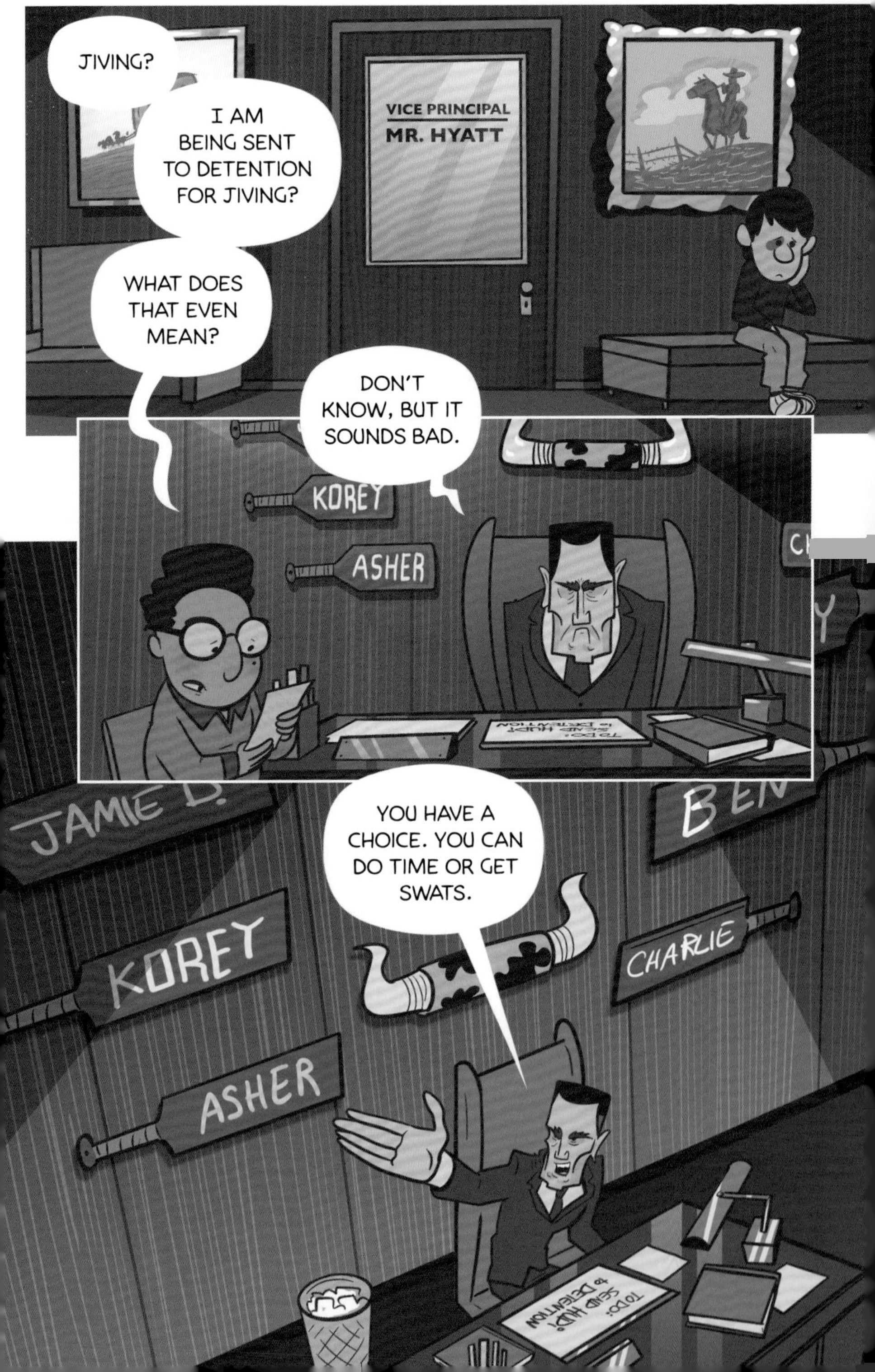
JIVING?
I AM BEING SENT TO DETENTION FOR JIVING?
VICE PRINCIPAL
MR. HYATT
WHAT DOES THAT EVEN MEAN?
DON'T KNOW, BUT IT SOUNDS BAD.
KOREY
ASHER
TO DO: SEND HUD! to DETENTION
JAMIE D.
BEN
YOU HAVE A CHOICE. YOU CAN DO TIME OR GET SWATS.
KOREY
CHARLIE
ASHER
TO DO: SEND HUD! to DETENTION

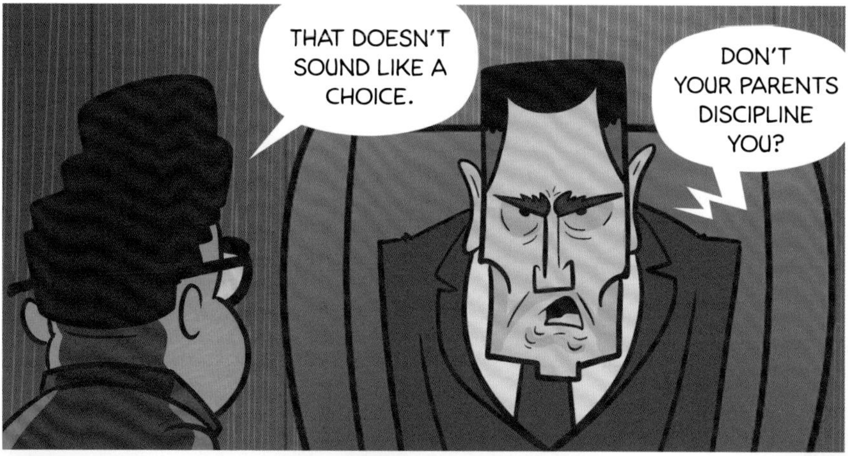
THAT DOESN'T SOUND LIKE A CHOICE.
DON'T YOUR PARENTS DISCIPLINE YOU?

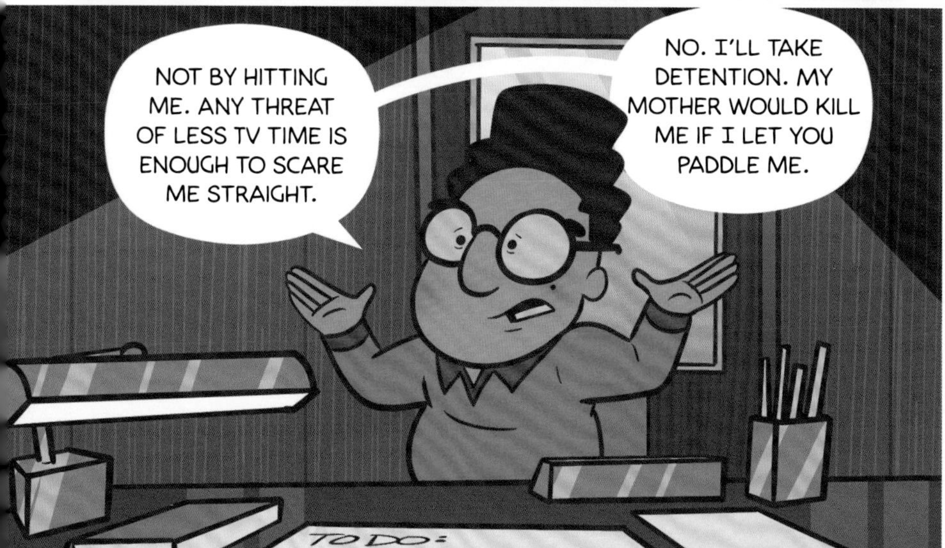
NOT BY HITTING ME. ANY THREAT OF LESS TV TIME IS ENOUGH TO SCARE ME STRAIGHT.
NO. I'LL TAKE DETENTION. MY MOTHER WOULD KILL ME IF I LET YOU PADDLE ME.
TO DO: SEND HUDI to DETENTION

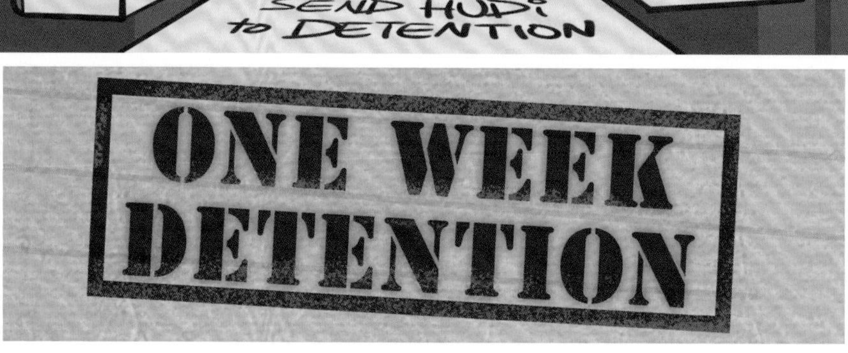
ONE WEEK DETENTION

HUDI on TRIAL

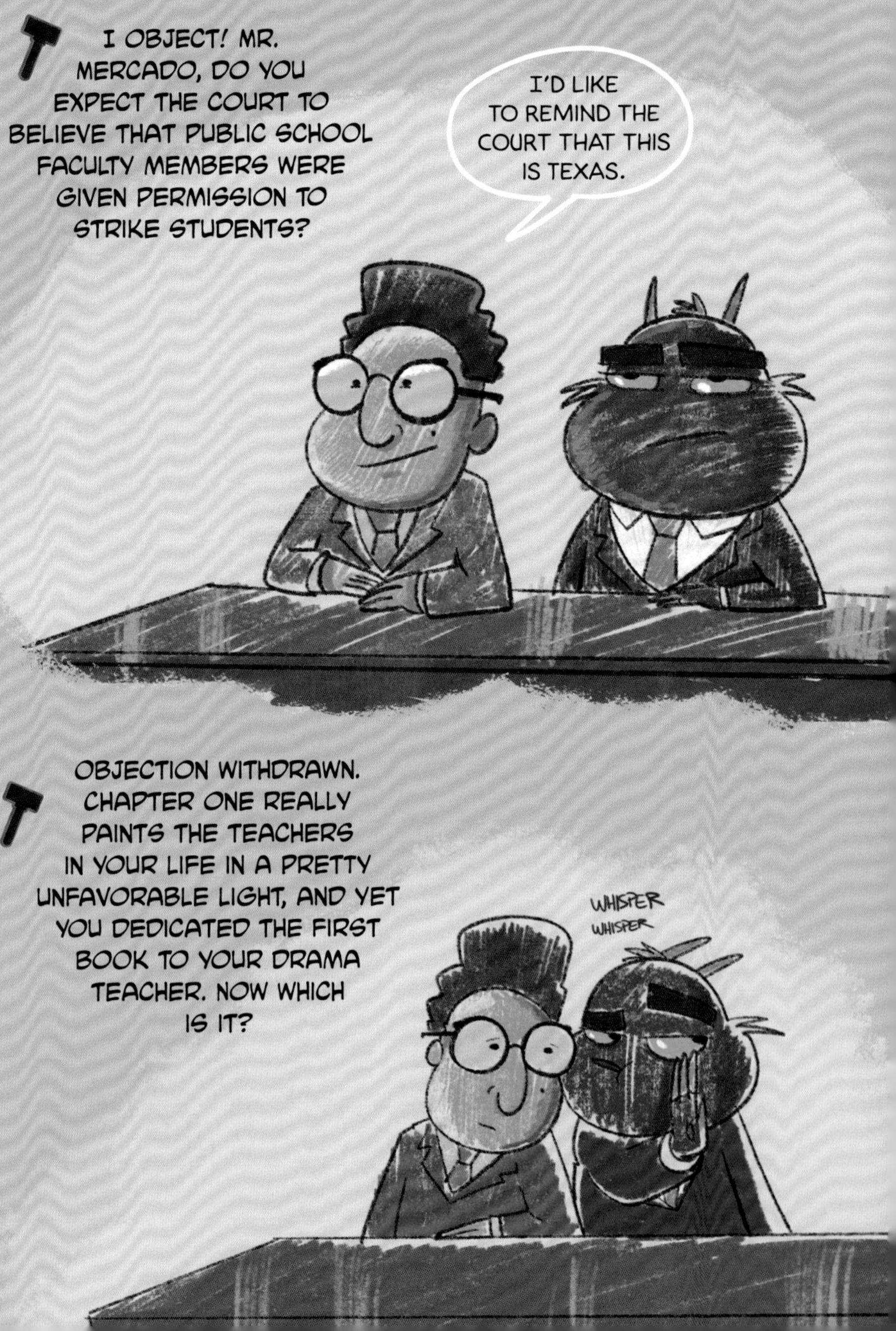

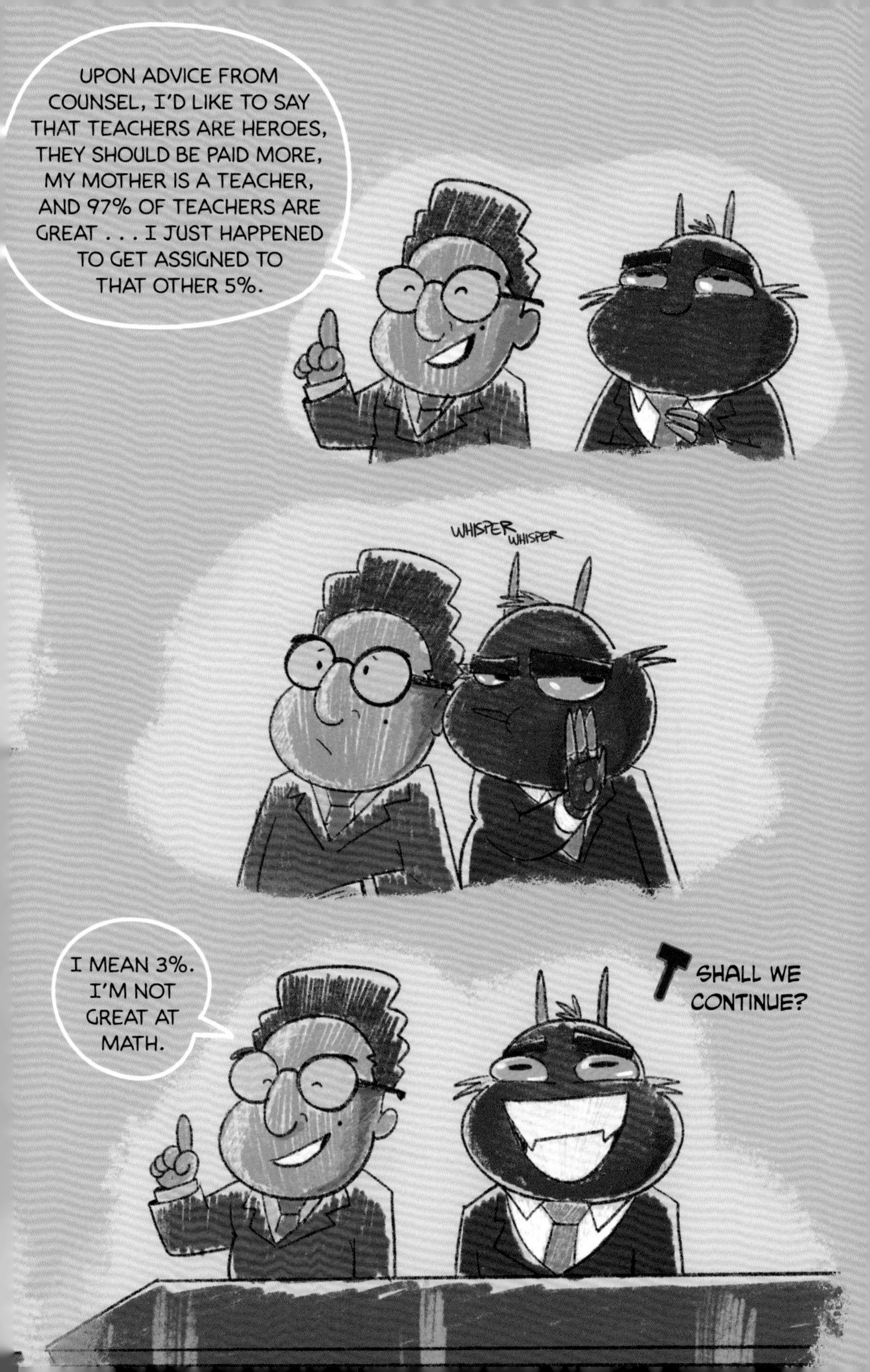
UPON ADVICE FROM COUNSEL, I'D LIKE TO SAY THAT TEACHERS ARE HEROES, THEY SHOULD BE PAID MORE, MY MOTHER IS A TEACHER, AND 97% OF TEACHERS ARE GREAT . . . I JUST HAPPENED TO GET ASSIGNED TO THAT OTHER 5%.
WHISPER WHISPER
I MEAN 3%. I'M NOT GREAT AT MATH.
SHALL WE CONTINUE?

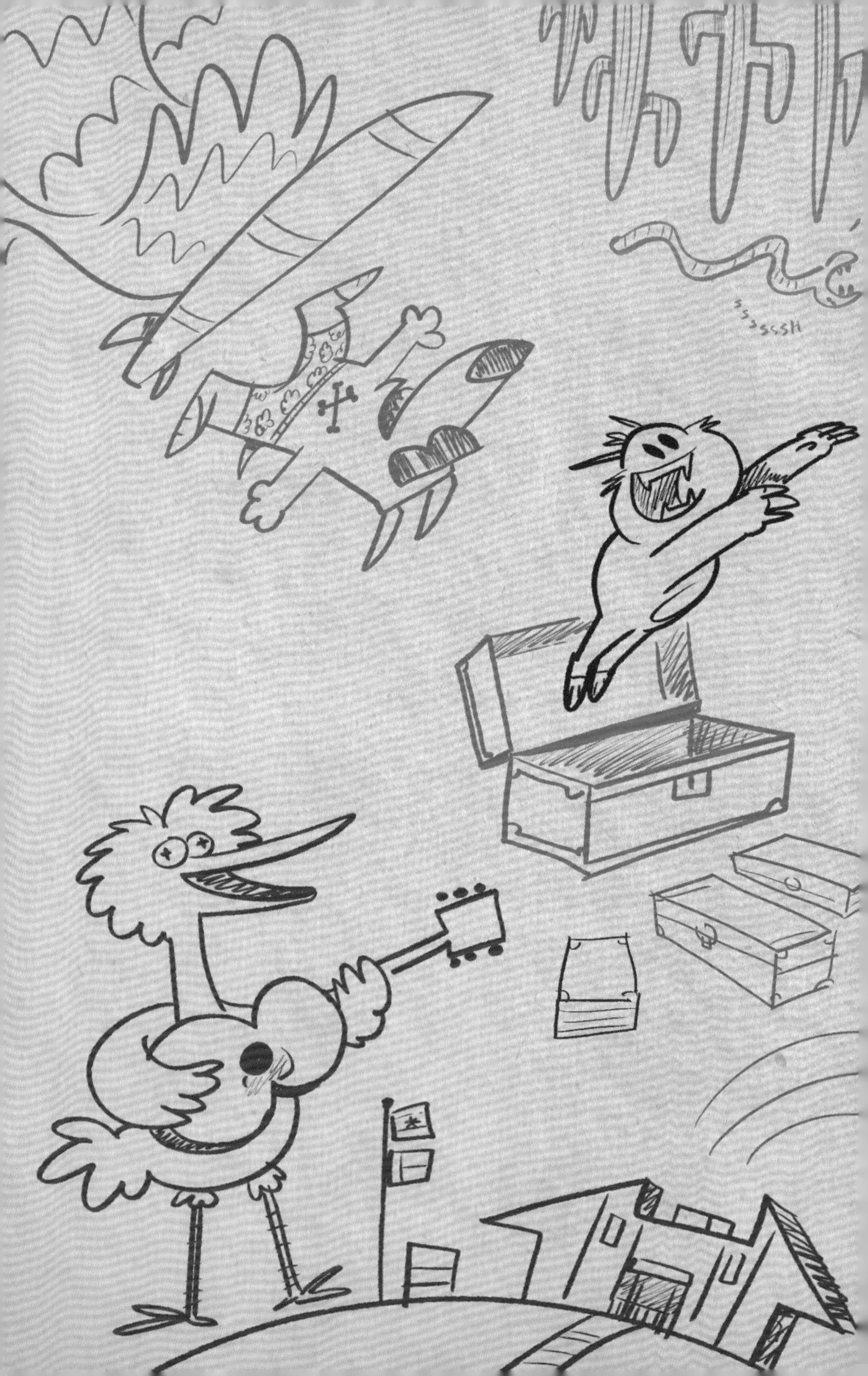
SSSSSSH

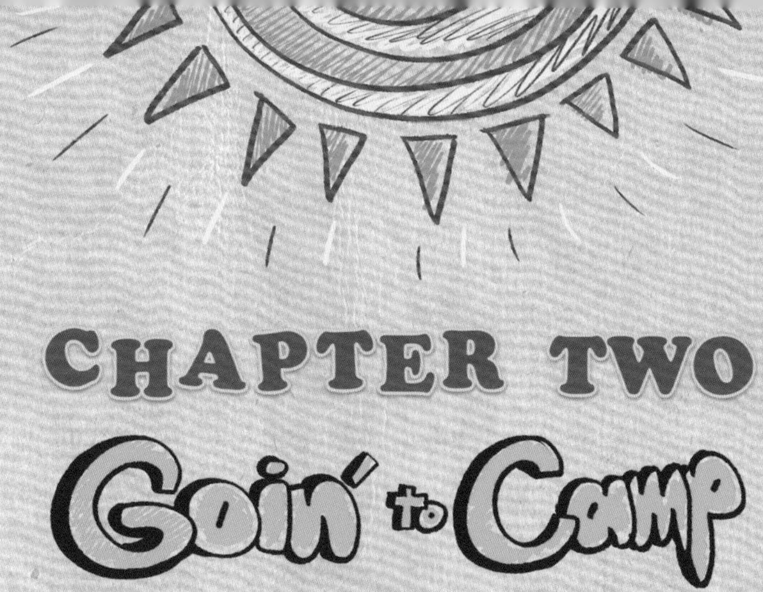

CHAPTER TWO

Goin' to Camp

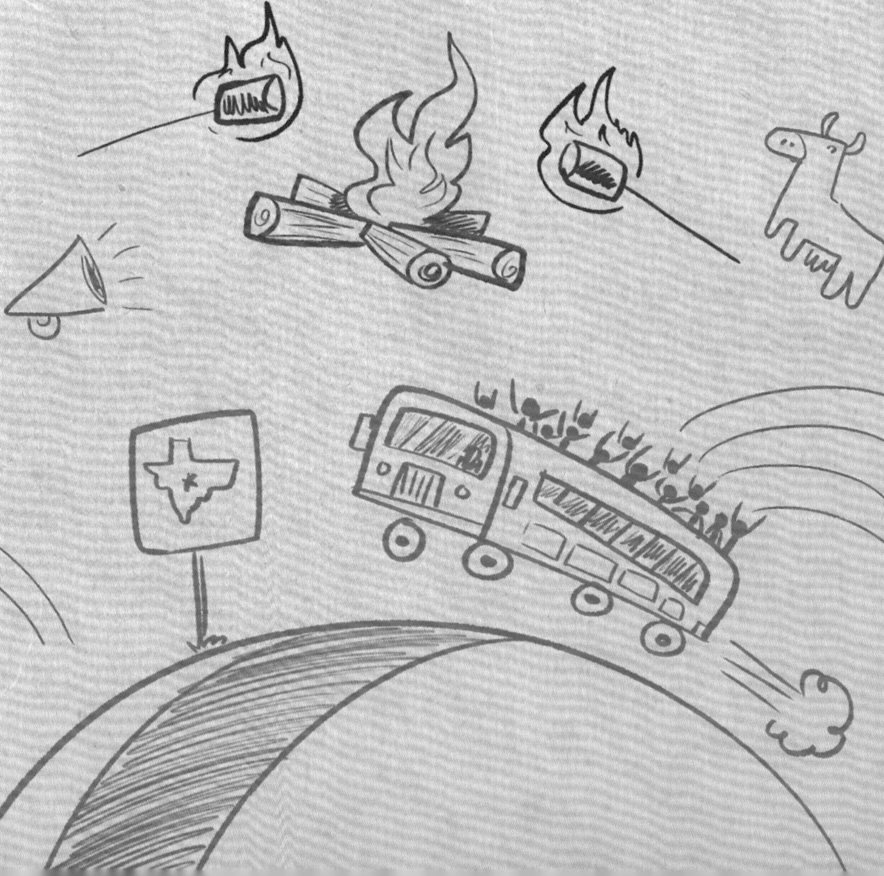

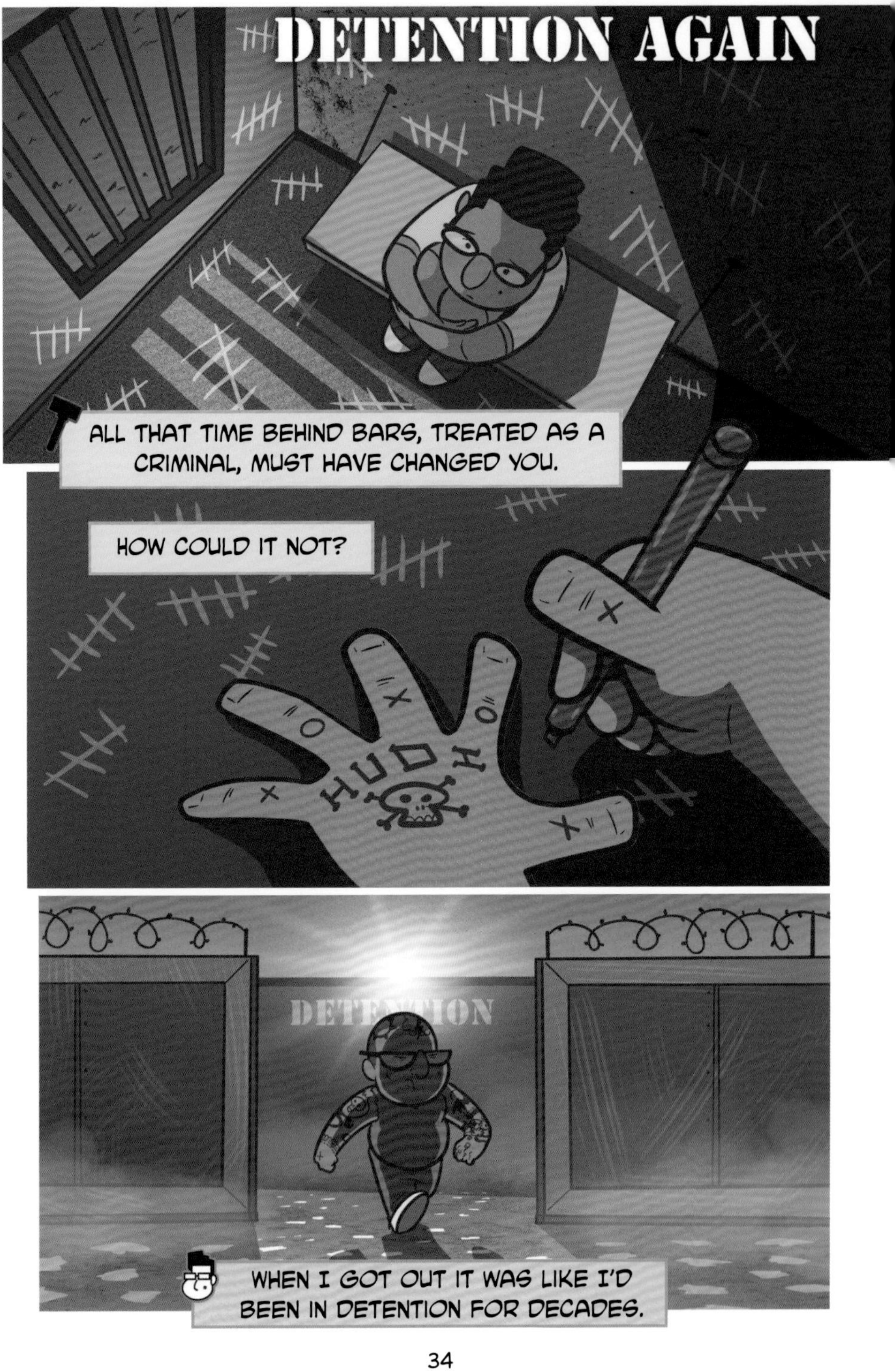
DETENTION AGAIN
ALL THAT TIME BEHIND BARS, TREATED AS A CRIMINAL, MUST HAVE CHANGED YOU.
HOW COULD IT NOT?
DETENTION
WHEN I GOT OUT IT WAS LIKE I'D BEEN IN DETENTION FOR DECADES.

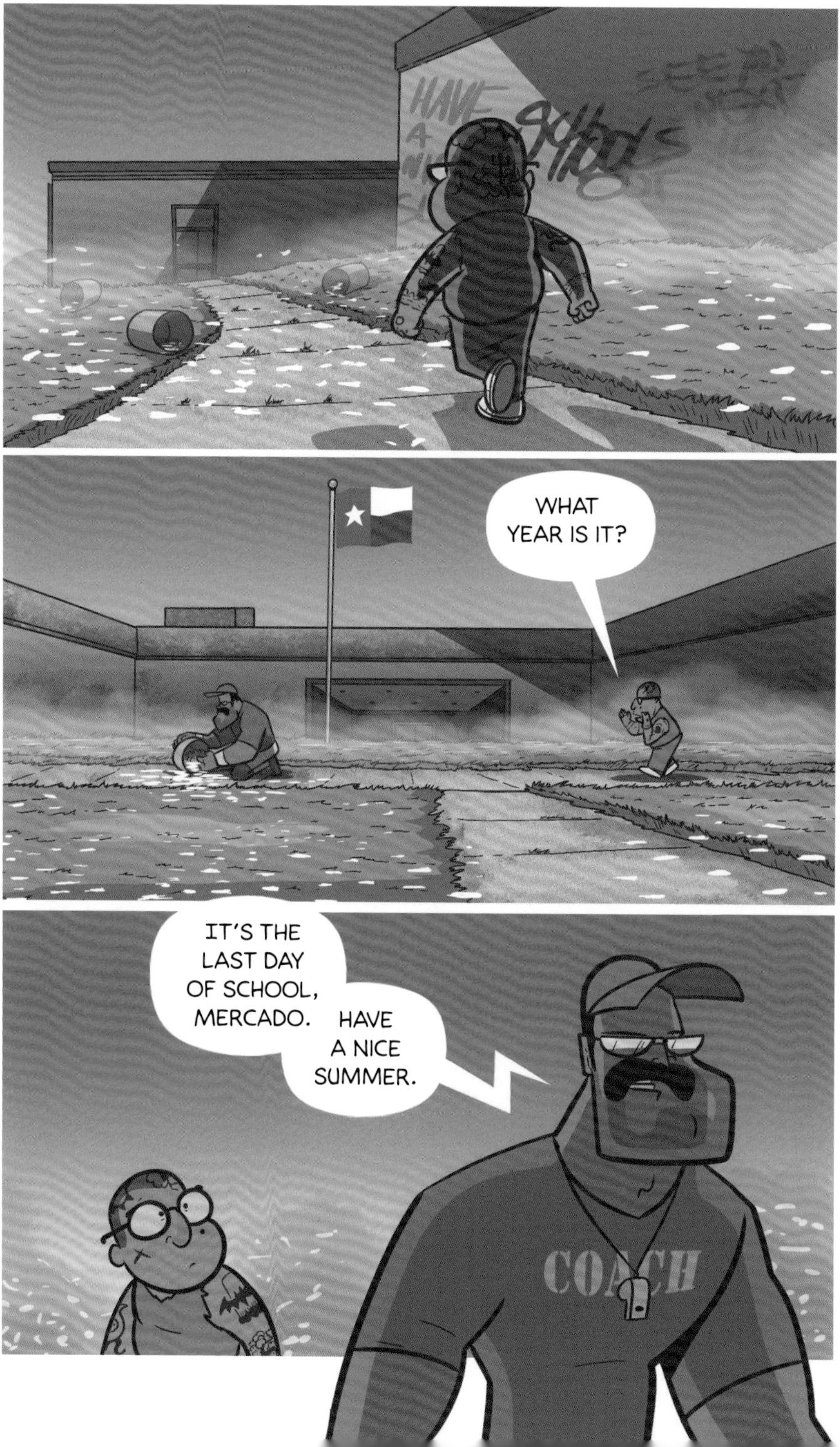
WHAT YEAR IS IT?
IT'S THE LAST DAY OF SCHOOL, MERCADO.
HAVE A NICE SUMMER.
COACH

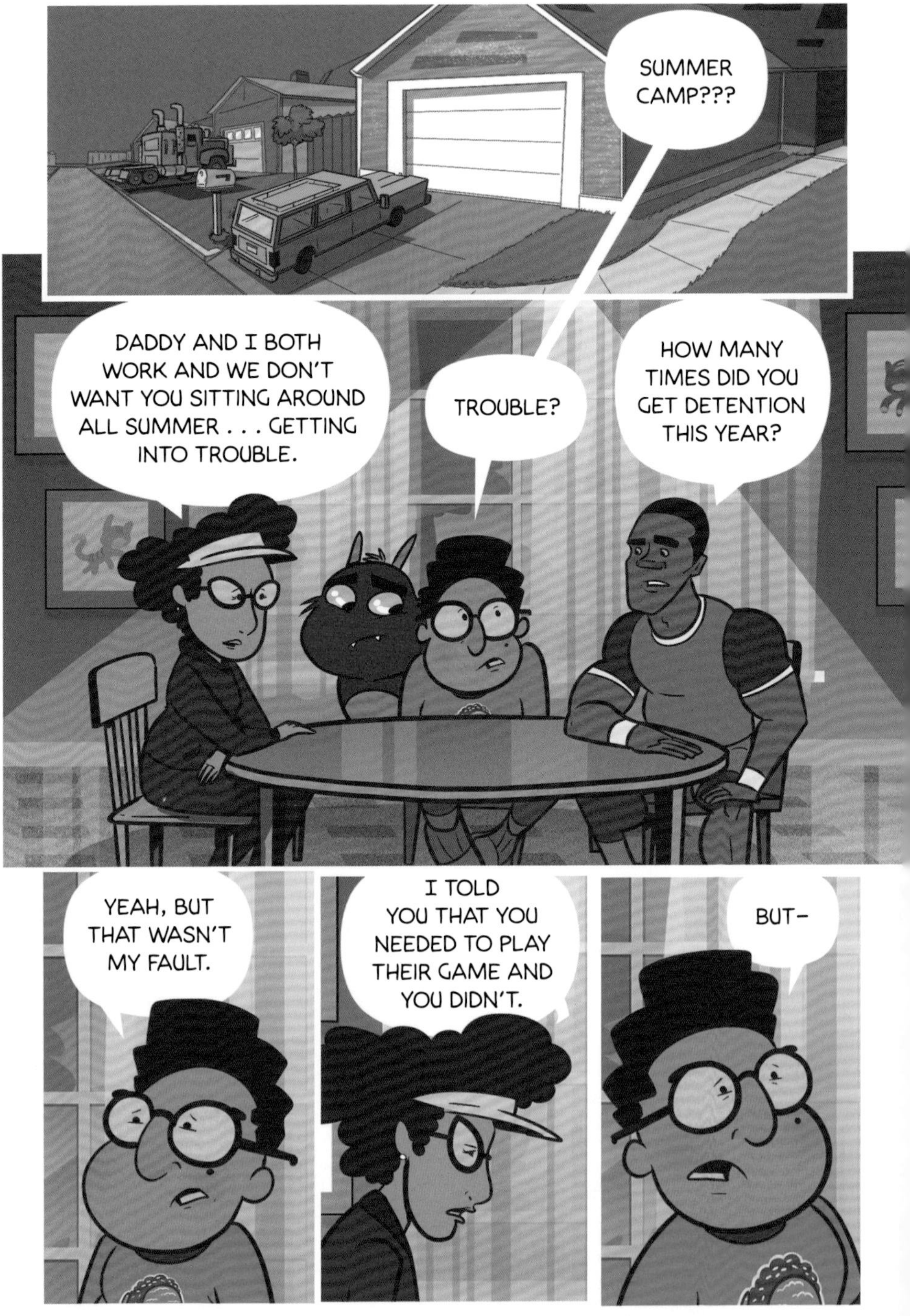
SUMMER CAMP???
DADDY AND I BOTH WORK AND WE DON'T WANT YOU SITTING AROUND ALL SUMMER . . . GETTING INTO TROUBLE.
TROUBLE?
HOW MANY TIMES DID YOU GET DETENTION THIS YEAR?
YEAH, BUT THAT WASN'T MY FAULT.
I TOLD YOU THAT YOU NEEDED TO PLAY THEIR GAME AND YOU DIDN'T.
BUT-

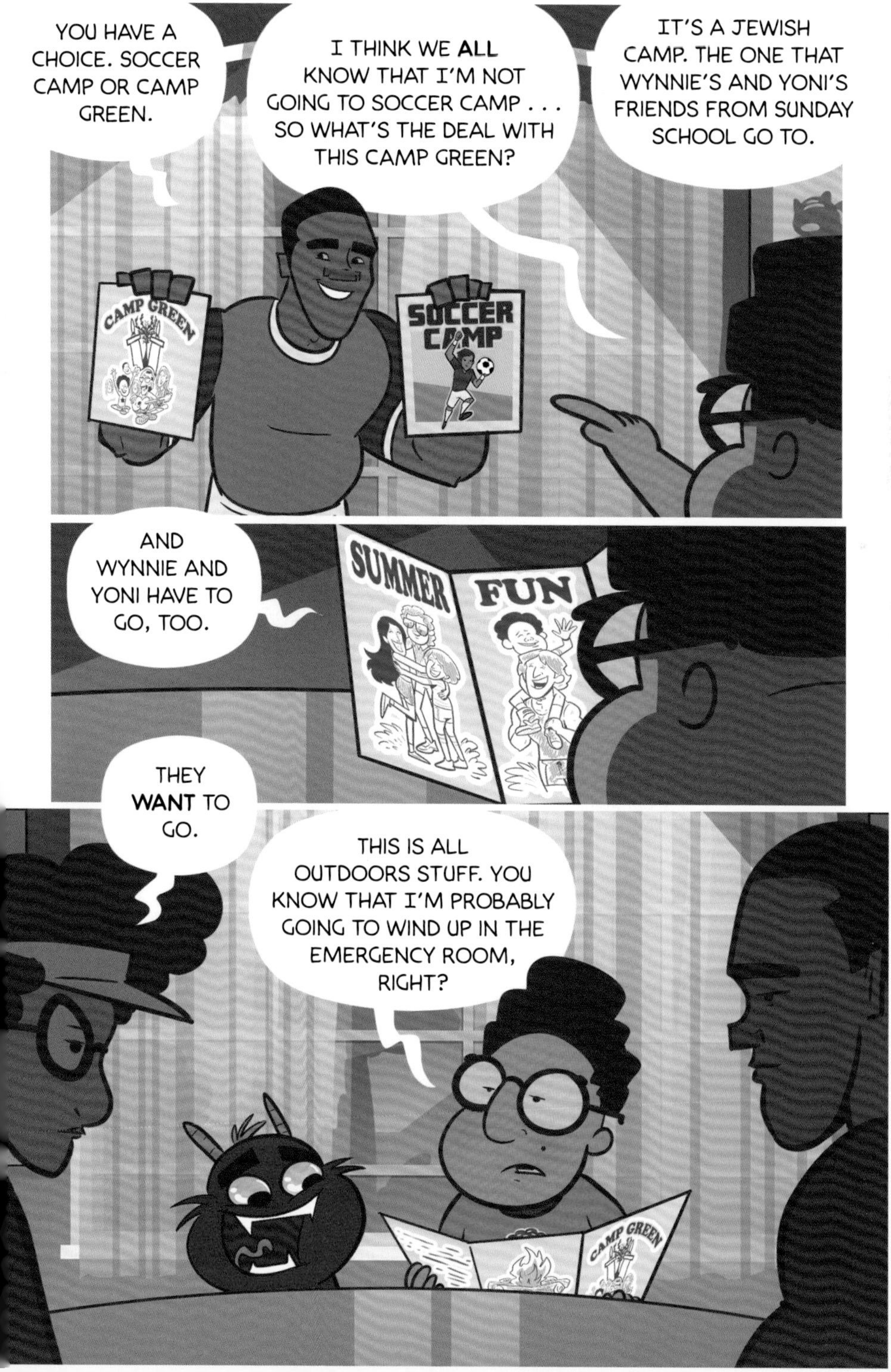
YOU HAVE A CHOICE. SOCCER CAMP OR CAMP GREEN.
I THINK WE **ALL** KNOW THAT I'M NOT GOING TO SOCCER CAMP . . . SO WHAT'S THE DEAL WITH THIS CAMP GREEN?
IT'S A JEWISH CAMP. THE ONE THAT WYNNIE'S AND YONI'S FRIENDS FROM SUNDAY SCHOOL GO TO.
CAMP GREEN
SOCCER CAMP
AND WYNNIE AND YONI HAVE TO GO, TOO.
SUMMER FUN
THEY **WANT** TO GO.
THIS IS ALL OUTDOORS STUFF. YOU KNOW THAT I'M PROBABLY GOING TO WIND UP IN THE EMERGENCY ROOM, RIGHT?
CAMP GREEN

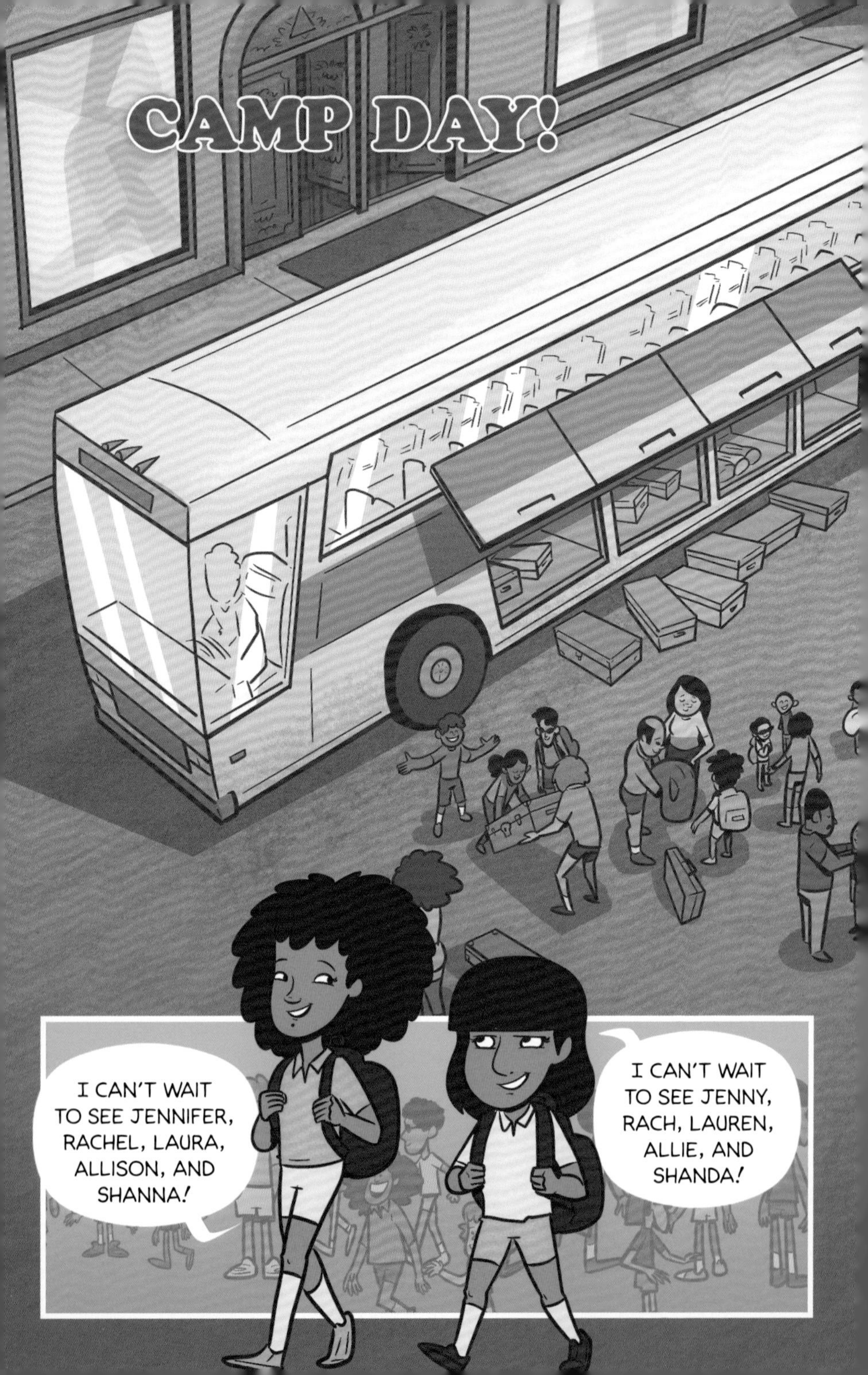
CAMP DAY!
I CAN'T WAIT TO SEE JENNIFER, RACHEL, LAURA, ALLISON, AND SHANNA!
I CAN'T WAIT TO SEE JENNY, RACH, LAUREN, ALLIE, AND SHANDA!

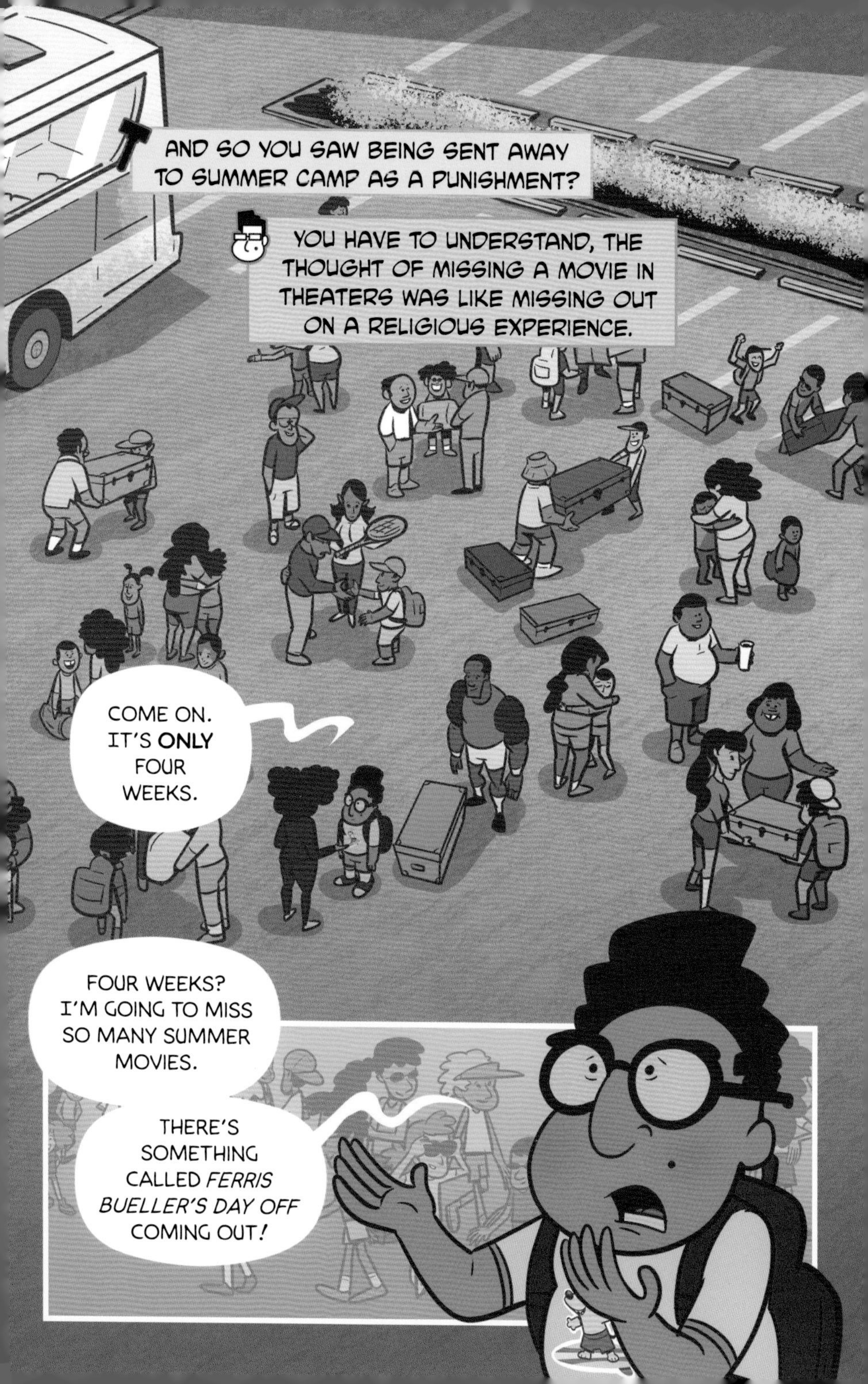
AND SO YOU SAW BEING SENT AWAY TO SUMMER CAMP AS A PUNISHMENT?
YOU HAVE TO UNDERSTAND, THE THOUGHT OF MISSING A MOVIE IN THEATERS WAS LIKE MISSING OUT ON A RELIGIOUS EXPERIENCE.
COME ON. IT'S **ONLY** FOUR WEEKS.
FOUR WEEKS? I'M GOING TO MISS SO MANY SUMMER MOVIES.
THERE'S SOMETHING CALLED *FERRIS BUELLER'S DAY OFF* COMING OUT*!*

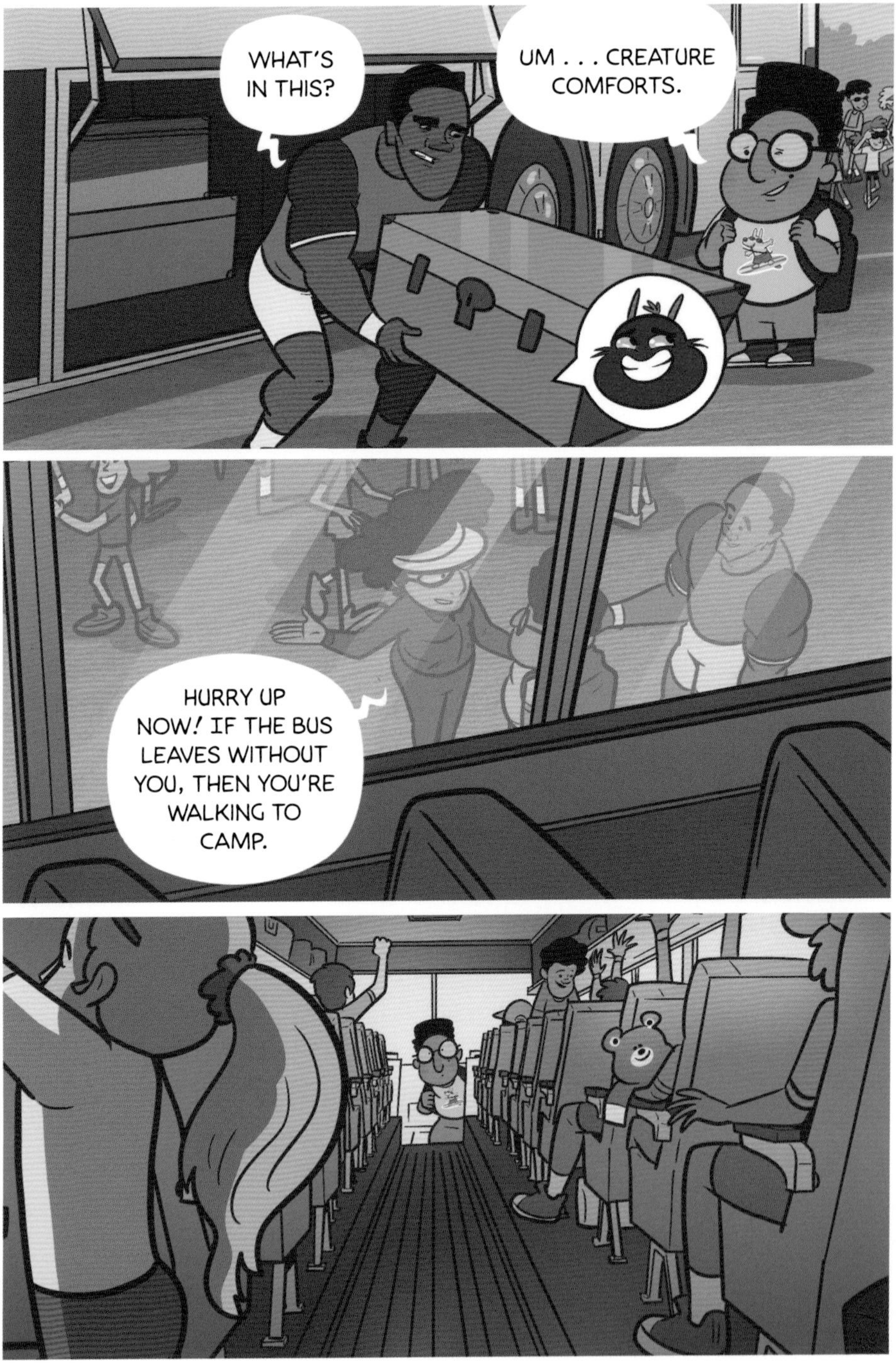
WHAT'S IN THIS?
UM . . . CREATURE COMFORTS.
HURRY UP NOW! IF THE BUS LEAVES WITHOUT YOU, THEN YOU'RE WALKING TO CAMP.

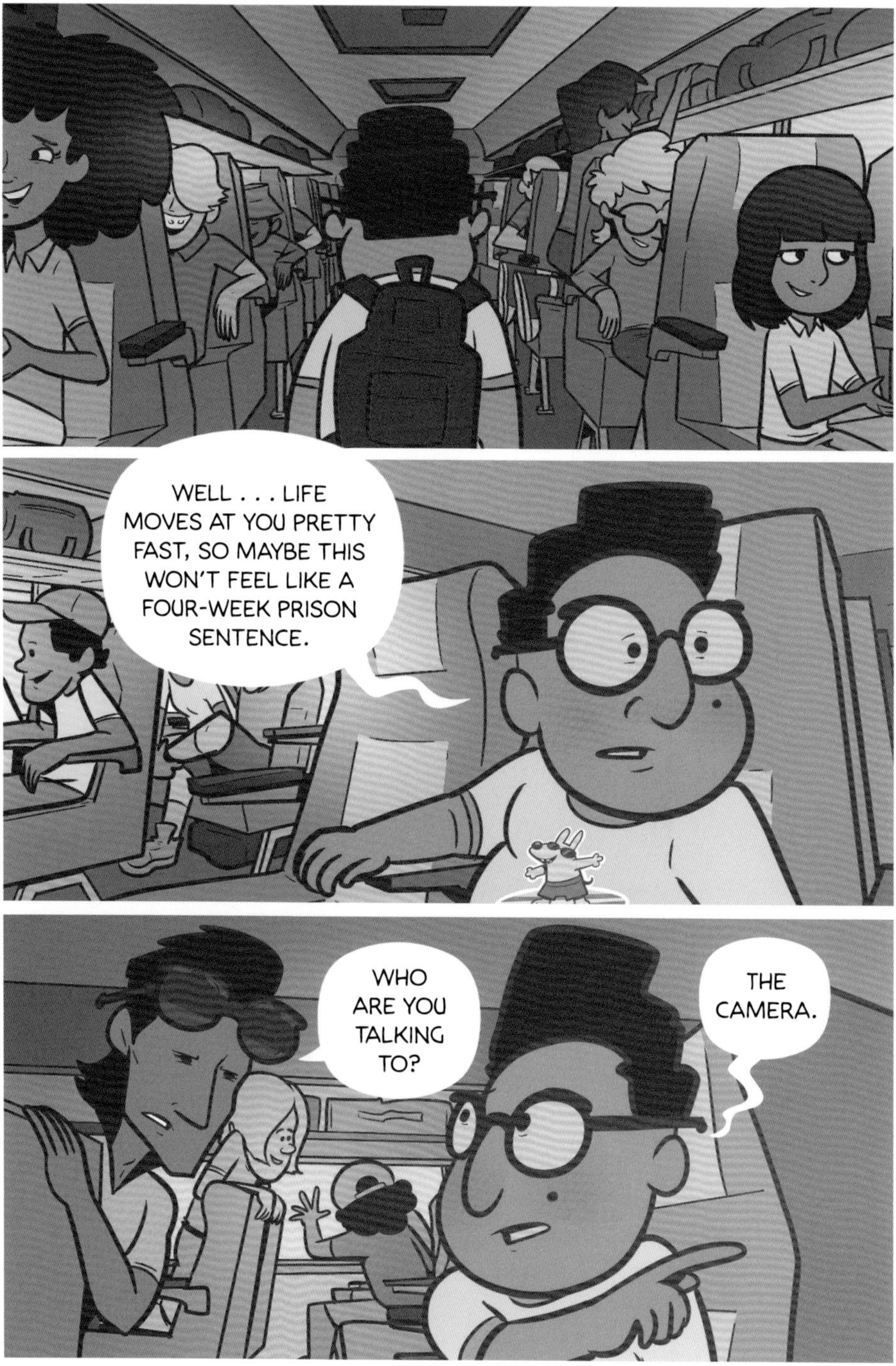
WELL . . . LIFE MOVES AT YOU PRETTY FAST, SO MAYBE THIS WON'T FEEL LIKE A FOUR-WEEK PRISON SENTENCE.
WHO ARE YOU TALKING TO?
THE CAMERA.

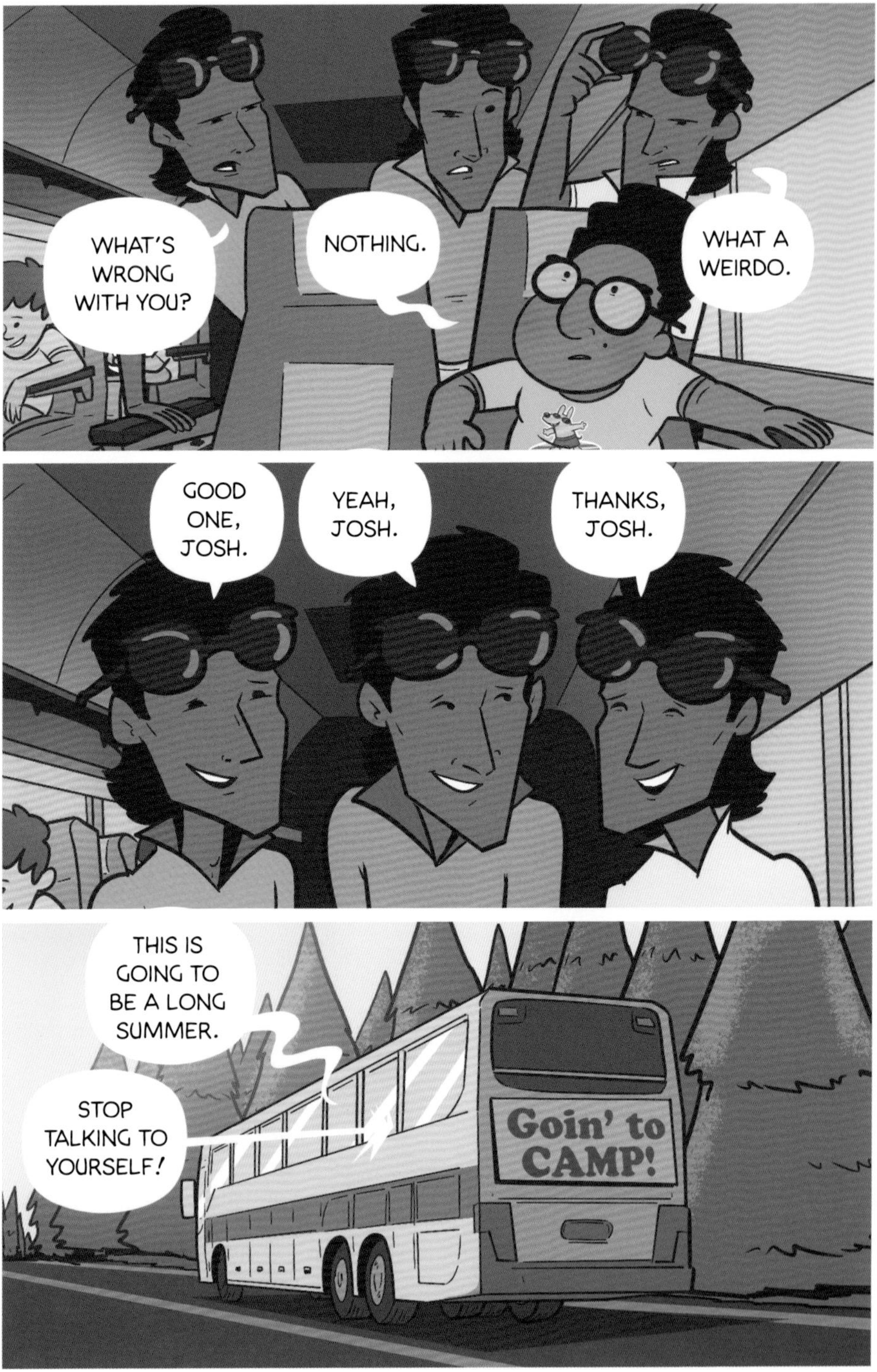
WHAT'S WRONG WITH YOU?
NOTHING.
WHAT A WEIRDO.
GOOD ONE, JOSH.
YEAH, JOSH.
THANKS, JOSH.
THIS IS GOING TO BE A LONG SUMMER.
STOP TALKING TO YOURSELF!
Goin' to CAMP!

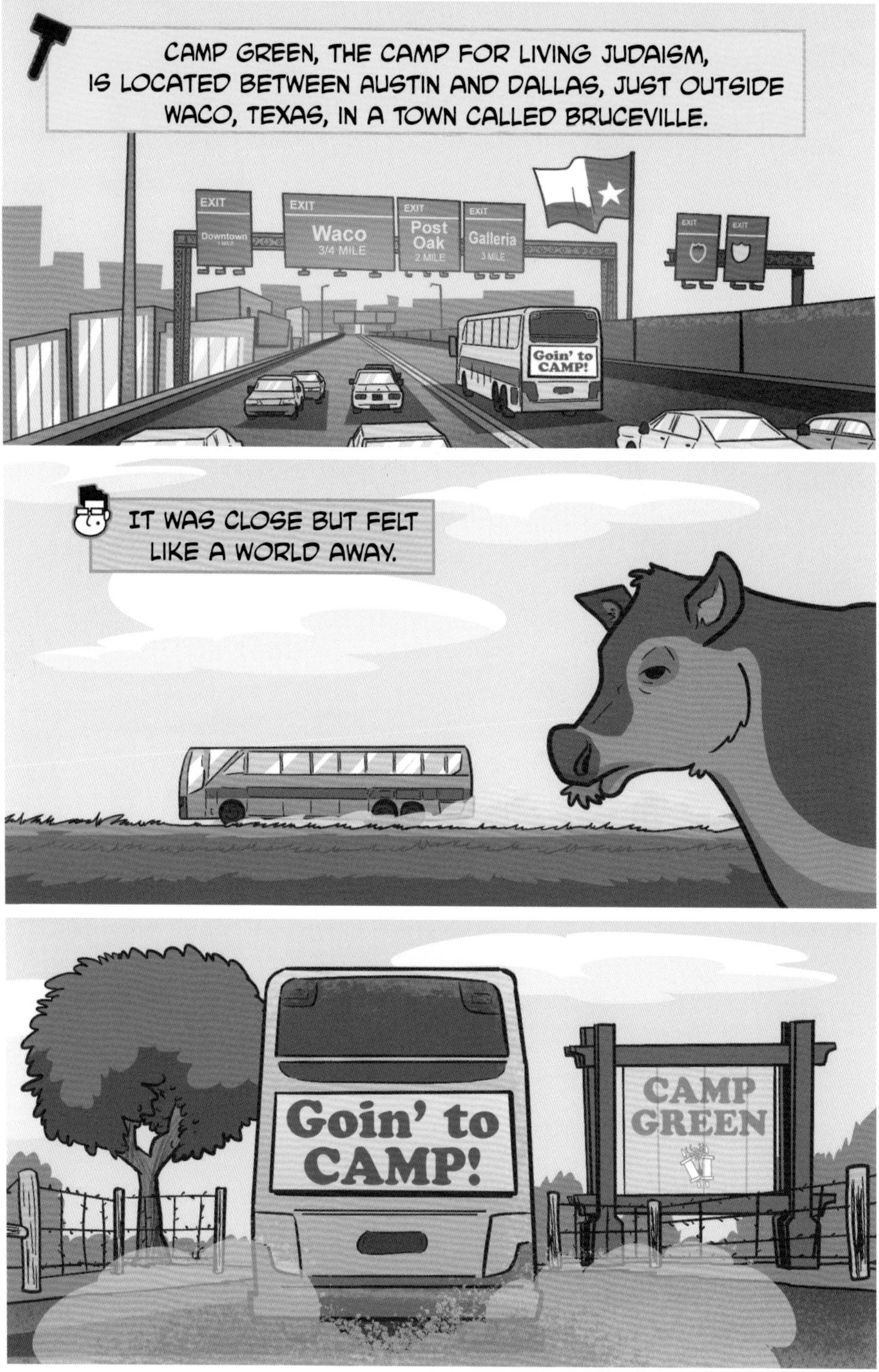
CAMP GREEN, THE CAMP FOR LIVING JUDAISM, IS LOCATED BETWEEN AUSTIN AND DALLAS, JUST OUTSIDE WACO, TEXAS, IN A TOWN CALLED BRUCEVILLE.
EXIT Downtown
EXIT Waco 3/4 MILE
EXIT Post Oak 2 MILE
EXIT Galleria 3 MILE
EXIT
EXIT
Goin' to CAMP!
IT WAS CLOSE BUT FELT LIKE A WORLD AWAY.
Goin' to CAMP!
CAMP GREEN

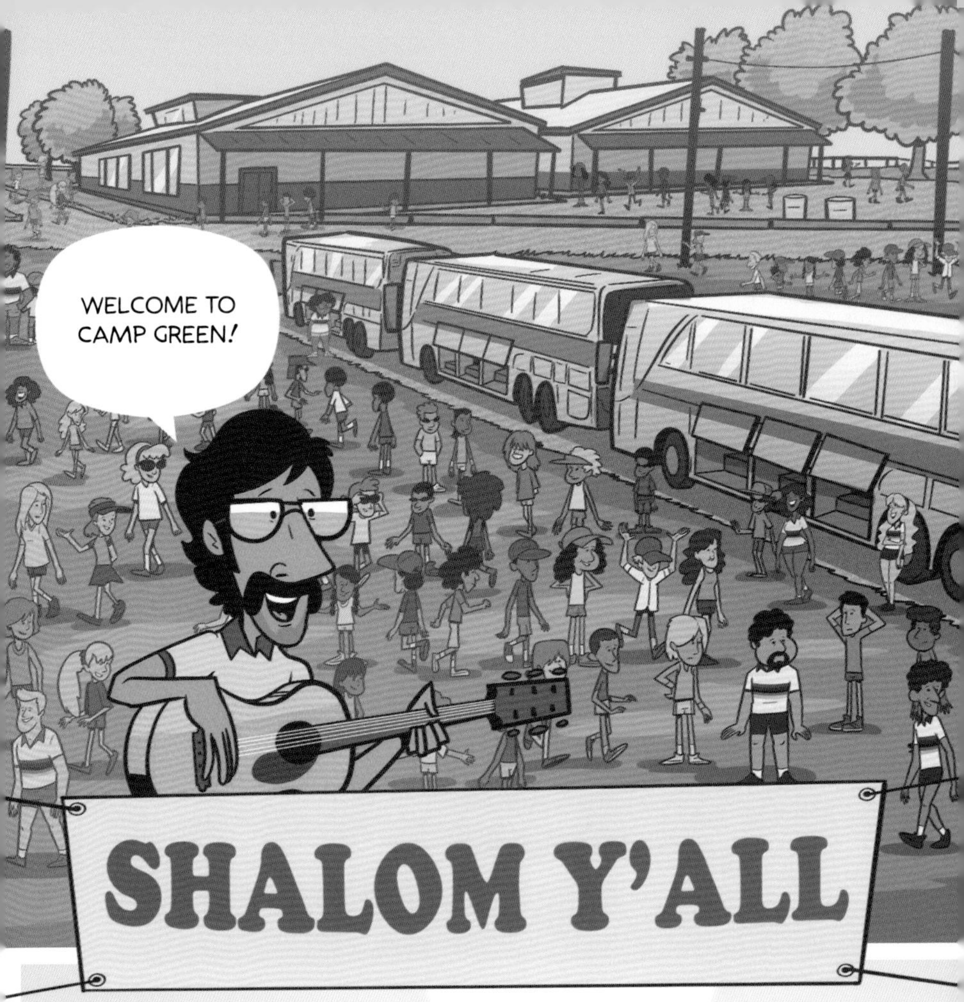
WELCOME TO CAMP GREEN!
SHALOM Y'ALL

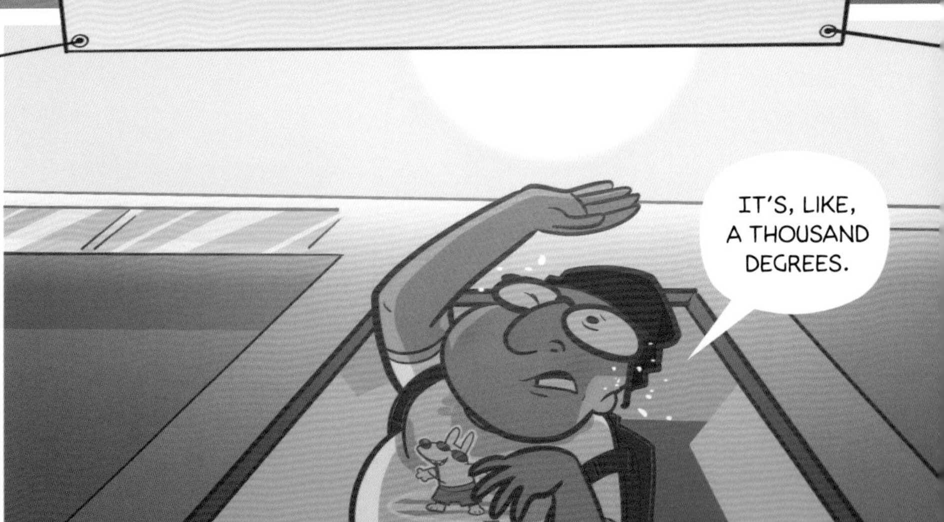
IT'S, LIKE, A THOUSAND DEGREES.

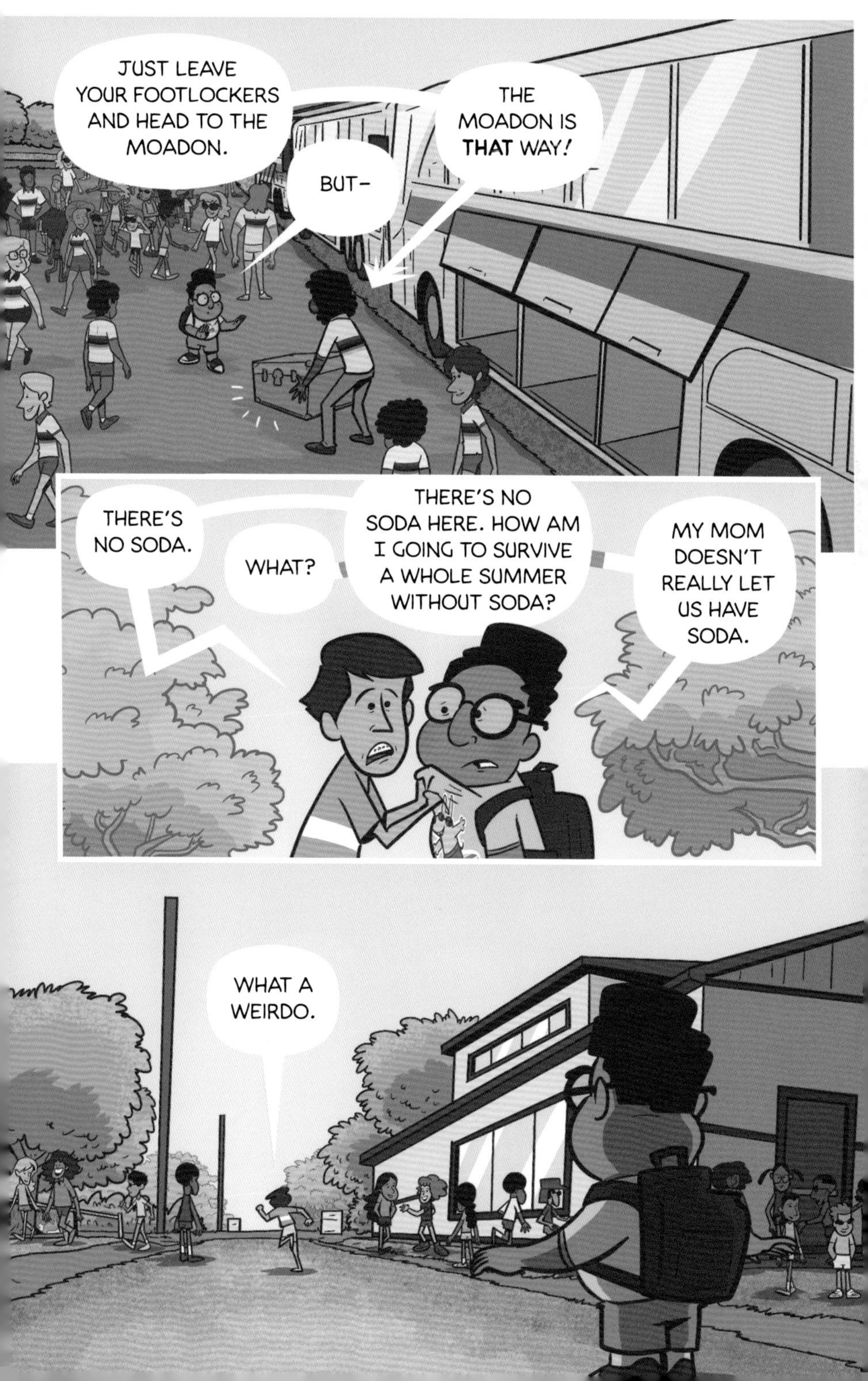
JUST LEAVE YOUR FOOTLOCKERS AND HEAD TO THE MOADON.
BUT-
THE MOADON IS **THAT** WAY!
THERE'S NO SODA.
WHAT?
THERE'S NO SODA HERE. HOW AM I GOING TO SURVIVE A WHOLE SUMMER WITHOUT SODA?
MY MOM DOESN'T REALLY LET US HAVE SODA.
WHAT A WEIRDO.

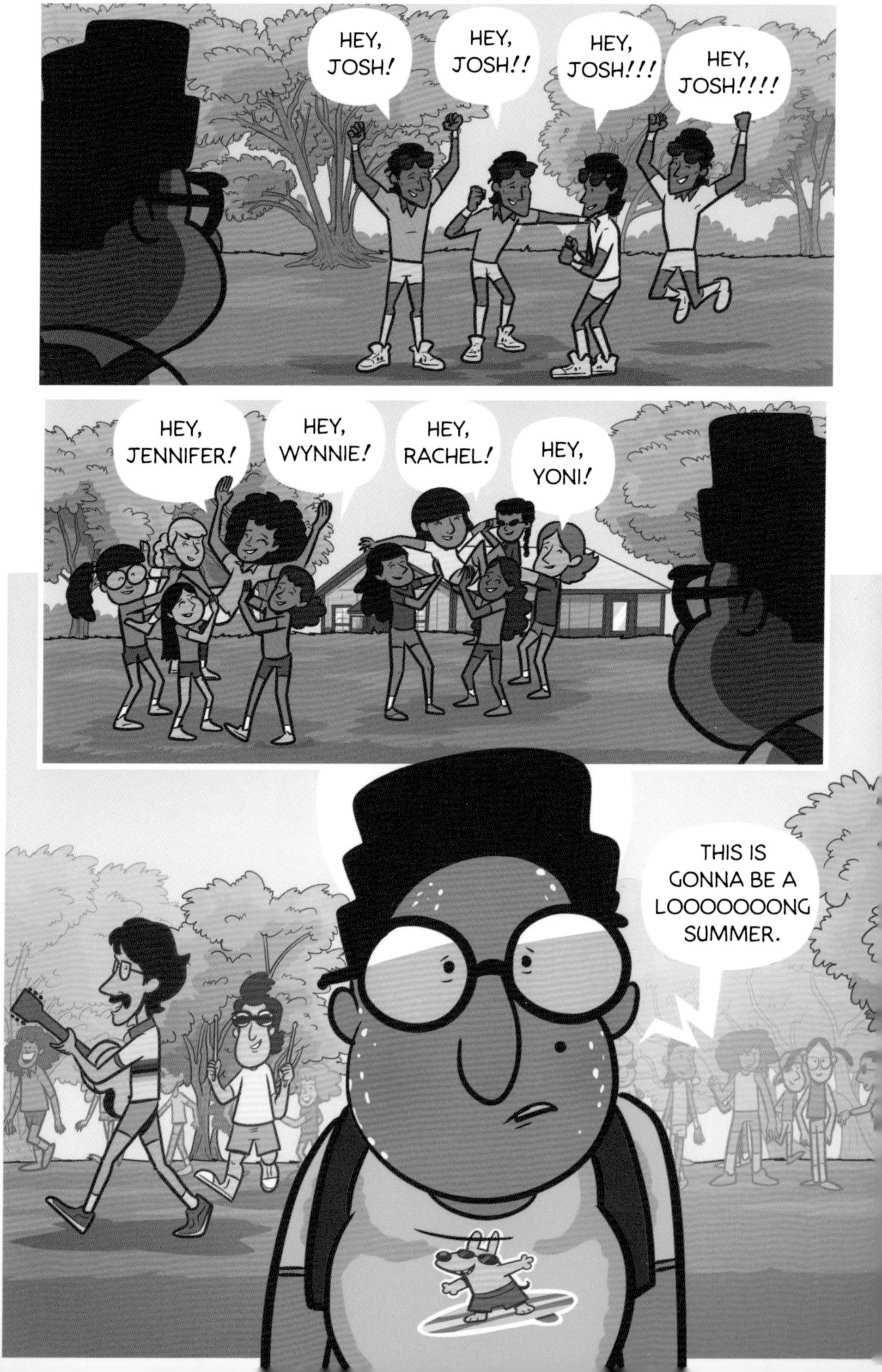
HEY, JOSH!
HEY, JOSH!!
HEY, JOSH!!!
HEY, JOSH!!!!
HEY, JENNIFER!
HEY, WYNNIE!
HEY, RACHEL!
HEY, YONI!
THIS IS GONNA BE A LOOOOOOONG SUMMER.

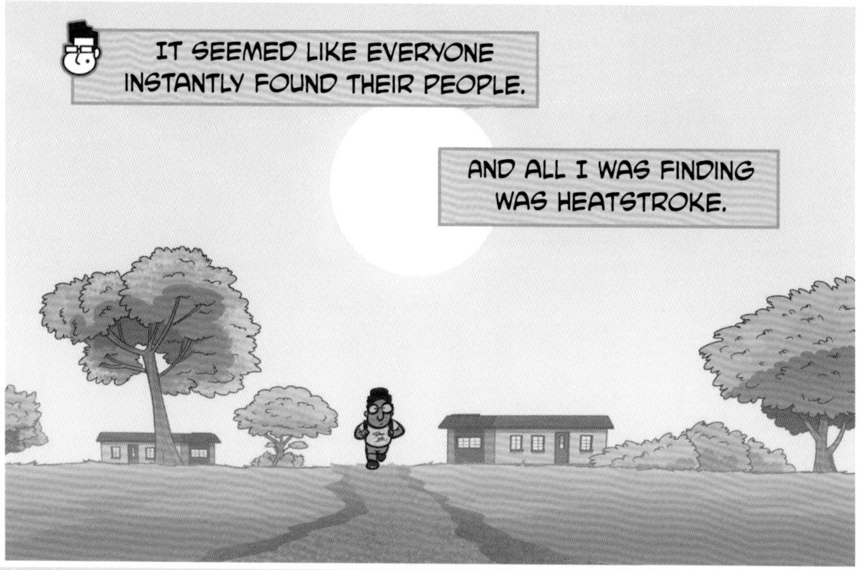
IT SEEMED LIKE EVERYONE INSTANTLY FOUND THEIR PEOPLE.
AND ALL I WAS FINDING WAS HEATSTROKE.

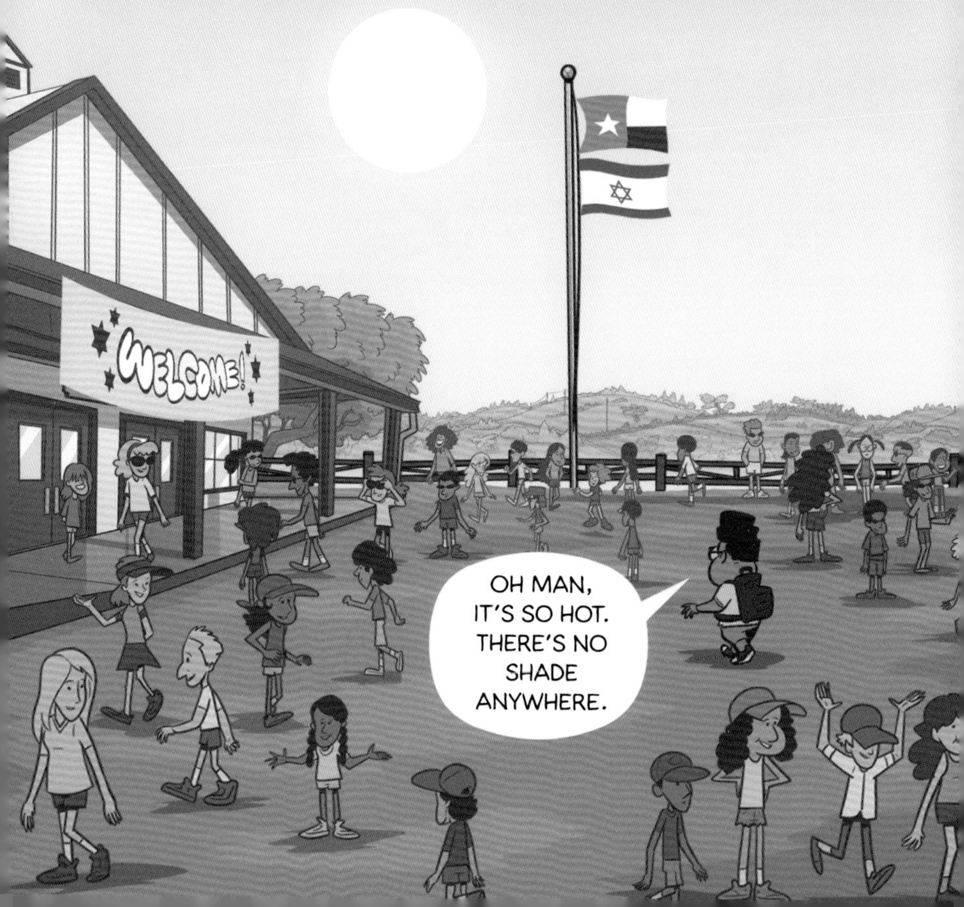
WELCOME!
OH MAN, IT'S SO HOT. THERE'S NO SHADE ANYWHERE.

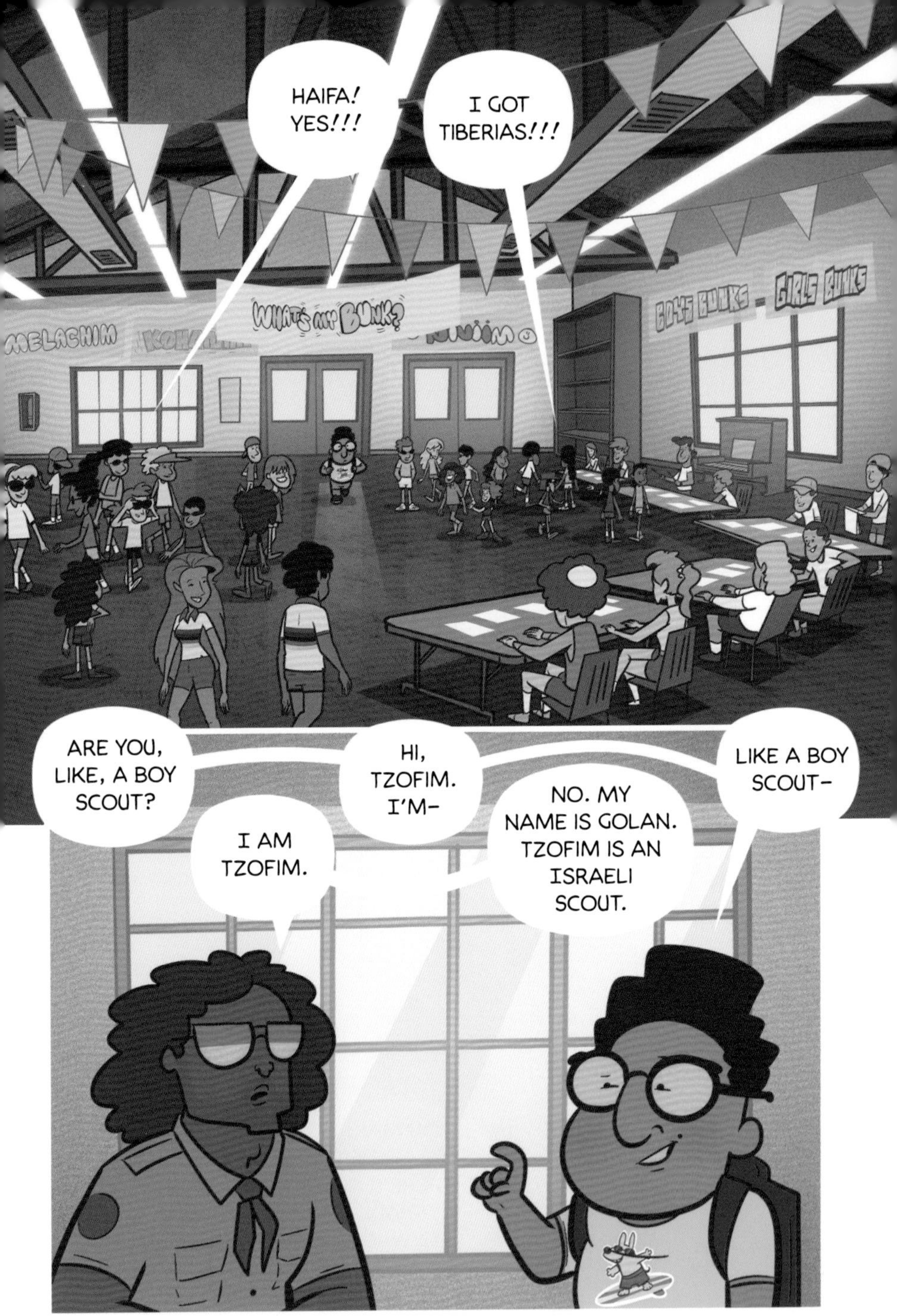
HAIFA! YES!!!
I GOT TIBERIAS!!!
WHAT'S MY BUNK?
MELACHIM
BOYS BUNKS
GIRLS BUNKS
ARE YOU, LIKE, A BOY SCOUT?
I AM TZOFIM.
HI, TZOFIM. I'M–
NO. MY NAME IS GOLAN. TZOFIM IS AN ISRAELI SCOUT.
LIKE A BOY SCOUT–

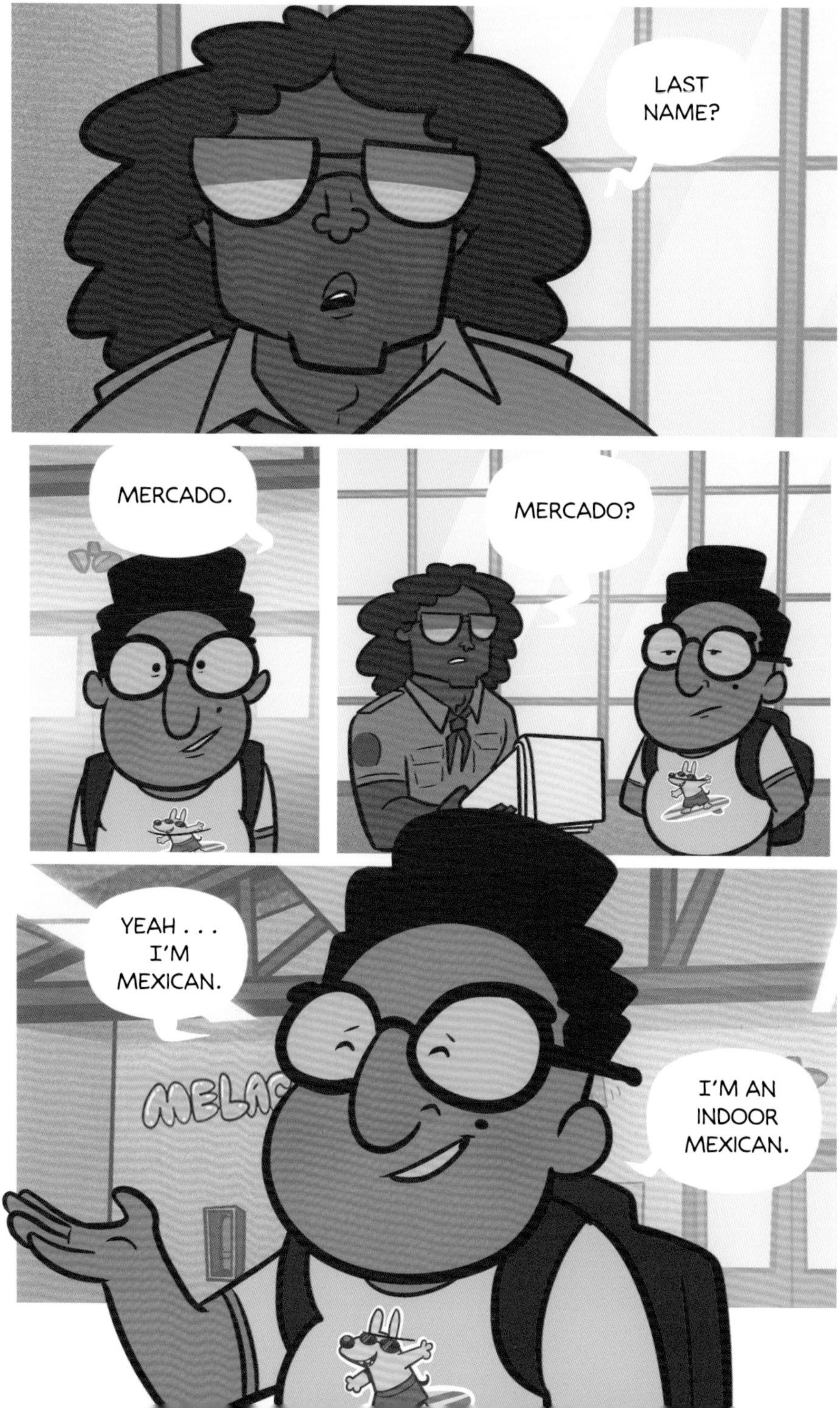
LAST NAME?
MERCADO.
MERCADO?
YEAH . . . I'M MEXICAN.
I'M AN INDOOR MEXICAN.

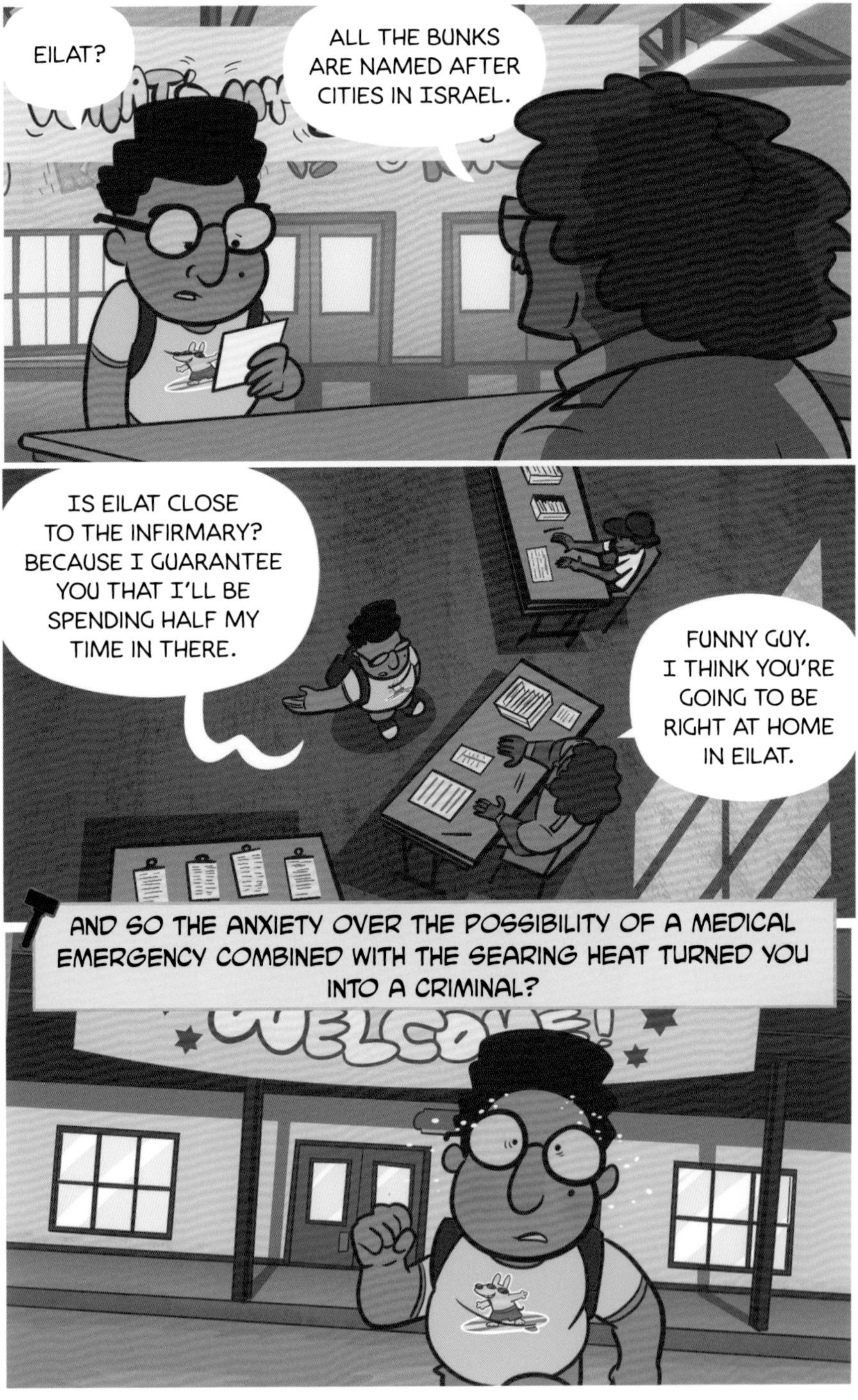
EILAT?
ALL THE BUNKS ARE NAMED AFTER CITIES IN ISRAEL.
IS EILAT CLOSE TO THE INFIRMARY? BECAUSE I GUARANTEE YOU THAT I'LL BE SPENDING HALF MY TIME IN THERE.
FUNNY GUY. I THINK YOU'RE GOING TO BE RIGHT AT HOME IN EILAT.
AND SO THE ANXIETY OVER THE POSSIBILITY OF A MEDICAL EMERGENCY COMBINED WITH THE SEARING HEAT TURNED YOU INTO A CRIMINAL?

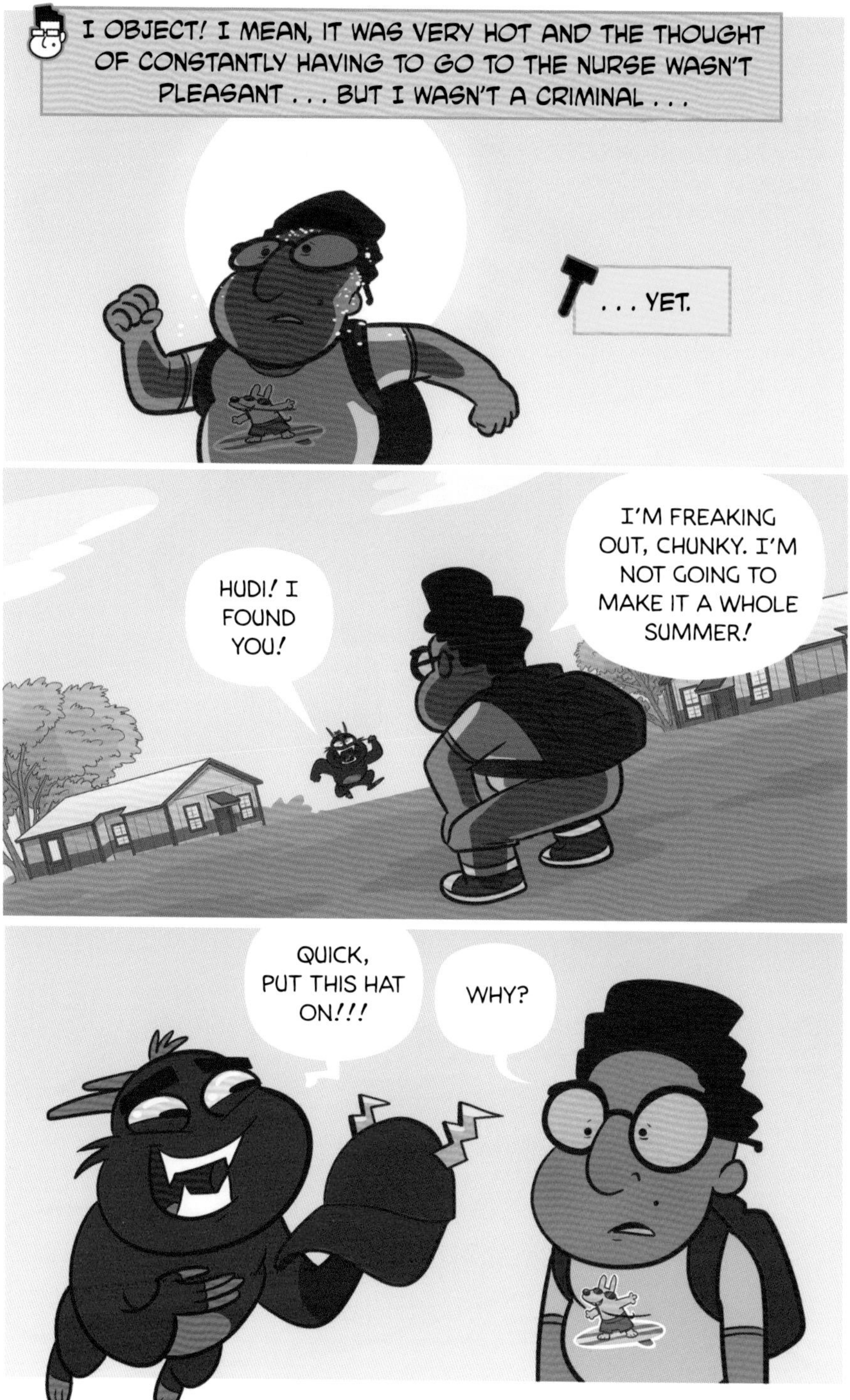
I OBJECT! I MEAN, IT WAS VERY HOT AND THE THOUGHT OF CONSTANTLY HAVING TO GO TO THE NURSE WASN'T PLEASANT . . . BUT I WASN'T A CRIMINAL . . .
. . . YET.
HUDI! I FOUND YOU!
I'M FREAKING OUT, CHUNKY. I'M NOT GOING TO MAKE IT A WHOLE SUMMER!
QUICK, PUT THIS HAT ON!!!
WHY?

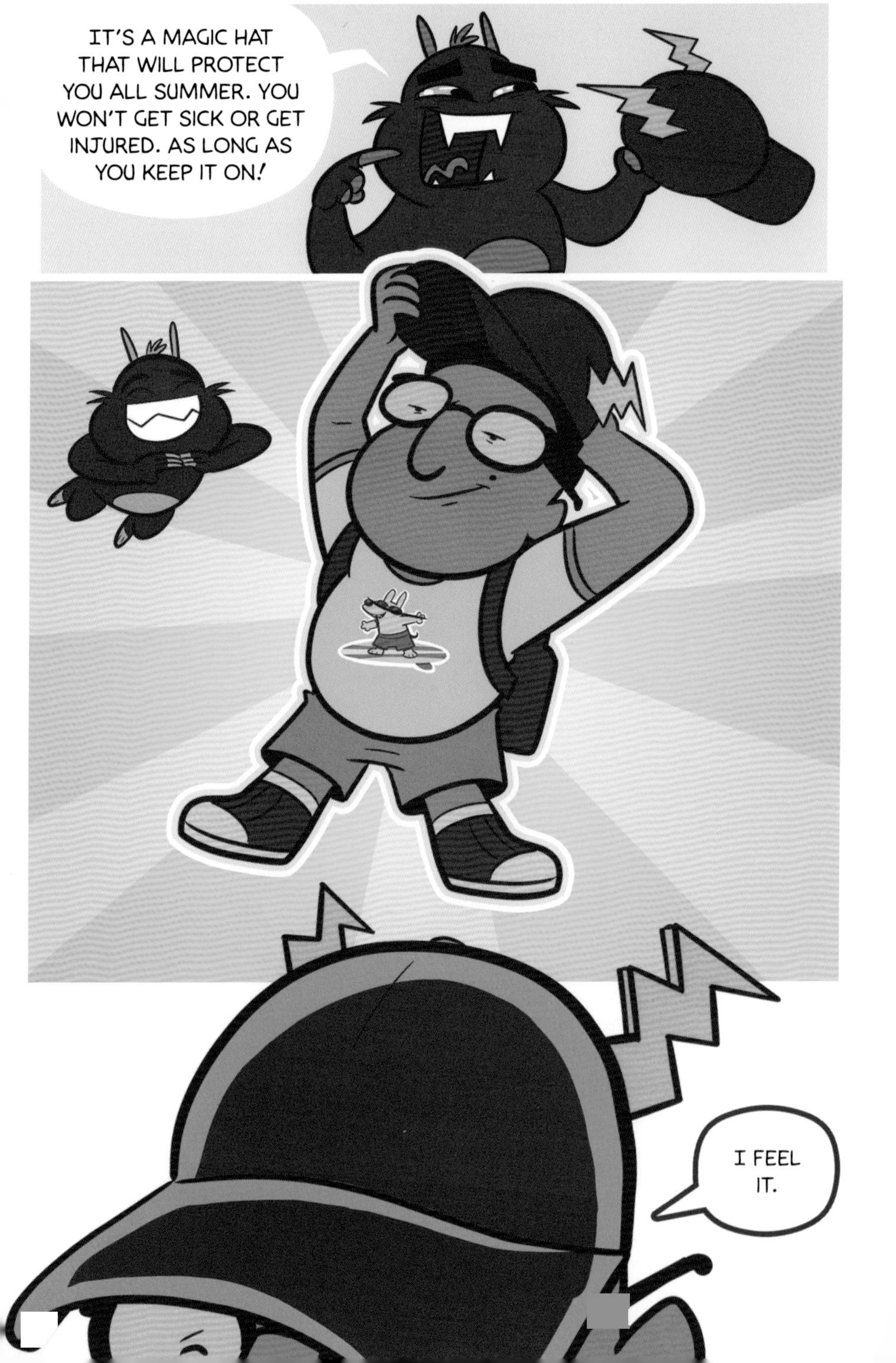
IT'S A MAGIC HAT THAT WILL PROTECT YOU ALL SUMMER. YOU WON'T GET SICK OR GET INJURED. AS LONG AS YOU KEEP IT ON!
I FEEL IT.

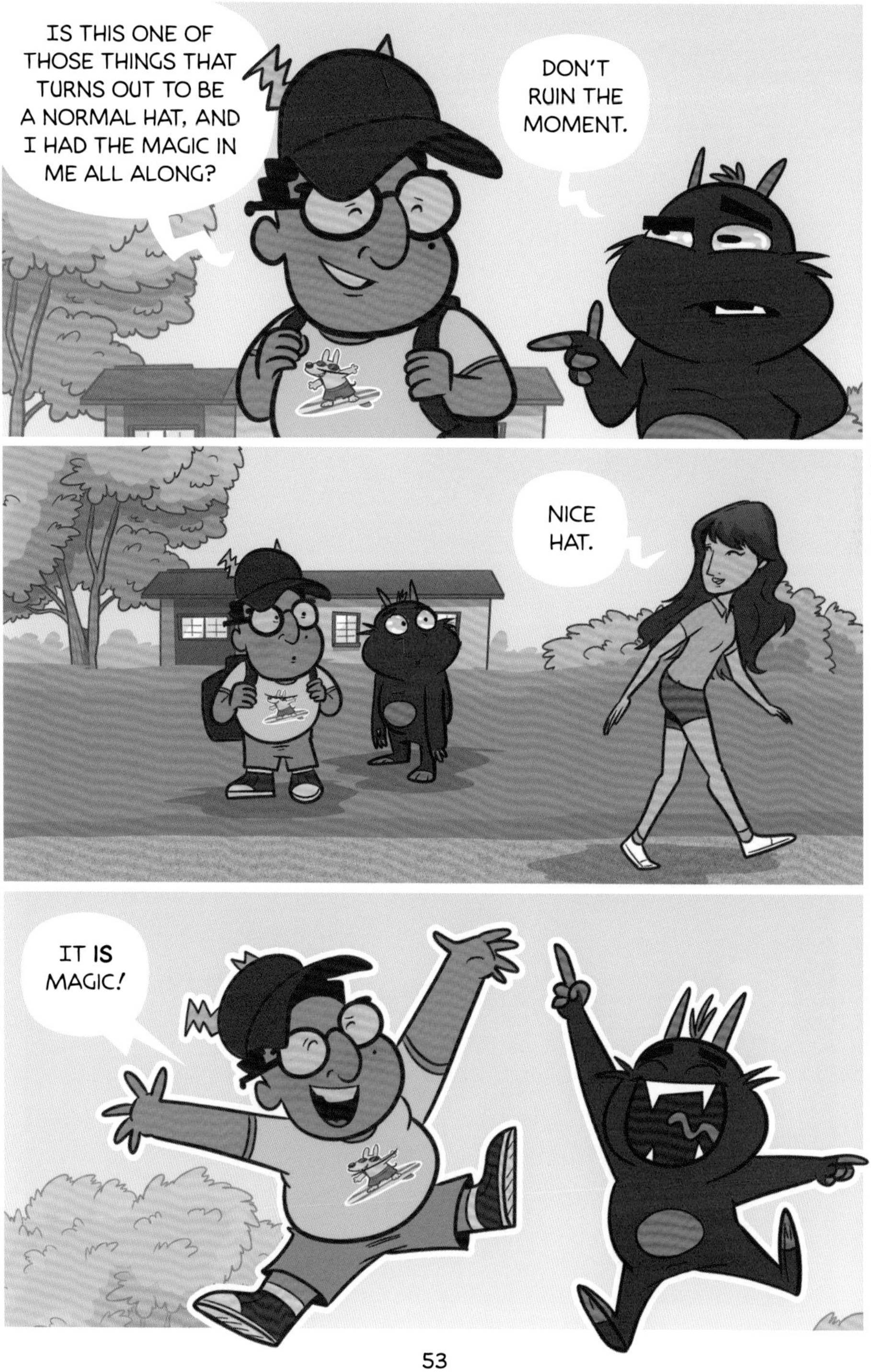
IS THIS ONE OF THOSE THINGS THAT TURNS OUT TO BE A NORMAL HAT, AND I HAD THE MAGIC IN ME ALL ALONG?
DON'T RUIN THE MOMENT.
NICE HAT.
IT **IS** MAGIC!

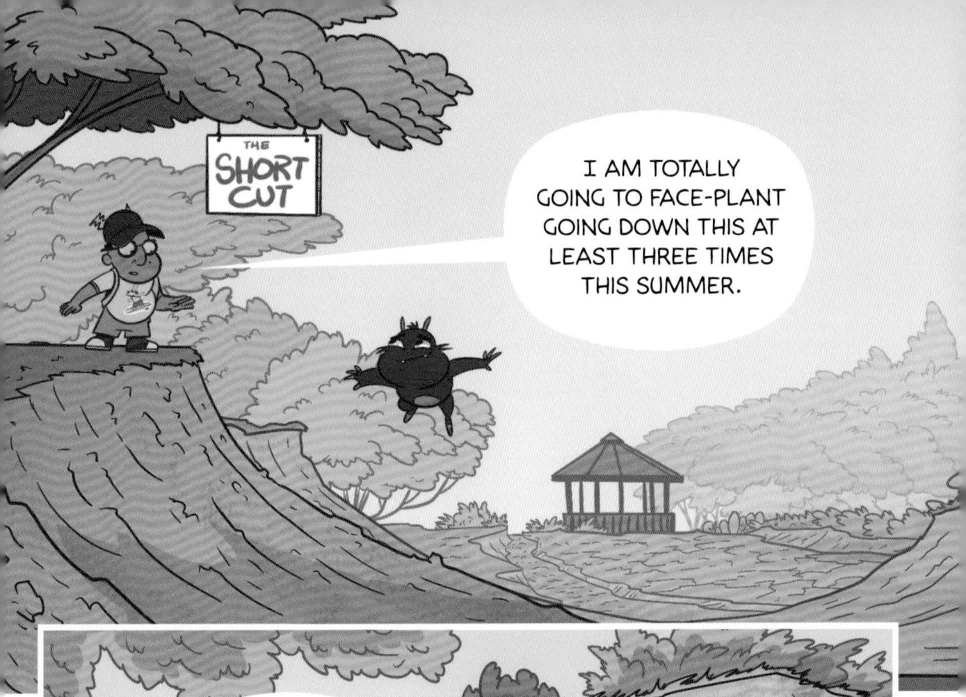
THE SHORT CUT
I AM TOTALLY GOING TO FACE-PLANT GOING DOWN THIS AT LEAST THREE TIMES THIS SUMMER.

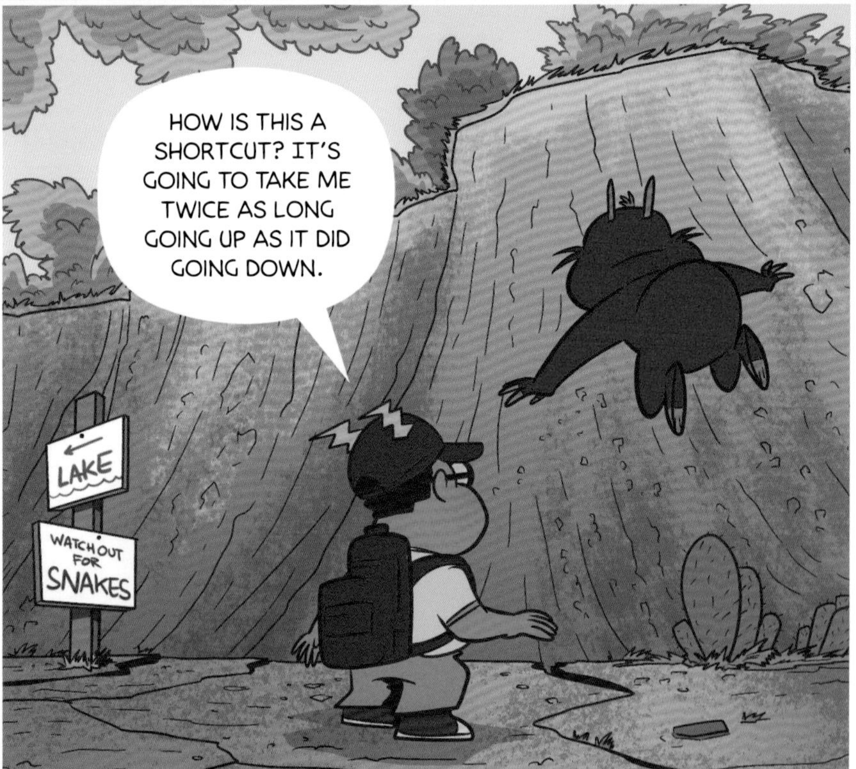
HOW IS THIS A SHORTCUT? IT'S GOING TO TAKE ME TWICE AS LONG GOING UP AS IT DID GOING DOWN.
LAKE
WATCH OUT FOR SNAKES

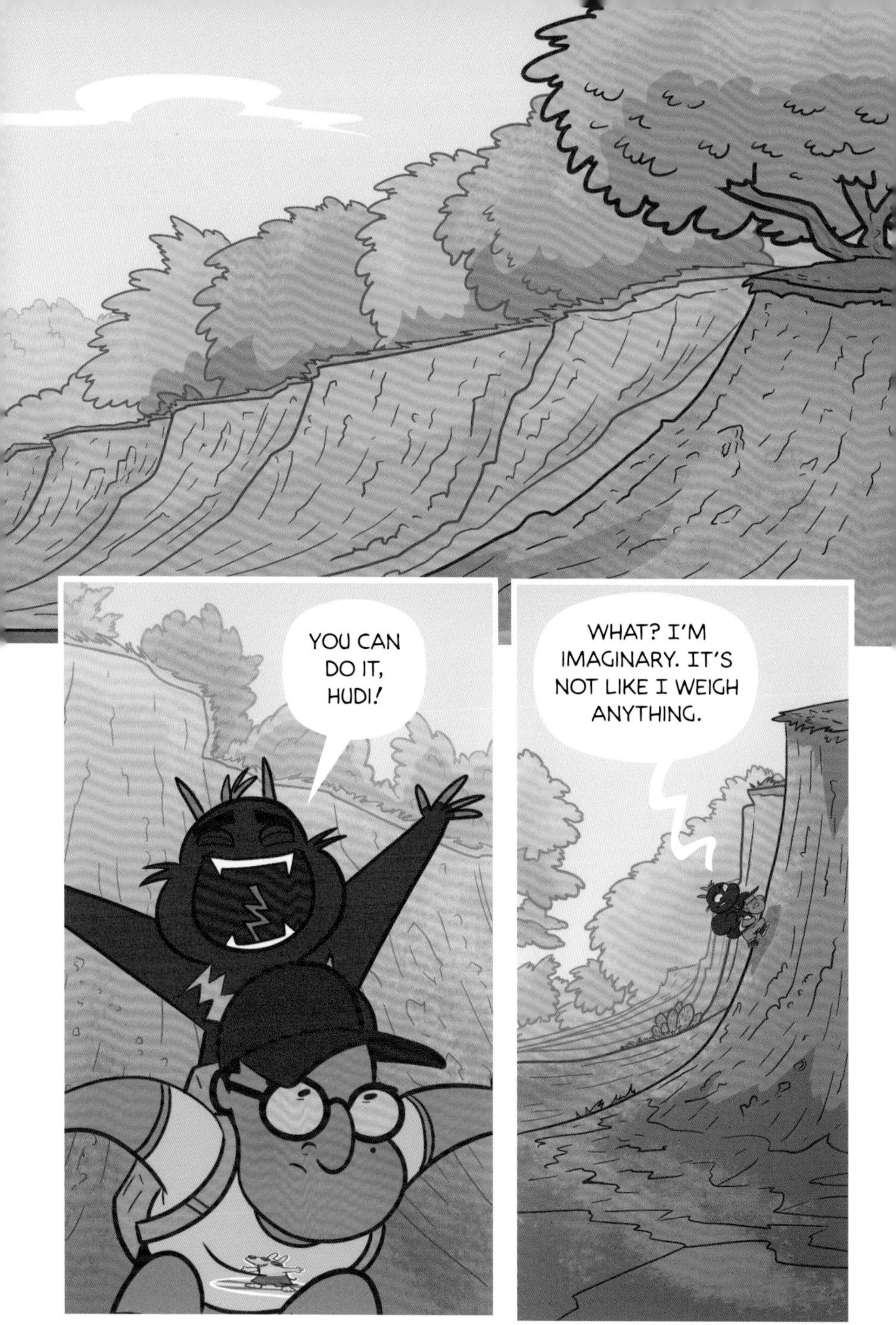
YOU CAN DO IT, HUDI!
WHAT? I'M IMAGINARY. IT'S NOT LIKE I WEIGH ANYTHING.

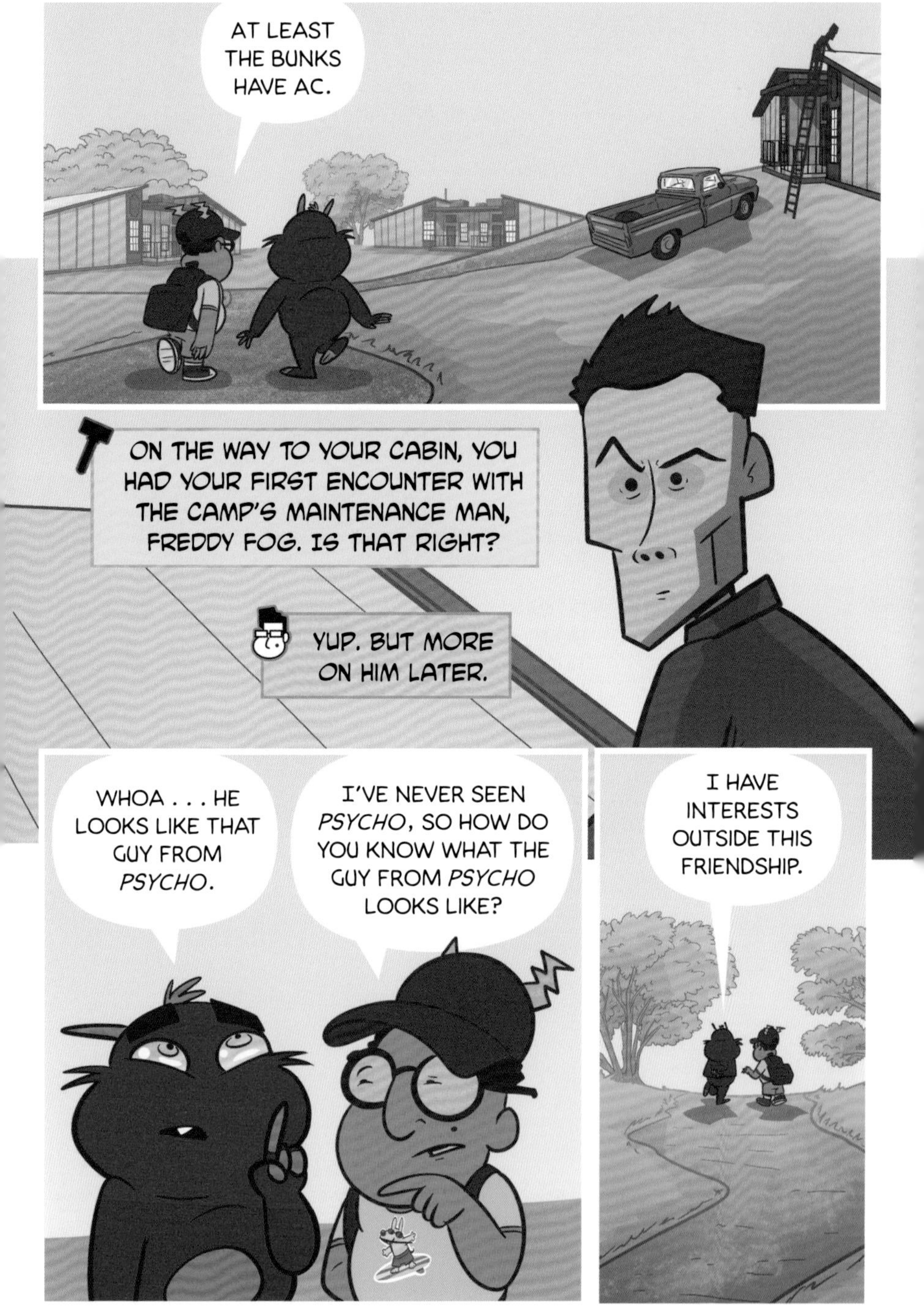
AT LEAST THE BUNKS HAVE AC.
ON THE WAY TO YOUR CABIN, YOU HAD YOUR FIRST ENCOUNTER WITH THE CAMP'S MAINTENANCE MAN, FREDDY FOG. IS THAT RIGHT?
YUP. BUT MORE ON HIM LATER.
WHOA . . . HE LOOKS LIKE THAT GUY FROM *PSYCHO*.
I'VE NEVER SEEN *PSYCHO*, SO HOW DO YOU KNOW WHAT THE GUY FROM *PSYCHO* LOOKS LIKE?
I HAVE INTERESTS OUTSIDE THIS FRIENDSHIP.

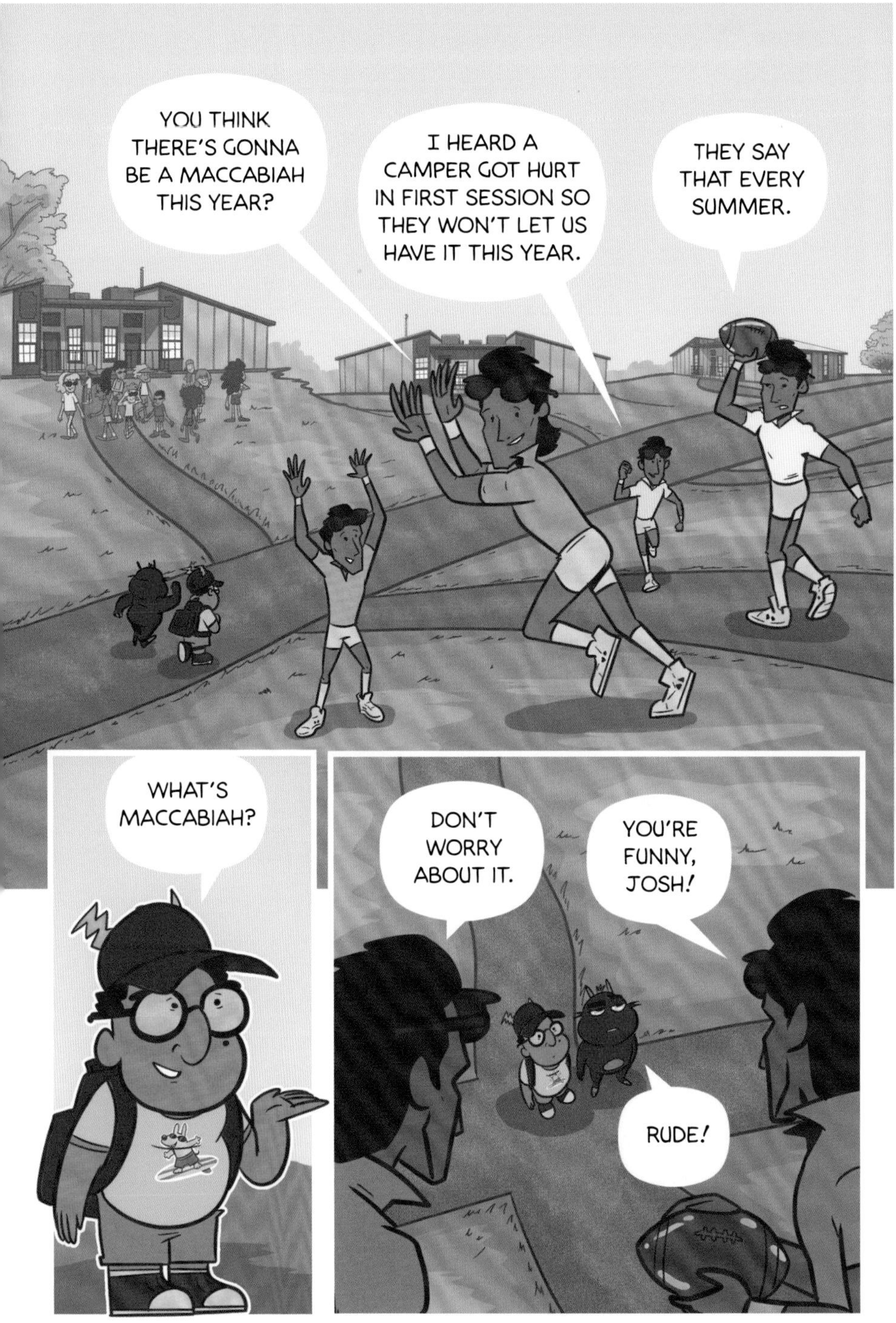
YOU THINK THERE'S GONNA BE A MACCABIAH THIS YEAR?
I HEARD A CAMPER GOT HURT IN FIRST SESSION SO THEY WON'T LET US HAVE IT THIS YEAR.
THEY SAY THAT EVERY SUMMER.
WHAT'S MACCABIAH?
DON'T WORRY ABOUT IT.
YOU'RE FUNNY, JOSH!
RUDE!

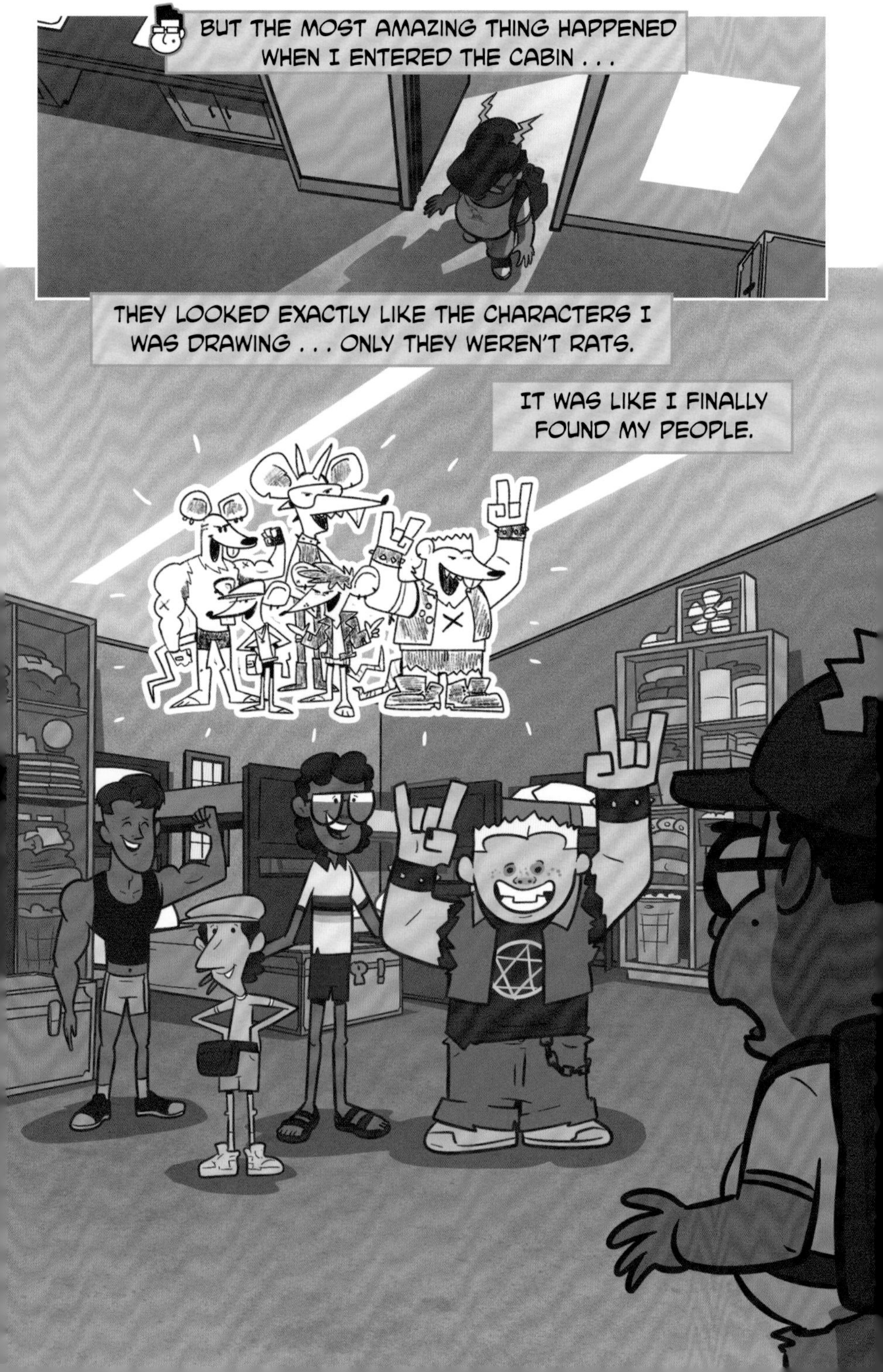
BUT THE MOST AMAZING THING HAPPENED WHEN I ENTERED THE CABIN . . .
THEY LOOKED EXACTLY LIKE THE CHARACTERS I WAS DRAWING . . . ONLY THEY WEREN'T RATS.
IT WAS LIKE I FINALLY FOUND MY PEOPLE.

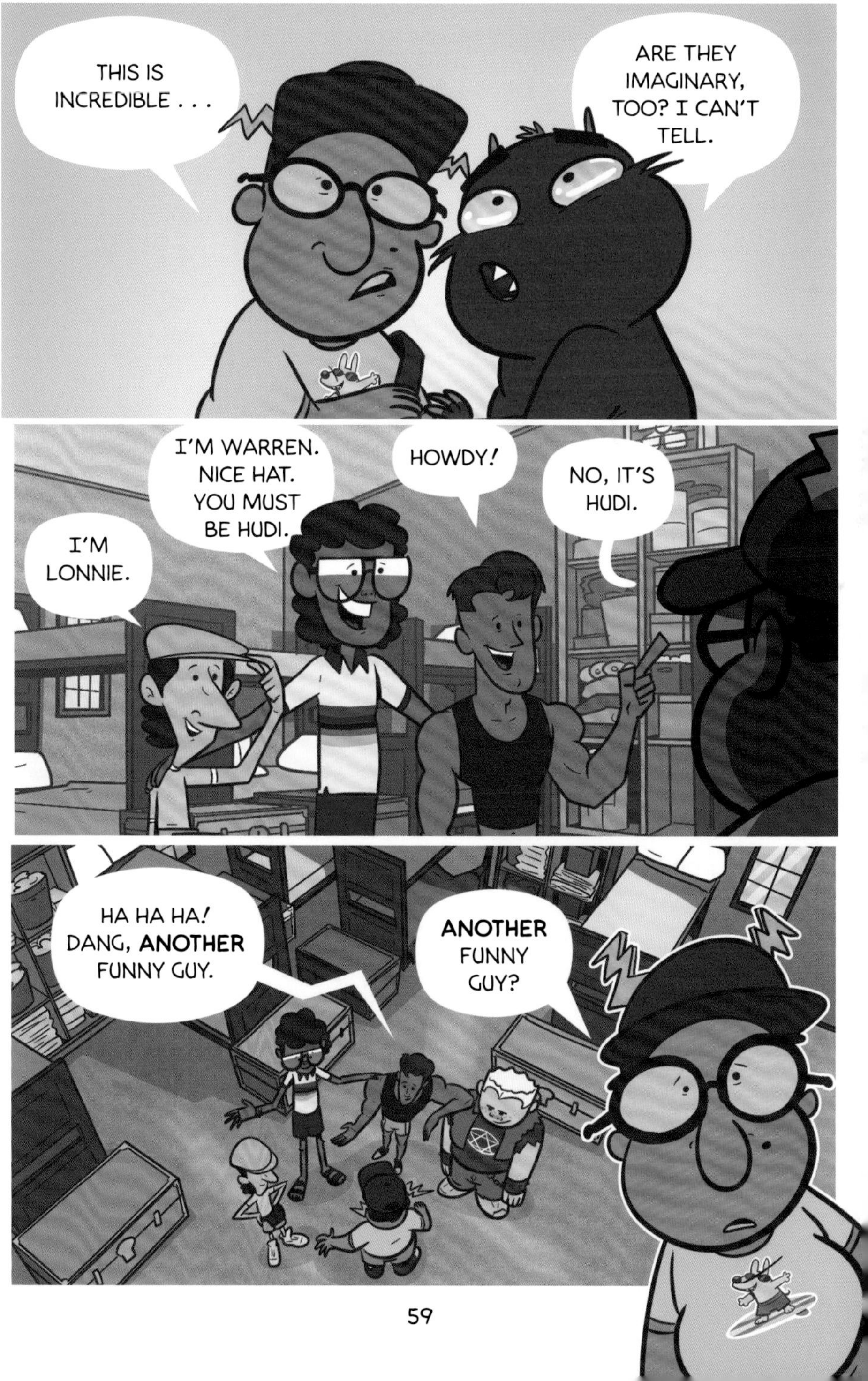
THIS IS INCREDIBLE . . .
ARE THEY IMAGINARY, TOO? I CAN'T TELL.
I'M LONNIE.
I'M WARREN. NICE HAT. YOU MUST BE HUDI.
HOWDY!
NO, IT'S HUDI.
HA HA HA! DANG, **ANOTHER** FUNNY GUY.
ANOTHER FUNNY GUY?

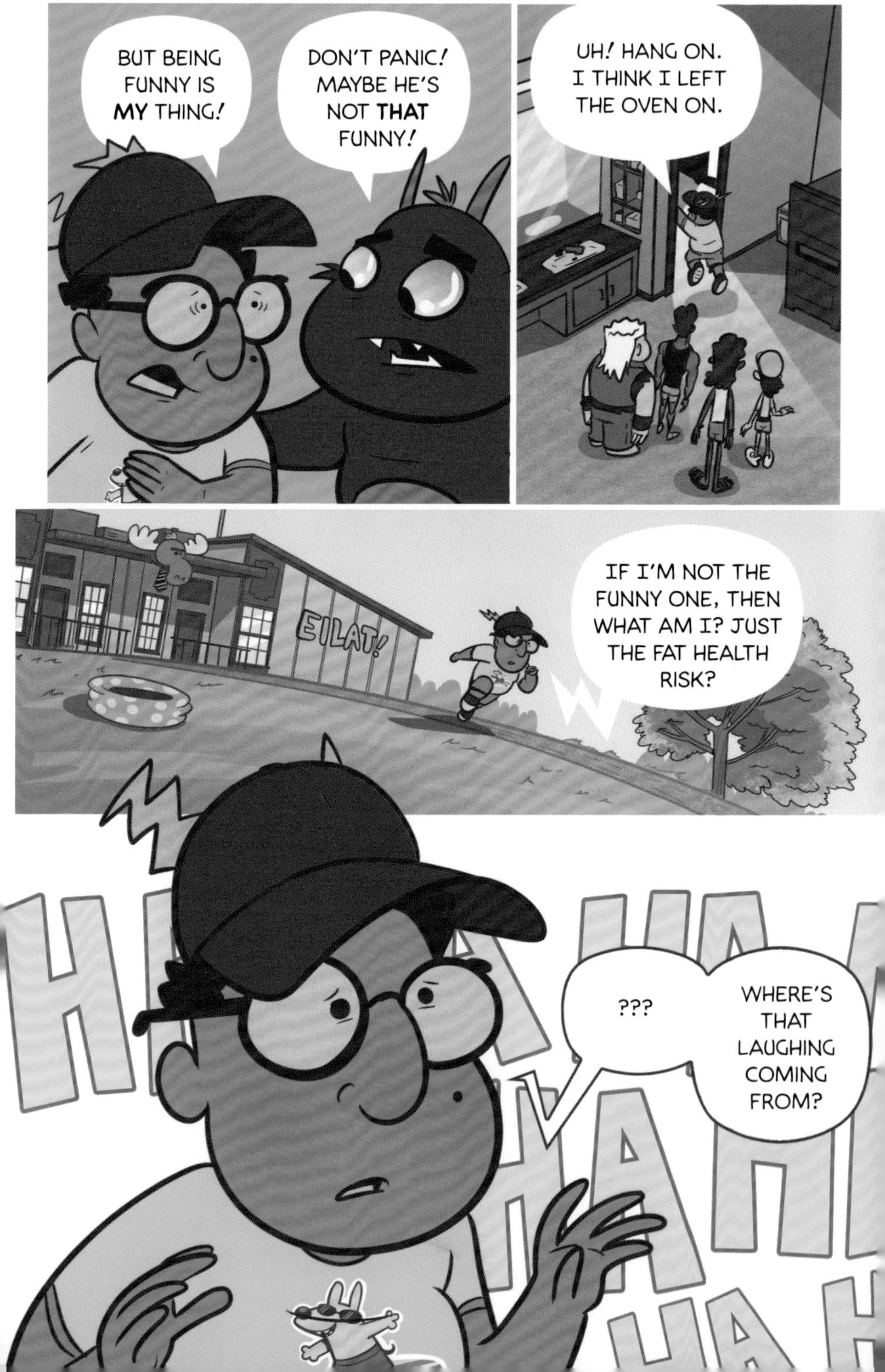
BUT BEING FUNNY IS **MY** THING!
DON'T PANIC! MAYBE HE'S NOT **THAT** FUNNY!
UH! HANG ON. I THINK I LEFT THE OVEN ON.
EILAT!
IF I'M NOT THE FUNNY ONE, THEN WHAT AM I? JUST THE FAT HEALTH RISK?
???
WHERE'S THAT LAUGHING COMING FROM?

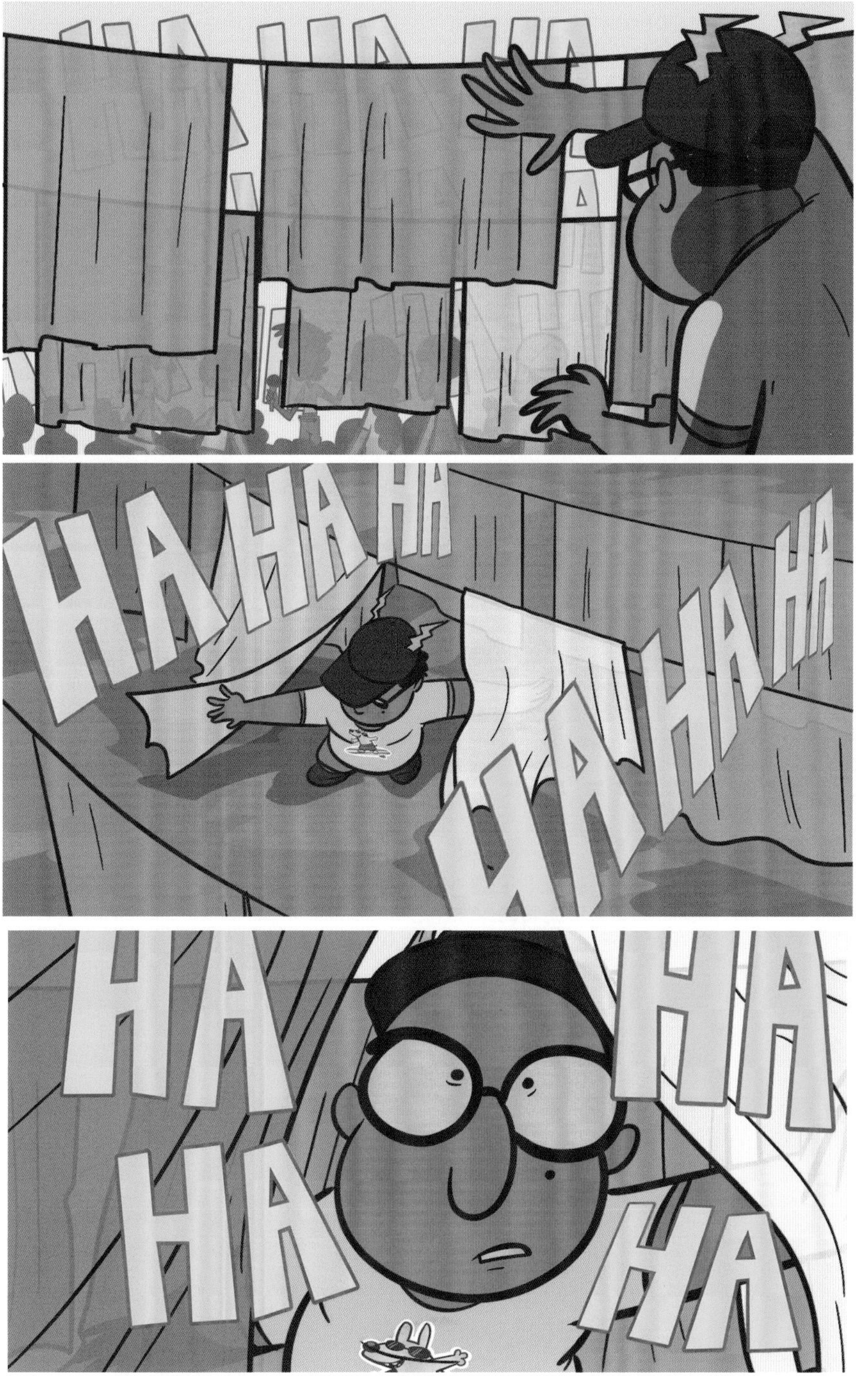
HA HA HA HA
HA HA HA HA
HA HA
HA HA
HA HA

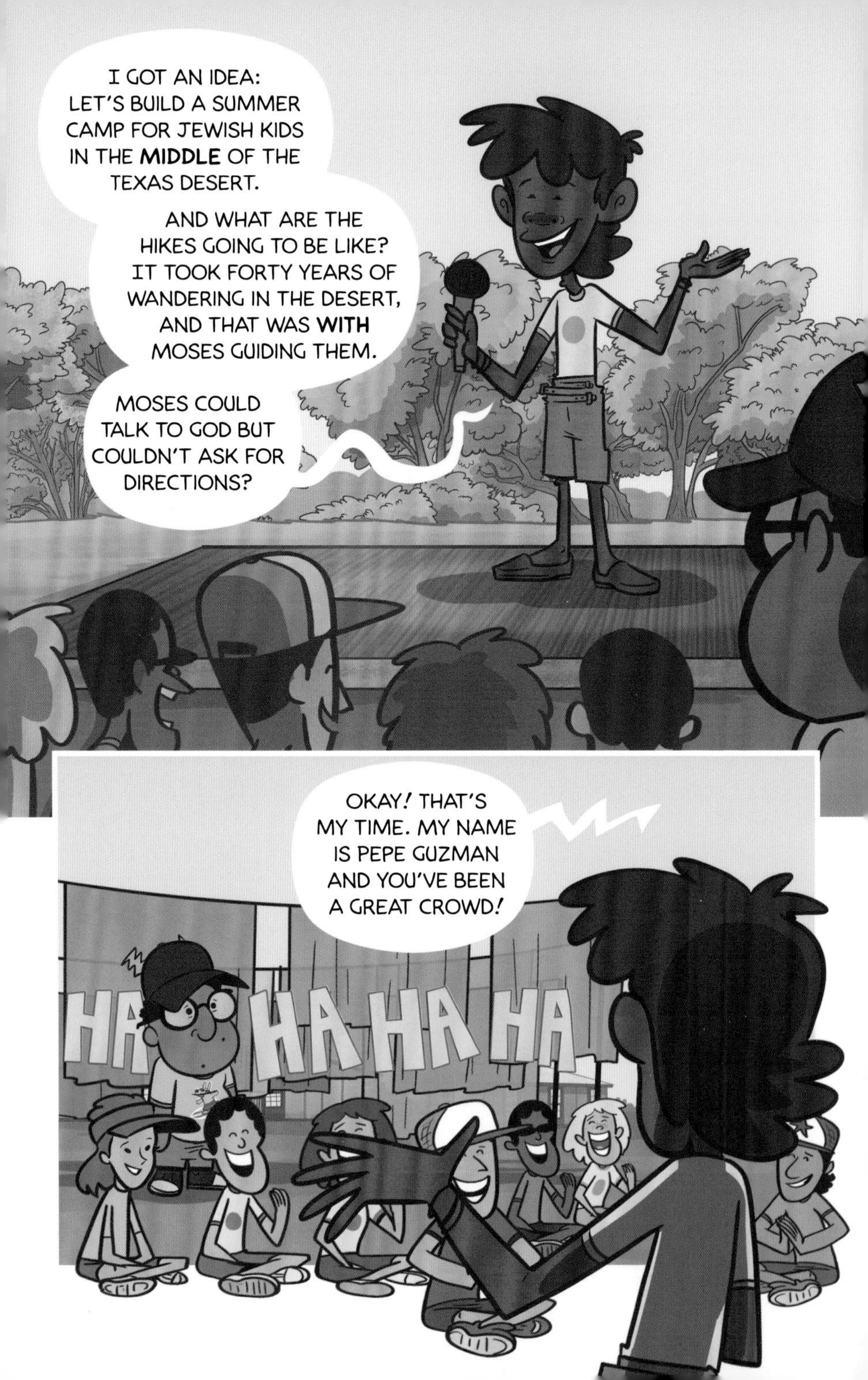
I GOT AN IDEA: LET'S BUILD A SUMMER CAMP FOR JEWISH KIDS IN THE **MIDDLE** OF THE TEXAS DESERT.
AND WHAT ARE THE HIKES GOING TO BE LIKE? IT TOOK FORTY YEARS OF WANDERING IN THE DESERT, AND THAT WAS **WITH** MOSES GUIDING THEM.
MOSES COULD TALK TO GOD BUT COULDN'T ASK FOR DIRECTIONS?
OKAY! THAT'S MY TIME. MY NAME IS PEPE GUZMAN AND YOU'VE BEEN A GREAT CROWD!
HA HA HA HA HA

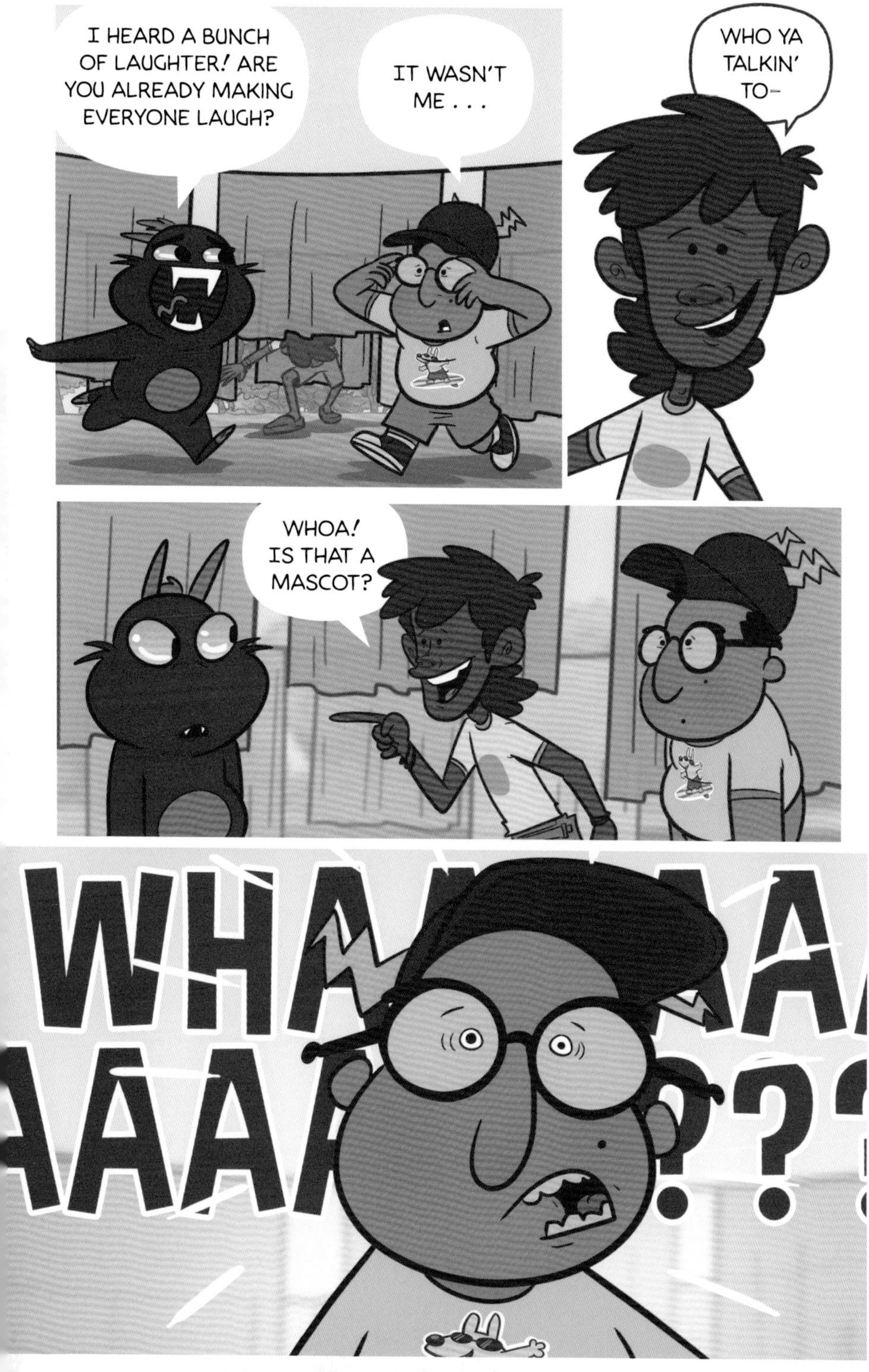
I HEARD A BUNCH OF LAUGHTER! ARE YOU ALREADY MAKING EVERYONE LAUGH?
IT WASN'T ME . . .
WHO YA TALKIN' TO–
WHOA! IS THAT A MASCOT?

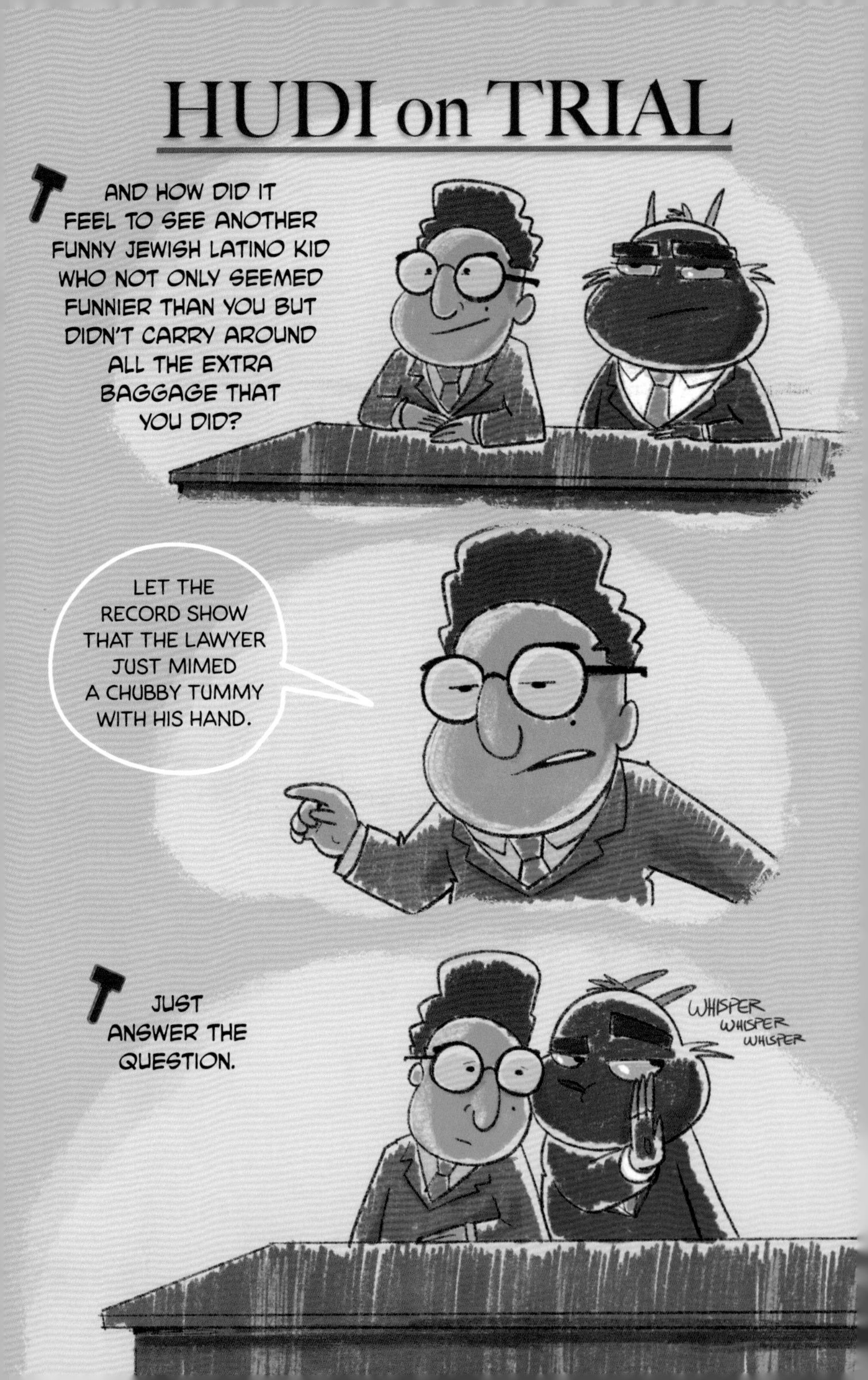
HUDI on TRIAL
AND HOW DID IT FEEL TO SEE ANOTHER FUNNY JEWISH LATINO KID WHO NOT ONLY SEEMED FUNNIER THAN YOU BUT DIDN'T CARRY AROUND ALL THE EXTRA BAGGAGE THAT YOU DID?
LET THE RECORD SHOW THAT THE LAWYER JUST MIMED A CHUBBY TUMMY WITH HIS HAND.
JUST ANSWER THE QUESTION.
WHISPER WHISPER WHISPER

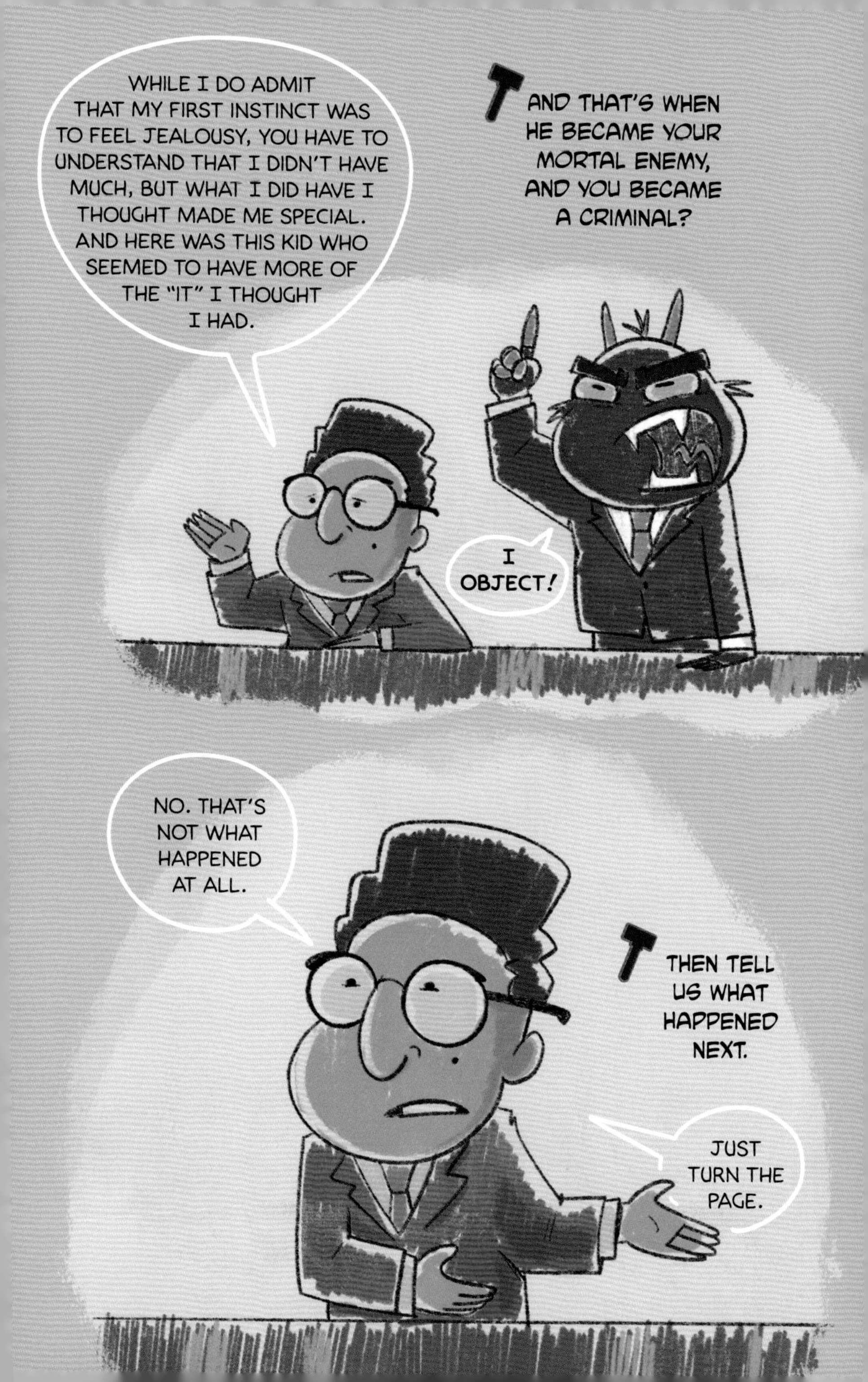
WHILE I DO ADMIT THAT MY FIRST INSTINCT WAS TO FEEL JEALOUSY, YOU HAVE TO UNDERSTAND THAT I DIDN'T HAVE MUCH, BUT WHAT I DID HAVE I THOUGHT MADE ME SPECIAL. AND HERE WAS THIS KID WHO SEEMED TO HAVE MORE OF THE "IT" I THOUGHT I HAD.
AND THAT'S WHEN HE BECAME YOUR MORTAL ENEMY, AND YOU BECAME A CRIMINAL?
I OBJECT!
NO. THAT'S NOT WHAT HAPPENED AT ALL.
THEN TELL US WHAT HAPPENED NEXT.
JUST TURN THE PAGE.

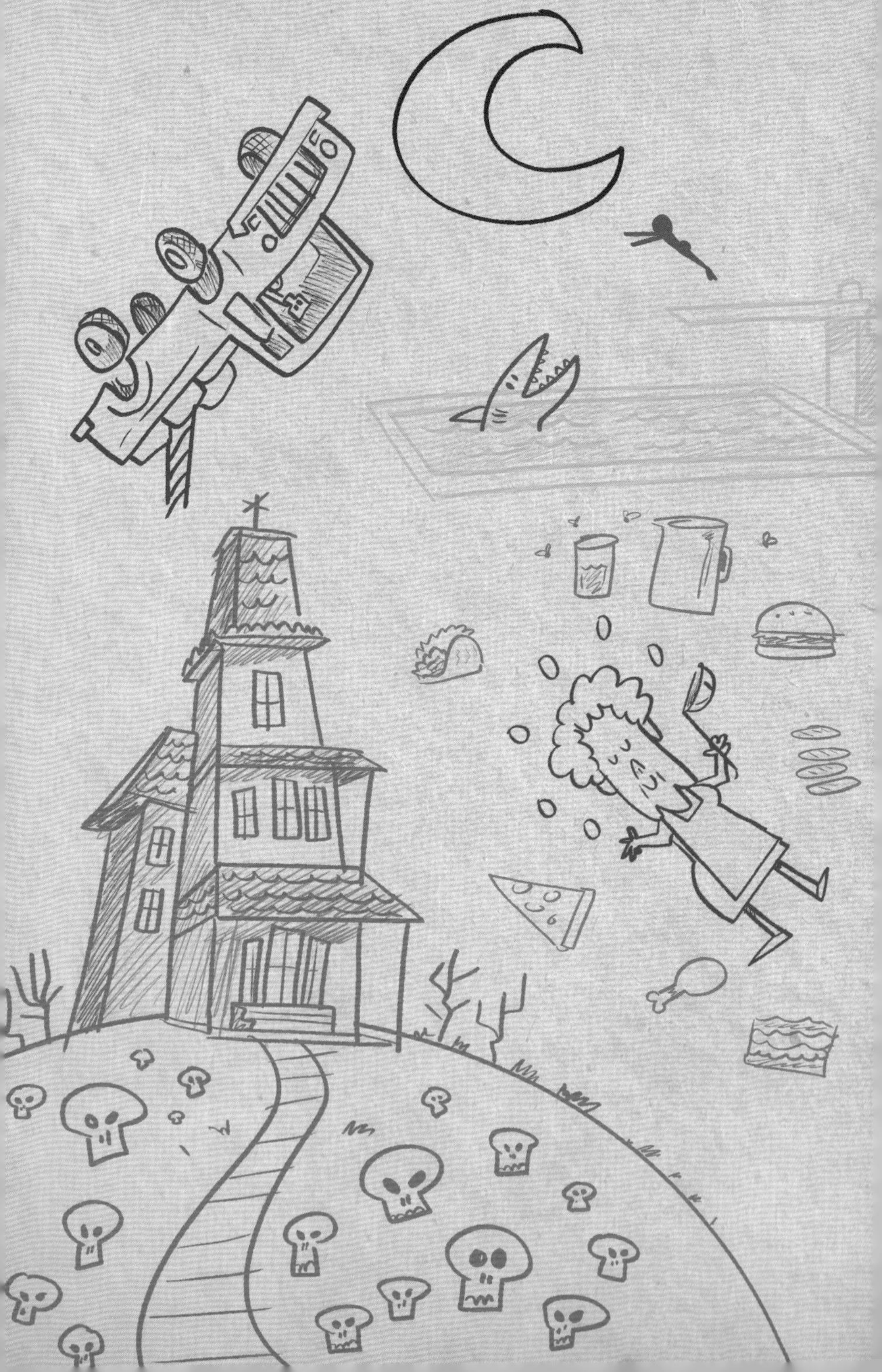

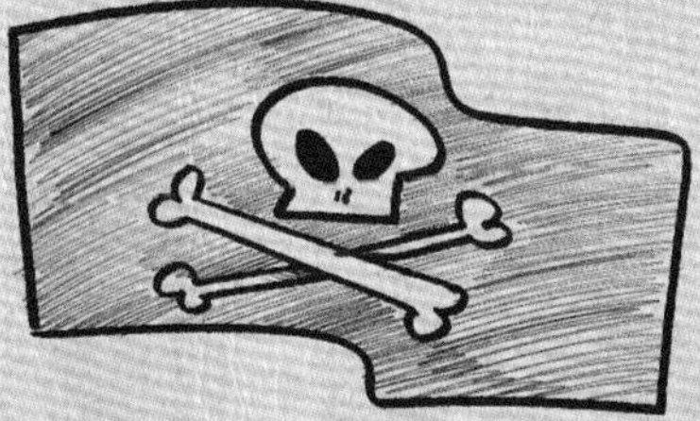

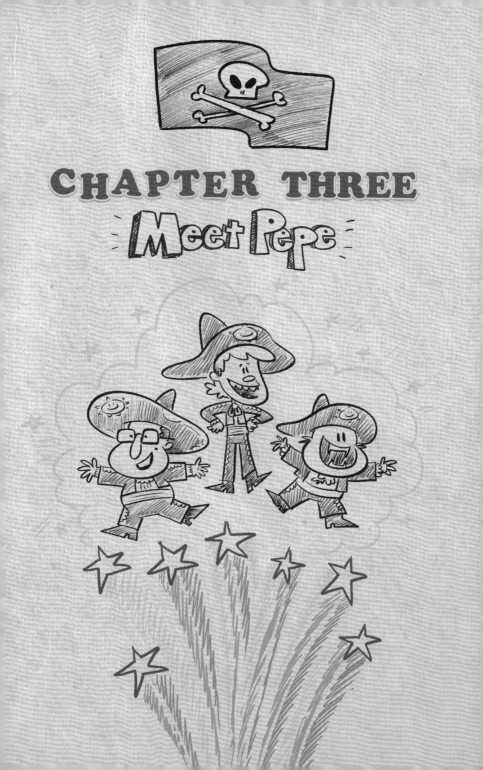

CHAPTER THREE

Meet Pepe

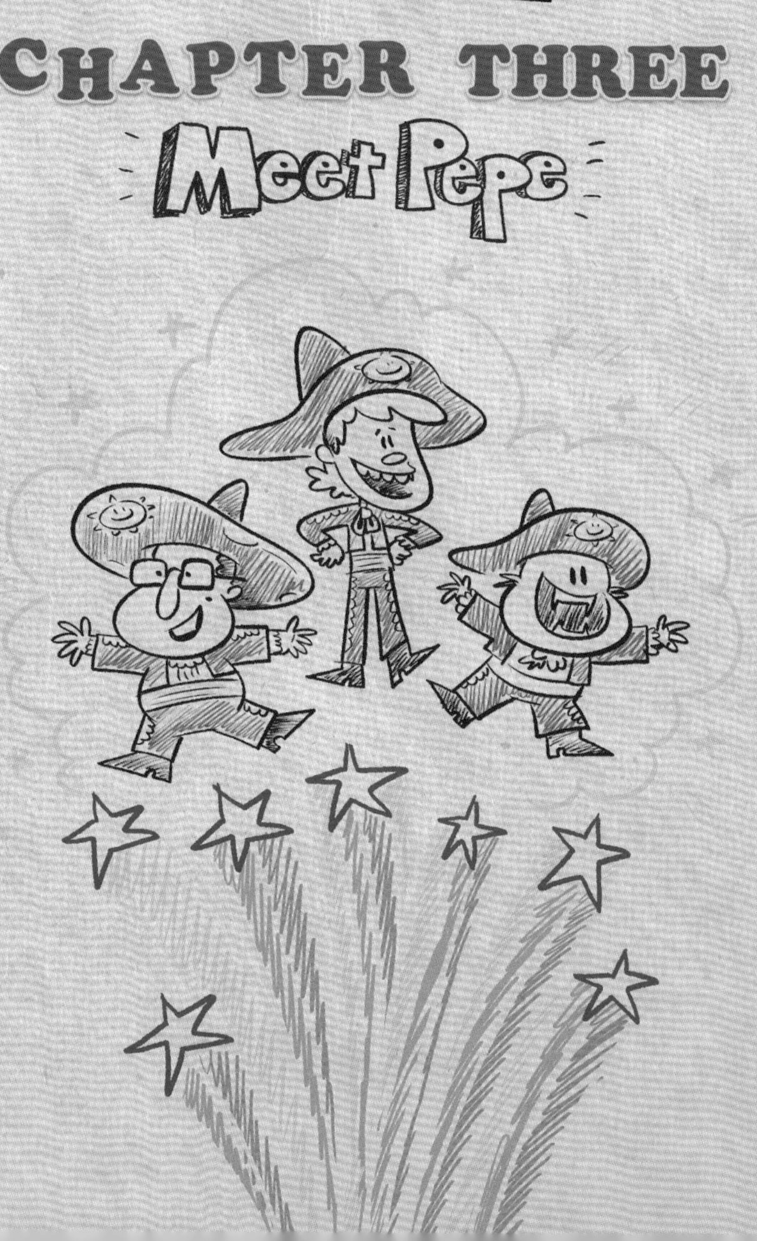

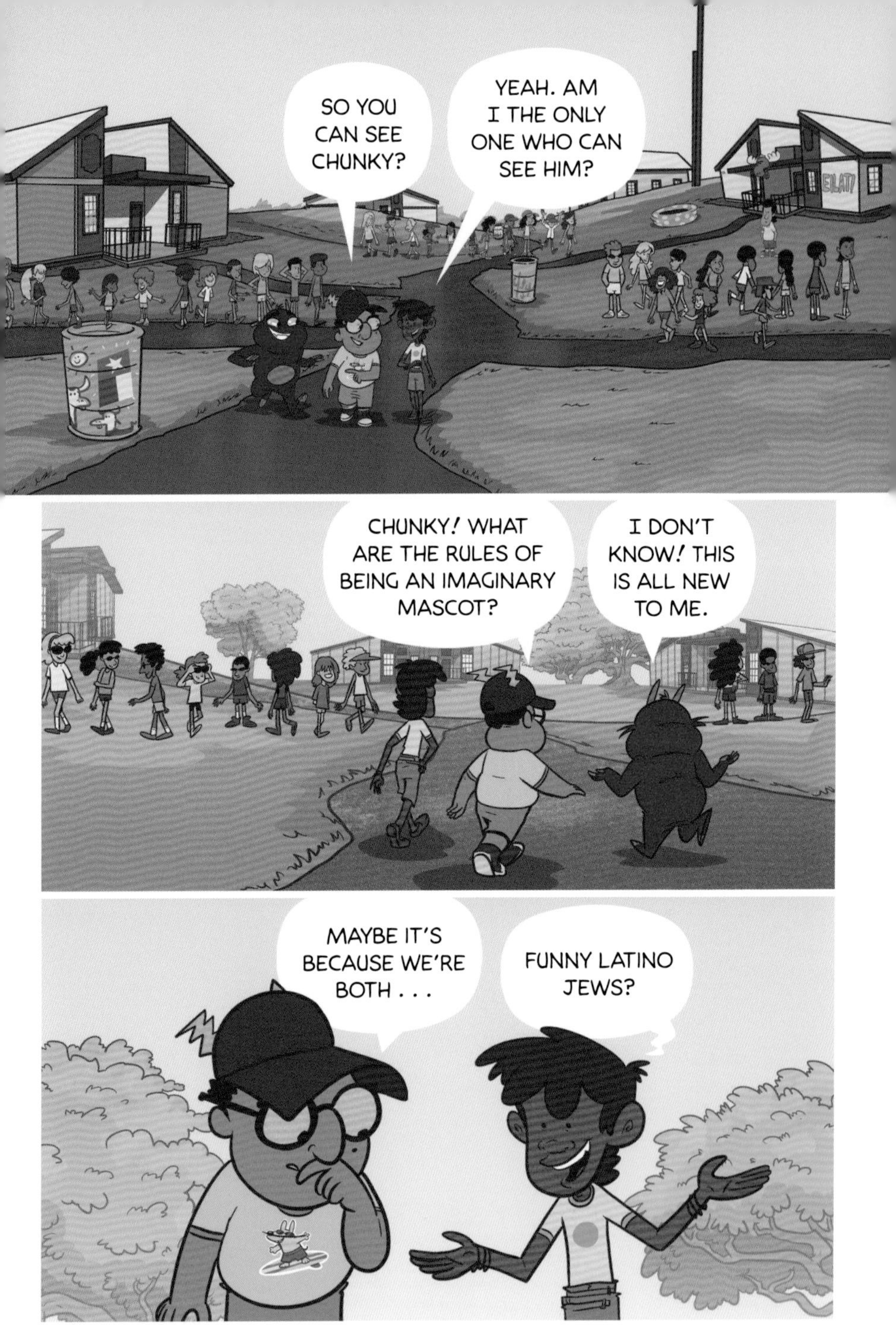
SO YOU CAN SEE CHUNKY?
YEAH. AM I THE ONLY ONE WHO CAN SEE HIM?
EILAT
CHUNKY! WHAT ARE THE RULES OF BEING AN IMAGINARY MASCOT?
I DON'T KNOW! THIS IS ALL NEW TO ME.
MAYBE IT'S BECAUSE WE'RE BOTH . . .
FUNNY LATINO JEWS?

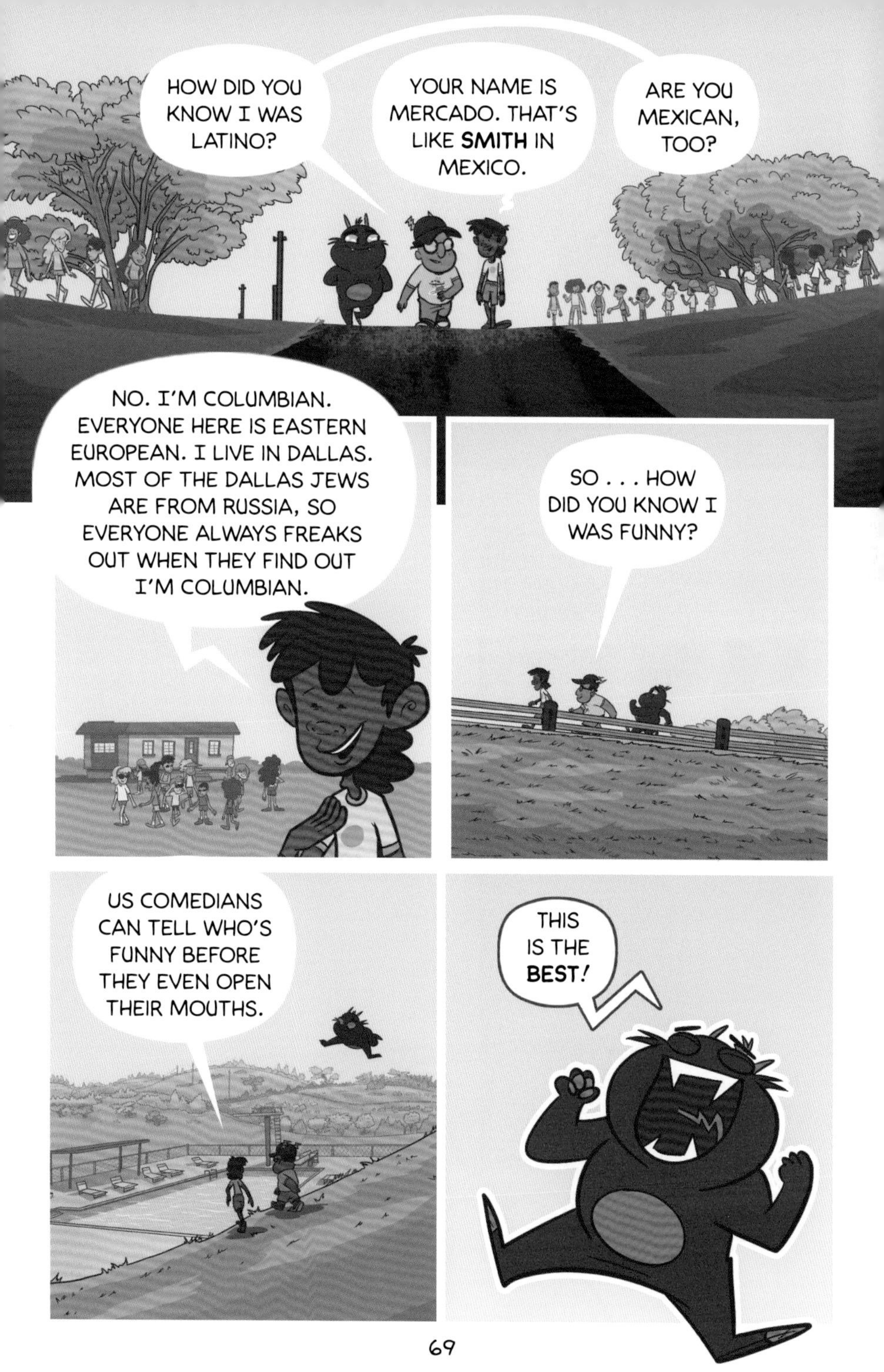
HOW DID YOU KNOW I WAS LATINO?
YOUR NAME IS MERCADO. THAT'S LIKE **SMITH** IN MEXICO.
ARE YOU MEXICAN, TOO?
NO. I'M COLUMBIAN. EVERYONE HERE IS EASTERN EUROPEAN. I LIVE IN DALLAS. MOST OF THE DALLAS JEWS ARE FROM RUSSIA, SO EVERYONE ALWAYS FREAKS OUT WHEN THEY FIND OUT I'M COLUMBIAN.
SO . . . HOW DID YOU KNOW I WAS FUNNY?
US COMEDIANS CAN TELL WHO'S FUNNY BEFORE THEY EVEN OPEN THEIR MOUTHS.
THIS IS THE **BEST**!

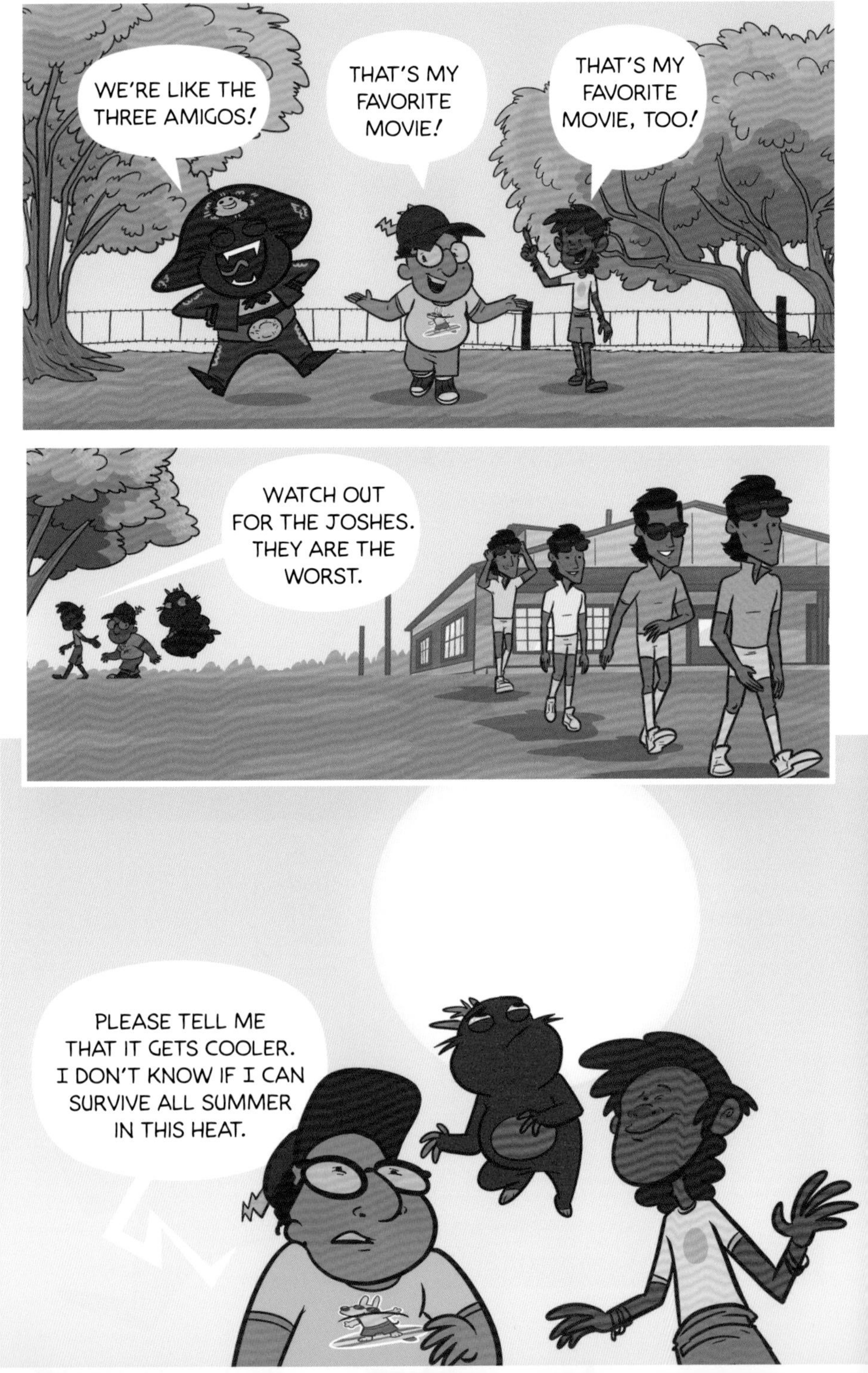
WE'RE LIKE THE THREE AMIGOS!
THAT'S MY FAVORITE MOVIE!
THAT'S MY FAVORITE MOVIE, TOO!
WATCH OUT FOR THE JOSHES. THEY ARE THE WORST.
PLEASE TELL ME THAT IT GETS COOLER. I DON'T KNOW IF I CAN SURVIVE ALL SUMMER IN THIS HEAT.

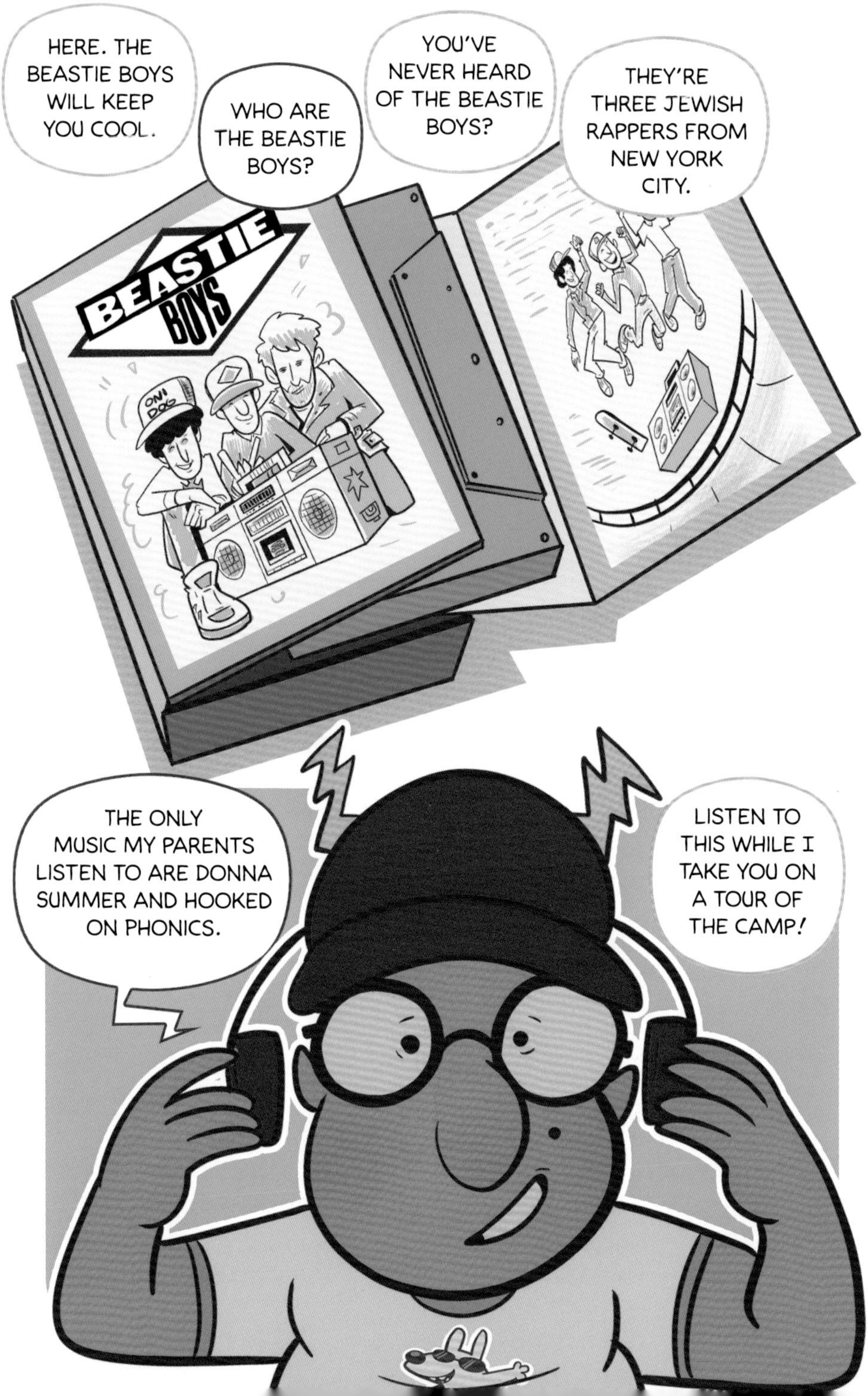
HERE. THE BEASTIE BOYS WILL KEEP YOU COOL.
WHO ARE THE BEASTIE BOYS?
YOU'VE NEVER HEARD OF THE BEASTIE BOYS?
THEY'RE THREE JEWISH RAPPERS FROM NEW YORK CITY.
BEASTIE BOYS
THE ONLY MUSIC MY PARENTS LISTEN TO ARE DONNA SUMMER AND HOOKED ON PHONICS.
LISTEN TO THIS WHILE I TAKE YOU ON A TOUR OF THE CAMP!

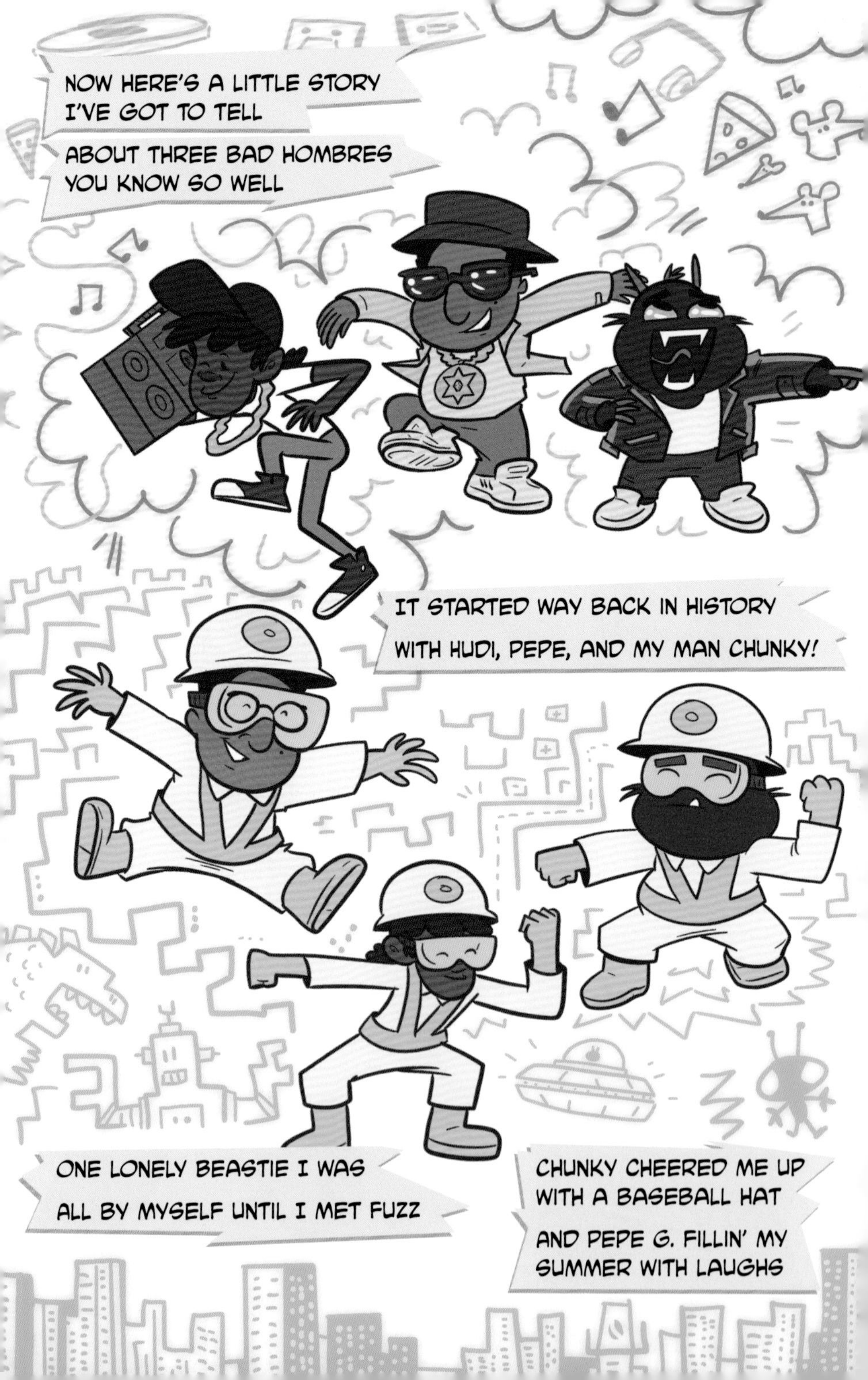
NOW HERE'S A LITTLE STORY I'VE GOT TO TELL
ABOUT THREE BAD HOMBRES YOU KNOW SO WELL
IT STARTED WAY BACK IN HISTORY
WITH HUDI, PEPE, AND MY MAN CHUNKY!
ONE LONELY BEASTIE I WAS
ALL BY MYSELF UNTIL I MET FUZZ
CHUNKY CHEERED ME UP WITH A BASEBALL HAT
AND PEPE G. FILLIN' MY SUMMER WITH LAUGHS

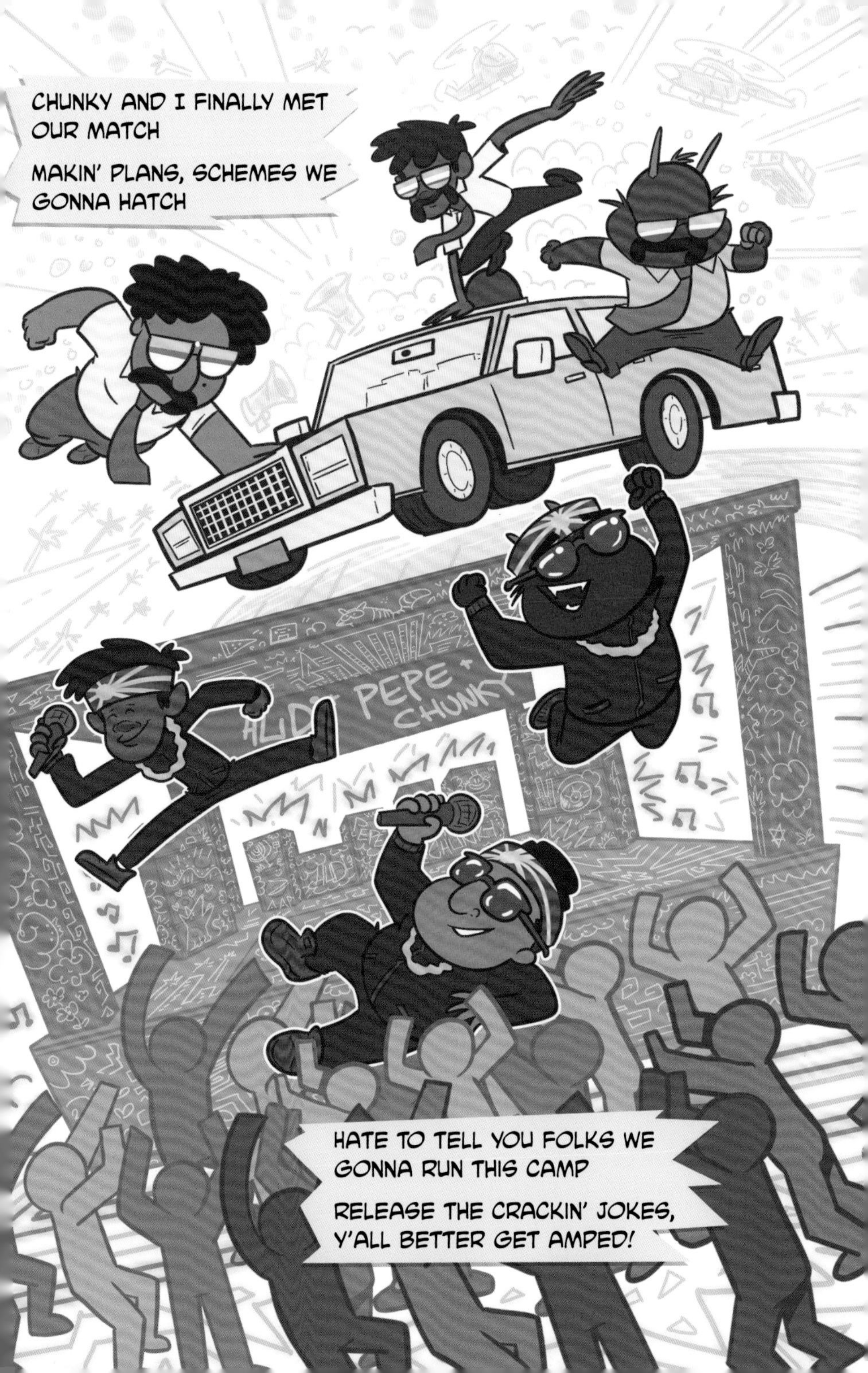
CHUNKY AND I FINALLY MET OUR MATCH
MAKIN' PLANS, SCHEMES WE GONNA HATCH
PEPE
CHUNKY
HATE TO TELL YOU FOLKS WE GONNA RUN THIS CAMP
RELEASE THE CRACKIN' JOKES, Y'ALL BETTER GET AMPED!

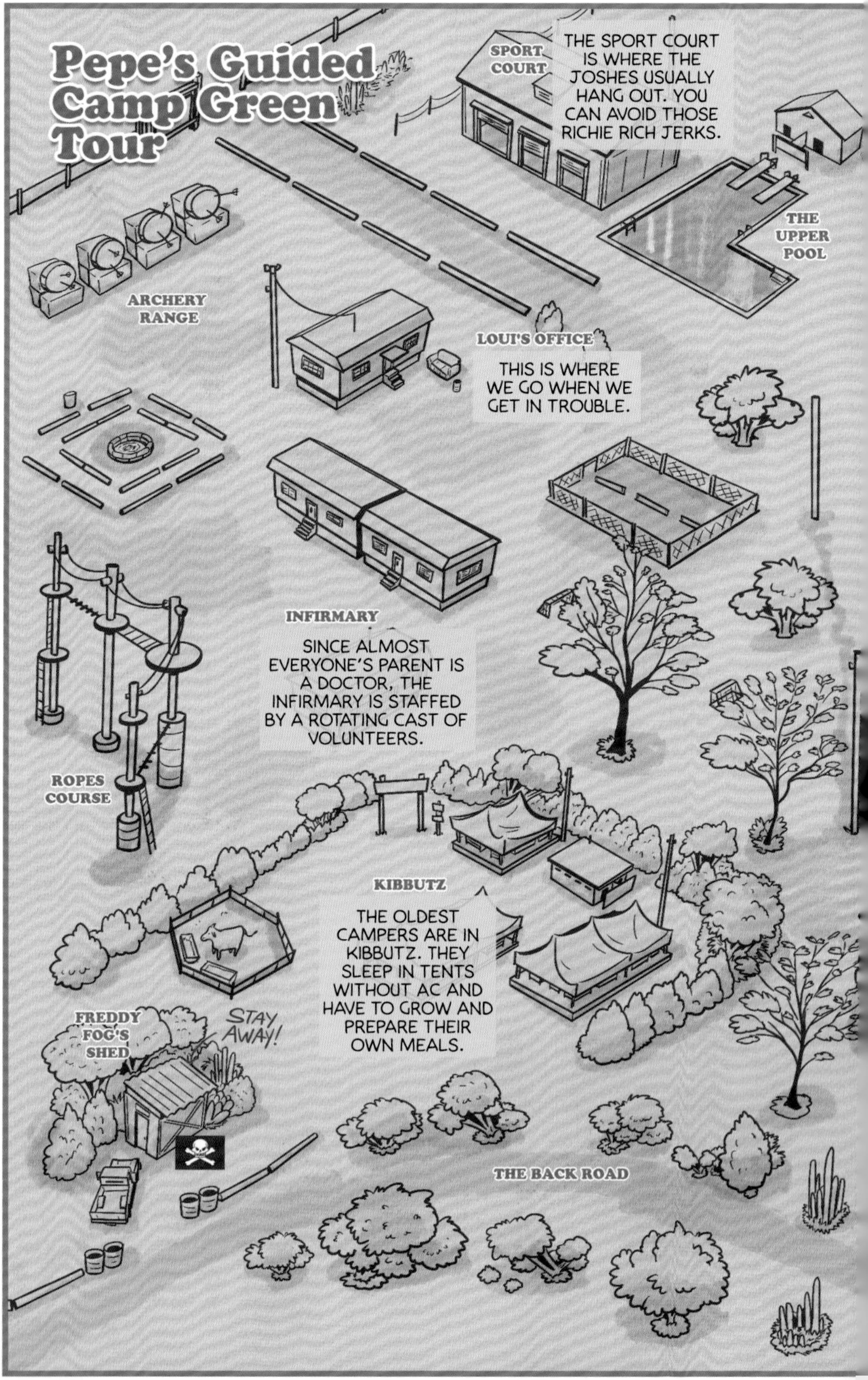
Pepe's Guided Camp Green Tour
SPORT COURT
THE SPORT COURT IS WHERE THE JOSHES USUALLY HANG OUT. YOU CAN AVOID THOSE RICHIE RICH JERKS.
THE UPPER POOL
ARCHERY RANGE
LOUI'S OFFICE
THIS IS WHERE WE GO WHEN WE GET IN TROUBLE.
INFIRMARY
SINCE ALMOST EVERYONE'S PARENT IS A DOCTOR, THE INFIRMARY IS STAFFED BY A ROTATING CAST OF VOLUNTEERS.
ROPES COURSE
KIBBUTZ
THE OLDEST CAMPERS ARE IN KIBBUTZ. THEY SLEEP IN TENTS WITHOUT AC AND HAVE TO GROW AND PREPARE THEIR OWN MEALS.
FREDDY FOG'S SHED
STAY AWAY!
THE BACK ROAD

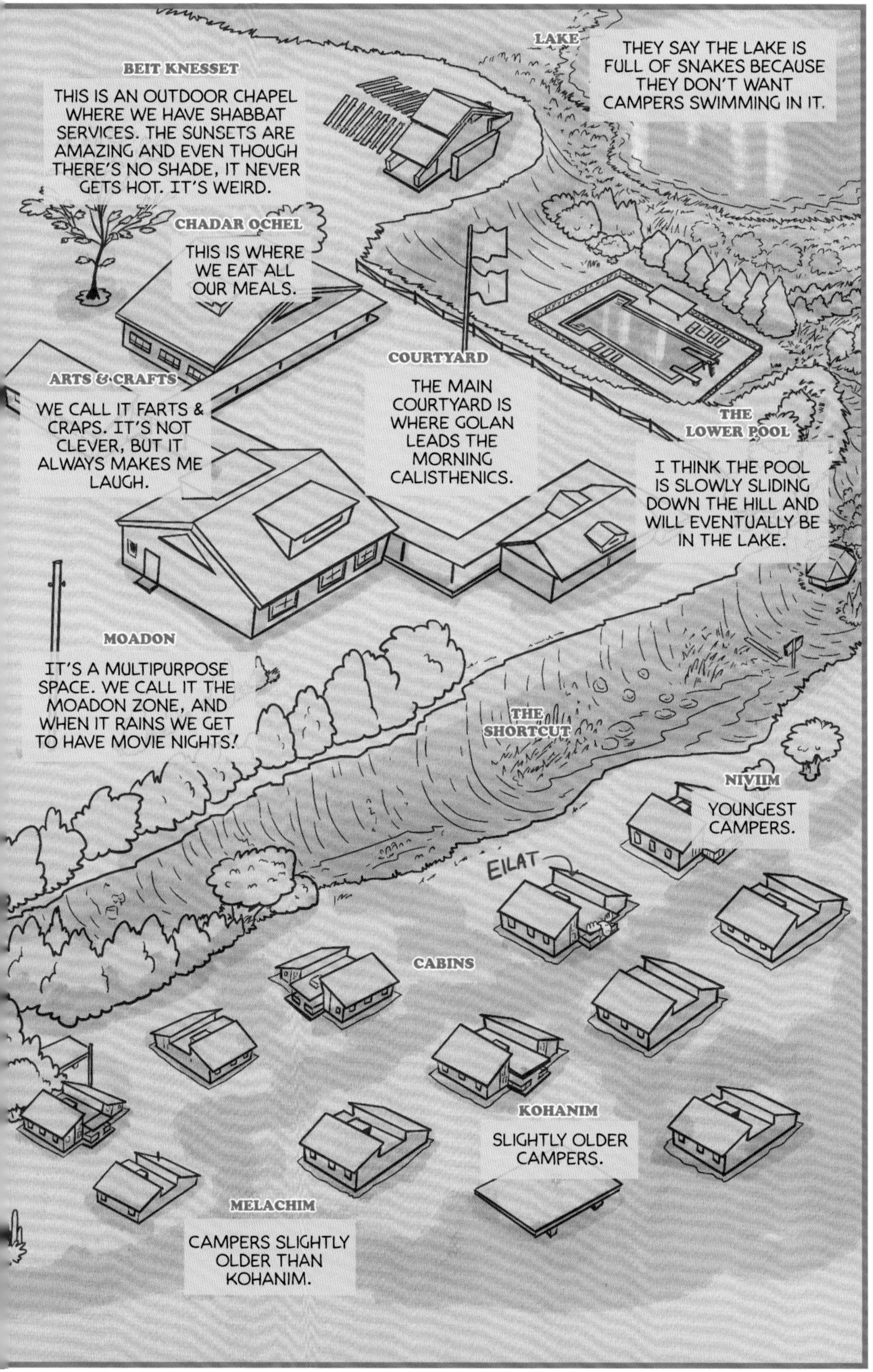
BEIT KNESSET
THIS IS AN OUTDOOR CHAPEL WHERE WE HAVE SHABBAT SERVICES. THE SUNSETS ARE AMAZING AND EVEN THOUGH THERE'S NO SHADE, IT NEVER GETS HOT. IT'S WEIRD.
LAKE
THEY SAY THE LAKE IS FULL OF SNAKES BECAUSE THEY DON'T WANT CAMPERS SWIMMING IN IT.
CHADAR OCHEL
THIS IS WHERE WE EAT ALL OUR MEALS.
ARTS & CRAFTS
WE CALL IT FARTS & CRAPS. IT'S NOT CLEVER, BUT IT ALWAYS MAKES ME LAUGH.
COURTYARD
THE MAIN COURTYARD IS WHERE GOLAN LEADS THE MORNING CALISTHENICS.
THE LOWER POOL
I THINK THE POOL IS SLOWLY SLIDING DOWN THE HILL AND WILL EVENTUALLY BE IN THE LAKE.
MOADON
IT'S A MULTIPURPOSE SPACE. WE CALL IT THE MOADON ZONE, AND WHEN IT RAINS WE GET TO HAVE MOVIE NIGHTS!
THE SHORTCUT
NIVIIM
YOUNGEST CAMPERS.
EILAT
CABINS
KOHANIM
SLIGHTLY OLDER CAMPERS.
MELACHIM
CAMPERS SLIGHTLY OLDER THAN KOHANIM.

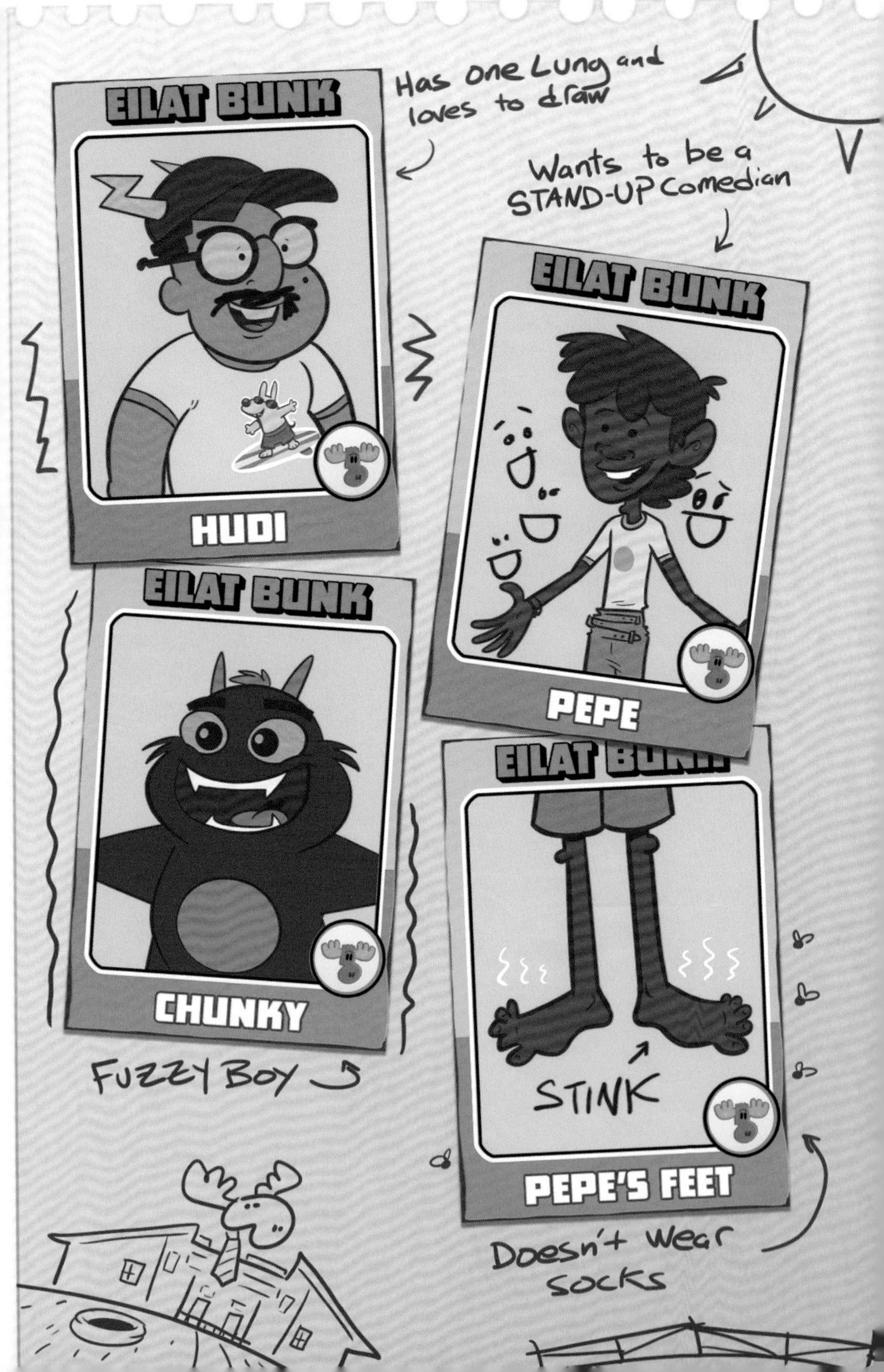
EILAT BUNK
HUDI
Has one Lung and loves to draw
Wants to be a STAND-UP Comedian
EILAT BUNK
PEPE
EILAT BUNK
CHUNKY
FUZZY BOY
EILAT BUNK
STINK
PEPE'S FEET
Doesn't wear socks

EILAT BUNK!!

EILAT BUNK
LEWIS

EILAT BUNK
WARREN

Older Camper
Not technically
in our Bunk but
he's a fellow
WEIRDO

~~EILAT~~ BUNK
RICKY

LOVES
HEAVY
METAL
&
LOVES TO
CUSS!

The Bunk's
Counselor
He used to be a
major Prankster
when he was a camper

BON-BON

EILAT BUNK
LONNIE

EILAT BUNK
ADAM

~~EILAT~~ BUNK
GOLAN

Always wears
that Old-Timey
NEWSIE CAP

HAS the
Thickest
TEXAS ACCENT
I have ever heard

In charge of
the BONFIRES.
He might burn the
whole camp down.

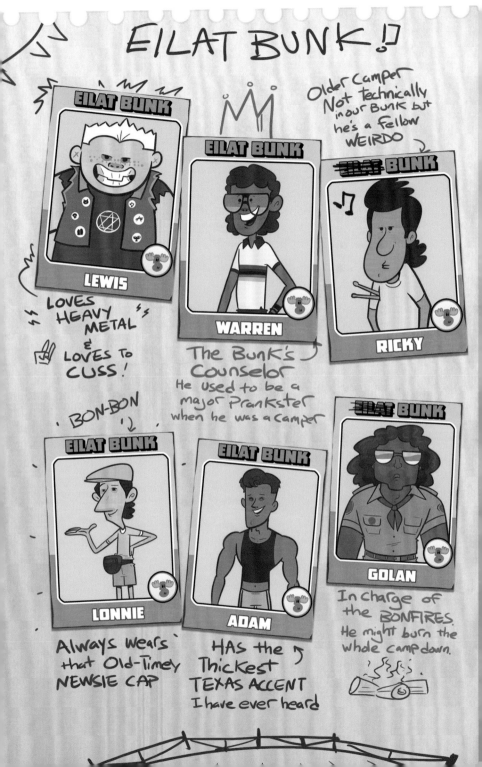

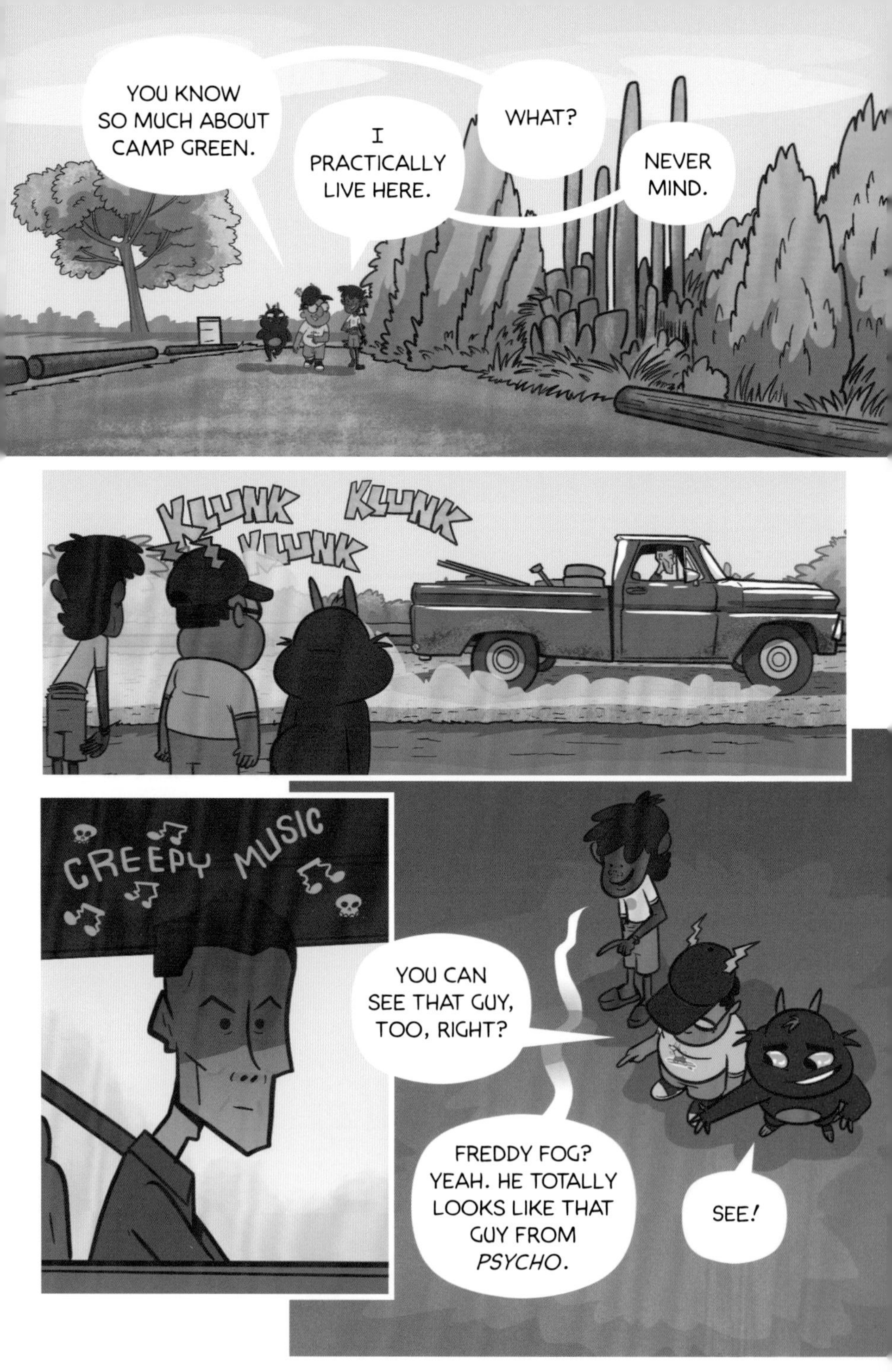
YOU KNOW SO MUCH ABOUT CAMP GREEN.
I PRACTICALLY LIVE HERE.
WHAT?
NEVER MIND.
KLUNK
KLUNK
KLUNK
CREEPY MUSIC
YOU CAN SEE THAT GUY, TOO, RIGHT?
FREDDY FOG? YEAH. HE TOTALLY LOOKS LIKE THAT GUY FROM *PSYCHO*.
SEE!

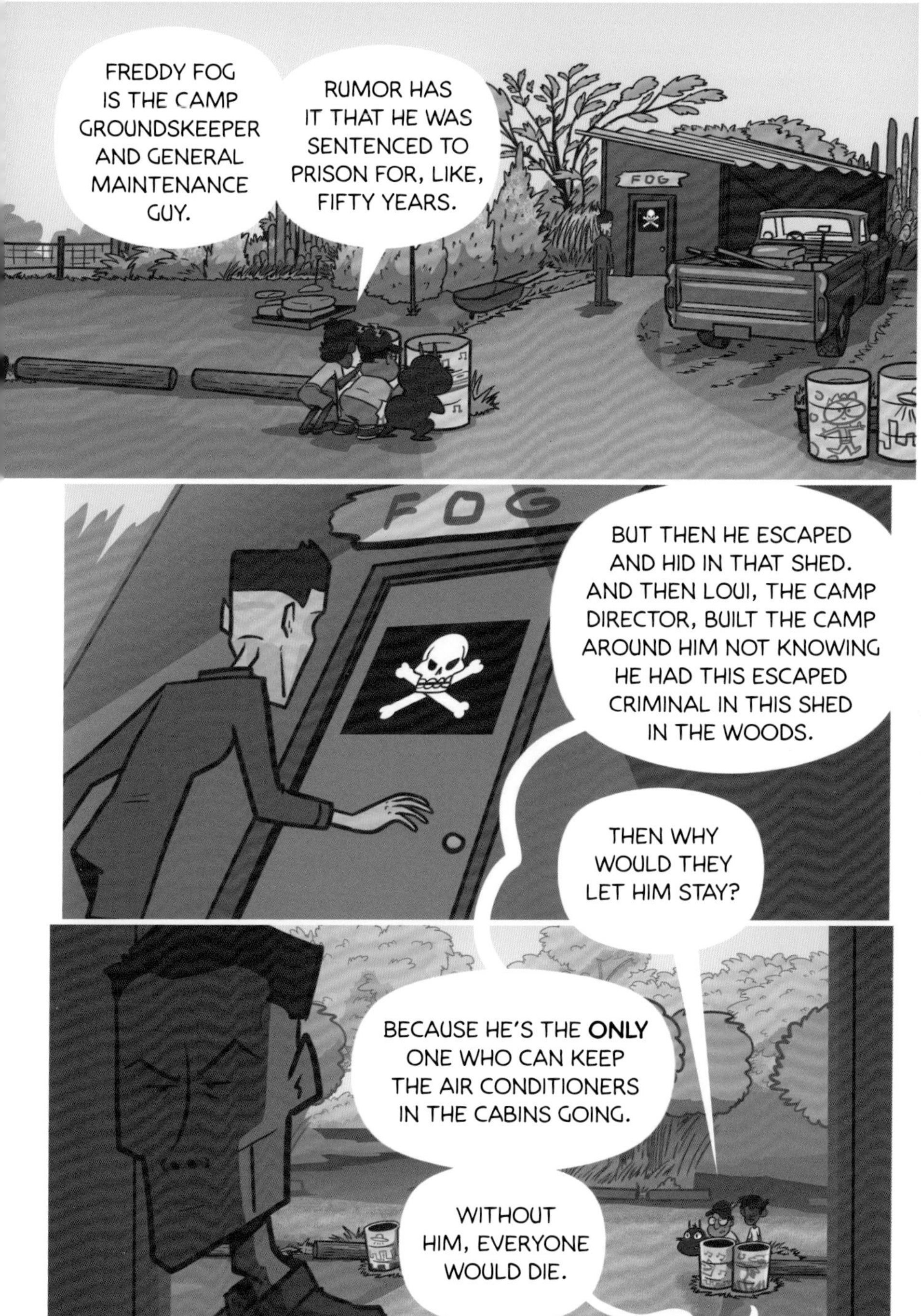
FREDDY FOG IS THE CAMP GROUNDSKEEPER AND GENERAL MAINTENANCE GUY.
RUMOR HAS IT THAT HE WAS SENTENCED TO PRISON FOR, LIKE, FIFTY YEARS.
FOG
FOG
BUT THEN HE ESCAPED AND HID IN THAT SHED. AND THEN LOUI, THE CAMP DIRECTOR, BUILT THE CAMP AROUND HIM NOT KNOWING HE HAD THIS ESCAPED CRIMINAL IN THIS SHED IN THE WOODS.
THEN WHY WOULD THEY LET HIM STAY?
BECAUSE HE'S THE **ONLY** ONE WHO CAN KEEP THE AIR CONDITIONERS IN THE CABINS GOING.
WITHOUT HIM, EVERYONE WOULD DIE.

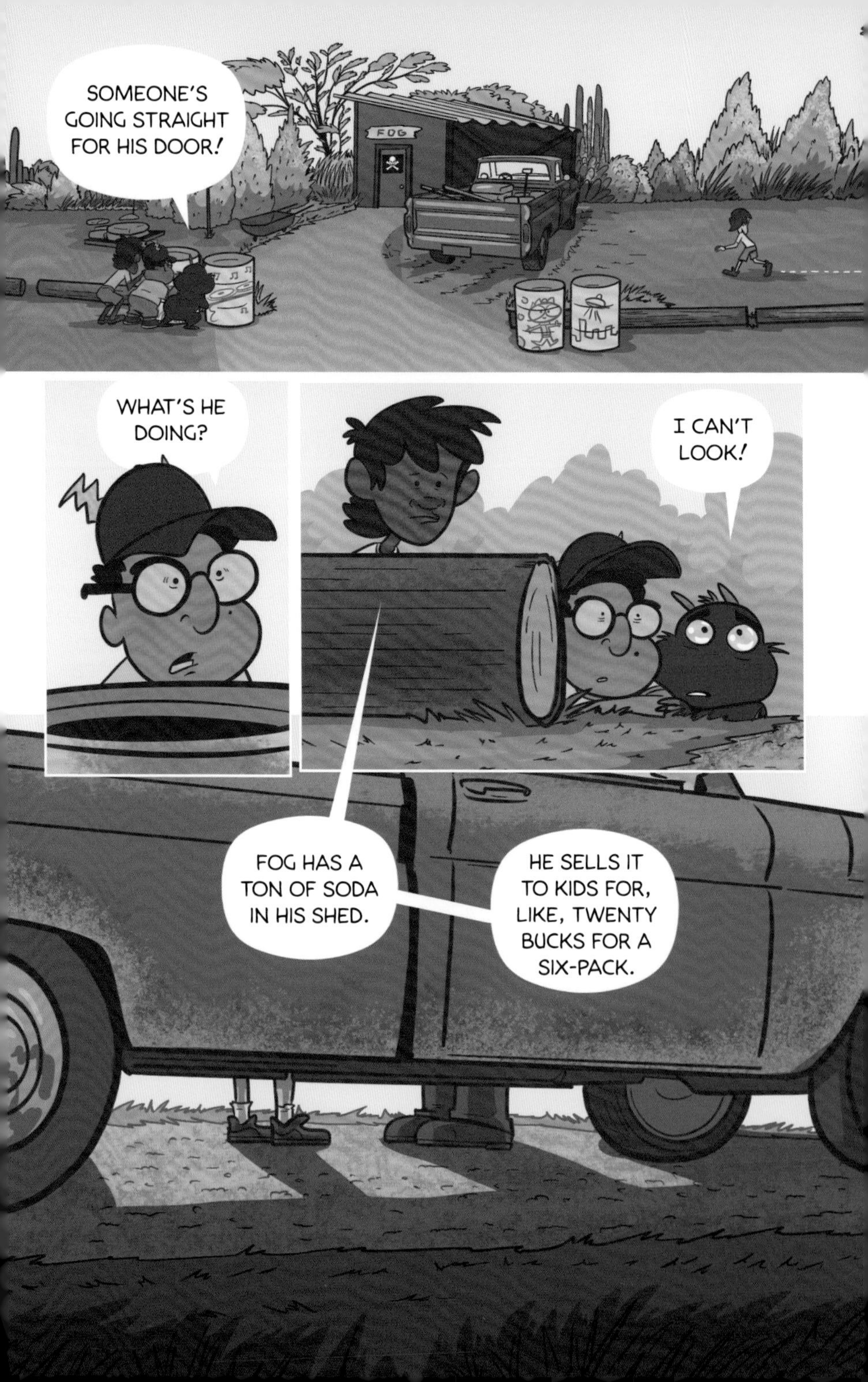
SOMEONE'S GOING STRAIGHT FOR HIS DOOR!
FOG
WHAT'S HE DOING?
I CAN'T LOOK!
FOG HAS A TON OF SODA IN HIS SHED.
HE SELLS IT TO KIDS FOR, LIKE, TWENTY BUCKS FOR A SIX-PACK.

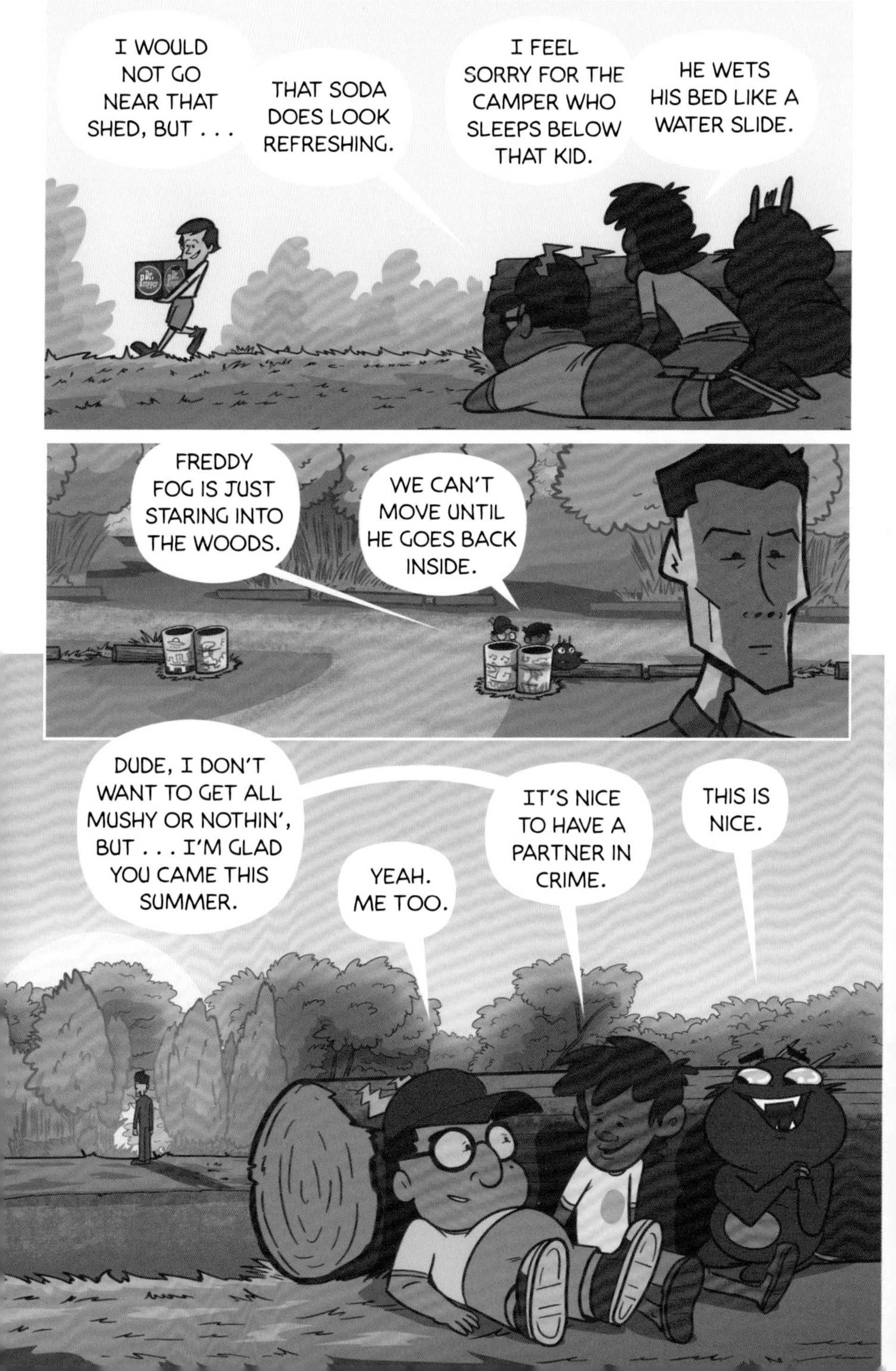
I WOULD NOT GO NEAR THAT SHED, BUT . . .
THAT SODA DOES LOOK REFRESHING.
I FEEL SORRY FOR THE CAMPER WHO SLEEPS BELOW THAT KID.
HE WETS HIS BED LIKE A WATER SLIDE.
FREDDY FOG IS JUST STARING INTO THE WOODS.
WE CAN'T MOVE UNTIL HE GOES BACK INSIDE.
DUDE, I DON'T WANT TO GET ALL MUSHY OR NOTHIN', BUT . . . I'M GLAD YOU CAME THIS SUMMER.
YEAH. ME TOO.
IT'S NICE TO HAVE A PARTNER IN CRIME.
THIS IS NICE.

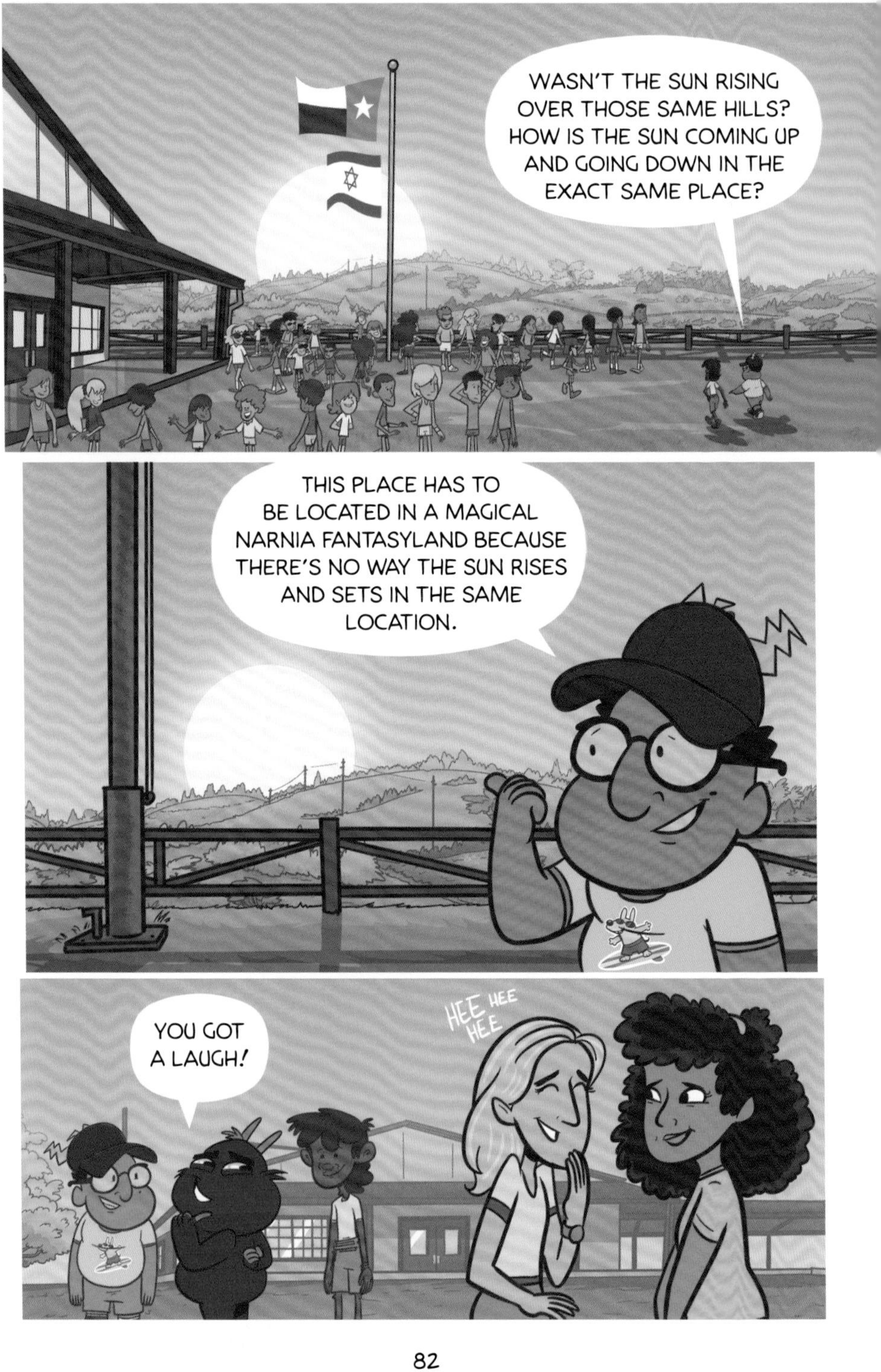
WASN'T THE SUN RISING OVER THOSE SAME HILLS? HOW IS THE SUN COMING UP AND GOING DOWN IN THE EXACT SAME PLACE?
THIS PLACE HAS TO BE LOCATED IN A MAGICAL NARNIA FANTASYLAND BECAUSE THERE'S NO WAY THE SUN RISES AND SETS IN THE SAME LOCATION.
YOU GOT A LAUGH!
HEE HEE HEE

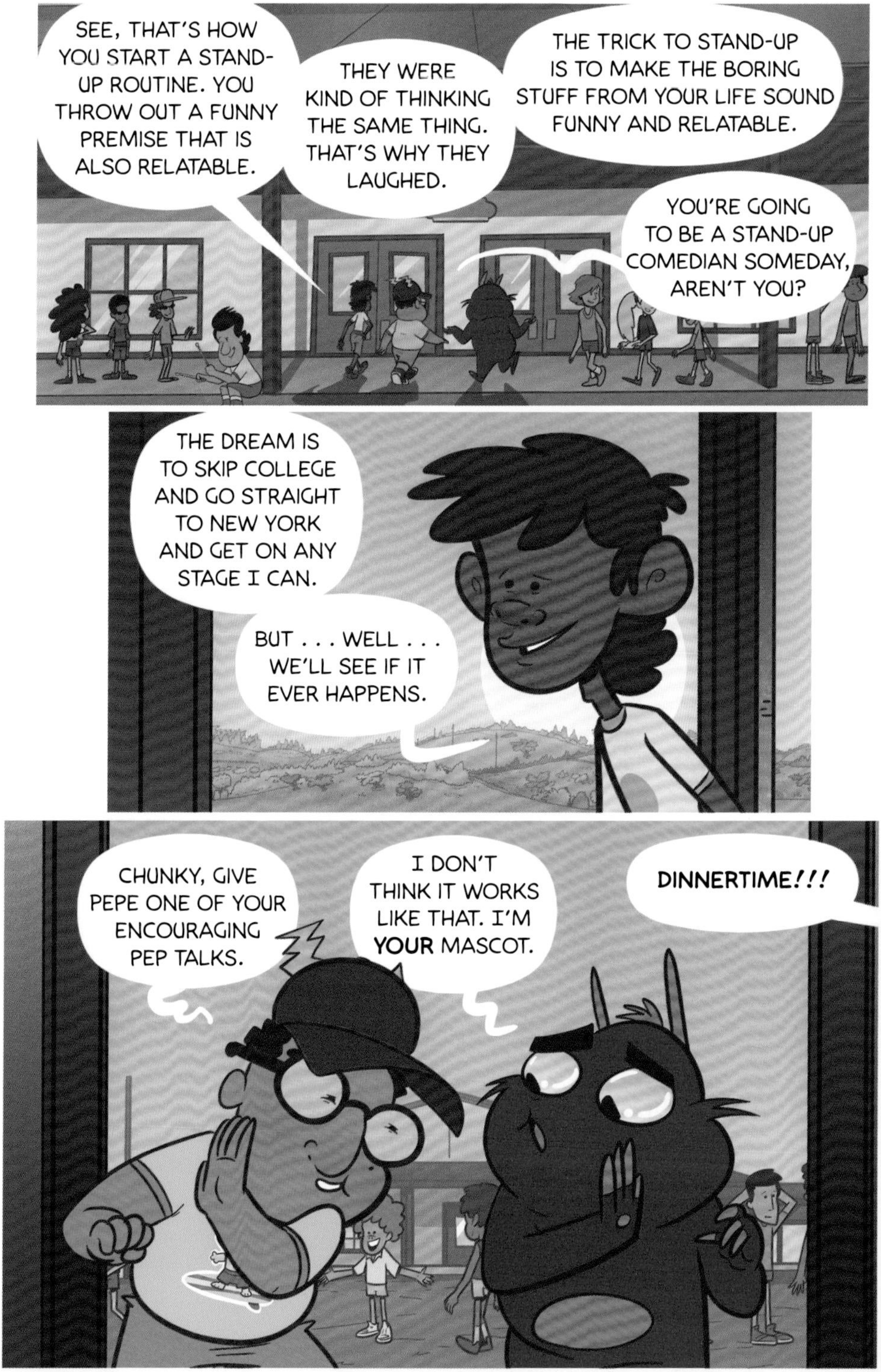
SEE, THAT'S HOW YOU START A STAND-UP ROUTINE. YOU THROW OUT A FUNNY PREMISE THAT IS ALSO RELATABLE.
THEY WERE KIND OF THINKING THE SAME THING. THAT'S WHY THEY LAUGHED.
THE TRICK TO STAND-UP IS TO MAKE THE BORING STUFF FROM YOUR LIFE SOUND FUNNY AND RELATABLE.
YOU'RE GOING TO BE A STAND-UP COMEDIAN SOMEDAY, AREN'T YOU?
THE DREAM IS TO SKIP COLLEGE AND GO STRAIGHT TO NEW YORK AND GET ON ANY STAGE I CAN.
BUT . . . WELL . . . WE'LL SEE IF IT EVER HAPPENS.
CHUNKY, GIVE PEPE ONE OF YOUR ENCOURAGING PEP TALKS.
I DON'T THINK IT WORKS LIKE THAT. I'M **YOUR** MASCOT.
DINNERTIME!!!

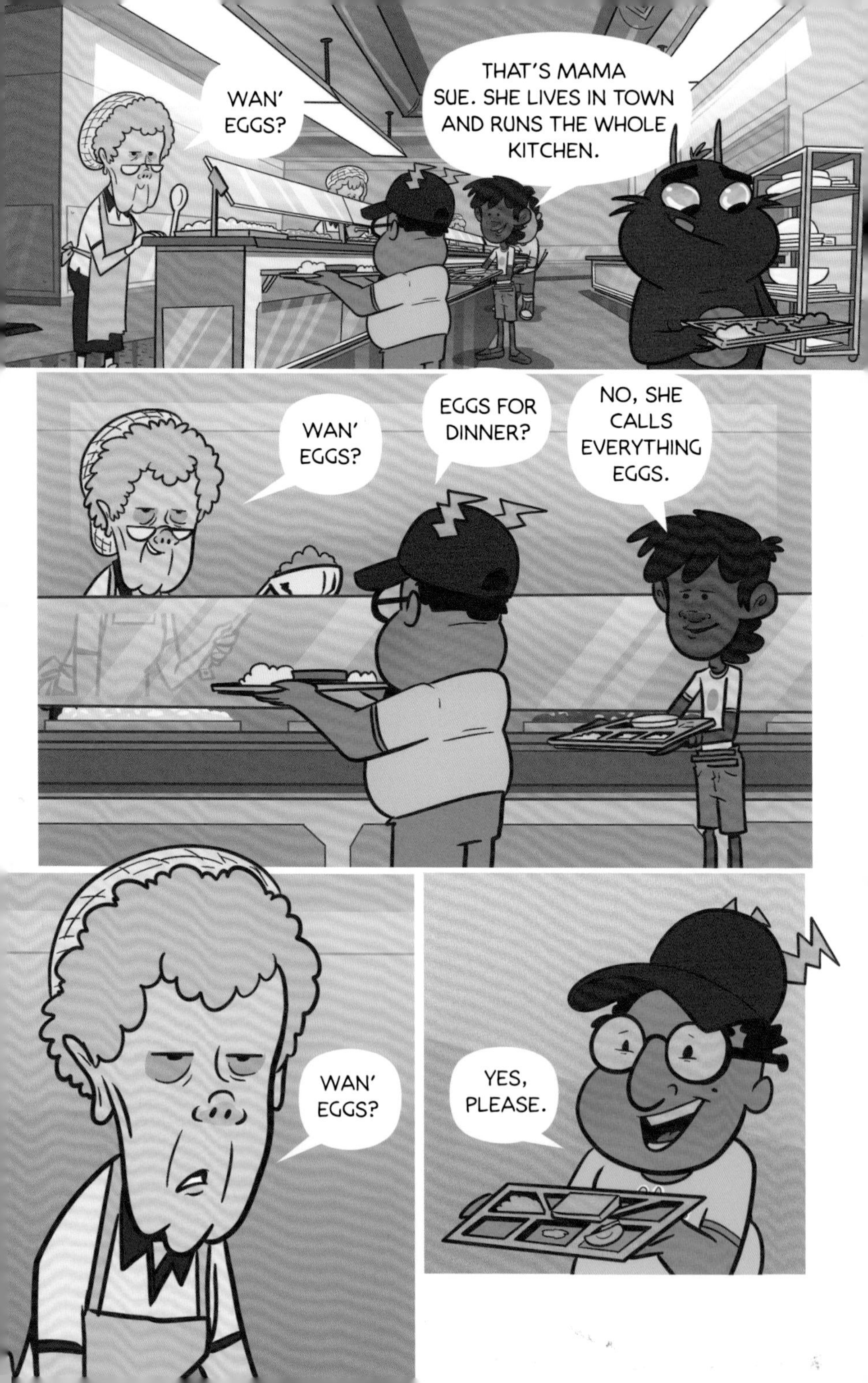
WAN' EGGS?
THAT'S MAMA SUE. SHE LIVES IN TOWN AND RUNS THE WHOLE KITCHEN.
WAN' EGGS?
EGGS FOR DINNER?
NO, SHE CALLS EVERYTHING EGGS.
WAN' EGGS?
YES, PLEASE.

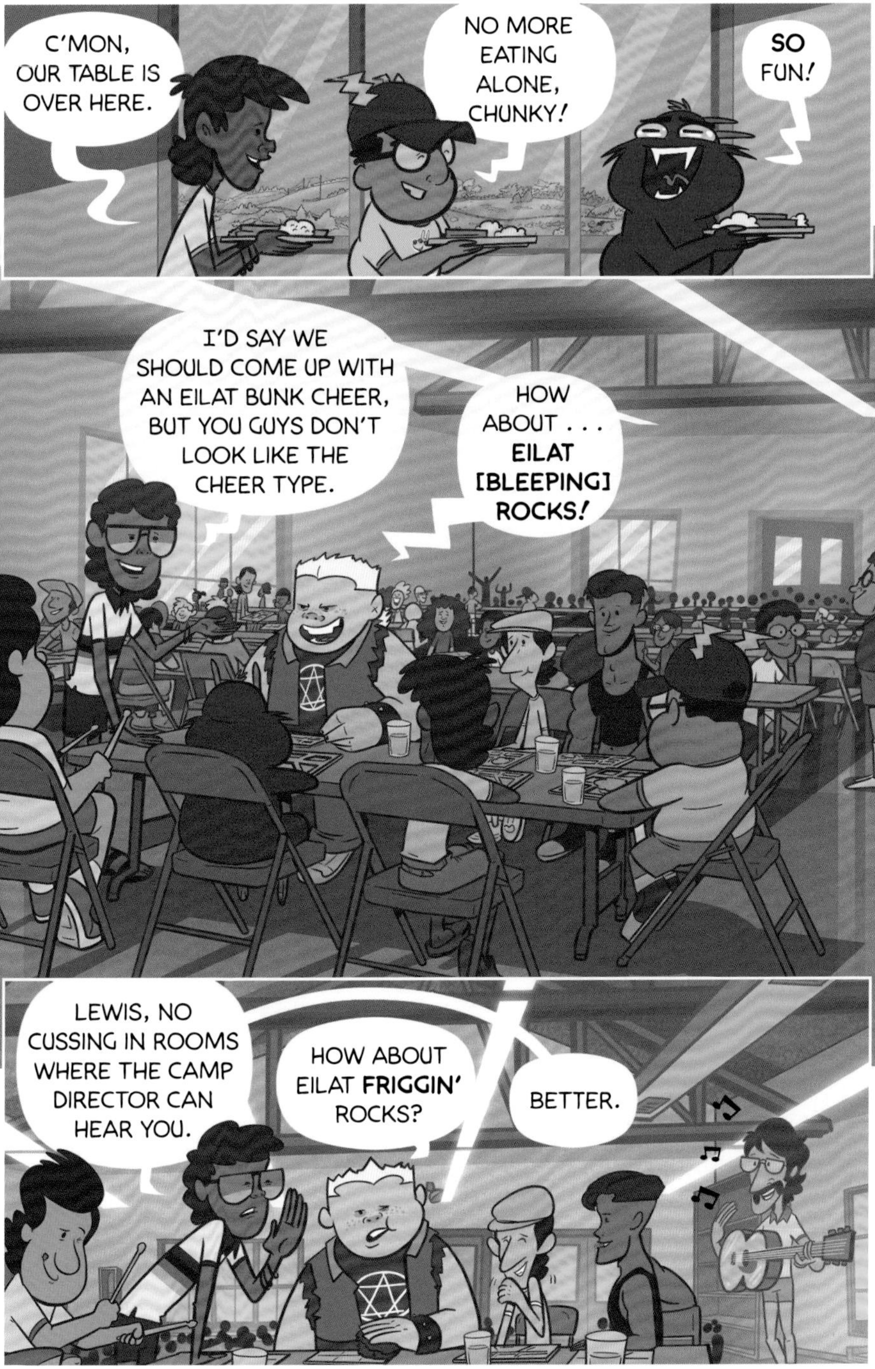
C'MON, OUR TABLE IS OVER HERE.
NO MORE EATING ALONE, CHUNKY!
SO FUN!
I'D SAY WE SHOULD COME UP WITH AN EILAT BUNK CHEER, BUT YOU GUYS DON'T LOOK LIKE THE CHEER TYPE.
HOW ABOUT . . . EILAT [BLEEPING] ROCKS!
LEWIS, NO CUSSING IN ROOMS WHERE THE CAMP DIRECTOR CAN HEAR YOU.
HOW ABOUT EILAT FRIGGIN' ROCKS?
BETTER.

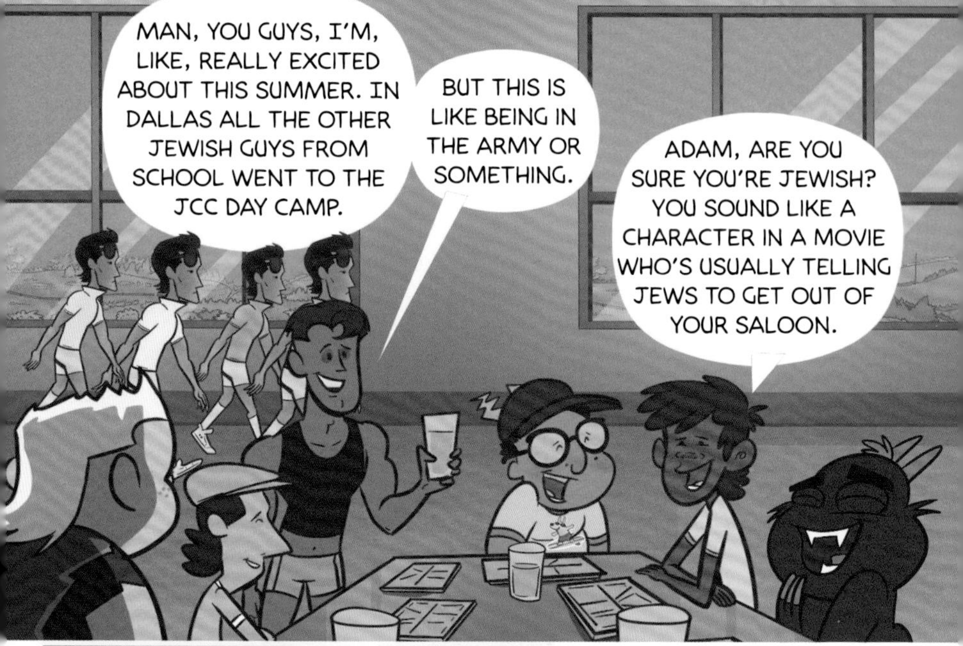

MAN, YOU GUYS, I'M, LIKE, REALLY EXCITED ABOUT THIS SUMMER. IN DALLAS ALL THE OTHER JEWISH GUYS FROM SCHOOL WENT TO THE JCC DAY CAMP.
BUT THIS IS LIKE BEING IN THE ARMY OR SOMETHING.
ADAM, ARE YOU SURE YOU'RE JEWISH? YOU SOUND LIKE A CHARACTER IN A MOVIE WHO'S USUALLY TELLING JEWS TO GET OUT OF YOUR SALOON.

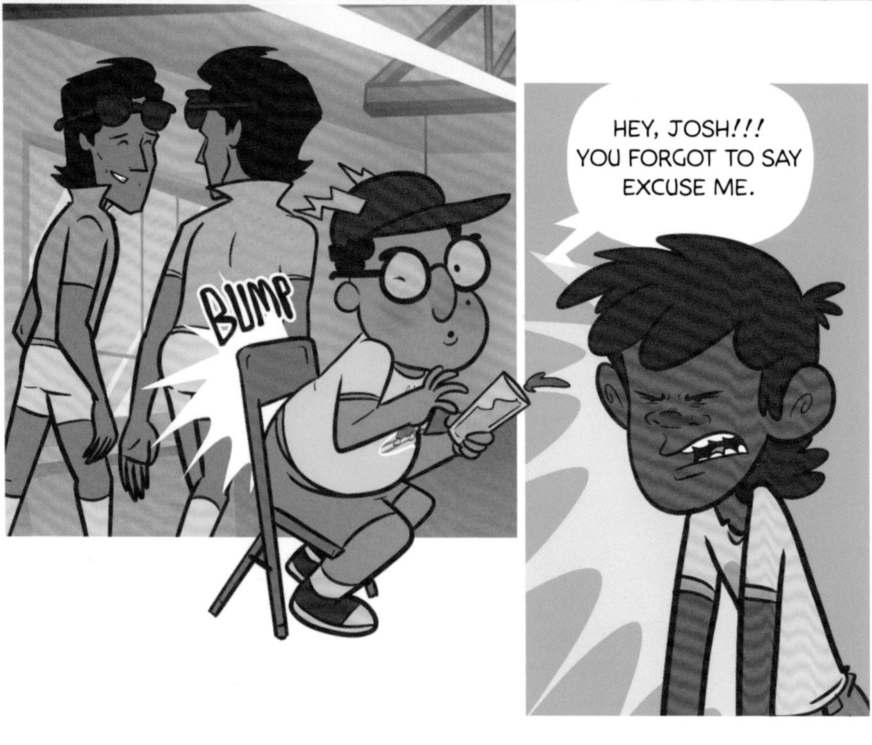

BUMP
HEY, JOSH!!! YOU FORGOT TO SAY EXCUSE ME.

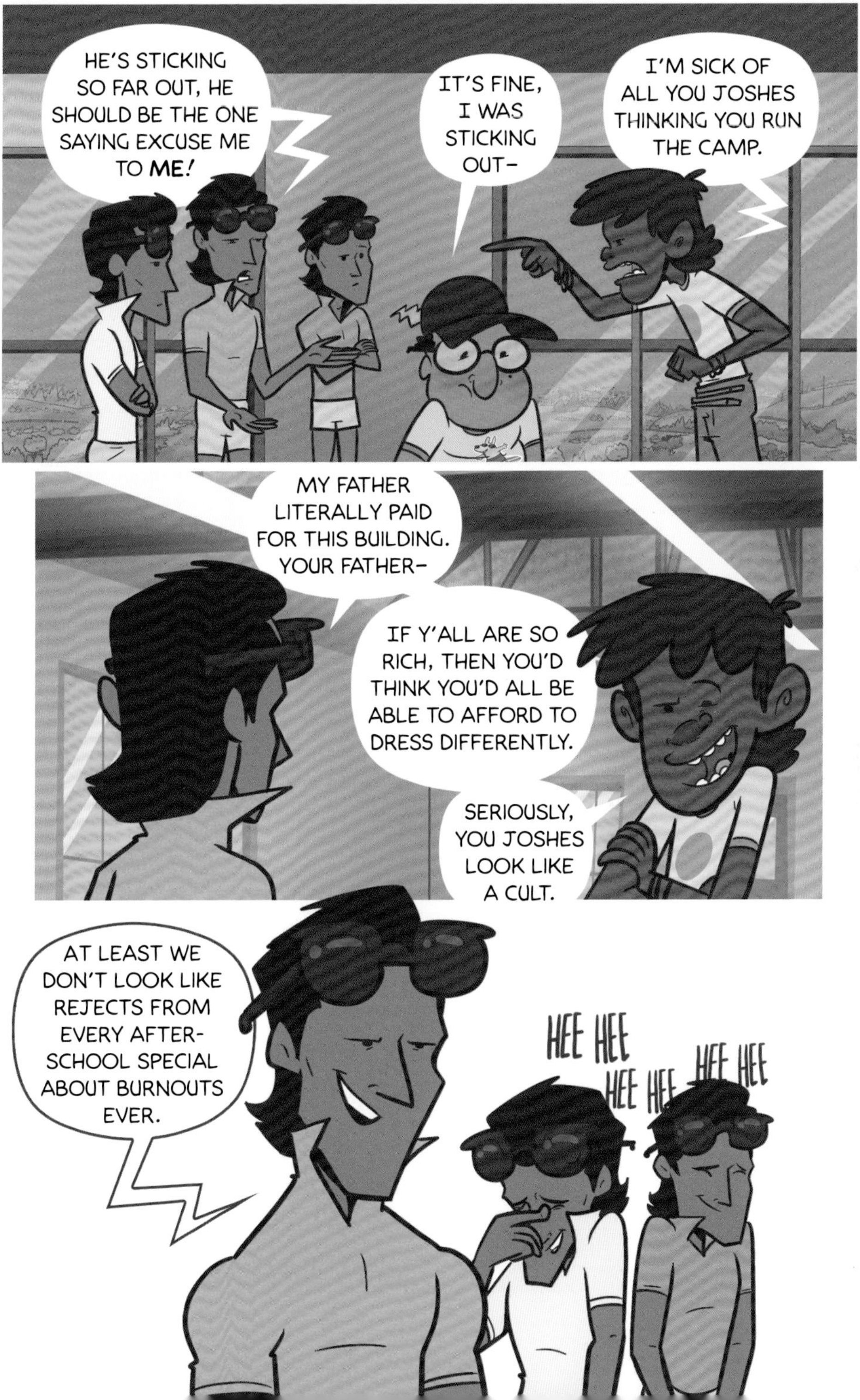
HE'S STICKING SO FAR OUT, HE SHOULD BE THE ONE SAYING EXCUSE ME TO **ME**!
IT'S FINE, I WAS STICKING OUT–
I'M SICK OF ALL YOU JOSHES THINKING YOU RUN THE CAMP.
MY FATHER LITERALLY PAID FOR THIS BUILDING. YOUR FATHER–
IF Y'ALL ARE SO RICH, THEN YOU'D THINK YOU'D ALL BE ABLE TO AFFORD TO DRESS DIFFERENTLY.
SERIOUSLY, YOU JOSHES LOOK LIKE A CULT.
AT LEAST WE DON'T LOOK LIKE REJECTS FROM EVERY AFTER-SCHOOL SPECIAL ABOUT BURNOUTS EVER.
HEE HEE
HEE HEE
HEE HEE

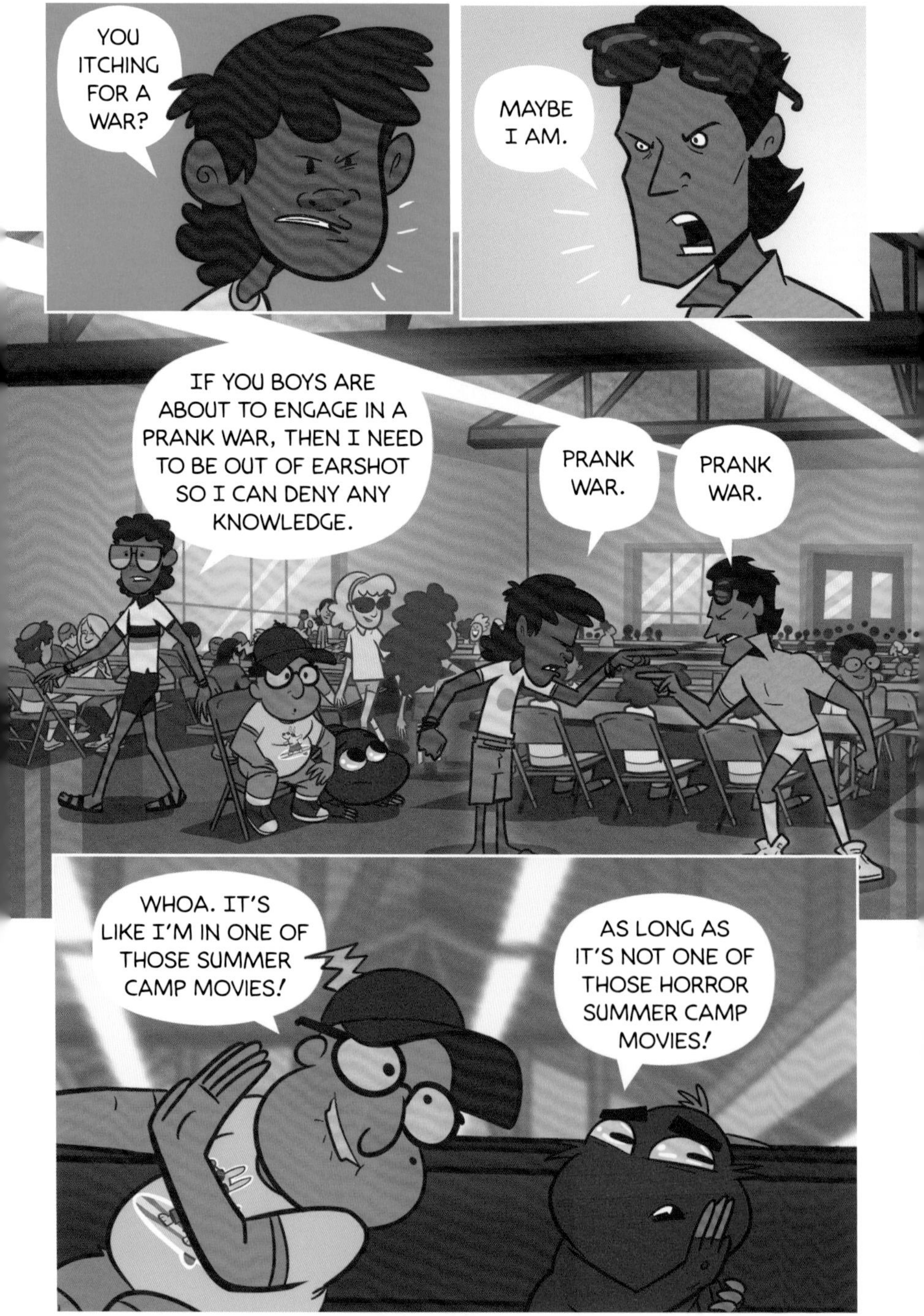
YOU ITCHING FOR A WAR?
MAYBE I AM.
IF YOU BOYS ARE ABOUT TO ENGAGE IN A PRANK WAR, THEN I NEED TO BE OUT OF EARSHOT SO I CAN DENY ANY KNOWLEDGE.
PRANK WAR.
PRANK WAR.
WHOA. IT'S LIKE I'M IN ONE OF THOSE SUMMER CAMP MOVIES!
AS LONG AS IT'S NOT ONE OF THOSE HORROR SUMMER CAMP MOVIES!

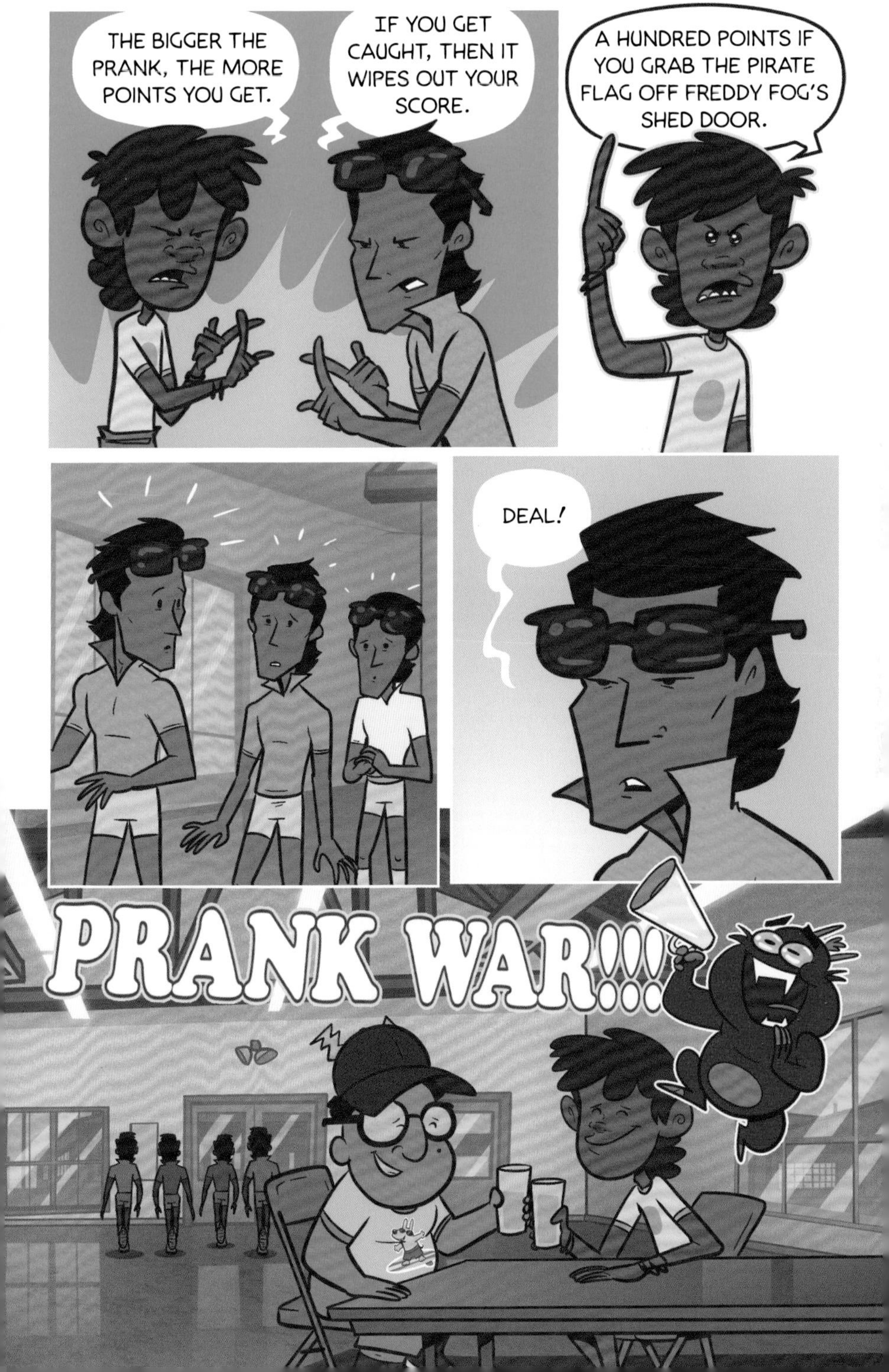
THE BIGGER THE PRANK, THE MORE POINTS YOU GET.
IF YOU GET CAUGHT, THEN IT WIPES OUT YOUR SCORE.
A HUNDRED POINTS IF YOU GRAB THE PIRATE FLAG OFF FREDDY FOG'S SHED DOOR.
DEAL!
PRANK WAR!!!

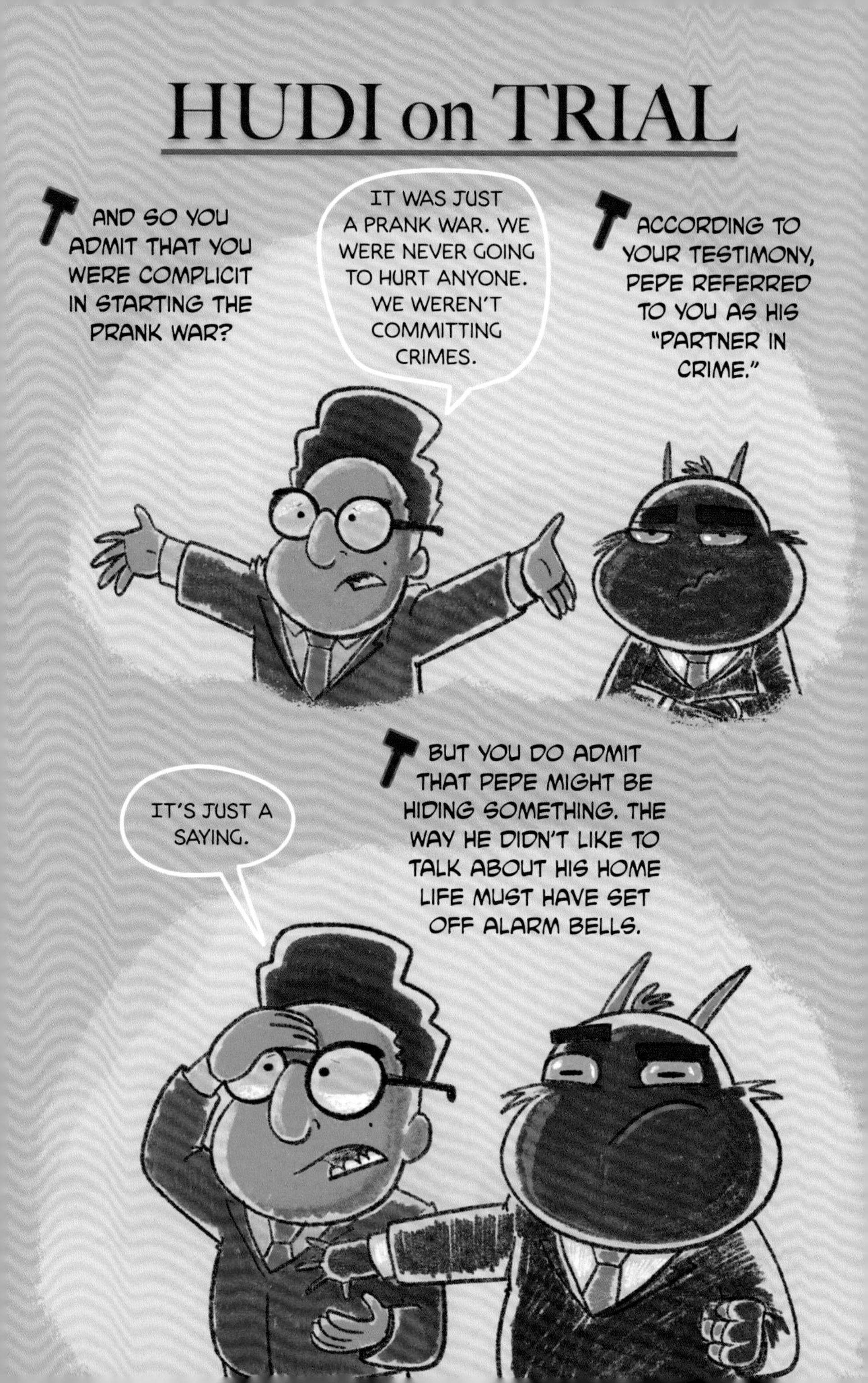
HUDI on TRIAL
AND SO YOU ADMIT THAT YOU WERE COMPLICIT IN STARTING THE PRANK WAR?
IT WAS JUST A PRANK WAR. WE WERE NEVER GOING TO HURT ANYONE. WE WEREN'T COMMITTING CRIMES.
ACCORDING TO YOUR TESTIMONY, PEPE REFERRED TO YOU AS HIS "PARTNER IN CRIME."
BUT YOU DO ADMIT THAT PEPE MIGHT BE HIDING SOMETHING. THE WAY HE DIDN'T LIKE TO TALK ABOUT HIS HOME LIFE MUST HAVE SET OFF ALARM BELLS.
IT'S JUST A SAYING.

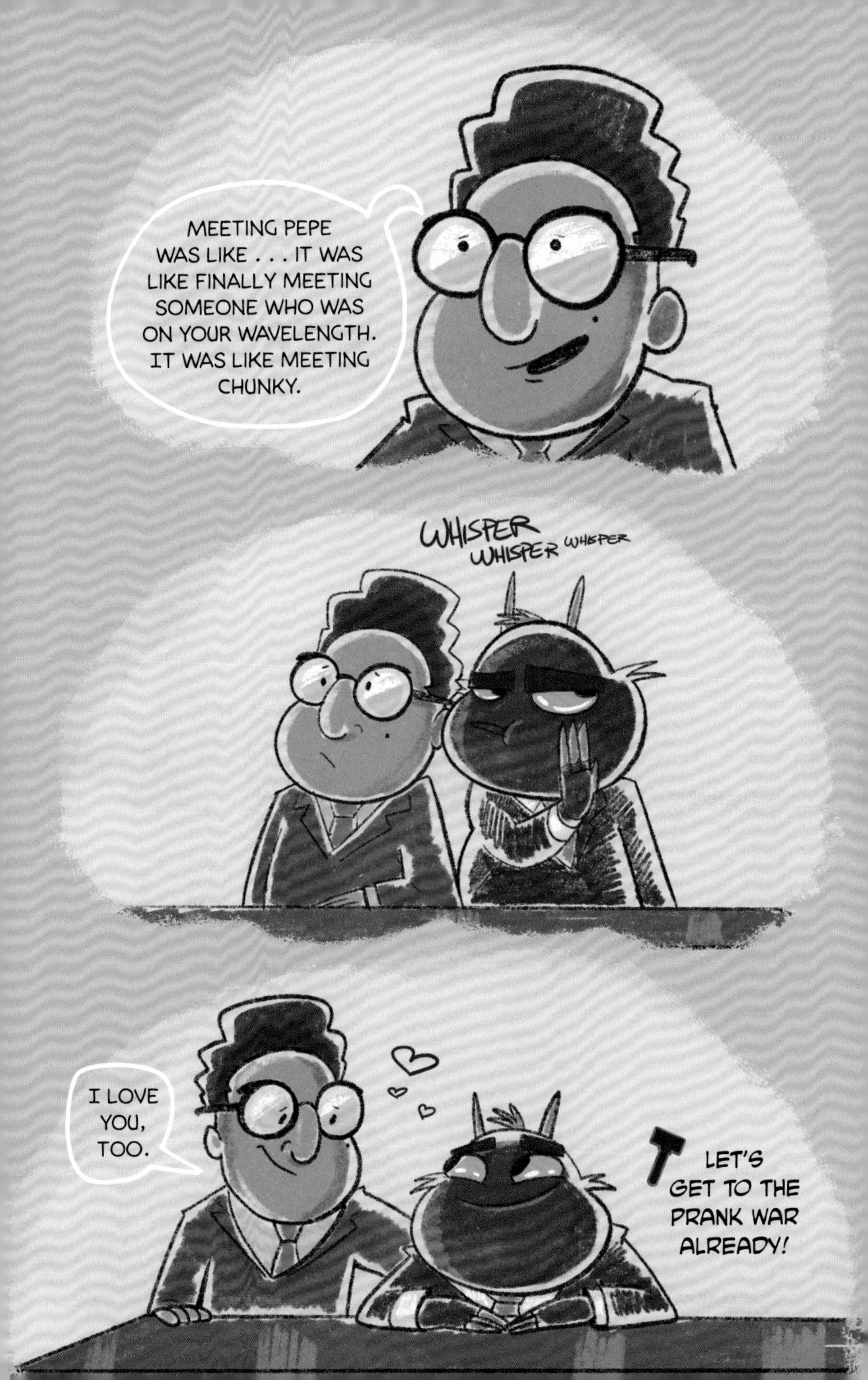
MEETING PEPE WAS LIKE . . . IT WAS LIKE FINALLY MEETING SOMEONE WHO WAS ON YOUR WAVELENGTH. IT WAS LIKE MEETING CHUNKY.
WHISPER WHISPER WHISPER
I LOVE YOU, TOO.
LET'S GET TO THE PRANK WAR ALREADY!

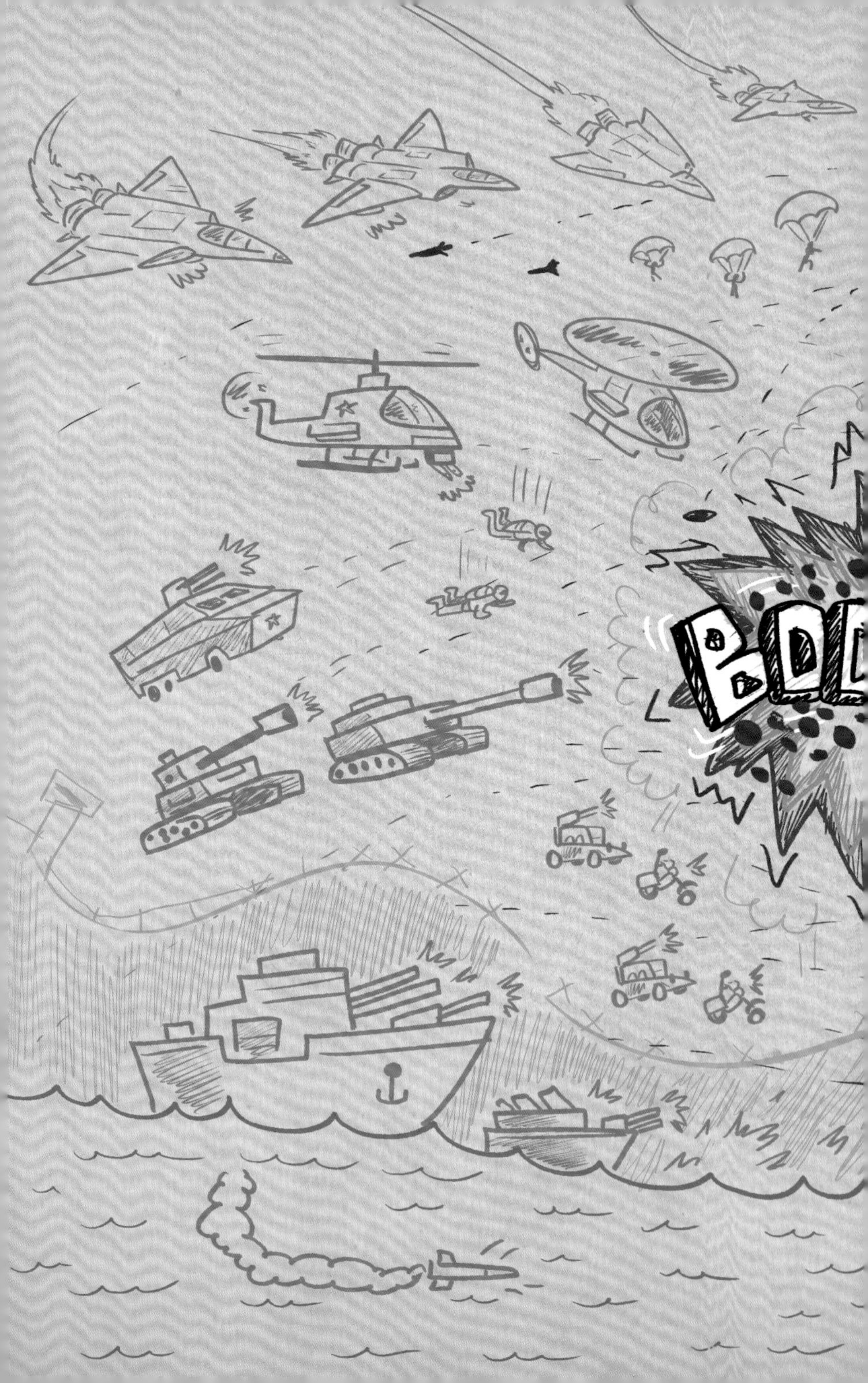
BO

CHAPTER FOUR

PRANK WAR

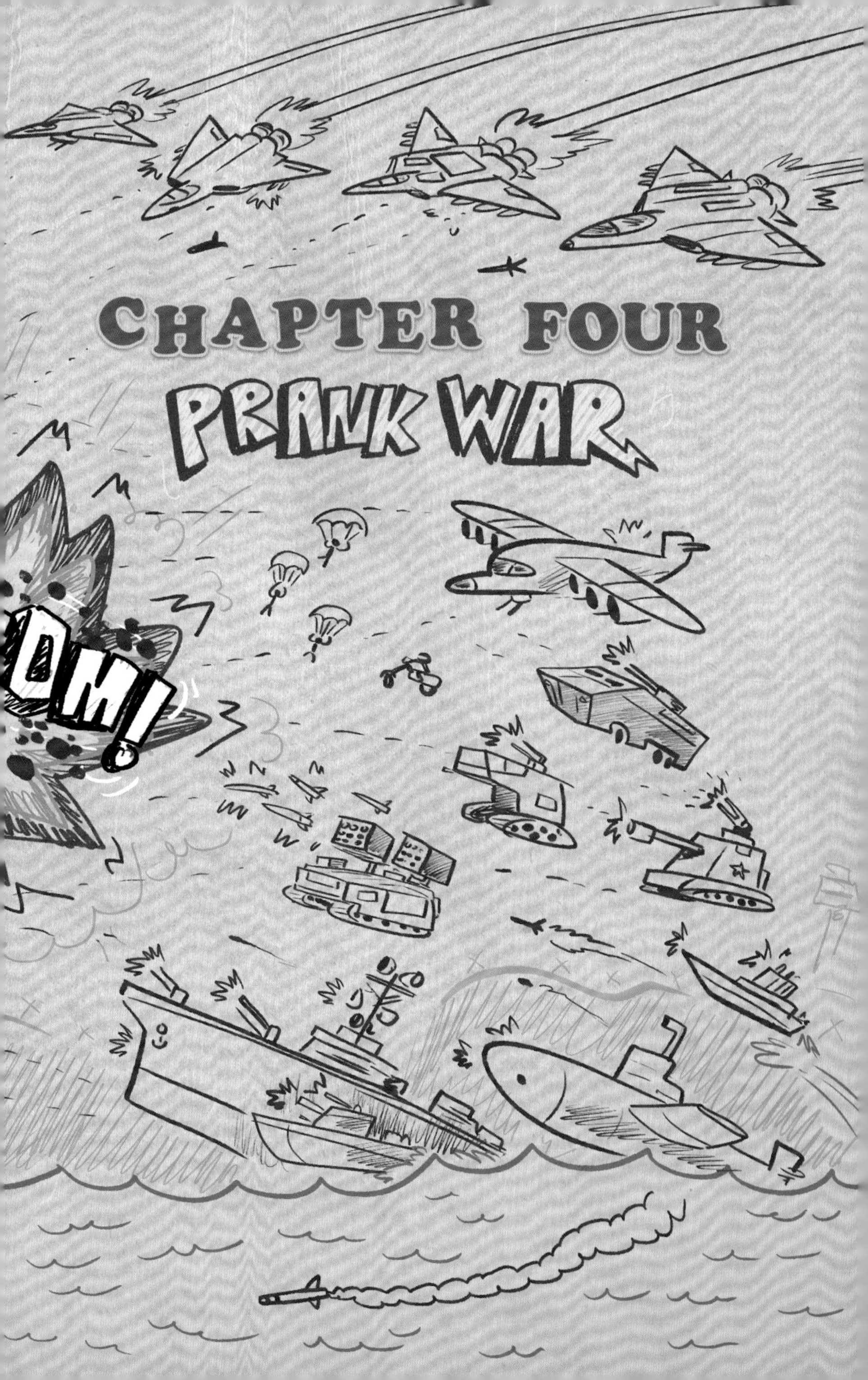

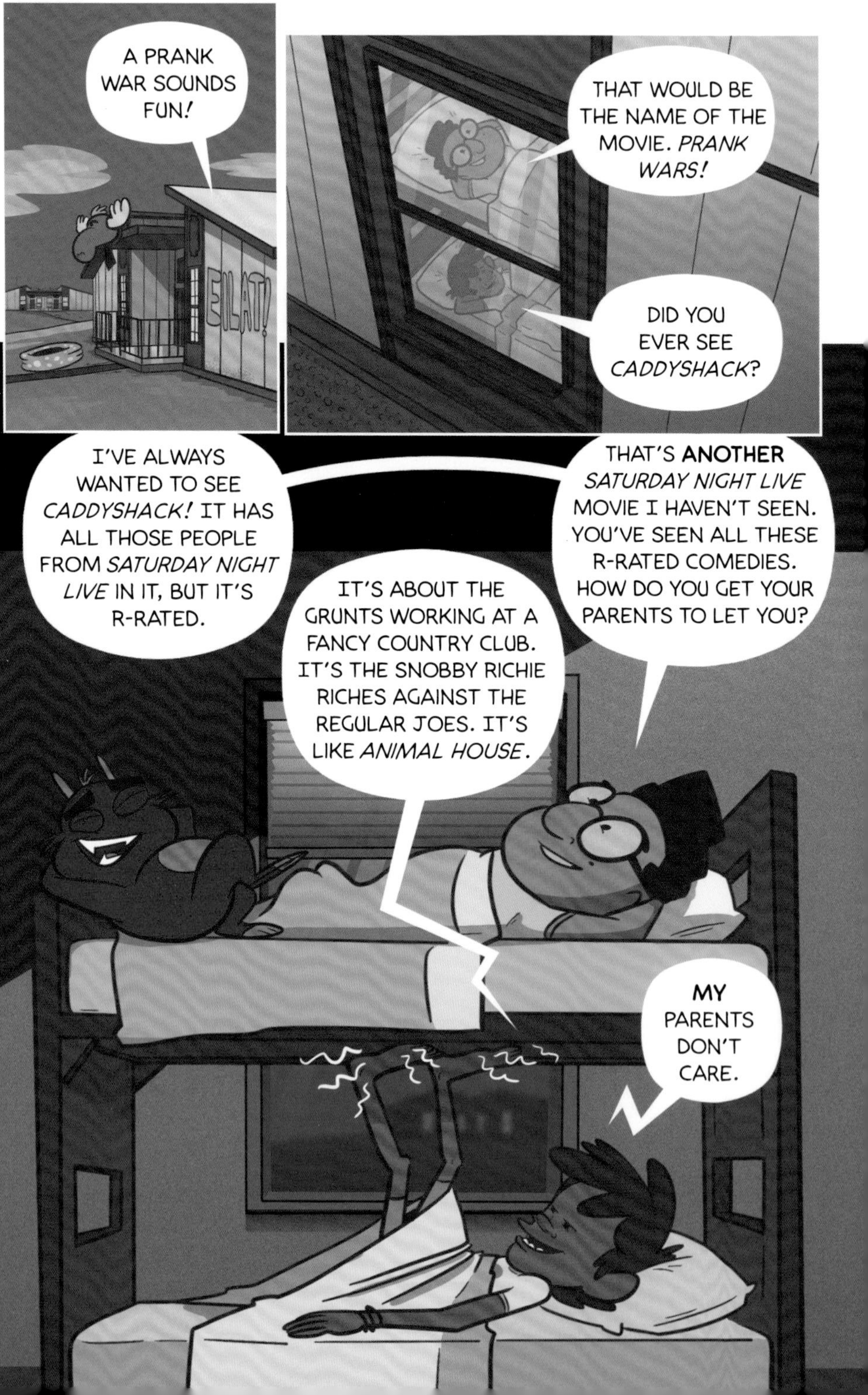
A PRANK WAR SOUNDS FUN!
THAT WOULD BE THE NAME OF THE MOVIE. *PRANK WARS!*
DID YOU EVER SEE *CADDYSHACK*?
EILAT!
I'VE ALWAYS WANTED TO SEE *CADDYSHACK!* IT HAS ALL THOSE PEOPLE FROM *SATURDAY NIGHT LIVE* IN IT, BUT IT'S R-RATED.
THAT'S **ANOTHER** *SATURDAY NIGHT LIVE* MOVIE I HAVEN'T SEEN. YOU'VE SEEN ALL THESE R-RATED COMEDIES. HOW DO YOU GET YOUR PARENTS TO LET YOU?
IT'S ABOUT THE GRUNTS WORKING AT A FANCY COUNTRY CLUB. IT'S THE SNOBBY RICHIE RICHES AGAINST THE REGULAR JOES. IT'S LIKE *ANIMAL HOUSE*.
MY PARENTS DON'T CARE.

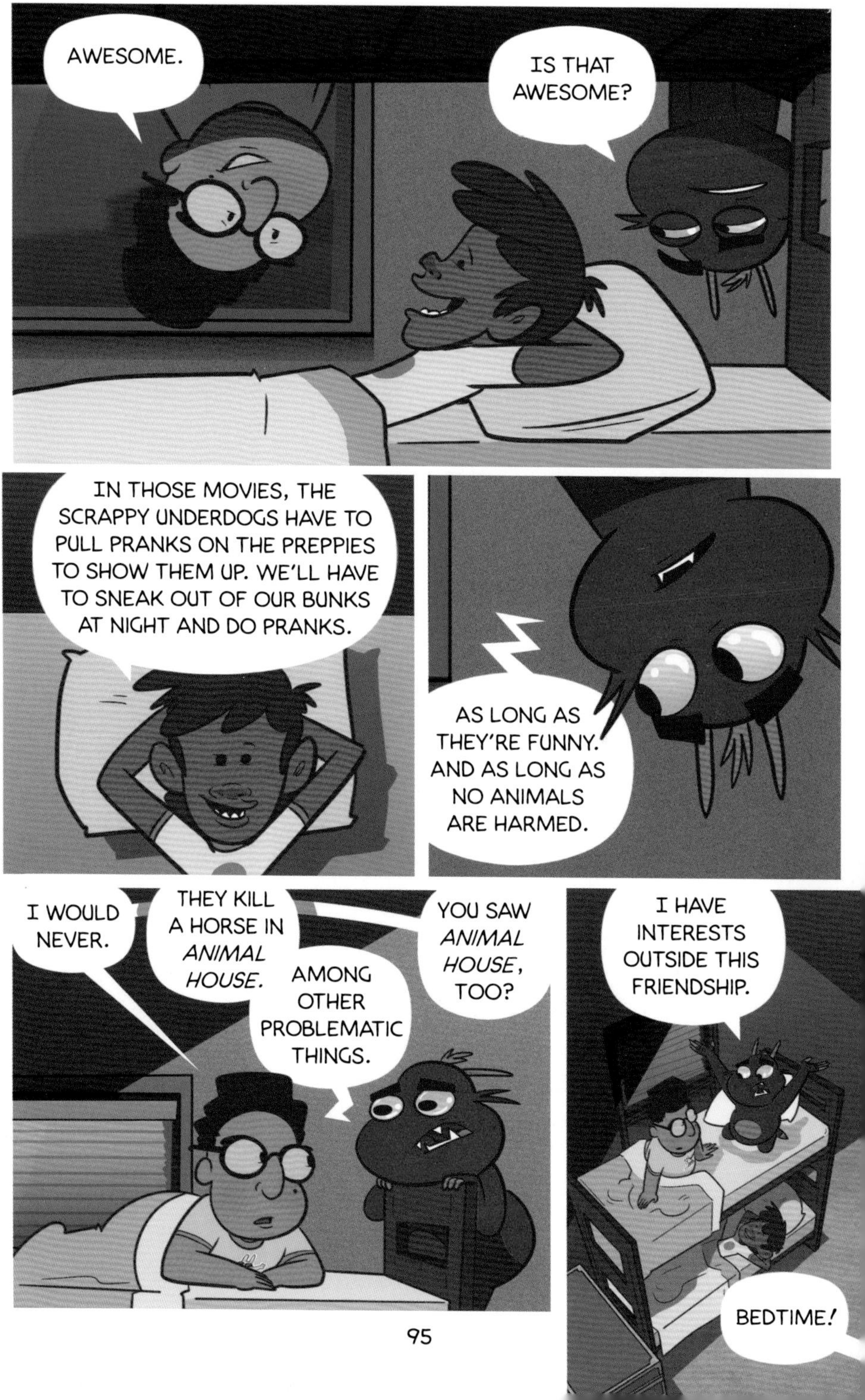
AWESOME.
IS THAT AWESOME?
IN THOSE MOVIES, THE SCRAPPY UNDERDOGS HAVE TO PULL PRANKS ON THE PREPPIES TO SHOW THEM UP. WE'LL HAVE TO SNEAK OUT OF OUR BUNKS AT NIGHT AND DO PRANKS.
AS LONG AS THEY'RE FUNNY. AND AS LONG AS NO ANIMALS ARE HARMED.
I WOULD NEVER.
THEY KILL A HORSE IN *ANIMAL HOUSE.*
AMONG OTHER PROBLEMATIC THINGS.
YOU SAW *ANIMAL HOUSE*, TOO?
I HAVE INTERESTS OUTSIDE THIS FRIENDSHIP.
BEDTIME!

PRANK WAR

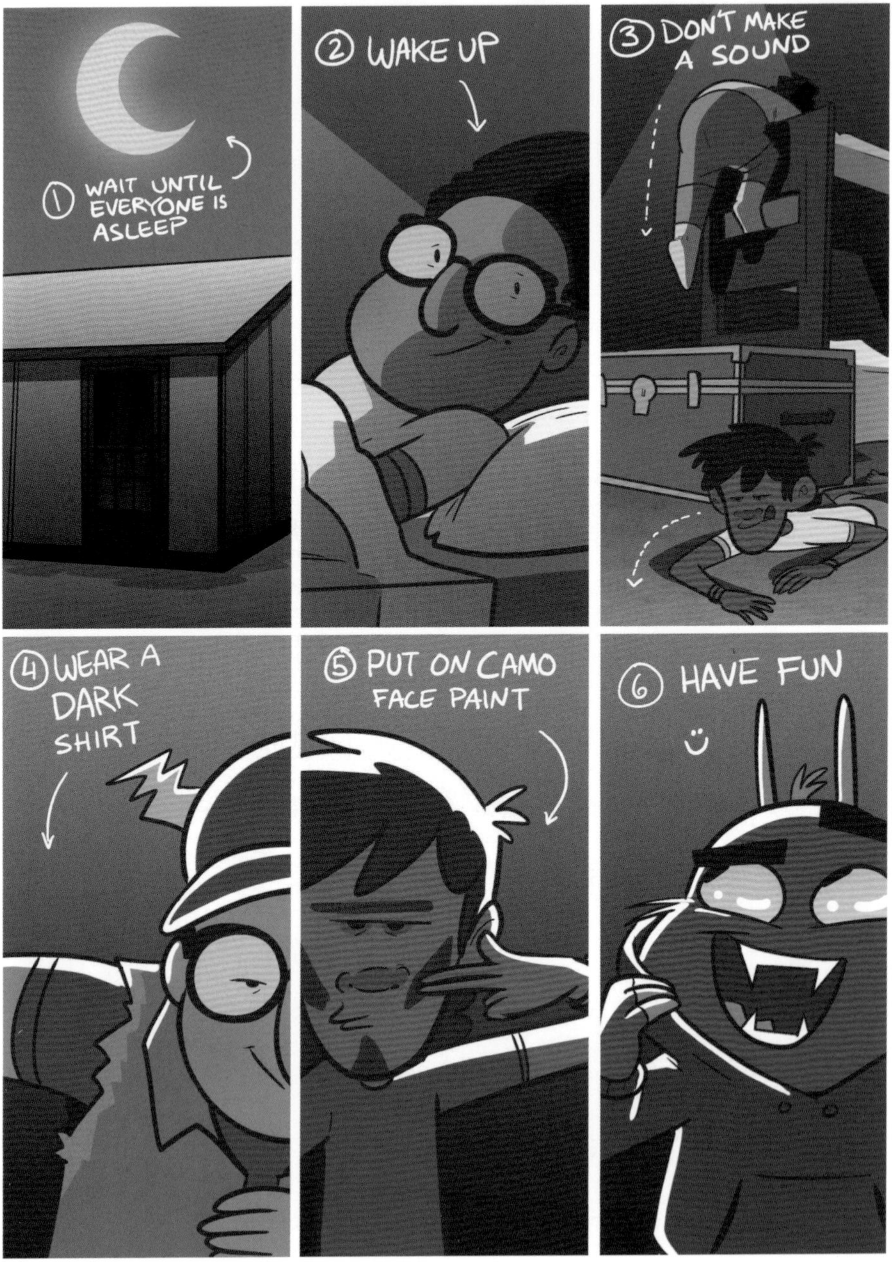
① WAIT UNTIL EVERYONE IS ASLEEP
② WAKE UP
③ DON'T MAKE A SOUND
④ WEAR A DARK SHIRT
⑤ PUT ON CAMO FACE PAINT
⑥ HAVE FUN
☺

NIGHT ONE

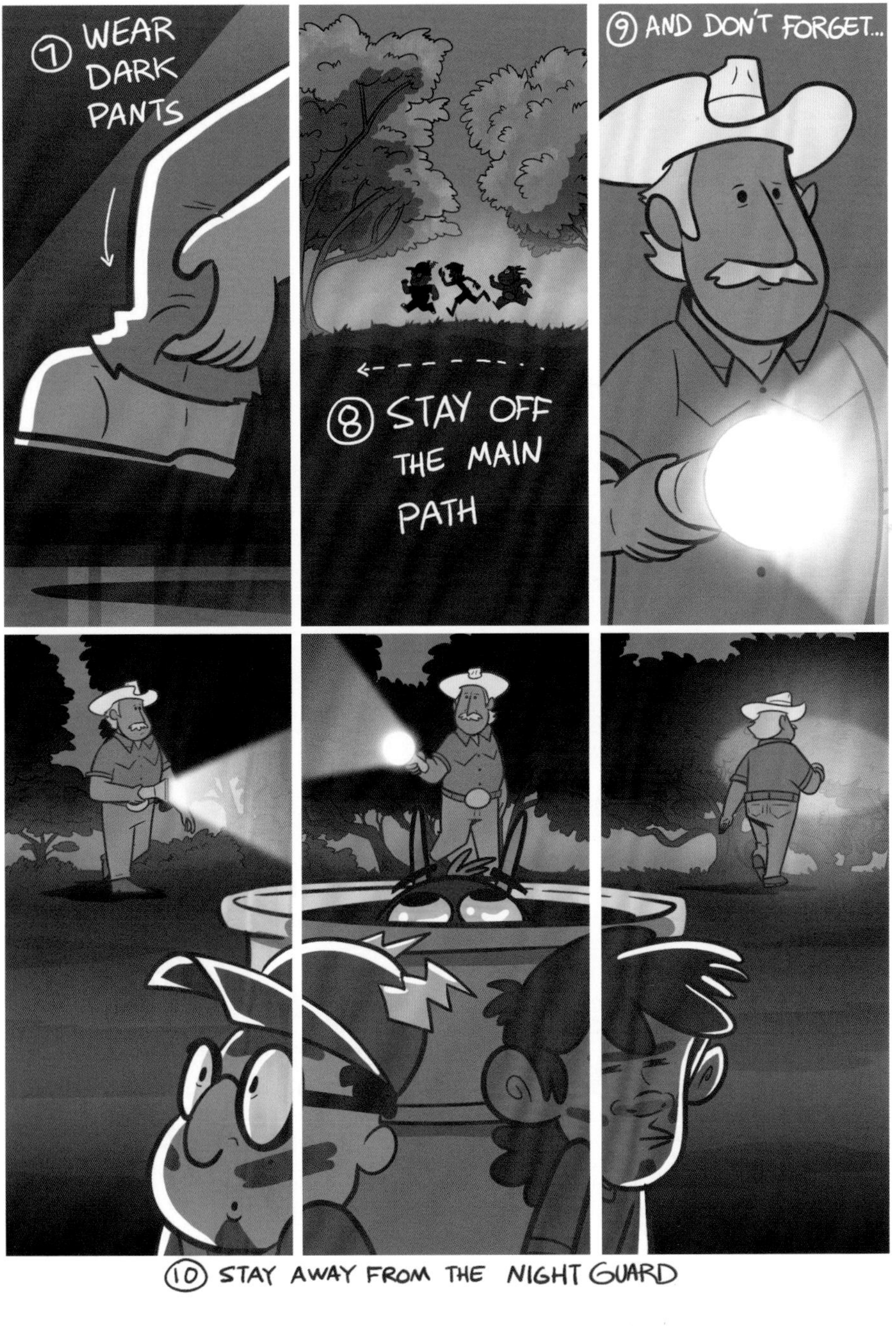

7 WEAR DARK PANTS
8 STAY OFF THE MAIN PATH
9 AND DON'T FORGET...
10 STAY AWAY FROM THE NIGHT GUARD

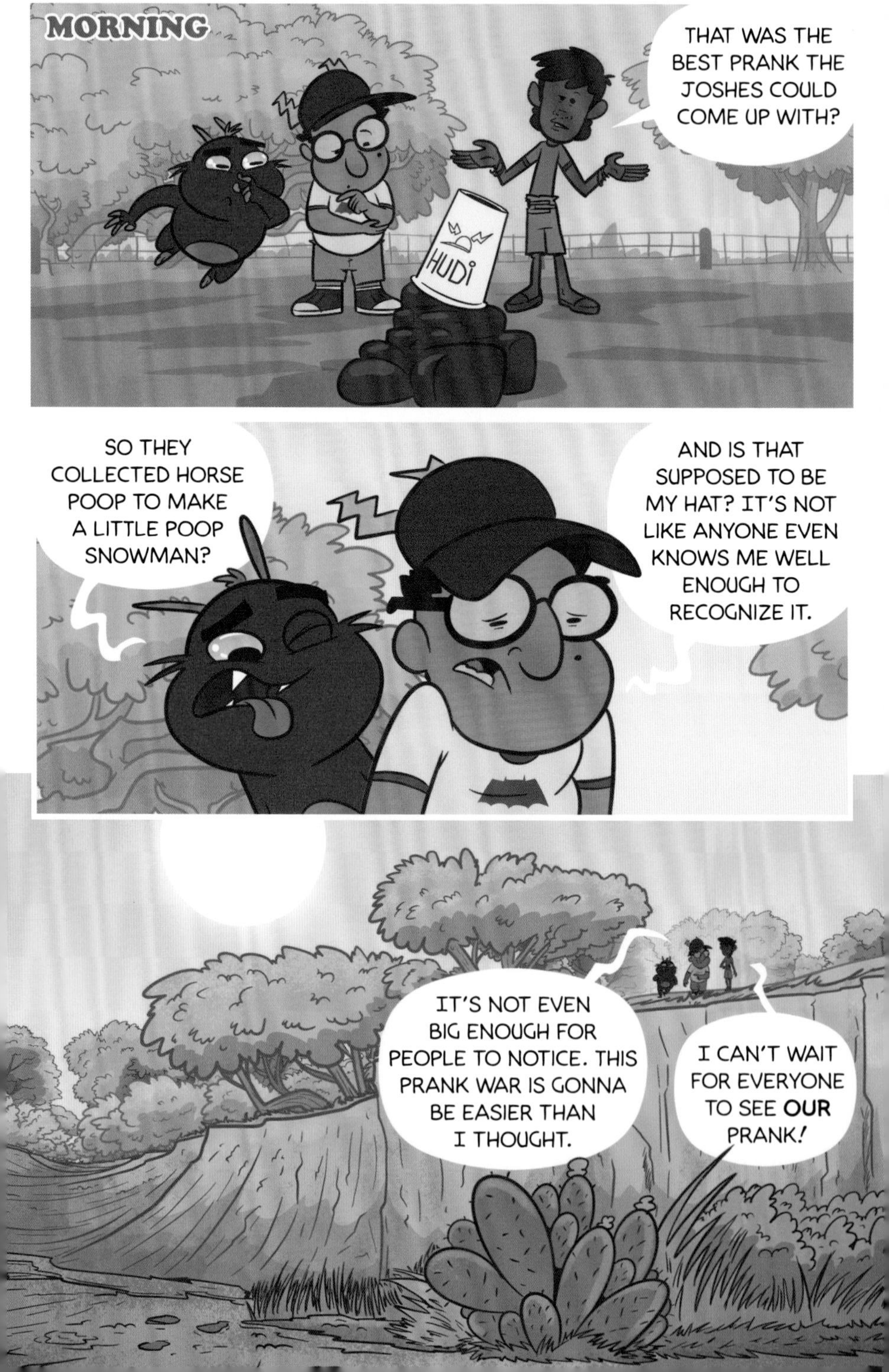
MORNING
THAT WAS THE BEST PRANK THE JOSHES COULD COME UP WITH?
HUDI
SO THEY COLLECTED HORSE POOP TO MAKE A LITTLE POOP SNOWMAN?
AND IS THAT SUPPOSED TO BE MY HAT? IT'S NOT LIKE ANYONE EVEN KNOWS ME WELL ENOUGH TO RECOGNIZE IT.
IT'S NOT EVEN BIG ENOUGH FOR PEOPLE TO NOTICE. THIS PRANK WAR IS GONNA BE EASIER THAN I THOUGHT.
I CAN'T WAIT FOR EVERYONE TO SEE **OUR** PRANK!

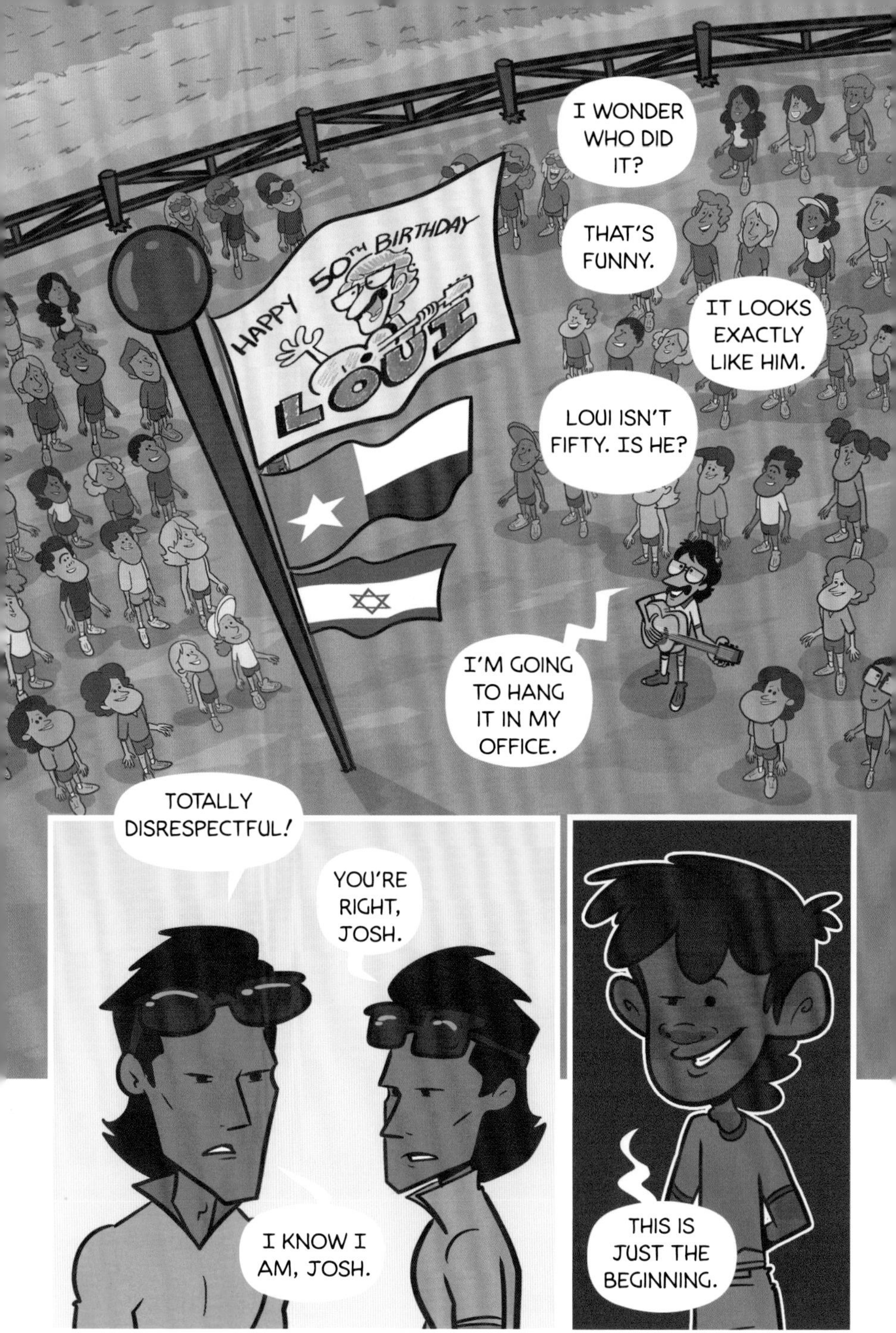
HAPPY 50TH BIRTHDAY
LOUI
I WONDER WHO DID IT?
THAT'S FUNNY.
IT LOOKS EXACTLY LIKE HIM.
LOUI ISN'T FIFTY. IS HE?
I'M GOING TO HANG IT IN MY OFFICE.
TOTALLY DISRESPECTFUL!
YOU'RE RIGHT, JOSH.
I KNOW I AM, JOSH.
THIS IS JUST THE BEGINNING.

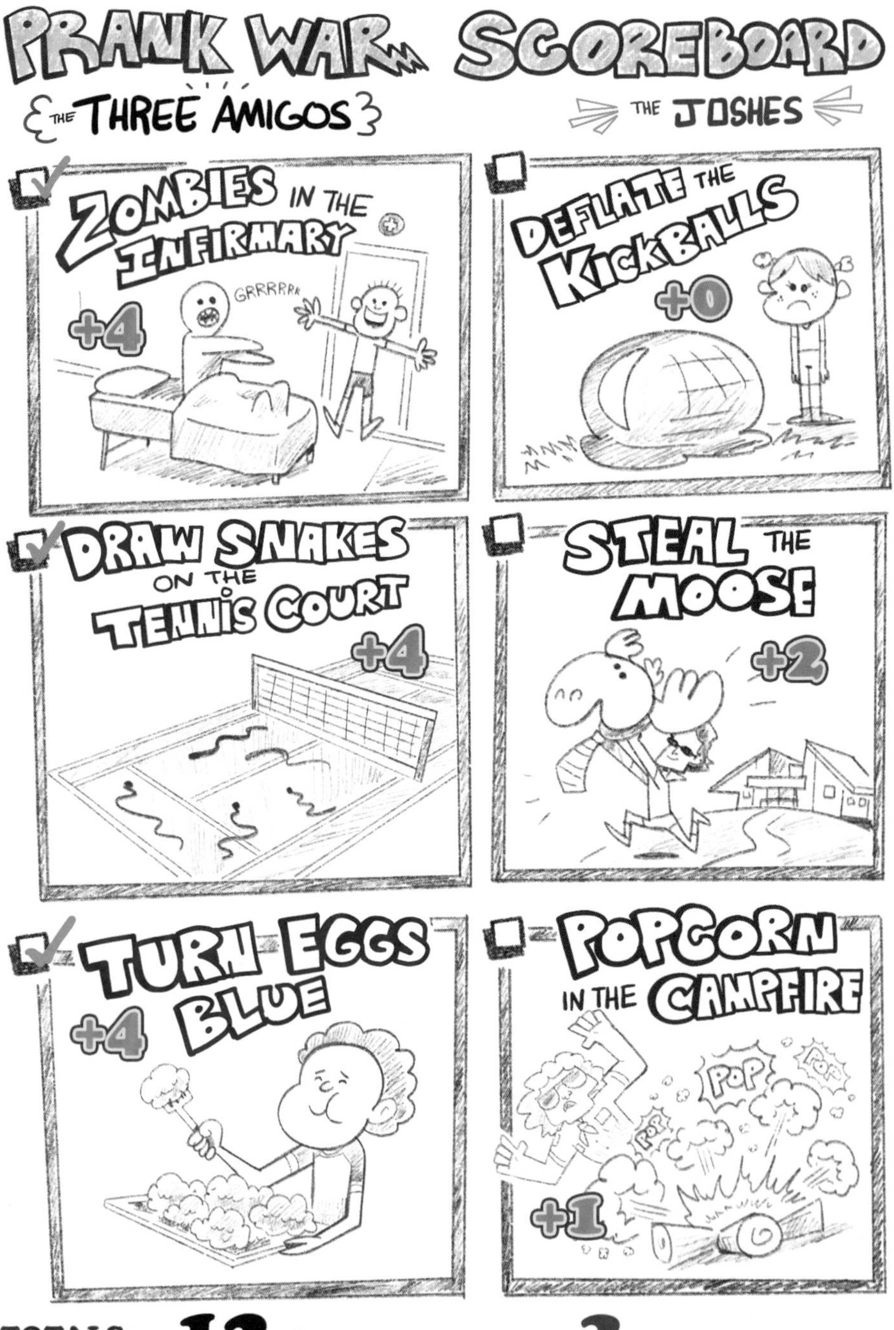
PRANK WAR SCOREBOARD
THE THREE AMIGOS
THE JOSHES
ZOMBIES IN THE INFIRMARY
+4
GRRRRRR
DEFLATE THE KICKBALLS
+0
DRAW SNAKES ON THE TENNIS COURT
+4
STEAL THE MOOSE
+2
TURN EGGS BLUE
+4
POPCORN IN THE CAMPFIRE
POP
POP
POP
+1

TOTALS: **12 Points** **3 Points**

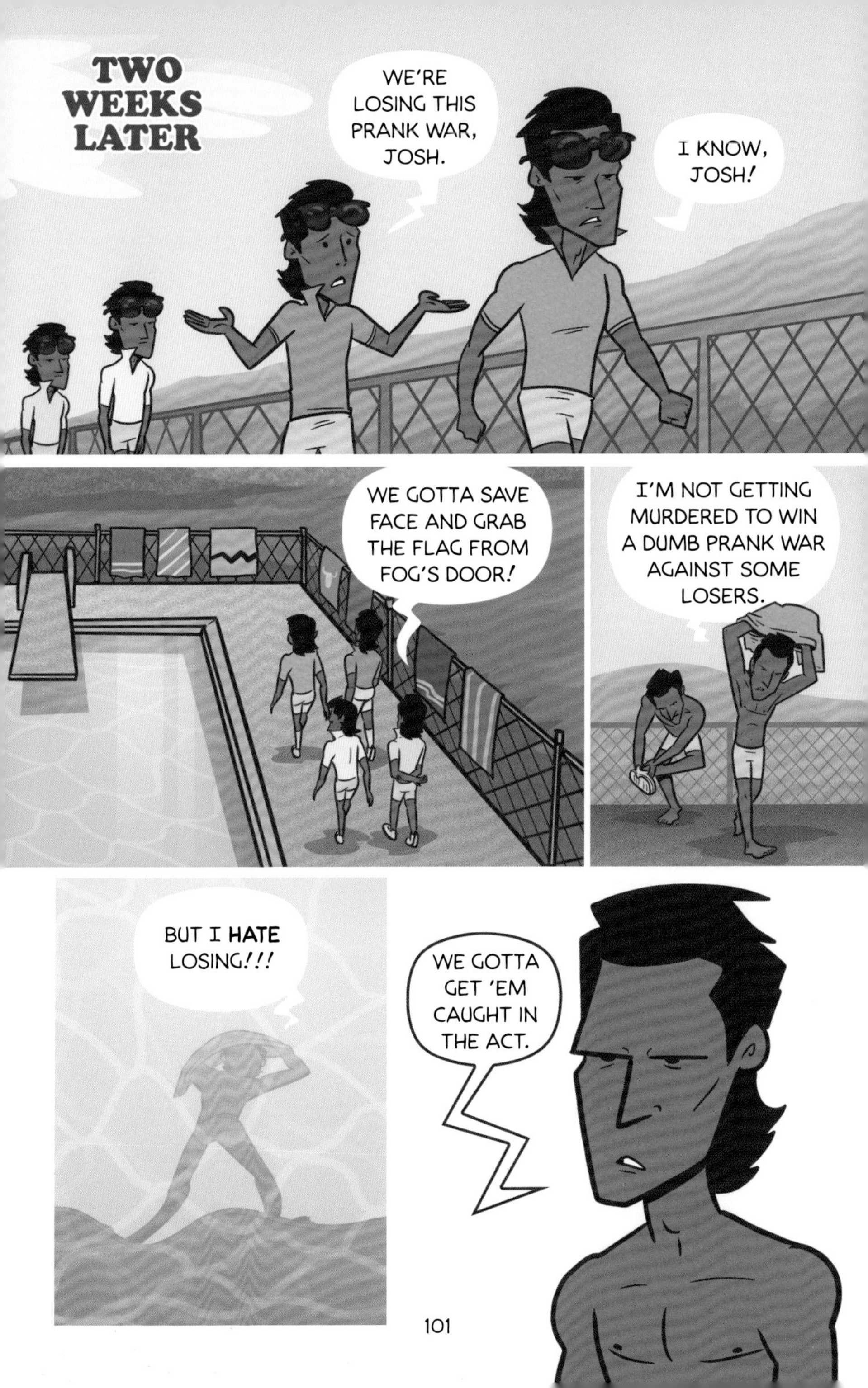
TWO WEEKS LATER
WE'RE LOSING THIS PRANK WAR, JOSH.
I KNOW, JOSH!
WE GOTTA SAVE FACE AND GRAB THE FLAG FROM FOG'S DOOR!
I'M NOT GETTING MURDERED TO WIN A DUMB PRANK WAR AGAINST SOME LOSERS.
BUT I **HATE** LOSING!!!
WE GOTTA GET 'EM CAUGHT IN THE ACT.

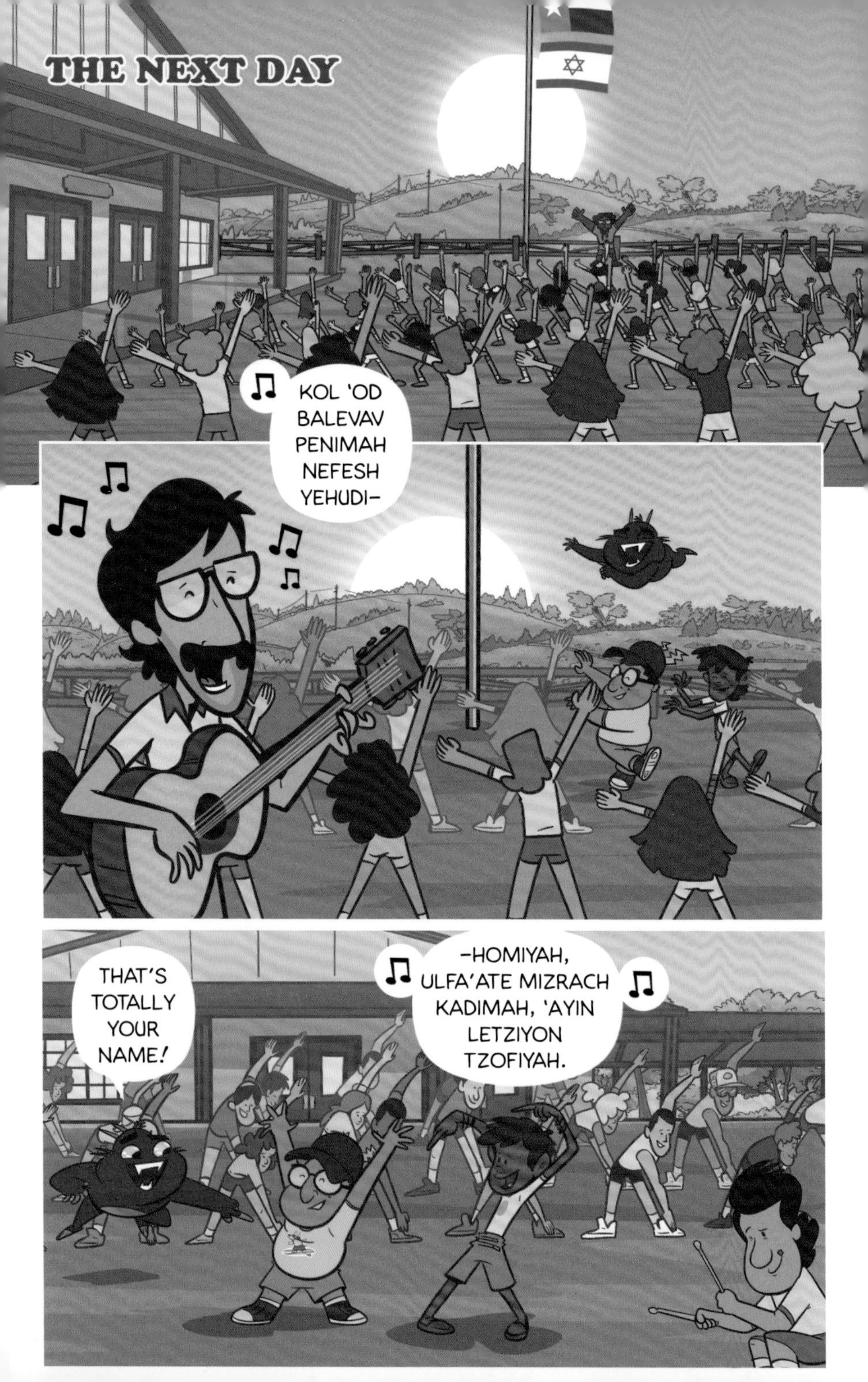
THE NEXT DAY
KOL 'OD BALEVAV PENIMAH NEFESH YEHUDI-
THAT'S TOTALLY YOUR NAME!
-HOMIYAH, ULFA'ATE MIZRACH KADIMAH, 'AYIN LETZIYON TZOFIYAH.

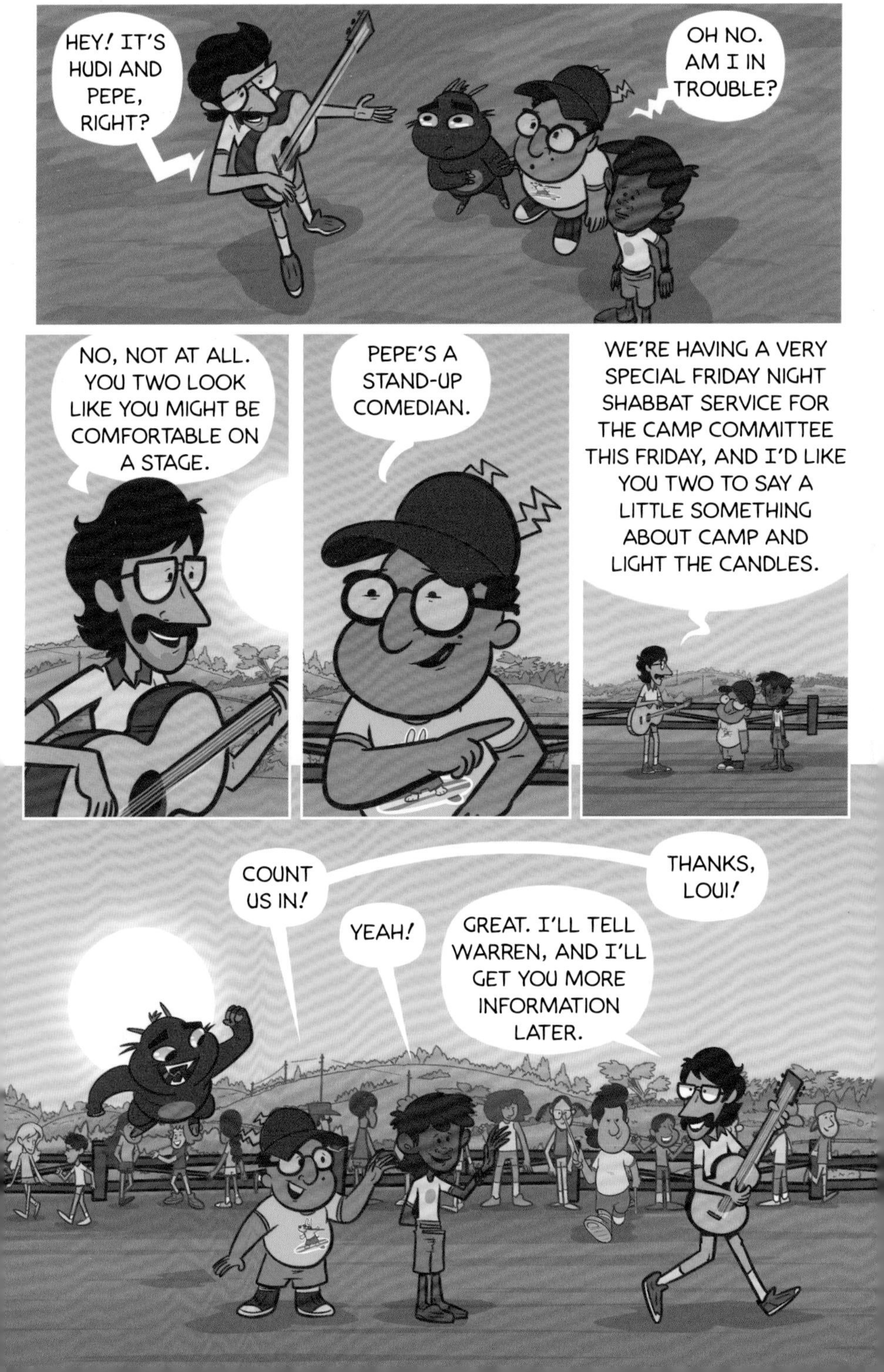
HEY! IT'S HUDI AND PEPE, RIGHT?
OH NO. AM I IN TROUBLE?
NO, NOT AT ALL. YOU TWO LOOK LIKE YOU MIGHT BE COMFORTABLE ON A STAGE.
PEPE'S A STAND-UP COMEDIAN.
WE'RE HAVING A VERY SPECIAL FRIDAY NIGHT SHABBAT SERVICE FOR THE CAMP COMMITTEE THIS FRIDAY, AND I'D LIKE YOU TWO TO SAY A LITTLE SOMETHING ABOUT CAMP AND LIGHT THE CANDLES.
COUNT US IN!
YEAH!
GREAT. I'LL TELL WARREN, AND I'LL GET YOU MORE INFORMATION LATER.
THANKS, LOUI!

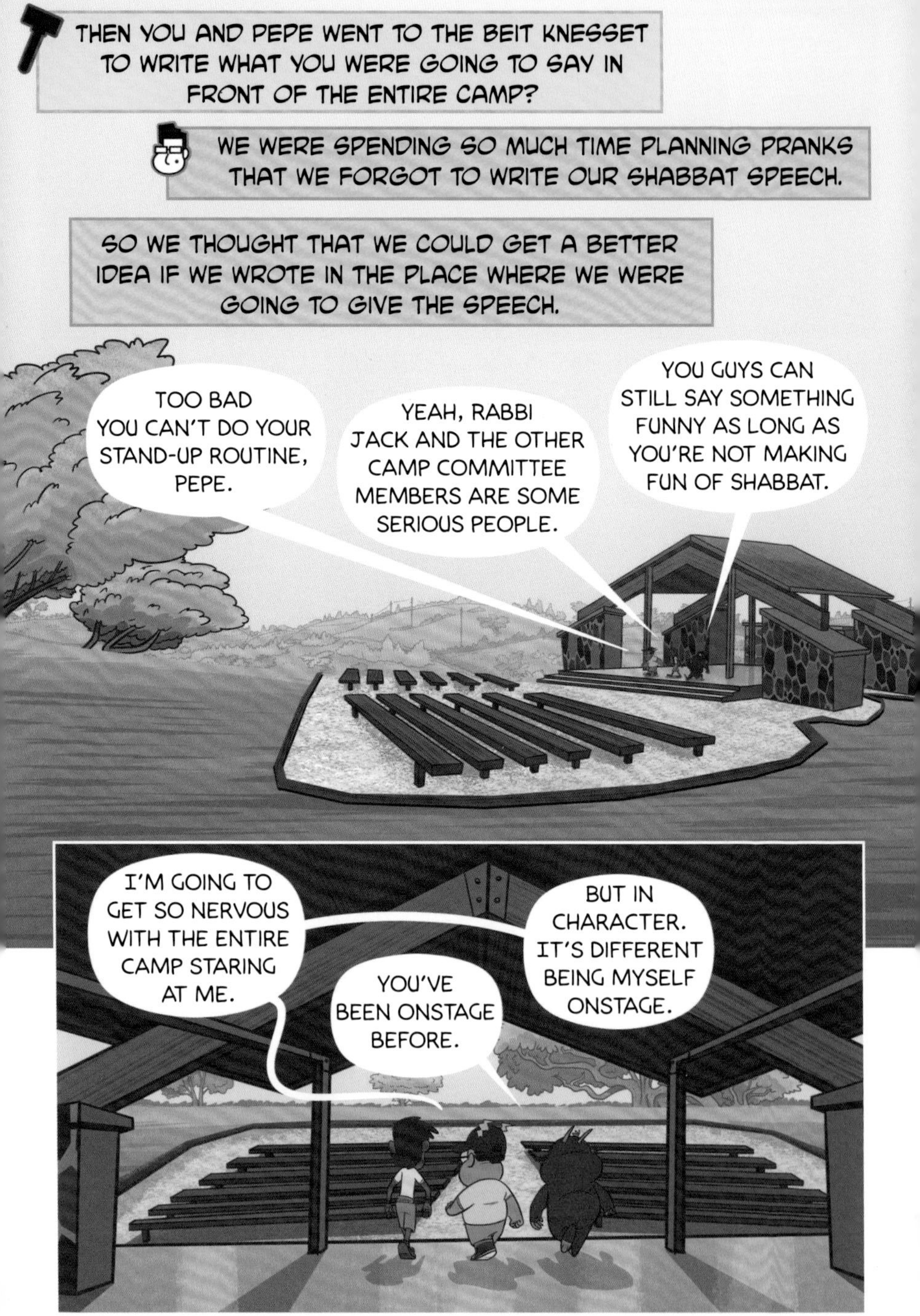
THEN YOU AND PEPE WENT TO THE BEIT KNESSET TO WRITE WHAT YOU WERE GOING TO SAY IN FRONT OF THE ENTIRE CAMP?
WE WERE SPENDING SO MUCH TIME PLANNING PRANKS THAT WE FORGOT TO WRITE OUR SHABBAT SPEECH.
SO WE THOUGHT THAT WE COULD GET A BETTER IDEA IF WE WROTE IN THE PLACE WHERE WE WERE GOING TO GIVE THE SPEECH.
TOO BAD YOU CAN'T DO YOUR STAND-UP ROUTINE, PEPE.
YEAH, RABBI JACK AND THE OTHER CAMP COMMITTEE MEMBERS ARE SOME SERIOUS PEOPLE.
YOU GUYS CAN STILL SAY SOMETHING FUNNY AS LONG AS YOU'RE NOT MAKING FUN OF SHABBAT.
I'M GOING TO GET SO NERVOUS WITH THE ENTIRE CAMP STARING AT ME.
YOU'VE BEEN ONSTAGE BEFORE.
BUT IN CHARACTER. IT'S DIFFERENT BEING MYSELF ONSTAGE.

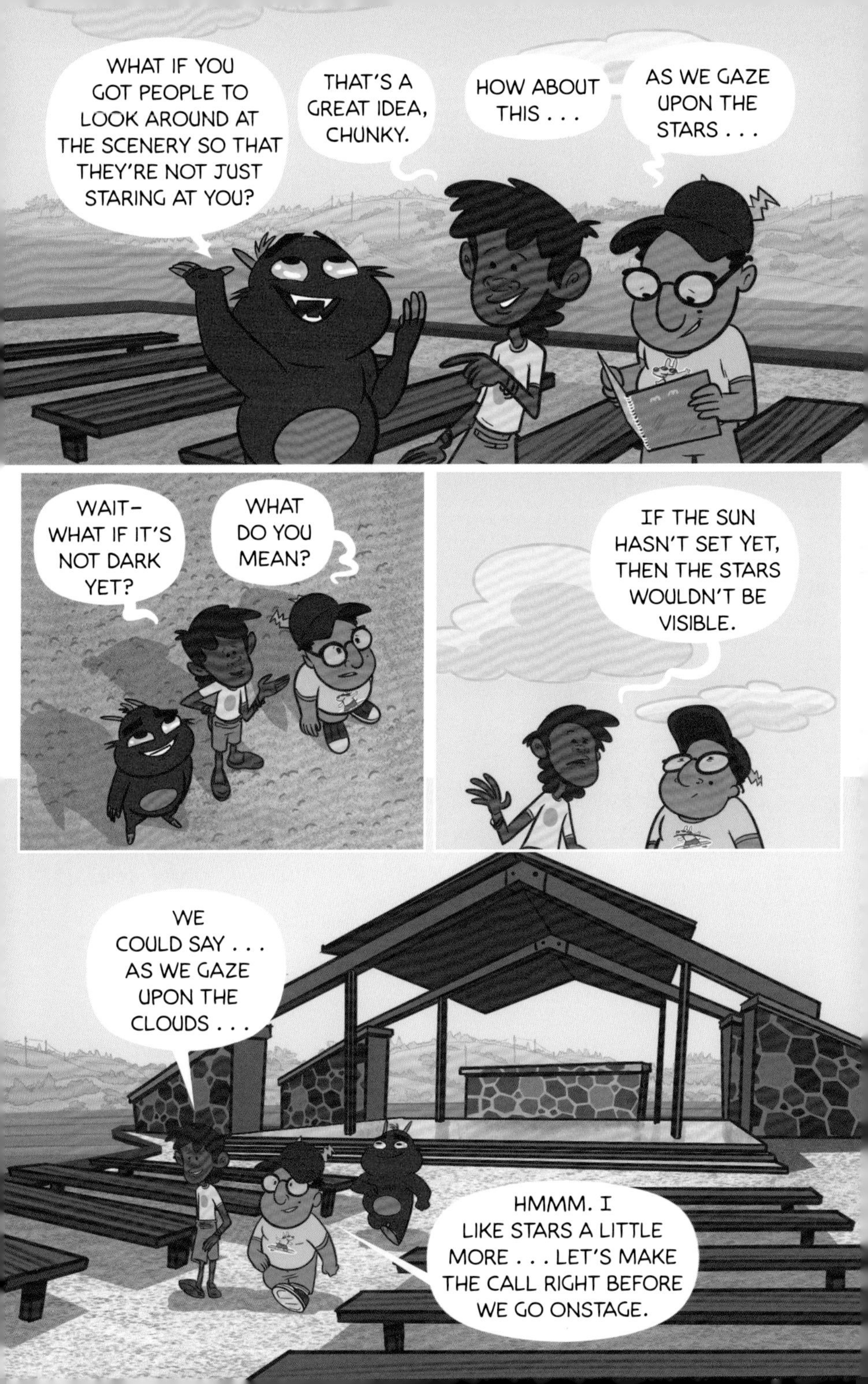
WHAT IF YOU GOT PEOPLE TO LOOK AROUND AT THE SCENERY SO THAT THEY'RE NOT JUST STARING AT YOU?
THAT'S A GREAT IDEA, CHUNKY.
HOW ABOUT THIS . . .
AS WE GAZE UPON THE STARS . . .
WAIT—WHAT IF IT'S NOT DARK YET?
WHAT DO YOU MEAN?
IF THE SUN HASN'T SET YET, THEN THE STARS WOULDN'T BE VISIBLE.
WE COULD SAY . . . AS WE GAZE UPON THE CLOUDS . . .
HMMM. I LIKE STARS A LITTLE MORE . . . LET'S MAKE THE CALL RIGHT BEFORE WE GO ONSTAGE.

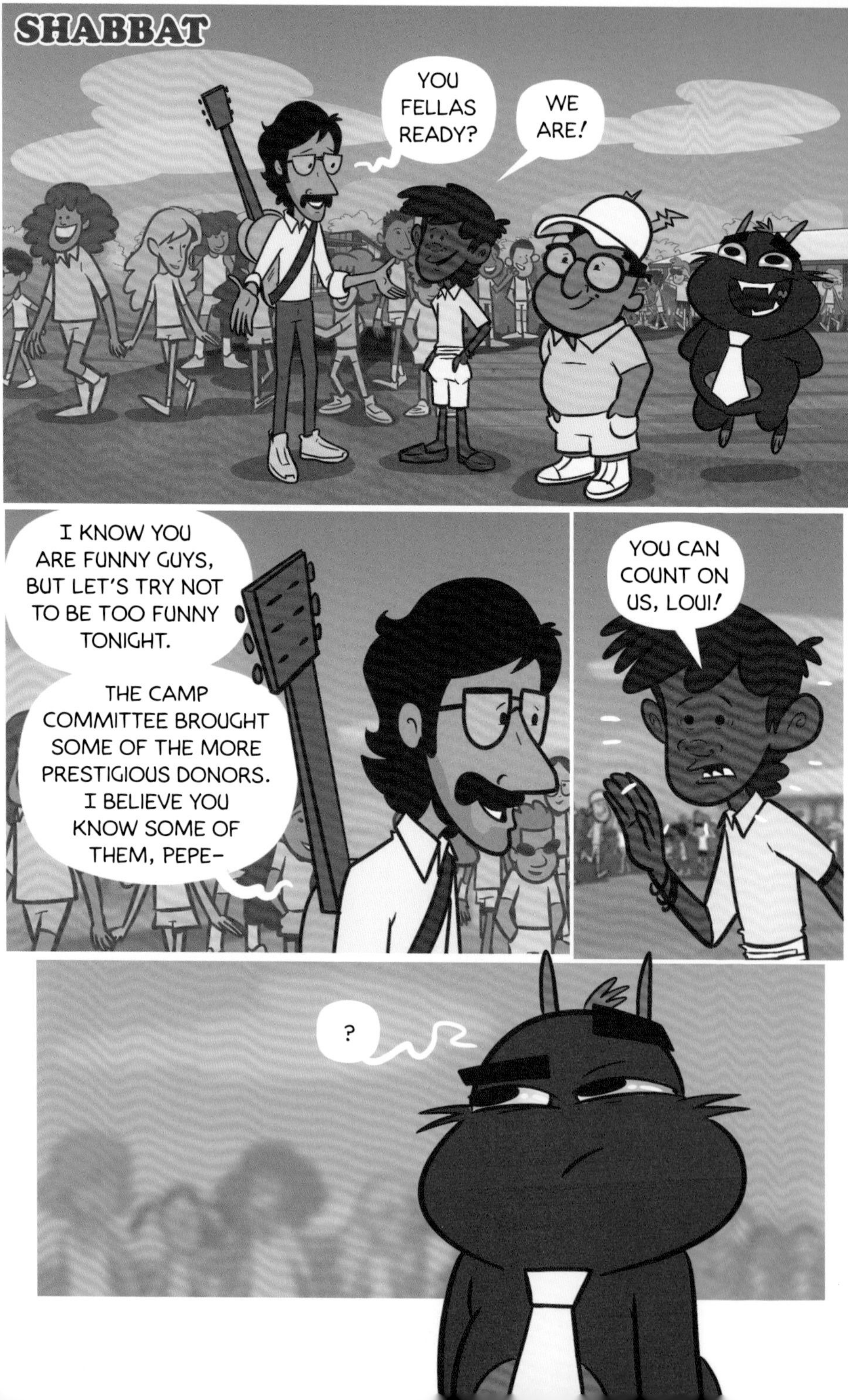
SHABBAT
YOU FELLAS READY?
WE ARE!
I KNOW YOU ARE FUNNY GUYS, BUT LET'S TRY NOT TO BE TOO FUNNY TONIGHT.
THE CAMP COMMITTEE BROUGHT SOME OF THE MORE PRESTIGIOUS DONORS. I BELIEVE YOU KNOW SOME OF THEM, PEPE-
YOU CAN COUNT ON US, LOUI!
?

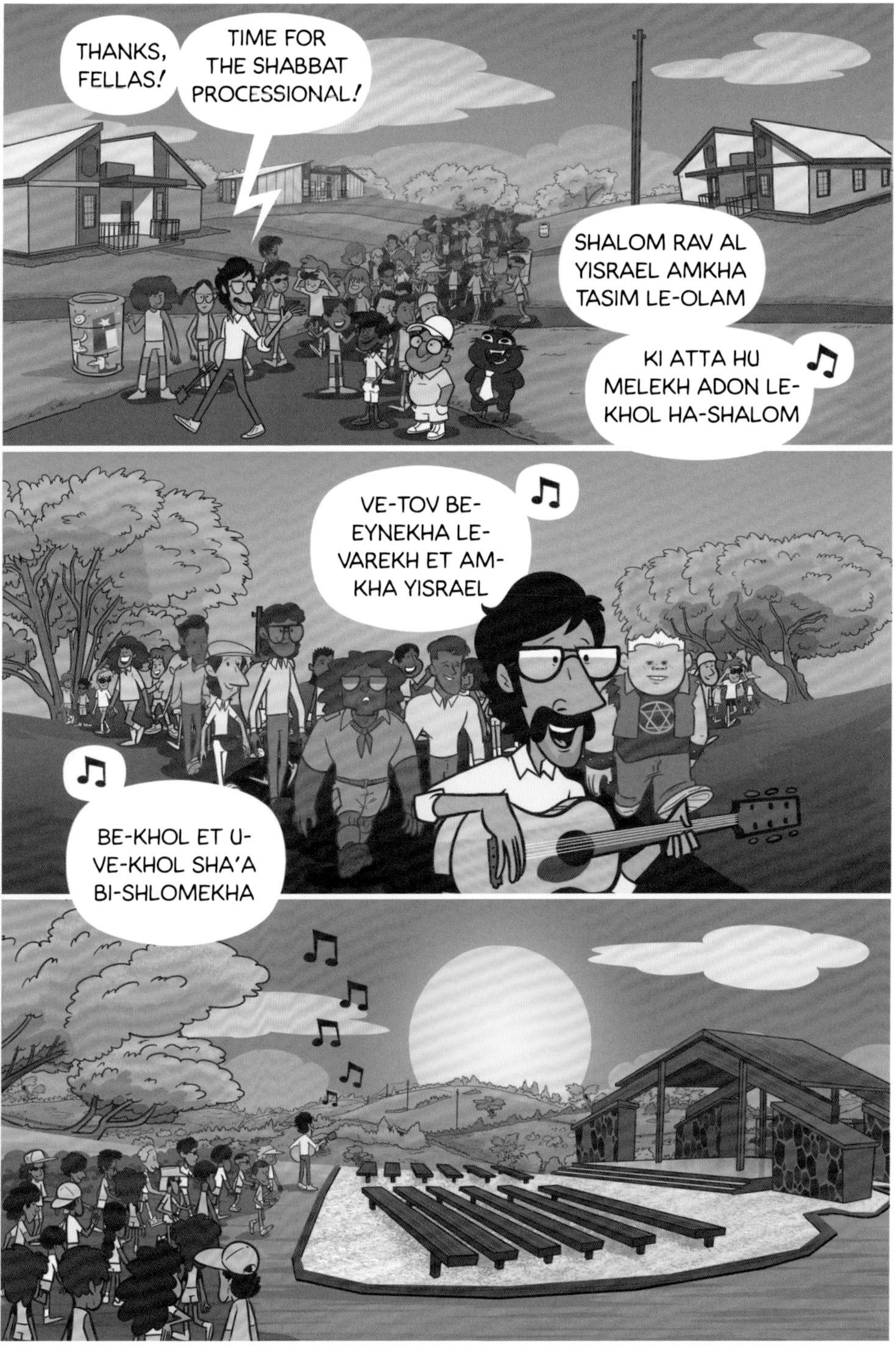
THANKS, FELLAS!
TIME FOR THE SHABBAT PROCESSIONAL!
SHALOM RAV AL YISRAEL AMKHA TASIM LE-OLAM
KI ATTA HU MELEKH ADON LE-KHOL HA-SHALOM
VE-TOV BE-EYNEKHA LE-VAREKH ET AM-KHA YISRAEL
BE-KHOL ET U-VE-KHOL SHA'A BI-SHLOMEKHA

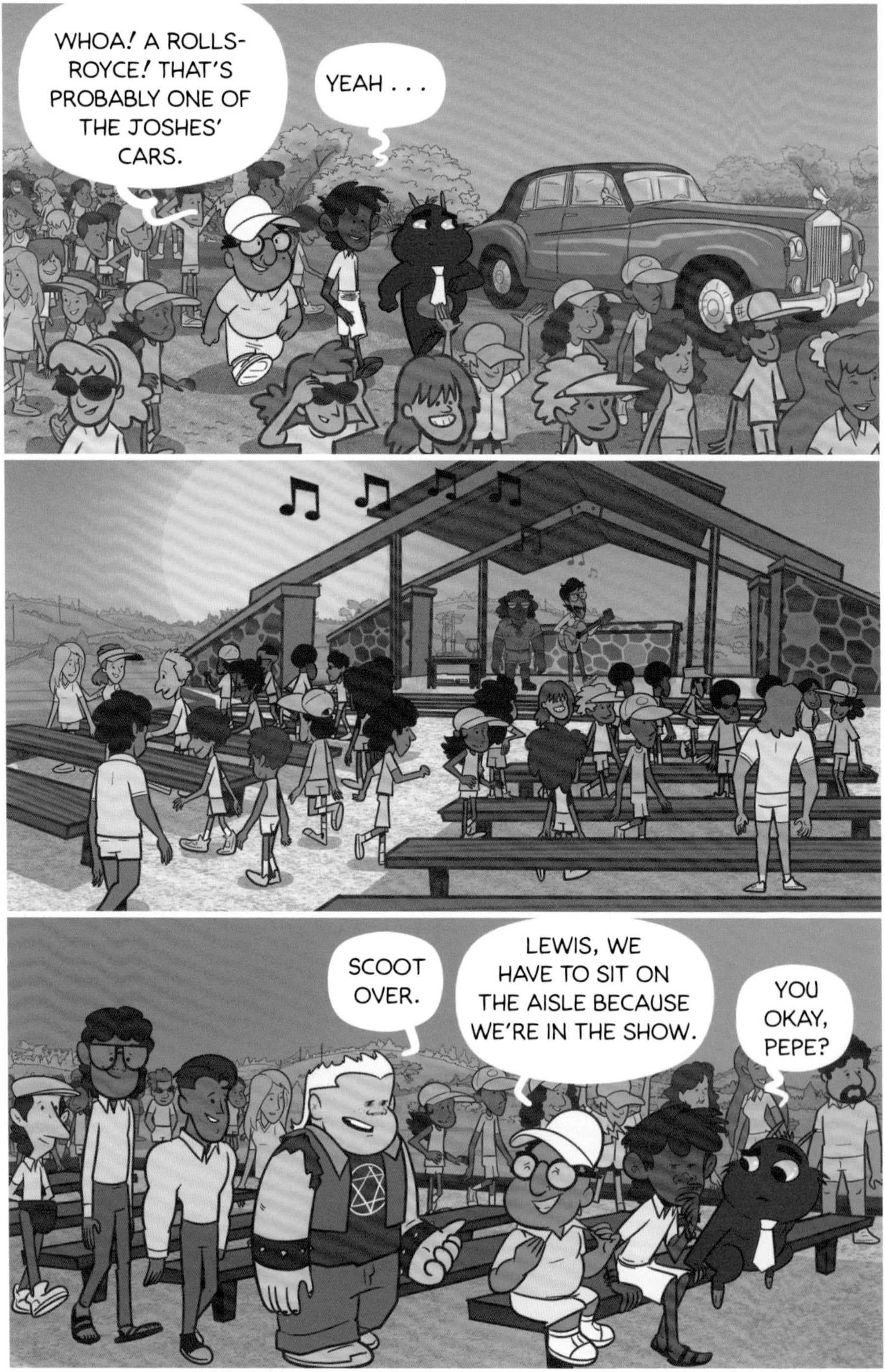
WHOA! A ROLLS-ROYCE! THAT'S PROBABLY ONE OF THE JOSHES' CARS.
YEAH . . .
SCOOT OVER.
LEWIS, WE HAVE TO SIT ON THE AISLE BECAUSE WE'RE IN THE SHOW.
YOU OKAY, PEPE?

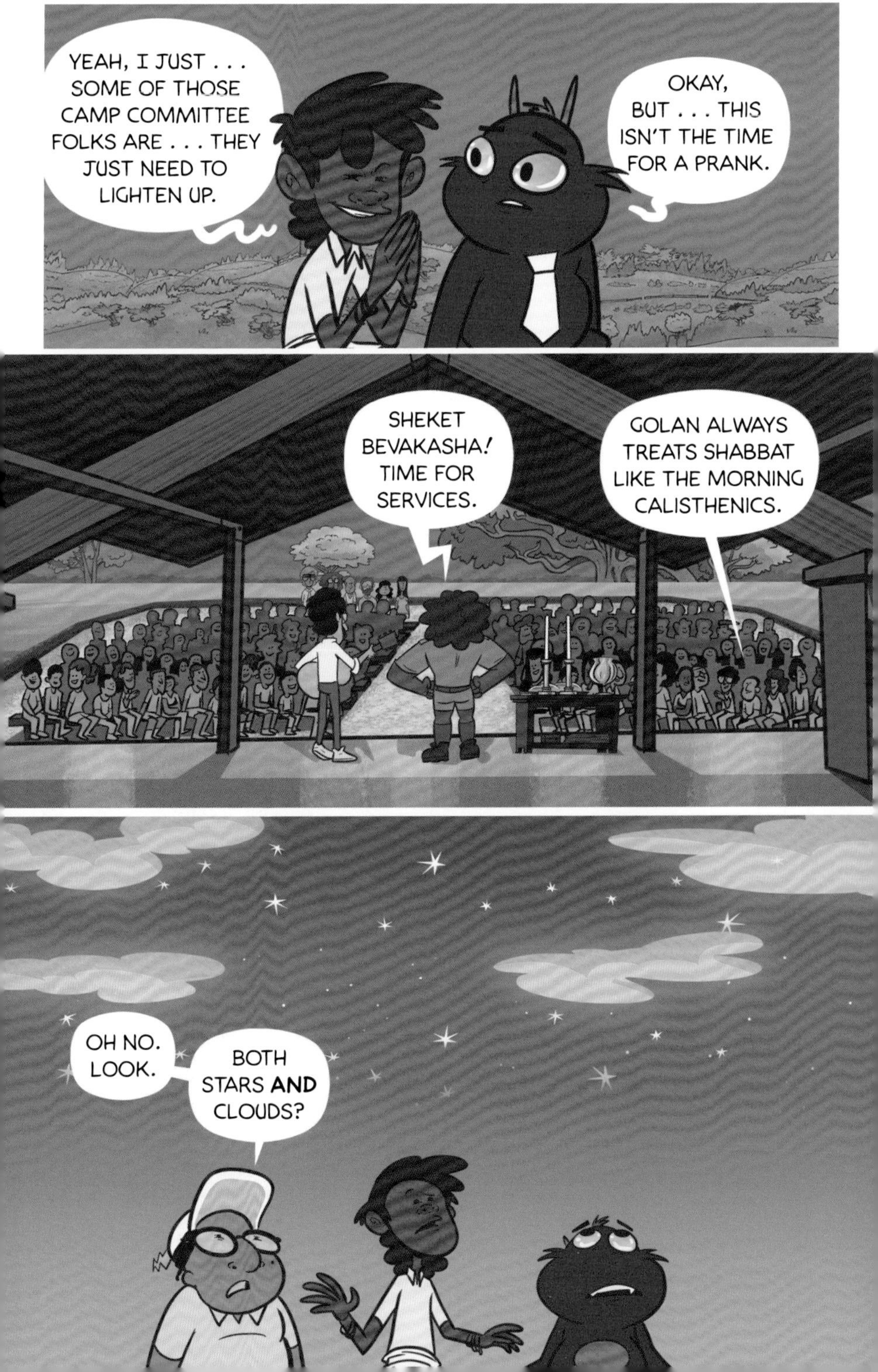
YEAH, I JUST . . . SOME OF THOSE CAMP COMMITTEE FOLKS ARE . . . THEY JUST NEED TO LIGHTEN UP.
OKAY, BUT . . . THIS ISN'T THE TIME FOR A PRANK.
SHEKET BEVAKASHA! TIME FOR SERVICES.
GOLAN ALWAYS TREATS SHABBAT LIKE THE MORNING CALISTHENICS.
OH NO. LOOK.
BOTH STARS **AND** CLOUDS?

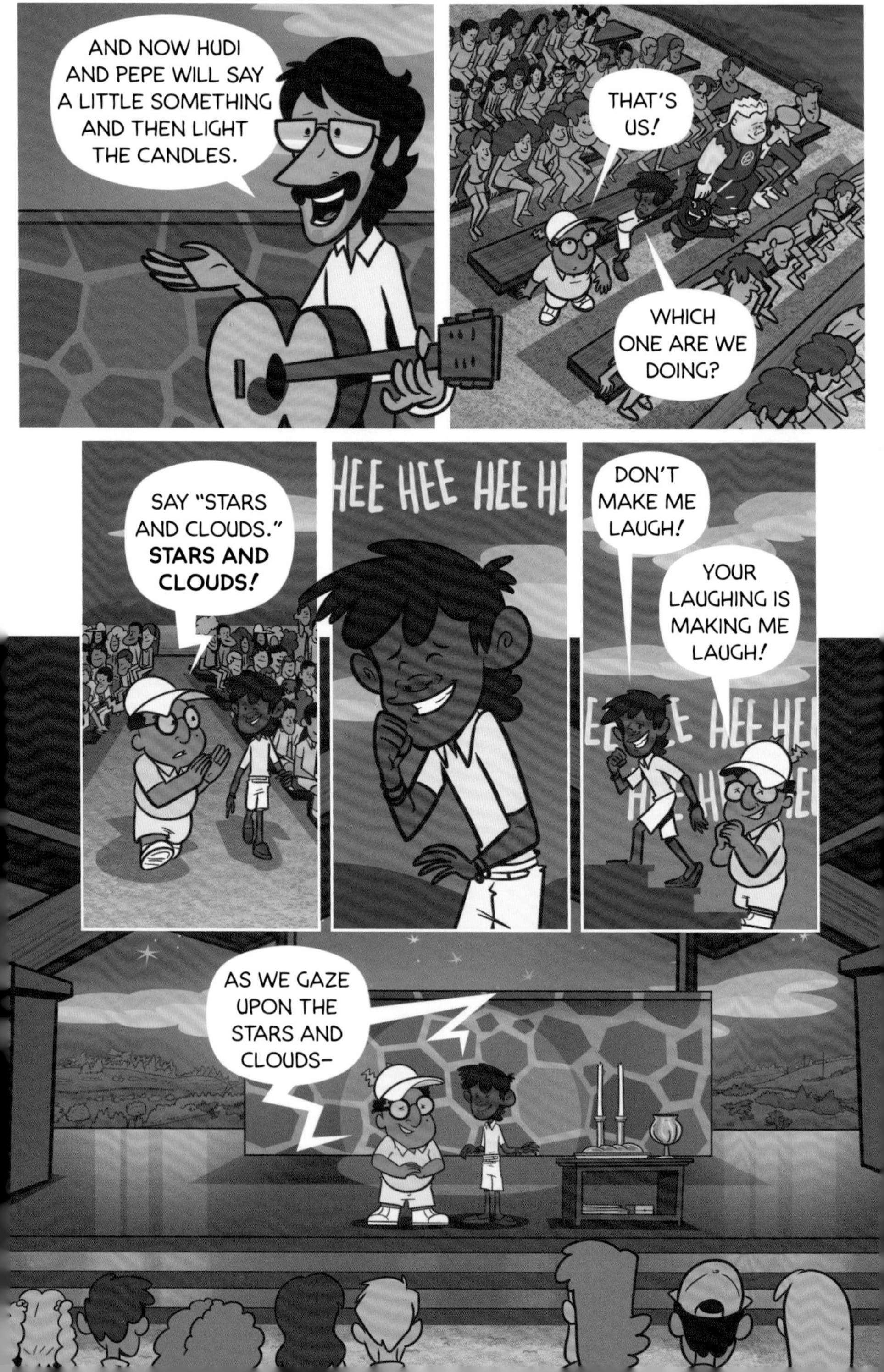
AND NOW HUDI AND PEPE WILL SAY A LITTLE SOMETHING AND THEN LIGHT THE CANDLES.
THAT'S US!
WHICH ONE ARE WE DOING?
SAY "STARS AND CLOUDS." **STARS AND CLOUDS!**
HEE HEE HEE HE
DON'T MAKE ME LAUGH!
YOUR LAUGHING IS MAKING ME LAUGH!
AS WE GAZE UPON THE STARS AND CLOUDS–

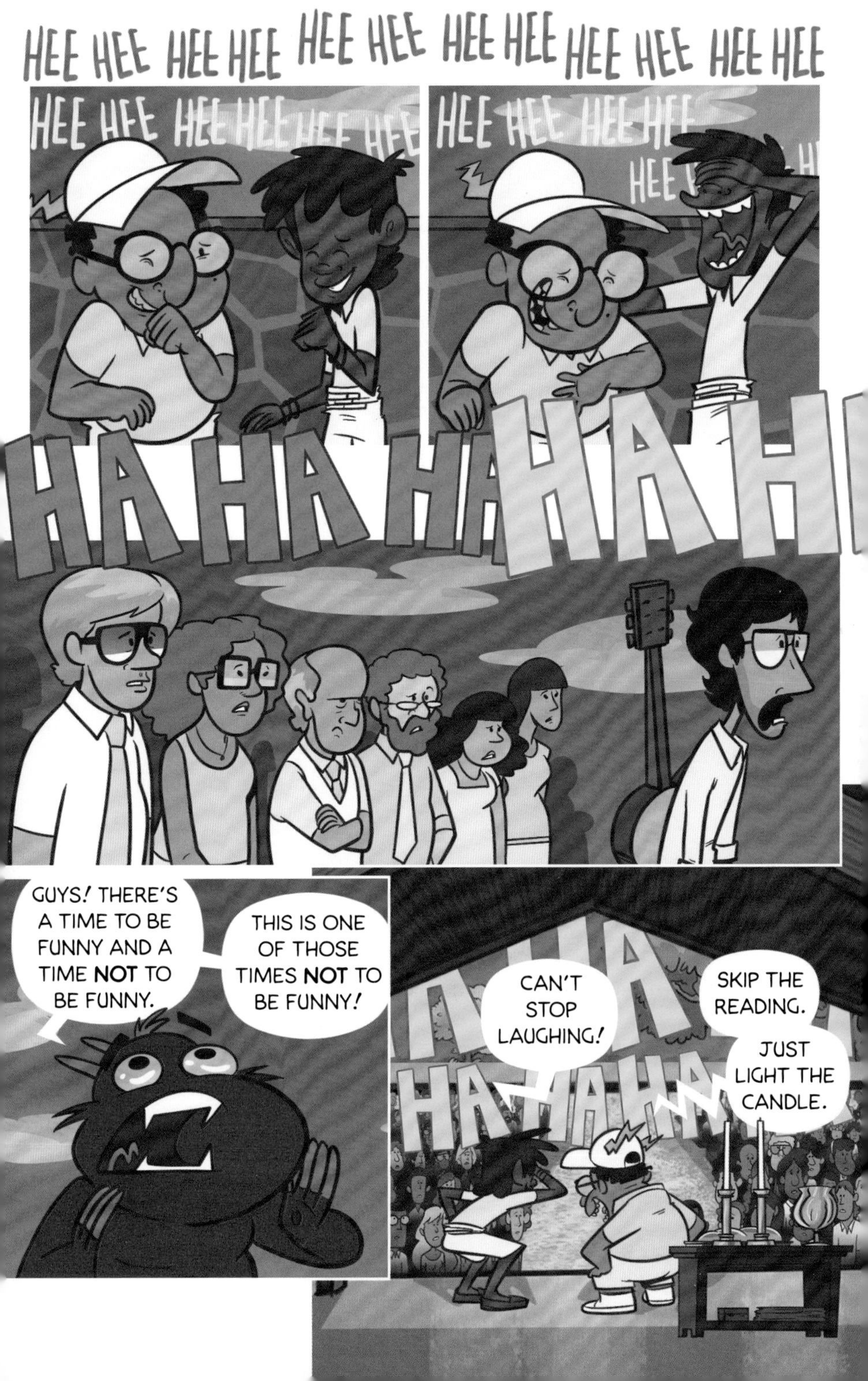
HEE HEE HEE HEE HEE HEE HEE HEE HEE HEE HEE HEE
HEE HEE HEE HEE
HEE HEE HEE HEE
HEE
HA HA HA HA HA HA
GUYS! THERE'S A TIME TO BE FUNNY AND A TIME **NOT** TO BE FUNNY.
THIS IS ONE OF THOSE TIMES **NOT** TO BE FUNNY!
CAN'T STOP LAUGHING!
SKIP THE READING.
JUST LIGHT THE CANDLE.

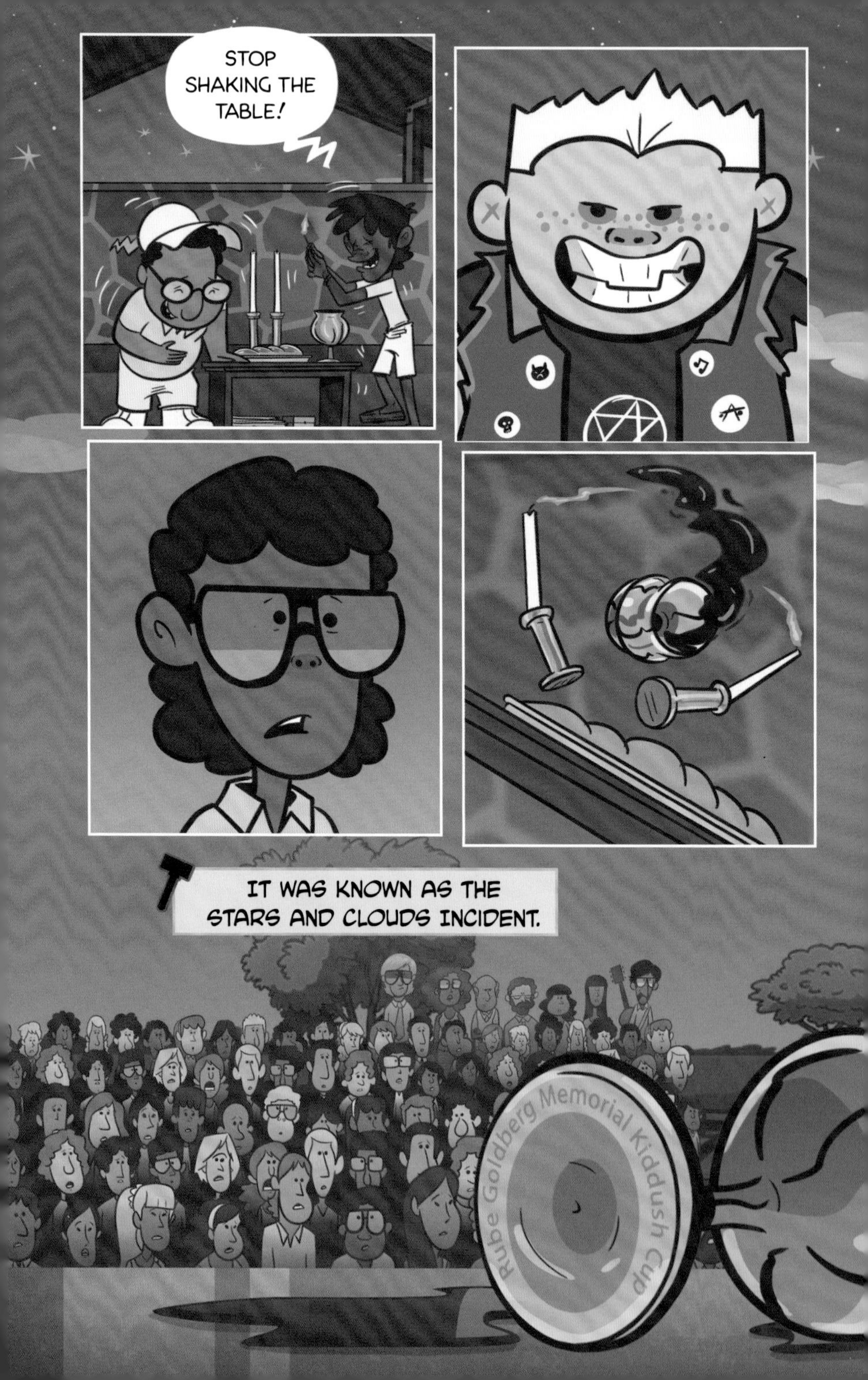
STOP SHAKING THE TABLE!
IT WAS KNOWN AS THE STARS AND CLOUDS INCIDENT.
Rube Goldberg Memorial Kiddush Cup

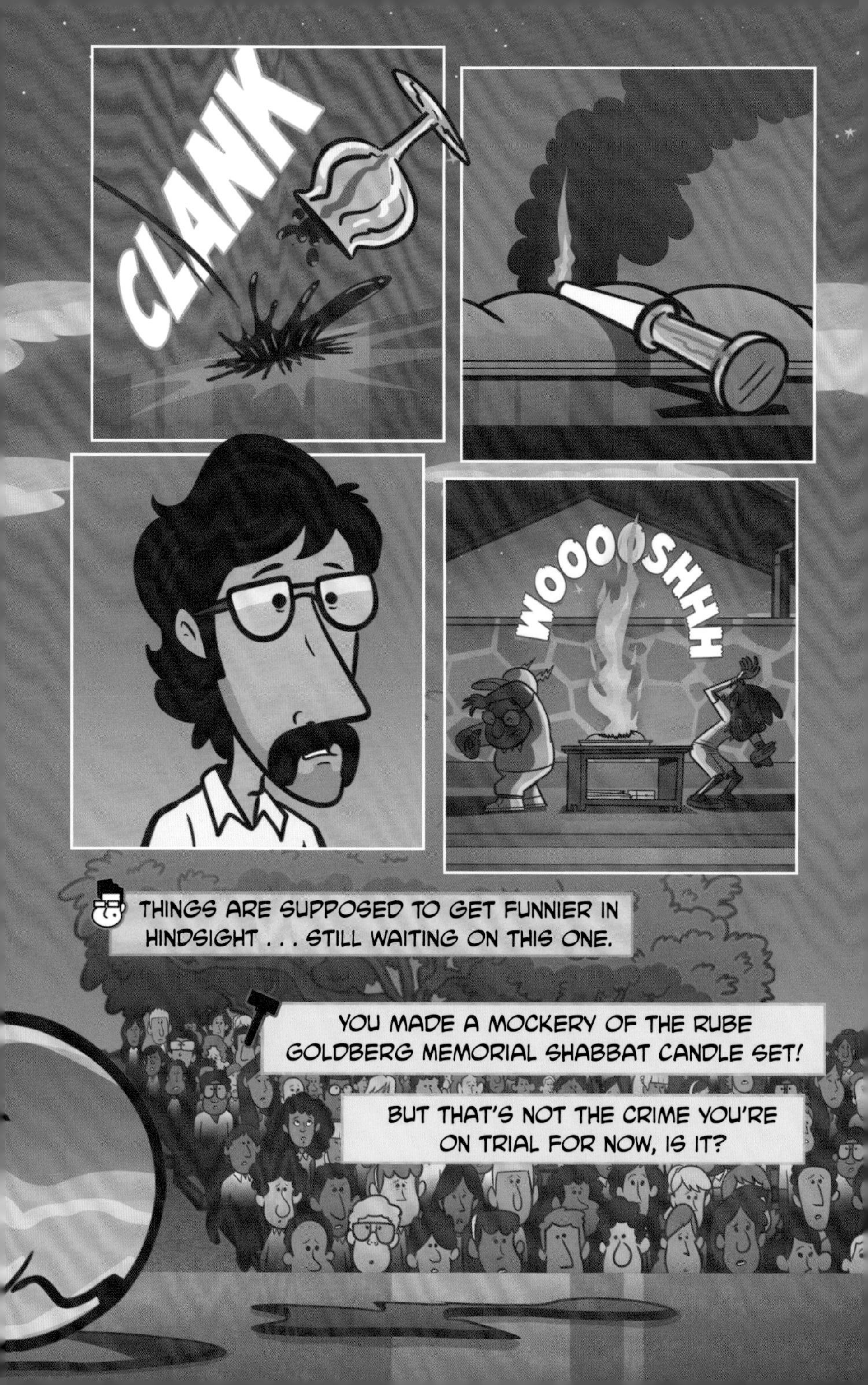
CLANK
WOOOOSHHH
THINGS ARE SUPPOSED TO GET FUNNIER IN HINDSIGHT . . . STILL WAITING ON THIS ONE.
YOU MADE A MOCKERY OF THE RUBE GOLDBERG MEMORIAL SHABBAT CANDLE SET!
BUT THAT'S NOT THE CRIME YOU'RE ON TRIAL FOR NOW, IS IT?

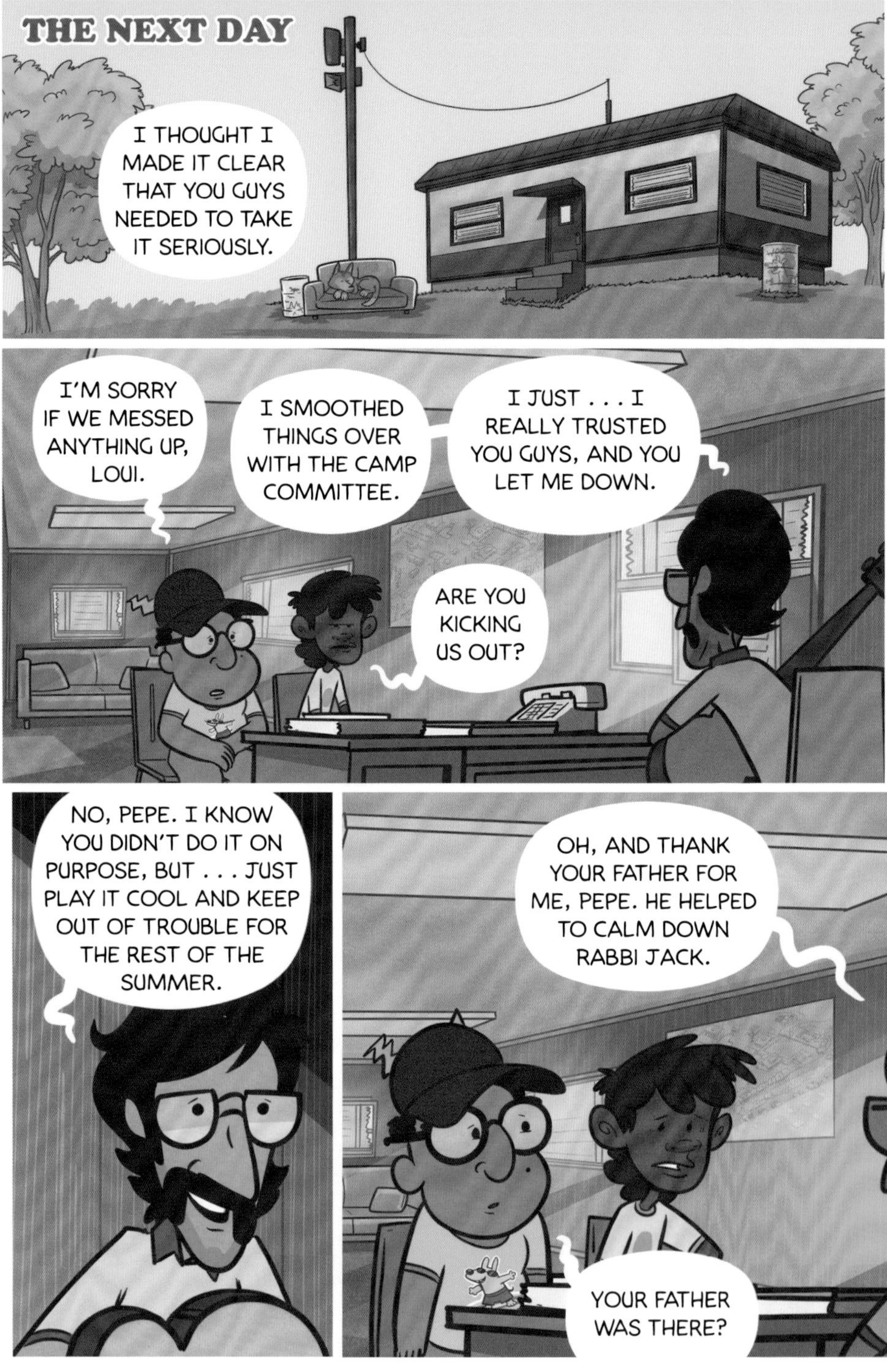
THE NEXT DAY
I THOUGHT I MADE IT CLEAR THAT YOU GUYS NEEDED TO TAKE IT SERIOUSLY.
I'M SORRY IF WE MESSED ANYTHING UP, LOUI.
I SMOOTHED THINGS OVER WITH THE CAMP COMMITTEE.
I JUST . . . I REALLY TRUSTED YOU GUYS, AND YOU LET ME DOWN.
ARE YOU KICKING US OUT?
NO, PEPE. I KNOW YOU DIDN'T DO IT ON PURPOSE, BUT . . . JUST PLAY IT COOL AND KEEP OUT OF TROUBLE FOR THE REST OF THE SUMMER.
OH, AND THANK YOUR FATHER FOR ME, PEPE. HE HELPED TO CALM DOWN RABBI JACK.
YOUR FATHER WAS THERE?

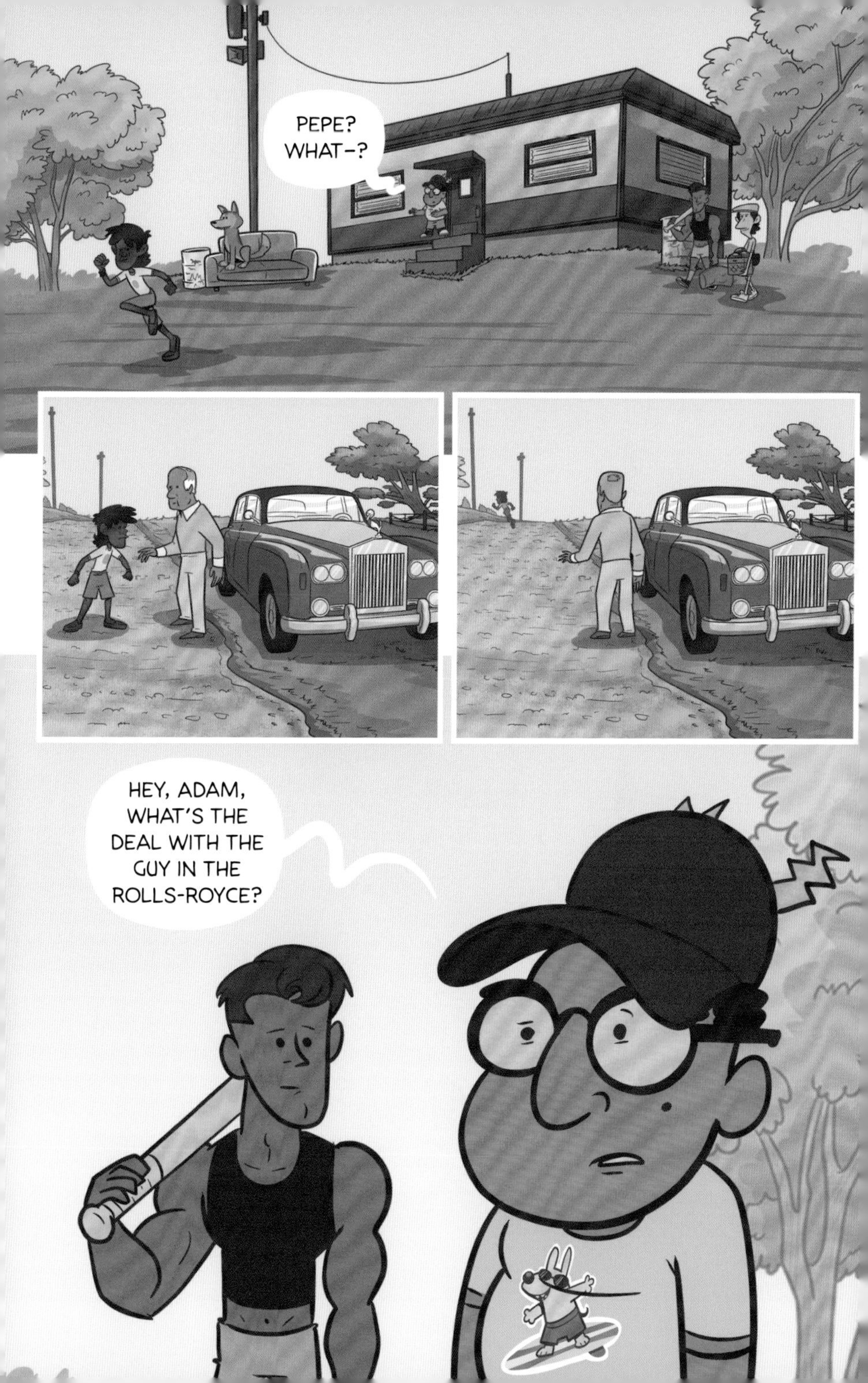
PEPE? WHAT–?
HEY, ADAM, WHAT'S THE DEAL WITH THE GUY IN THE ROLLS-ROYCE?

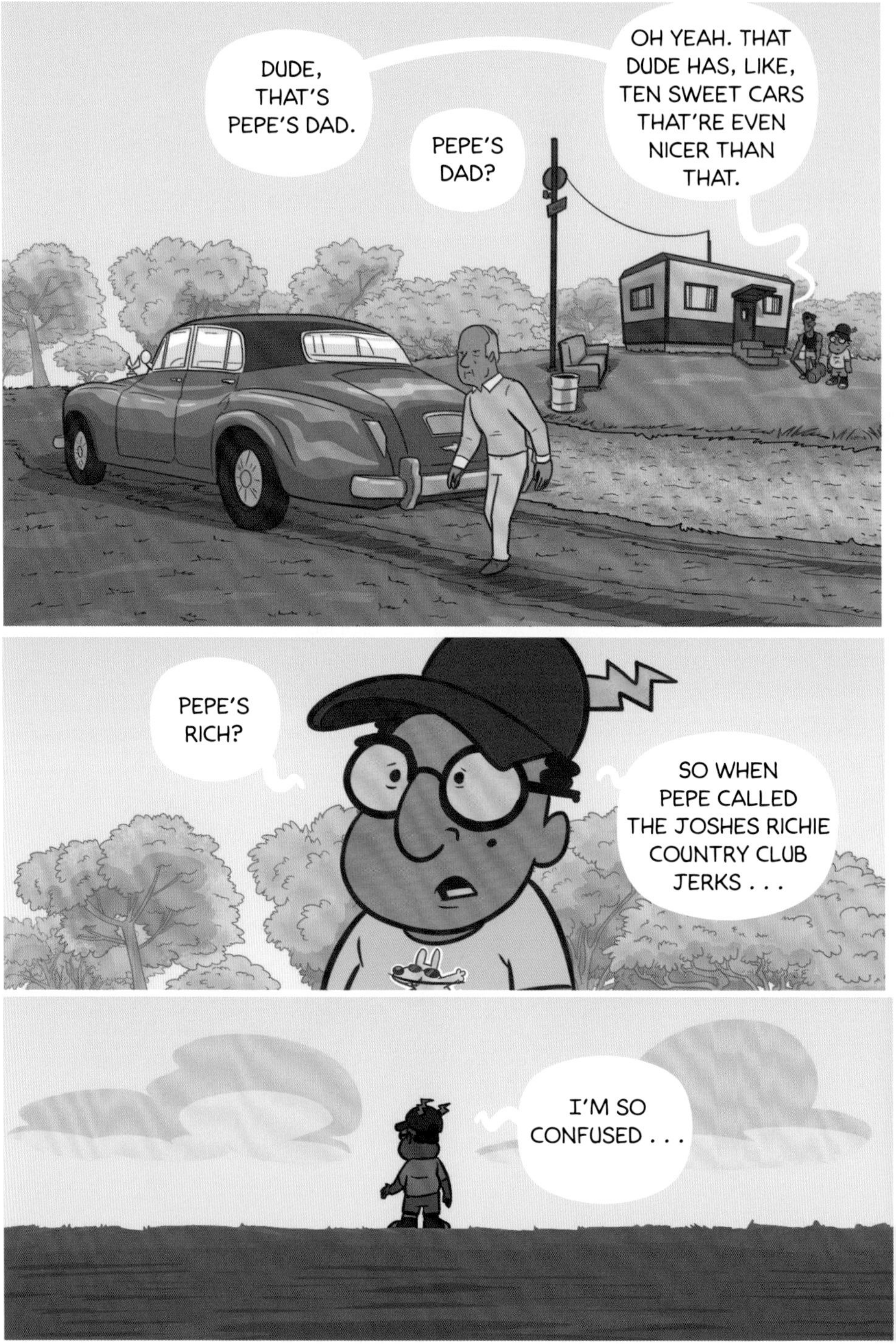
DUDE, THAT'S PEPE'S DAD.
PEPE'S DAD?
OH YEAH. THAT DUDE HAS, LIKE, TEN SWEET CARS THAT'RE EVEN NICER THAN THAT.
PEPE'S RICH?
SO WHEN PEPE CALLED THE JOSHES RICHIE COUNTRY CLUB JERKS . . .
I'M SO CONFUSED . . .

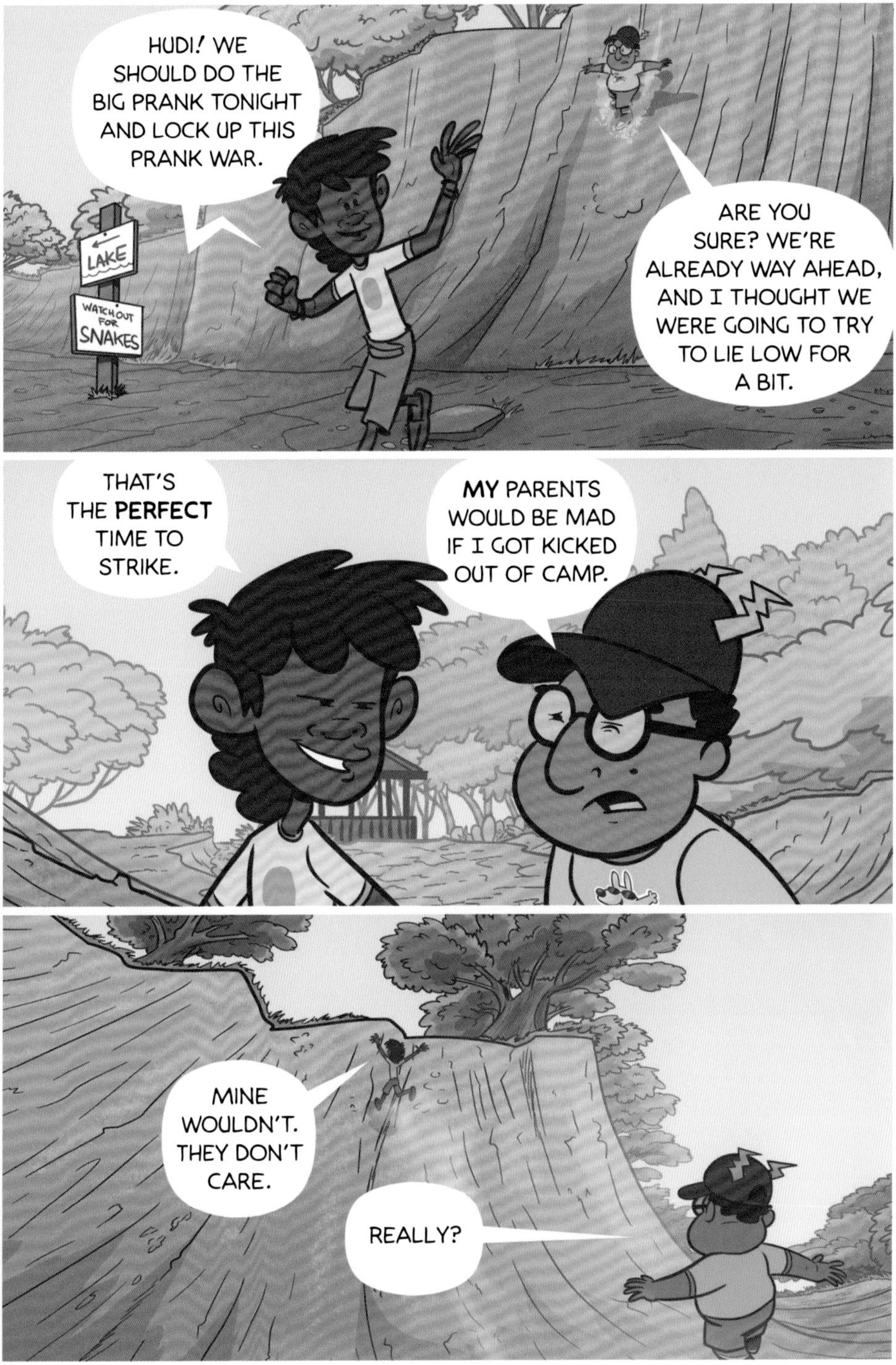
HUDI! WE SHOULD DO THE BIG PRANK TONIGHT AND LOCK UP THIS PRANK WAR.
LAKE
WATCH OUT FOR SNAKES
ARE YOU SURE? WE'RE ALREADY WAY AHEAD, AND I THOUGHT WE WERE GOING TO TRY TO LIE LOW FOR A BIT.
THAT'S THE **PERFECT** TIME TO STRIKE.
MY PARENTS WOULD BE MAD IF I GOT KICKED OUT OF CAMP.
MINE WOULDN'T. THEY DON'T CARE.
REALLY?

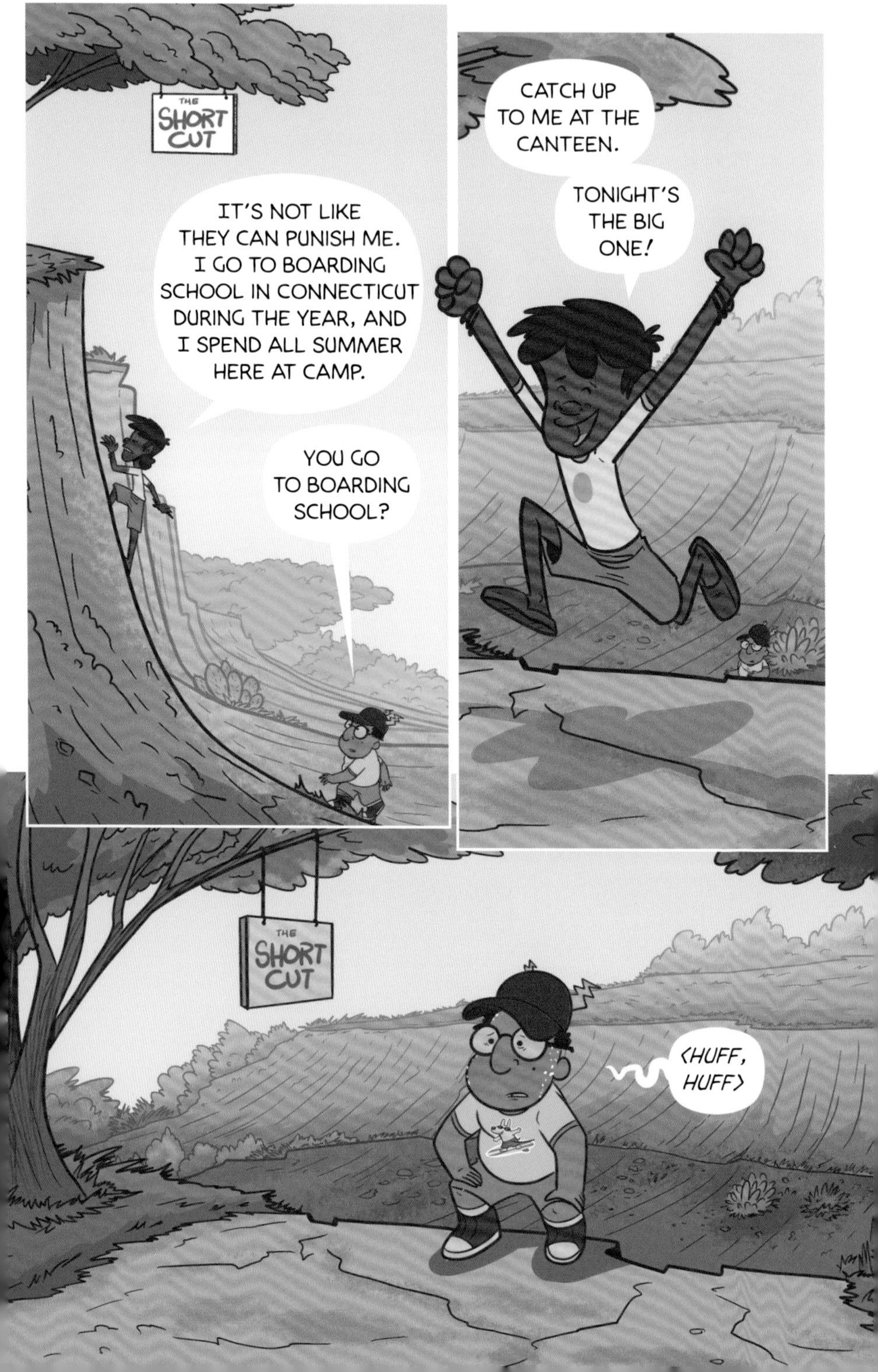
THE SHORT CUT
IT'S NOT LIKE THEY CAN PUNISH ME. I GO TO BOARDING SCHOOL IN CONNECTICUT DURING THE YEAR, AND I SPEND ALL SUMMER HERE AT CAMP.
YOU GO TO BOARDING SCHOOL?
CATCH UP TO ME AT THE CANTEEN.
TONIGHT'S THE BIG ONE!
THE SHORT CUT
<HUFF, HUFF>

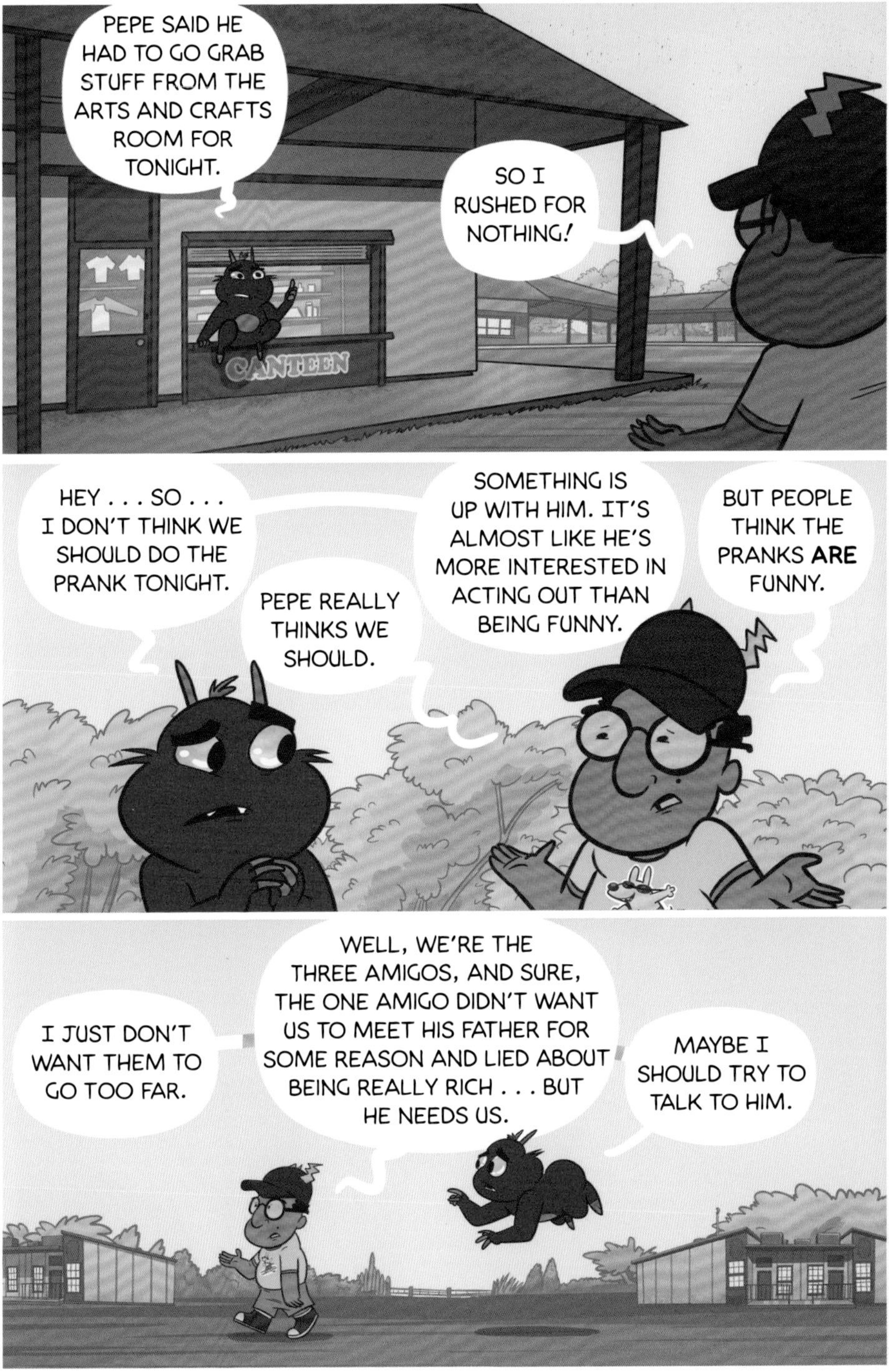
PEPE SAID HE HAD TO GO GRAB STUFF FROM THE ARTS AND CRAFTS ROOM FOR TONIGHT.
SO I RUSHED FOR NOTHING!
CANTEEN
HEY . . . SO . . . I DON'T THINK WE SHOULD DO THE PRANK TONIGHT.
PEPE REALLY THINKS WE SHOULD.
SOMETHING IS UP WITH HIM. IT'S ALMOST LIKE HE'S MORE INTERESTED IN ACTING OUT THAN BEING FUNNY.
BUT PEOPLE THINK THE PRANKS **ARE** FUNNY.
I JUST DON'T WANT THEM TO GO TOO FAR.
WELL, WE'RE THE THREE AMIGOS, AND SURE, THE ONE AMIGO DIDN'T WANT US TO MEET HIS FATHER FOR SOME REASON AND LIED ABOUT BEING REALLY RICH . . . BUT HE NEEDS US.
MAYBE I SHOULD TRY TO TALK TO HIM.

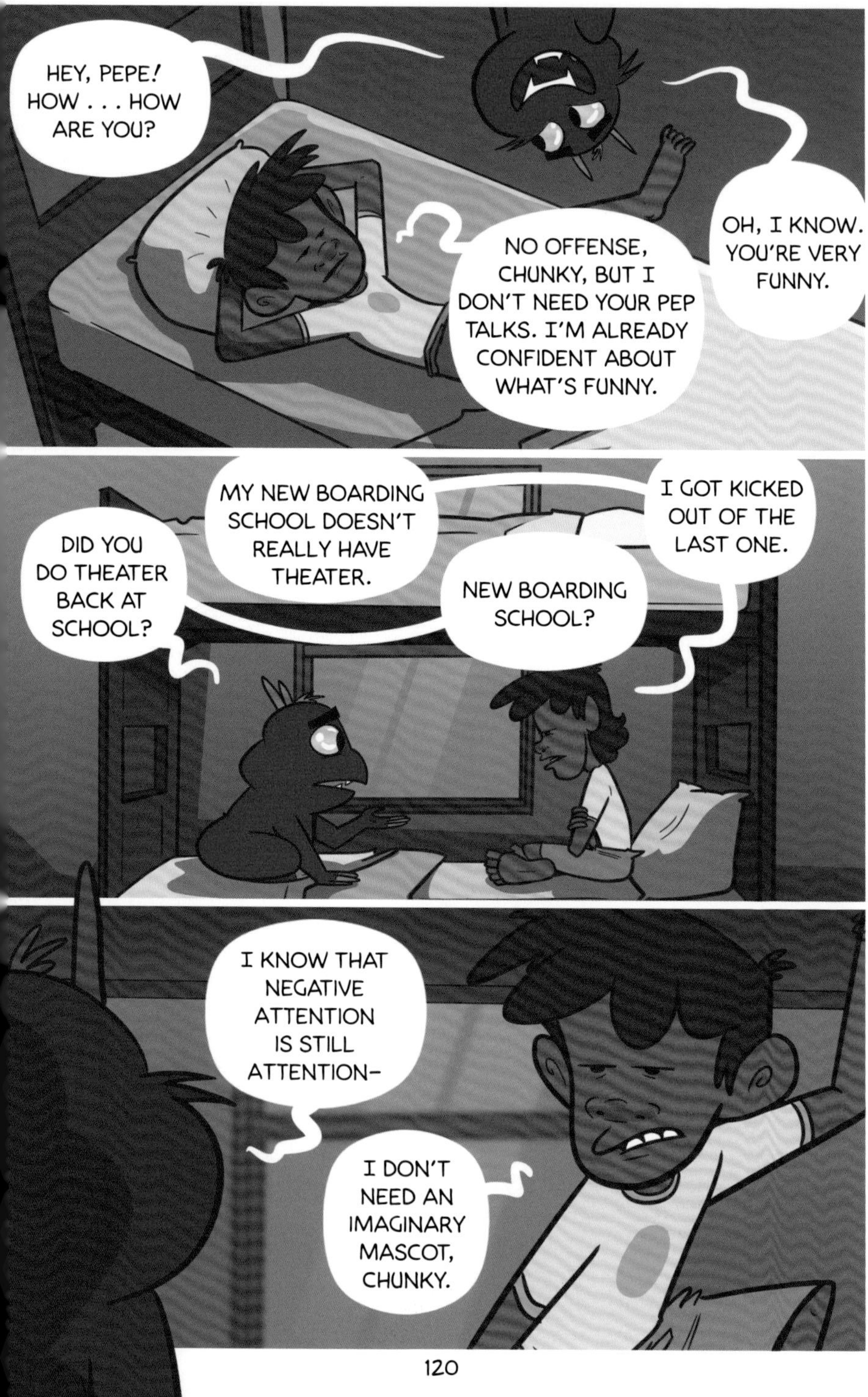
HEY, PEPE! HOW . . . HOW ARE YOU?
OH, I KNOW. YOU'RE VERY FUNNY.
NO OFFENSE, CHUNKY, BUT I DON'T NEED YOUR PEP TALKS. I'M ALREADY CONFIDENT ABOUT WHAT'S FUNNY.
DID YOU DO THEATER BACK AT SCHOOL?
MY NEW BOARDING SCHOOL DOESN'T REALLY HAVE THEATER.
I GOT KICKED OUT OF THE LAST ONE.
NEW BOARDING SCHOOL?
I KNOW THAT NEGATIVE ATTENTION IS STILL ATTENTION–
I DON'T NEED AN IMAGINARY MASCOT, CHUNKY.

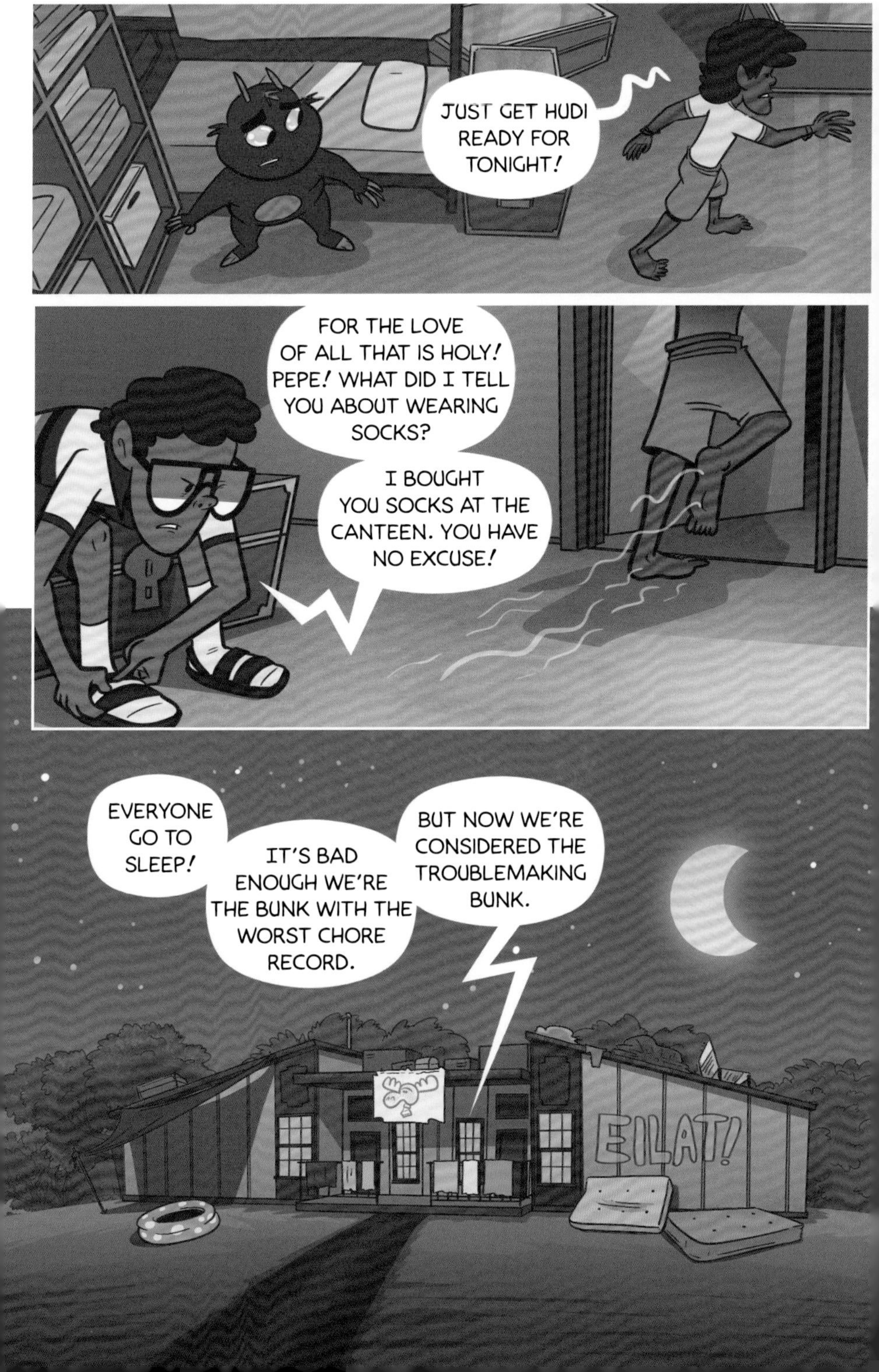
JUST GET HUDI READY FOR TONIGHT!
FOR THE LOVE OF ALL THAT IS HOLY! PEPE! WHAT DID I TELL YOU ABOUT WEARING SOCKS?
I BOUGHT YOU SOCKS AT THE CANTEEN. YOU HAVE NO EXCUSE!
EVERYONE GO TO SLEEP!
IT'S BAD ENOUGH WE'RE THE BUNK WITH THE WORST CHORE RECORD.
BUT NOW WE'RE CONSIDERED THE TROUBLEMAKING BUNK.
EILAT!

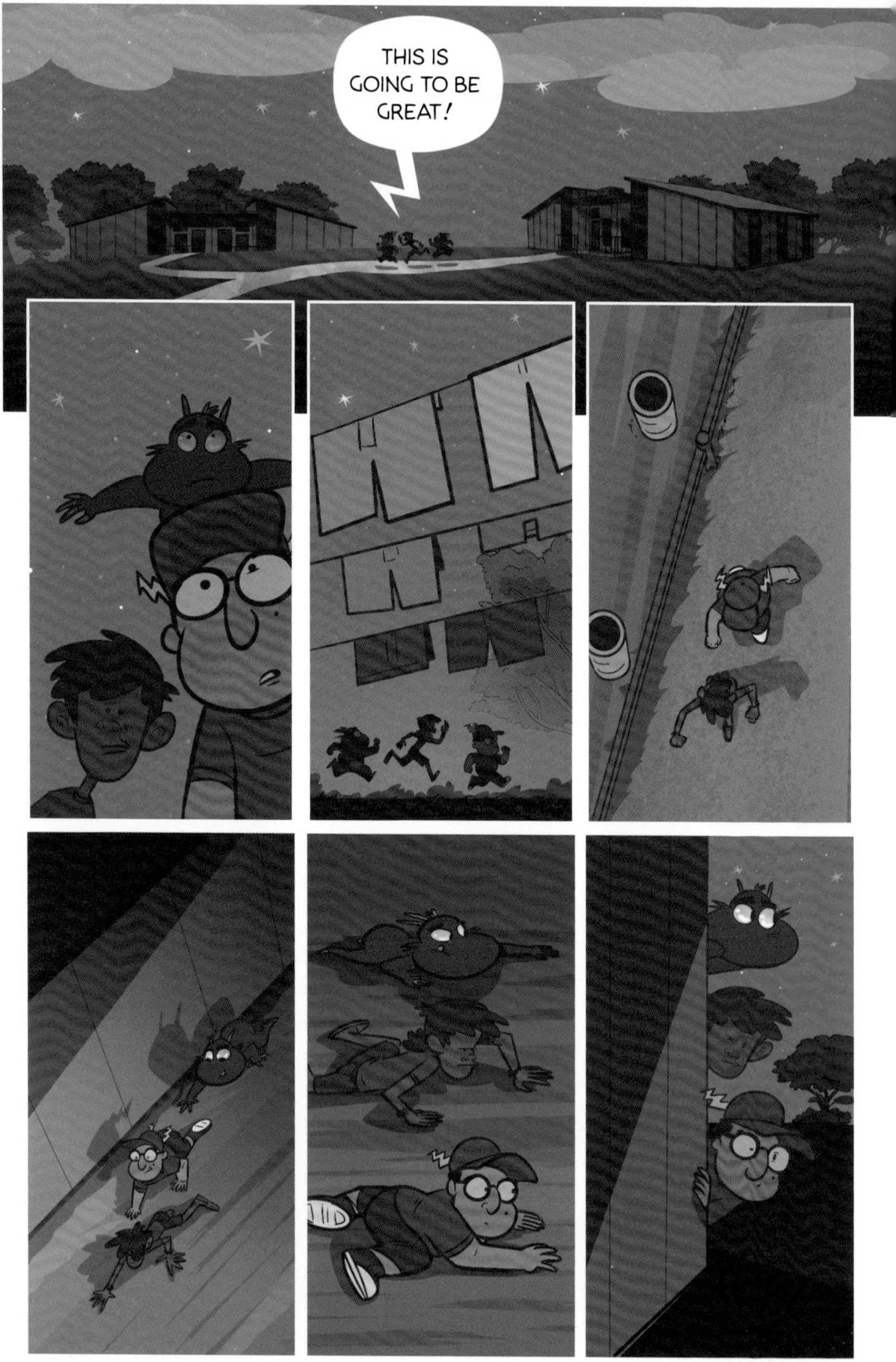
THIS IS GOING TO BE GREAT!

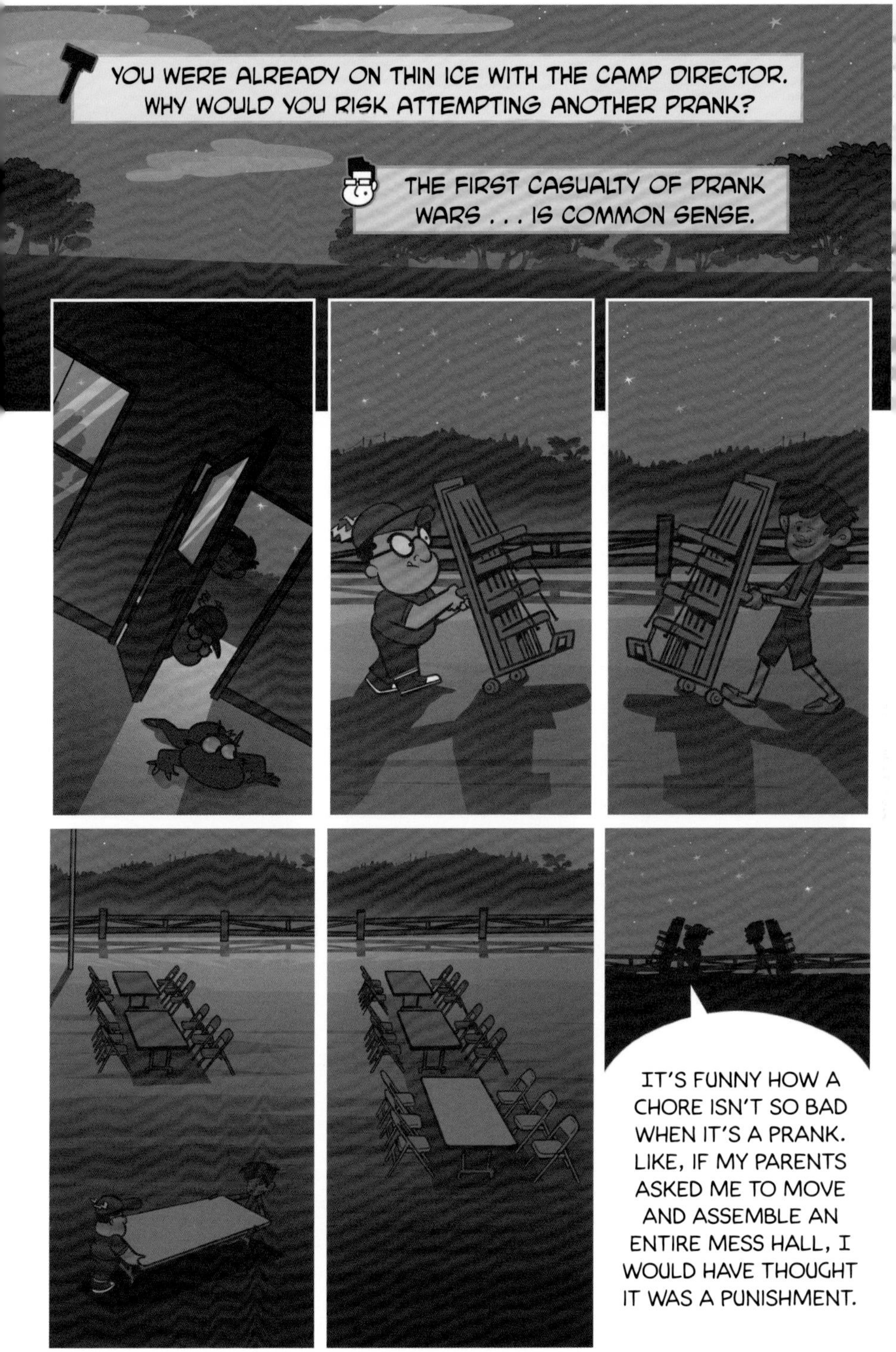
YOU WERE ALREADY ON THIN ICE WITH THE CAMP DIRECTOR. WHY WOULD YOU RISK ATTEMPTING ANOTHER PRANK?
THE FIRST CASUALTY OF PRANK WARS . . . IS COMMON SENSE.
IT'S FUNNY HOW A CHORE ISN'T SO BAD WHEN IT'S A PRANK. LIKE, IF MY PARENTS ASKED ME TO MOVE AND ASSEMBLE AN ENTIRE MESS HALL, I WOULD HAVE THOUGHT IT WAS A PUNISHMENT.

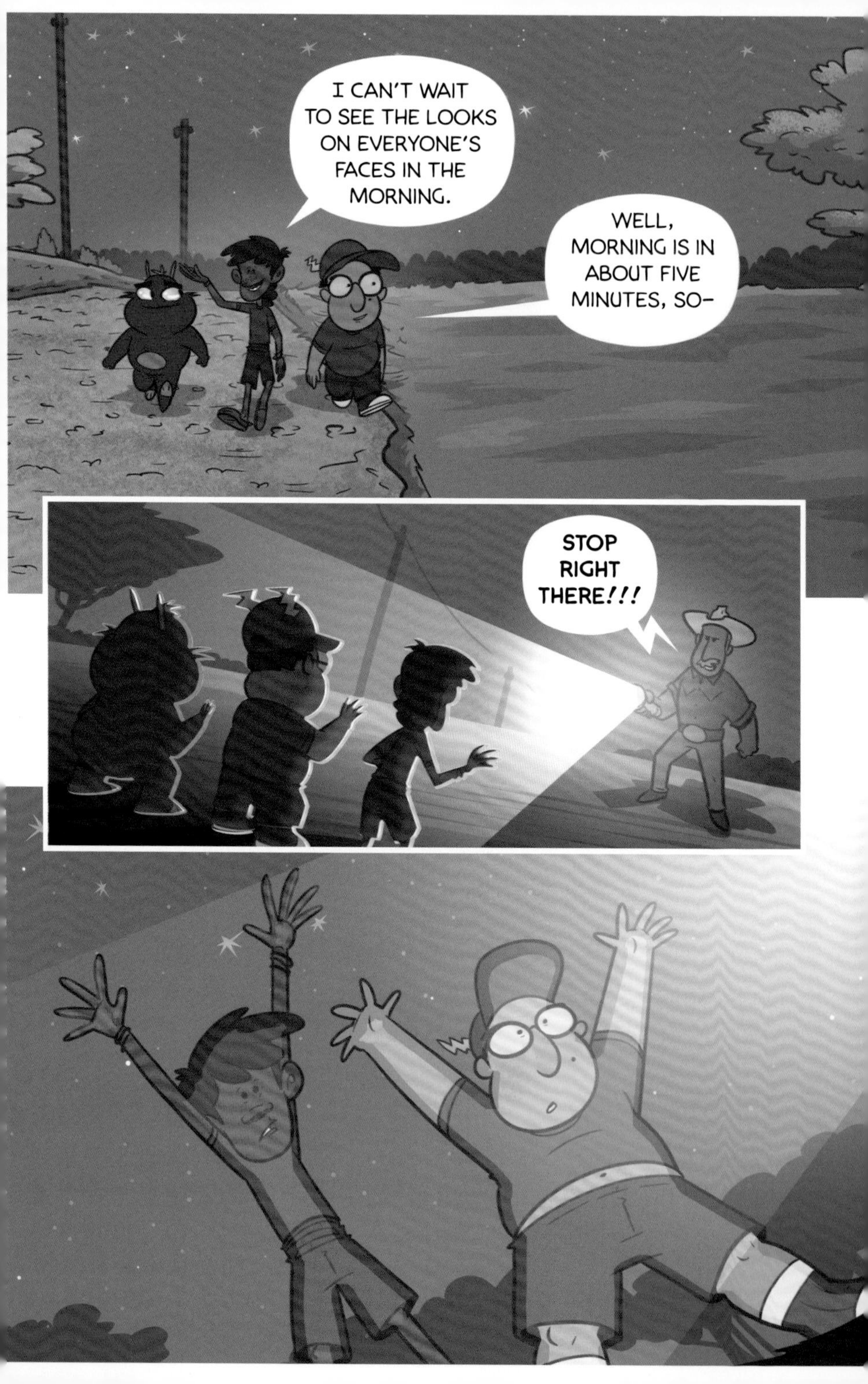
I CAN'T WAIT TO SEE THE LOOKS ON EVERYONE'S FACES IN THE MORNING.
WELL, MORNING IS IN ABOUT FIVE MINUTES, SO–
STOP RIGHT THERE!!!

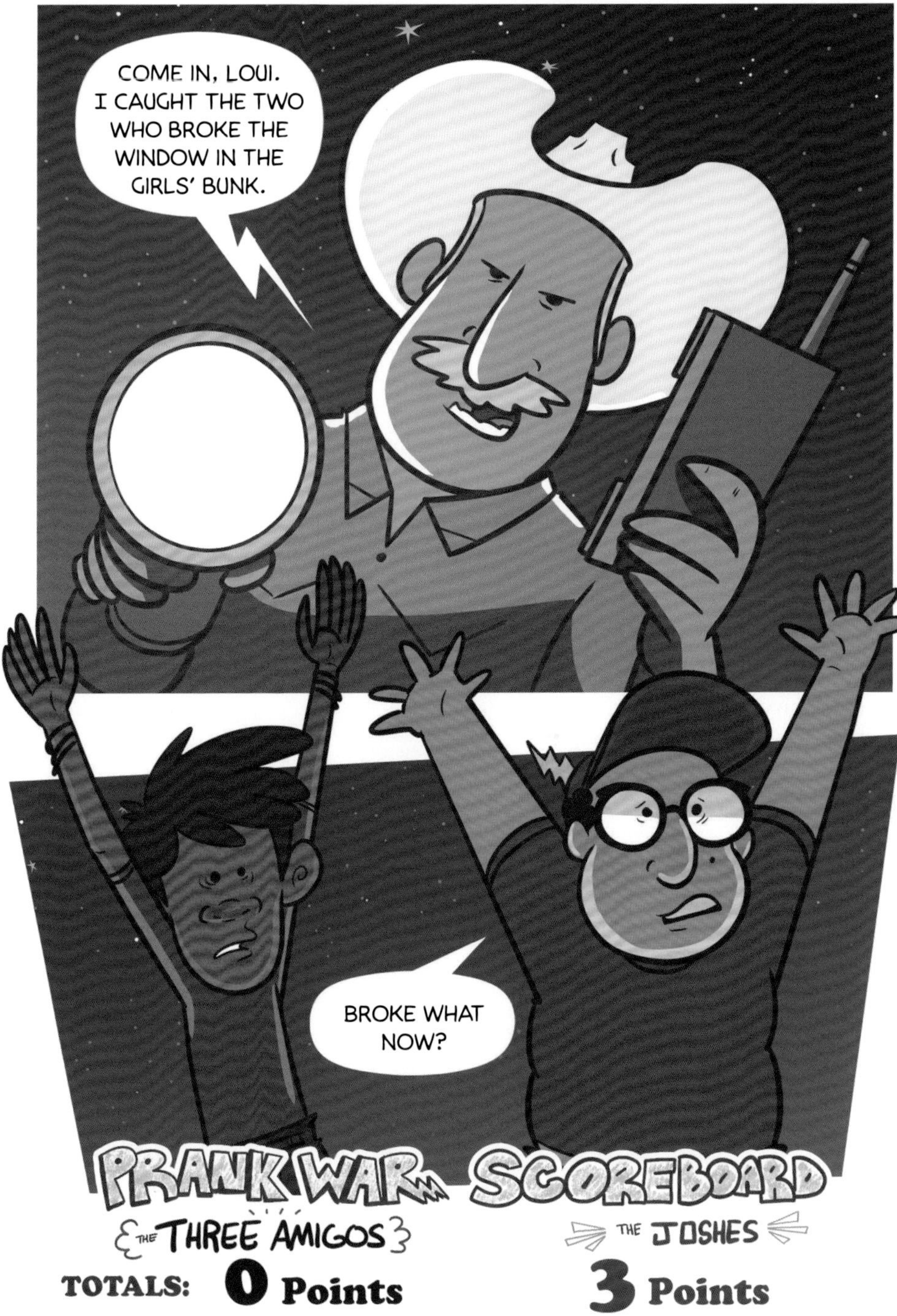
COME IN, LOUI. I CAUGHT THE TWO WHO BROKE THE WINDOW IN THE GIRLS' BUNK.
BROKE WHAT NOW?
PRANK WAR SCOREBOARD
THE THREE AMIGOS
THE JOSHES
TOTALS: 0 Points
3 Points

HUDI on TRIAL

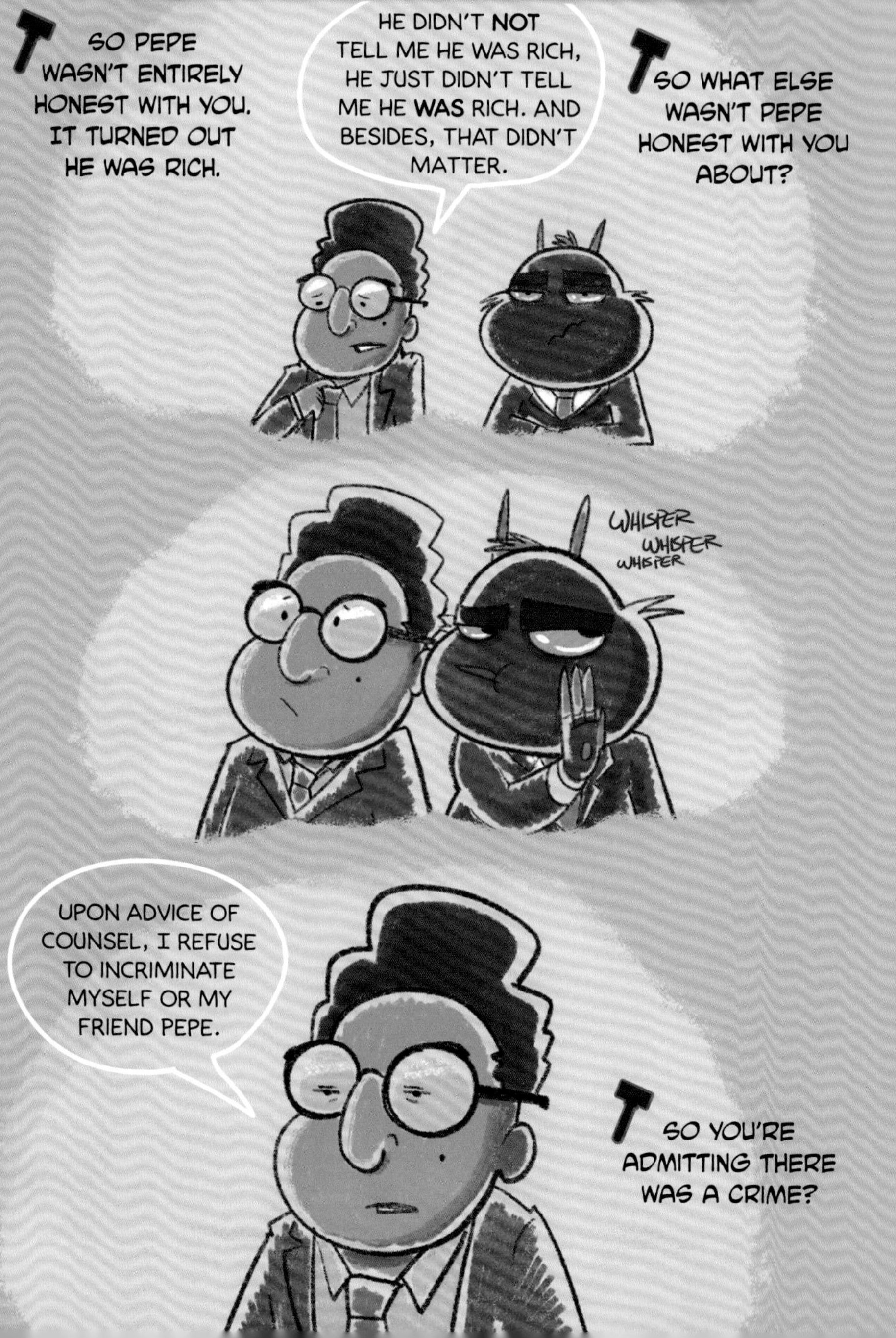

SO PEPE WASN'T ENTIRELY HONEST WITH YOU. IT TURNED OUT HE WAS RICH.
HE DIDN'T **NOT** TELL ME HE WAS RICH, HE JUST DIDN'T TELL ME HE **WAS** RICH. AND BESIDES, THAT DIDN'T MATTER.
SO WHAT ELSE WASN'T PEPE HONEST WITH YOU ABOUT?
WHISPER WHISPER WHISPER
UPON ADVICE OF COUNSEL, I REFUSE TO INCRIMINATE MYSELF OR MY FRIEND PEPE.
SO YOU'RE ADMITTING THERE WAS A CRIME?

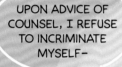

WHISPER
WHISPER
WHISPER

UPON ADVICE OF COUNSEL, I REFUSE TO INCRIMINATE MYSELF—

SEEMS LIKE YOU'RE LISTENING TO CHUNKY NOW WHEN YOU SHOULD HAVE BEEN LISTENING TO HIM ALL ALONG.

I MEAN . . . THEY'RE NOT WRONG.

CAN WE JUST GET BACK TO THE STORY? IT'S LIKE I'M ON TRIAL OVER HERE.

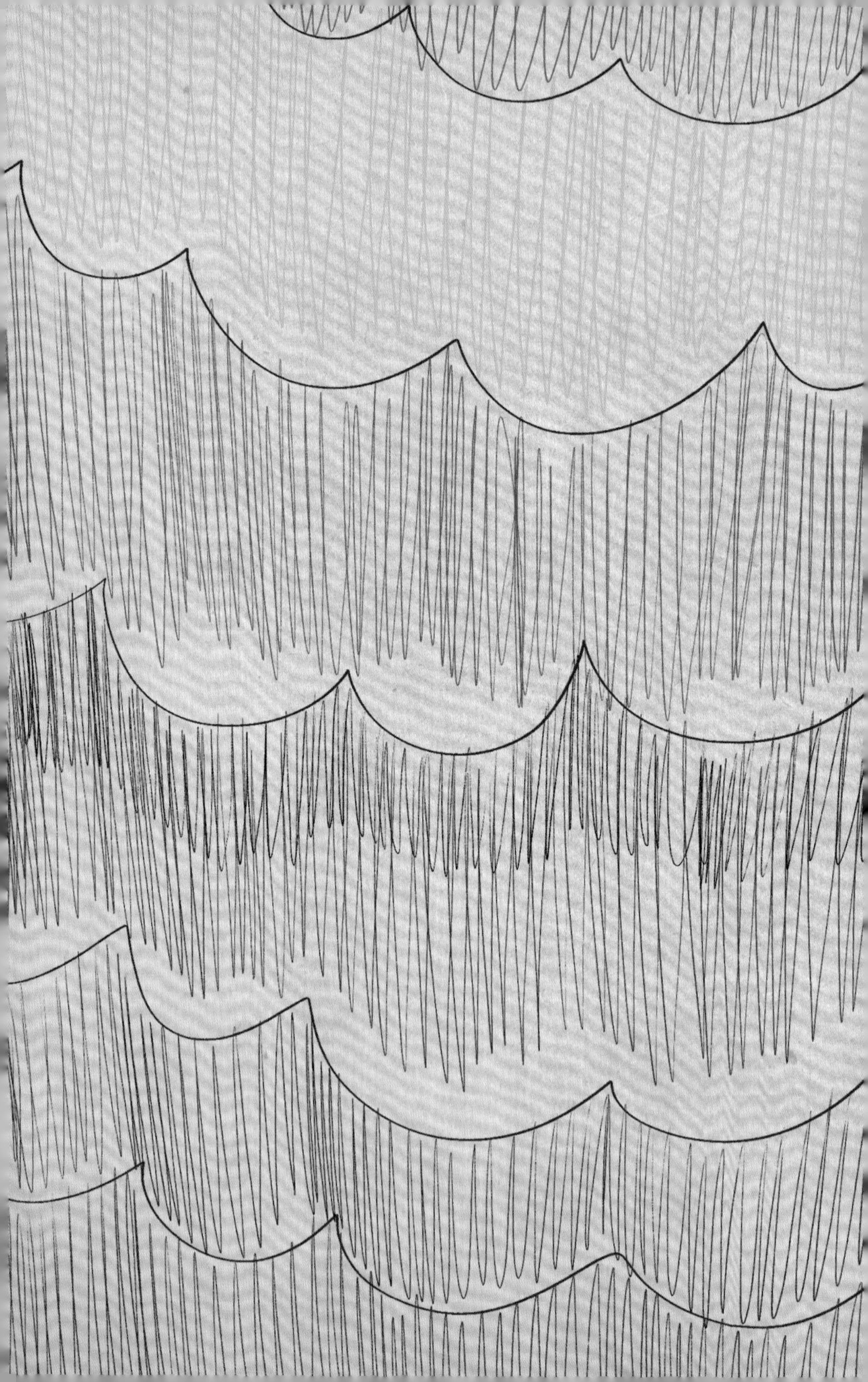

CHAPTER FIVE
STORM CLOUDS

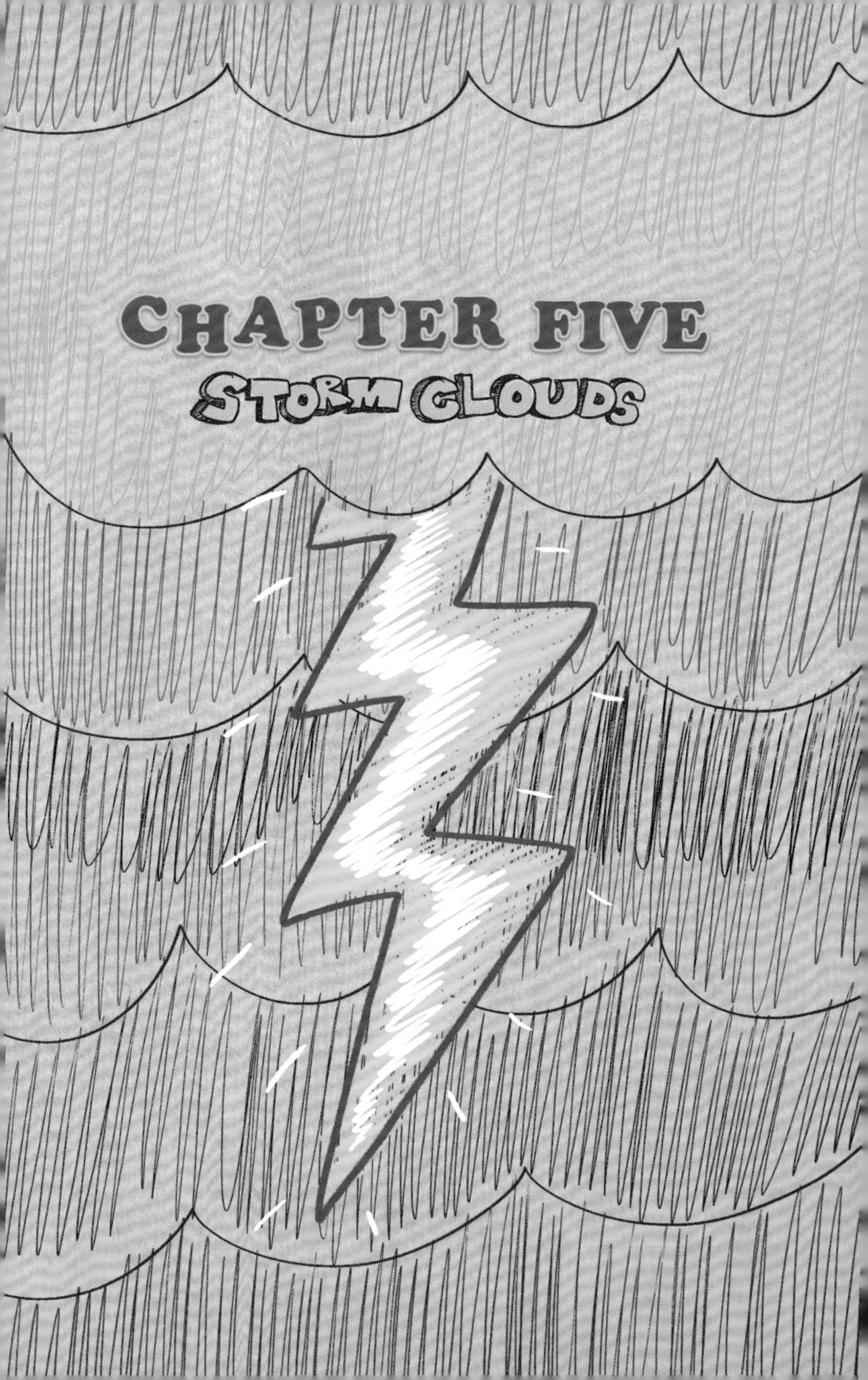

THIS IS **JUST** LIKE SCHOOL BACK HOME. WE'RE GETTING BLAMED FOR CRIMES WE DIDN'T COMMIT.
THERE'S THIS VICE PRINCIPAL WHO HAS IT IN FOR ME. I THOUGHT AT JEWISH CAMP I WOULD AT LEAST CATCH A BREAK.
THEY'LL NEVER LET US WIN!
WHY WOULD THEY EVEN THINK IT WAS US WHO BROKE THE WINDOW?

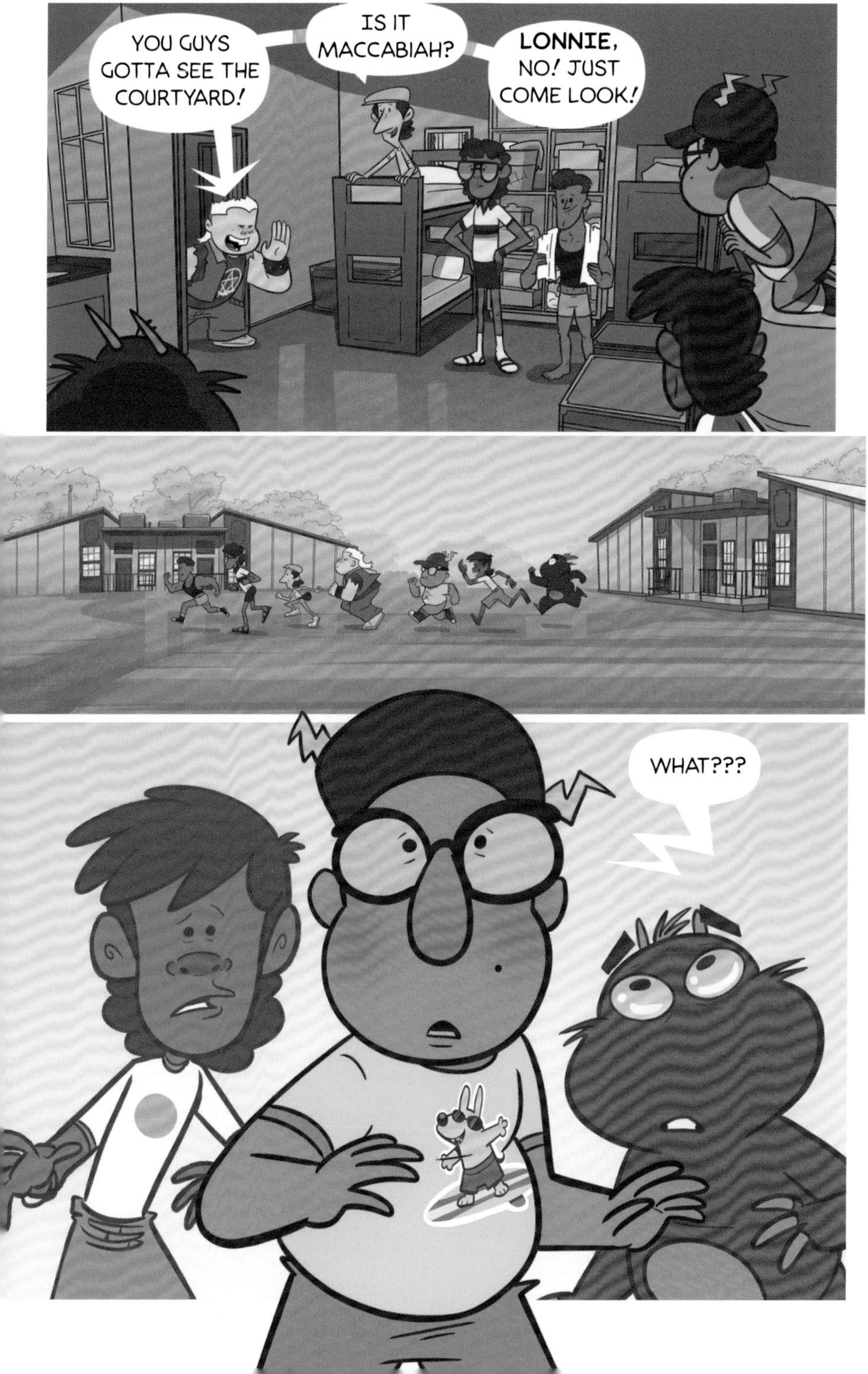
YOU GUYS GOTTA SEE THE COURTYARD!
IS IT MACCABIAH?
LONNIE, NO! JUST COME LOOK!
WHAT???

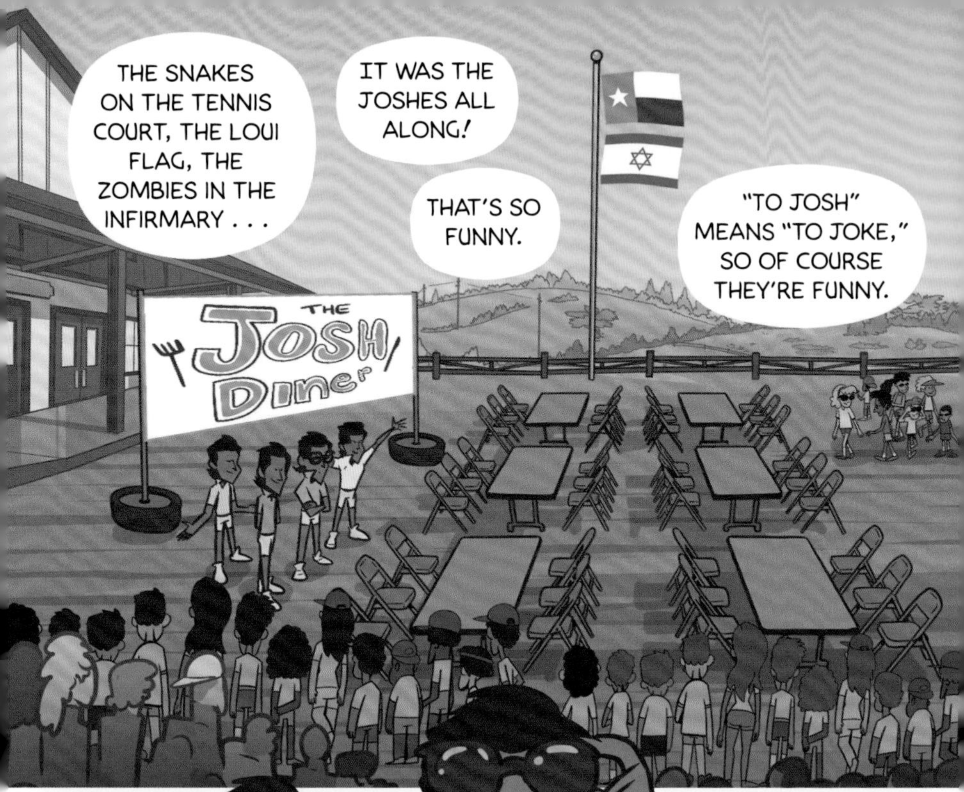
THE SNAKES ON THE TENNIS COURT, THE LOUI FLAG, THE ZOMBIES IN THE INFIRMARY . . .
IT WAS THE JOSHES ALL ALONG!
THAT'S SO FUNNY.
"TO JOSH" MEANS "TO JOKE," SO OF COURSE THEY'RE FUNNY.
THE JOSH Diner

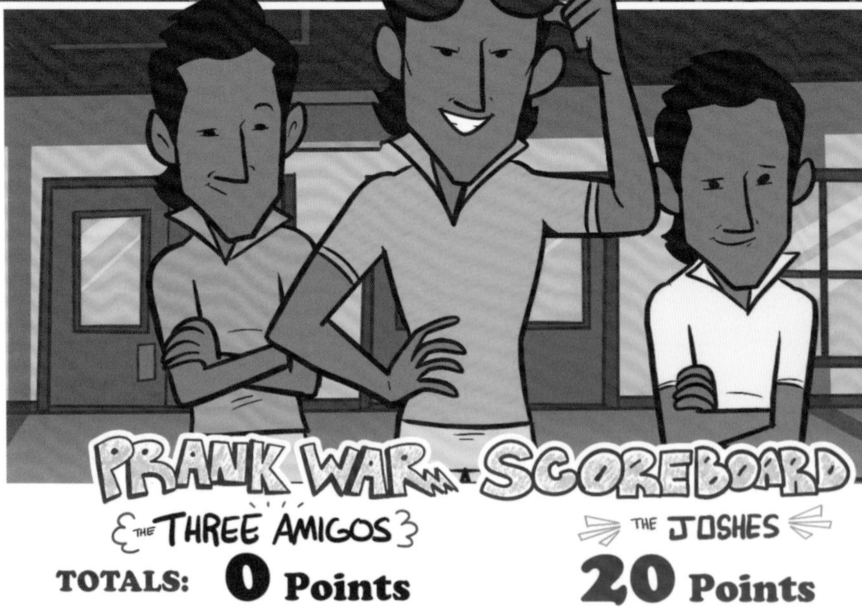
PRANK WAR SCOREBOARD
THE THREE AMIGOS
THE JOSHES
TOTALS: 0 Points
20 Points

THE JOSH DINER? THAT'S NOT EVEN FUNNY.
JOSH'S NOSHES . . . NOW THAT'S FUNNY. AND THAT'S JUST THE FIRST THING OFF THE TOP OF MY HEAD.
THEY STOLE OUR PRANK!
BUT ISN'T STEALING A PRANK CONSIDERED A PRANK?
NOW THIS IS THE RIGHT KIND OF PRANK, UNLIKE THE WINDOW THAT WAS SMASHED LAST NIGHT.
LOUI SAYS THE BROKEN WINDOW WAS THE SECOND STRIKE. NOW THE TWO OF YOU ARE ON HORSE DUTY.
HORSE DUTY?

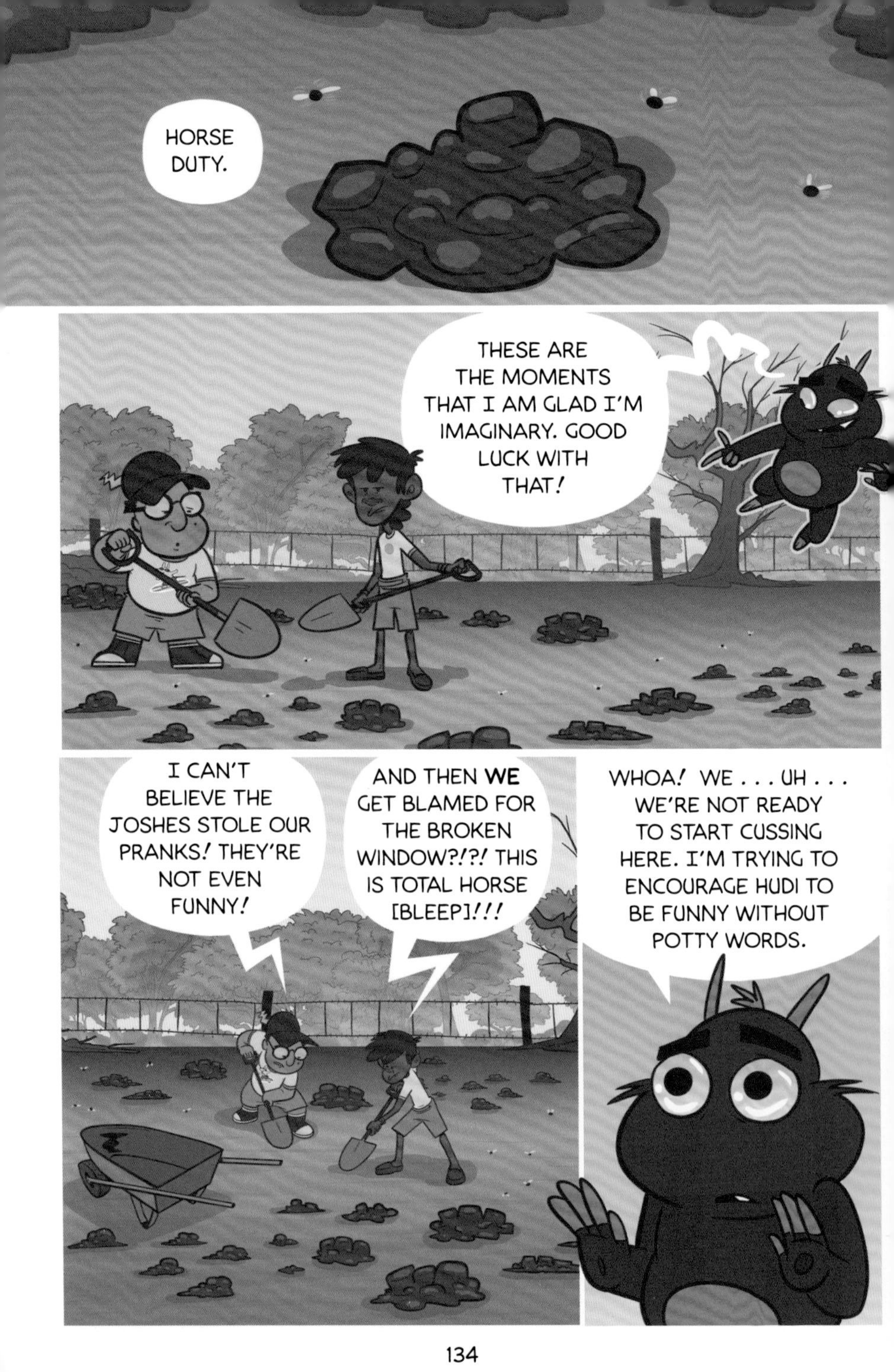
HORSE DUTY.
THESE ARE THE MOMENTS THAT I AM GLAD I'M IMAGINARY. GOOD LUCK WITH THAT!
I CAN'T BELIEVE THE JOSHES STOLE OUR PRANKS! THEY'RE NOT EVEN FUNNY!
AND THEN **WE** GET BLAMED FOR THE BROKEN WINDOW?!?! THIS IS TOTAL HORSE [BLEEP]!!!
WHOA! WE . . . UH . . . WE'RE NOT READY TO START CUSSING HERE. I'M TRYING TO ENCOURAGE HUDI TO BE FUNNY WITHOUT POTTY WORDS.

IT'S ALL RIGHT, CHUNKY. PEPE'S JUSTIFIABLY UPSET.
HEY, PEPE, CHEER UP. AT LEAST WE DIDN'T GET KICKED OUT.
THAT DOESN'T MATTER. I GOT KICKED OUT OF ONE BOARDING SCHOOL LAST YEAR AND ALL MY PARENTS DID WAS SEND ME TO ANOTHER ONE.
I HAVE A BROTHER AND A SISTER WHO ARE FIFTEEN YEARS OLDER THAN ME. THEY TREAT ME LIKE A STRANGER. THEY NEVER HAD TO GO TO BOARDING SCHOOL.
RUMBLE
RUMBLE
RUMBLE
RUMBLE
RUMBLE
RUMBLE

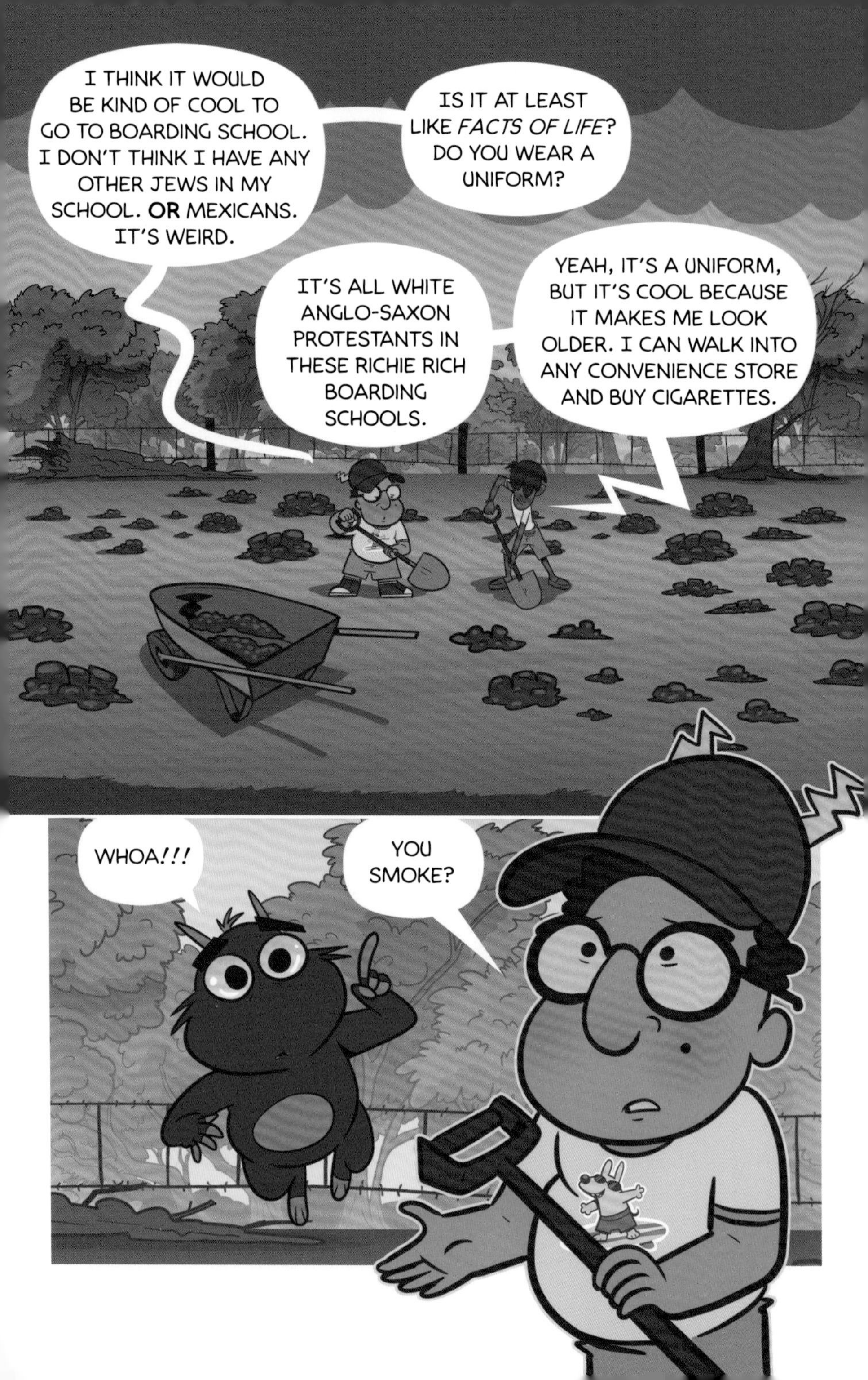
I THINK IT WOULD BE KIND OF COOL TO GO TO BOARDING SCHOOL. I DON'T THINK I HAVE ANY OTHER JEWS IN MY SCHOOL. **OR** MEXICANS. IT'S WEIRD.
IS IT AT LEAST LIKE *FACTS OF LIFE*? DO YOU WEAR A UNIFORM?
IT'S ALL WHITE ANGLO-SAXON PROTESTANTS IN THESE RICHIE RICH BOARDING SCHOOLS.
YEAH, IT'S A UNIFORM, BUT IT'S COOL BECAUSE IT MAKES ME LOOK OLDER. I CAN WALK INTO ANY CONVENIENCE STORE AND BUY CIGARETTES.
WHOA!!!
YOU SMOKE?

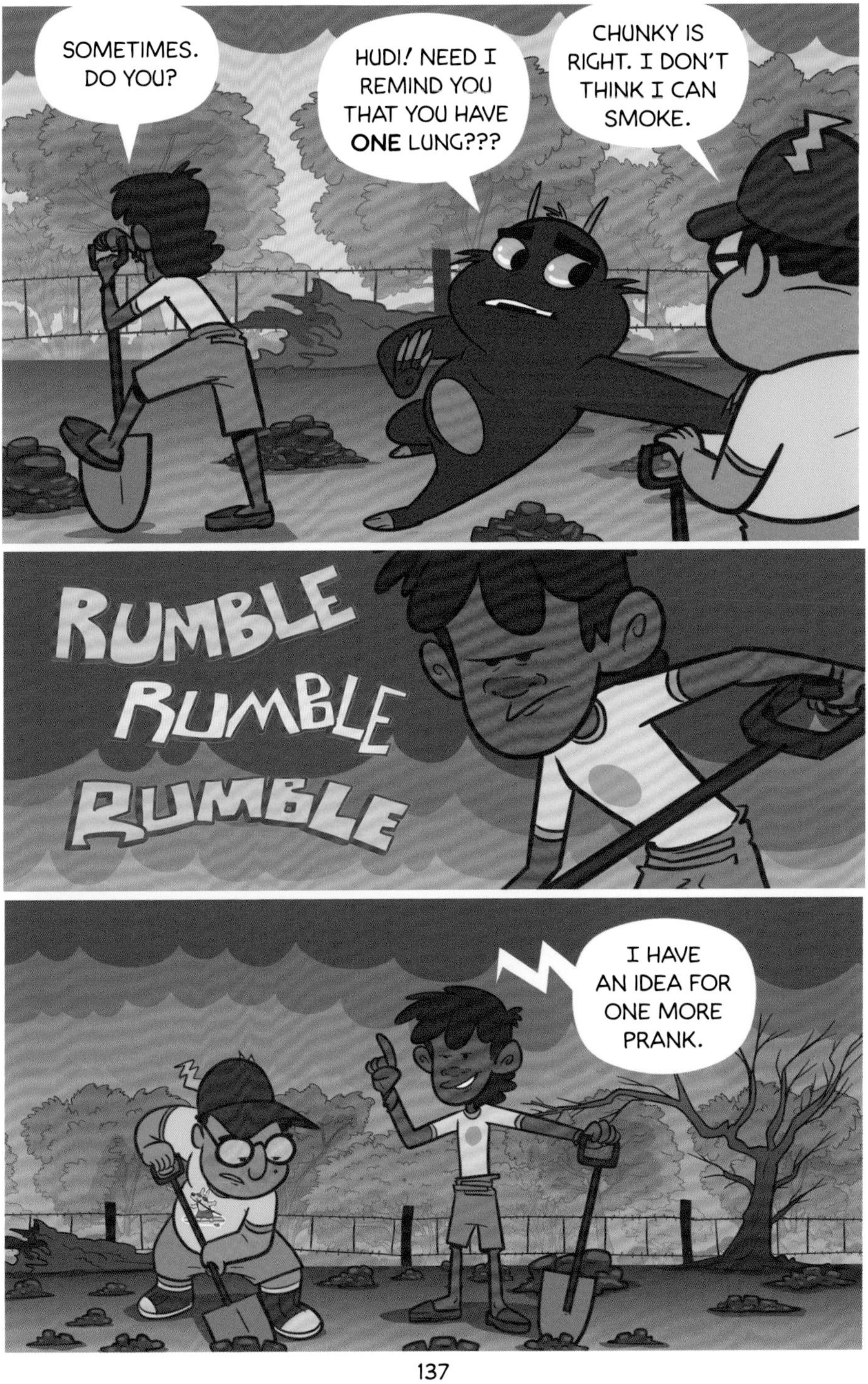
SOMETIMES. DO YOU?
HUDI! NEED I REMIND YOU THAT YOU HAVE **ONE** LUNG???
CHUNKY IS RIGHT. I DON'T THINK I CAN SMOKE.
RUMBLE RUMBLE RUMBLE
I HAVE AN IDEA FOR ONE MORE PRANK.

I DON'T THINK WE SHOULD–
WE GOTTA PRANK THE JOSHES. IF WE PRANK THE JOSHES, THEN EVERYONE WILL KNOW THEY LIED AND WE GET ALL THE POINTS BACK.
BUT–
COME ON! WE HAVE TO! WE'RE GETTING PUNISHED ANYWAY. WE MIGHT AS WELL GET THE CREDIT.
WHAM
WE WILL **NEVER** BE ACCEPTED IN THEIR CLUBS!

ALL RIGHT! STORM'S COMING! WE DON'T WANT TO BE OUT HERE WITH METAL SHOVELS.
OKAY, PEPE.
WE'LL DO THE PRANK.

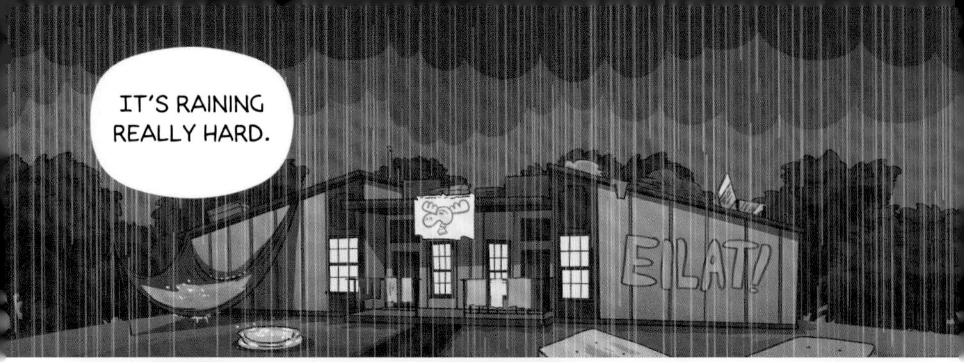
IT'S RAINING REALLY HARD.
EILAT!

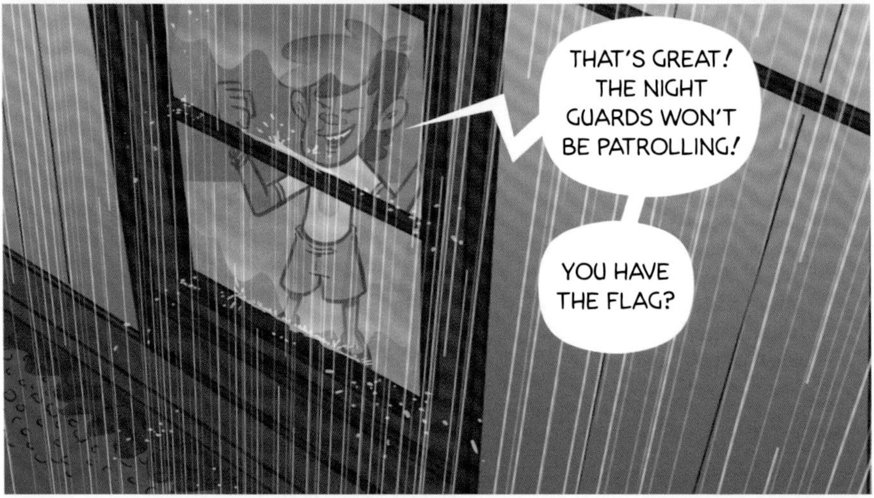
THAT'S GREAT! THE NIGHT GUARDS WON'T BE PATROLLING!
YOU HAVE THE FLAG?

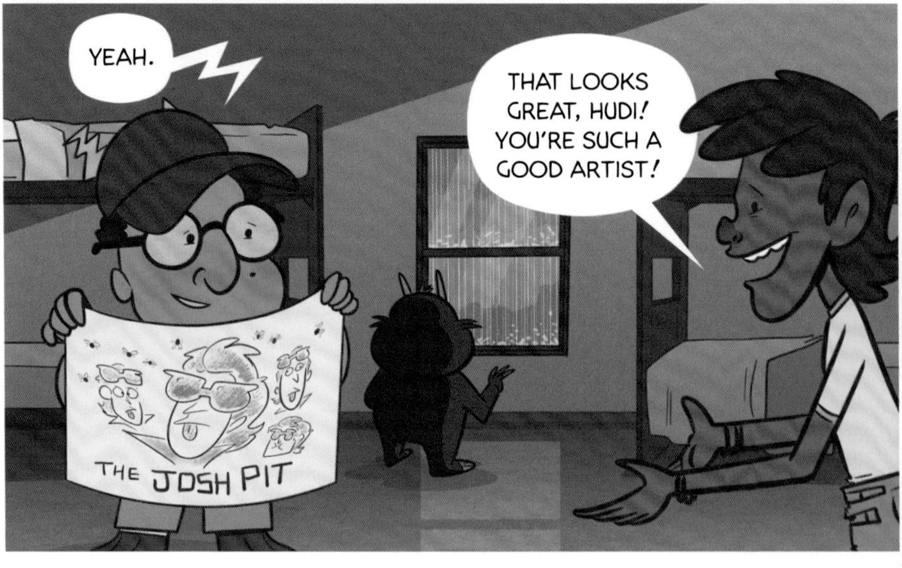
YEAH.
THAT LOOKS GREAT, HUDI! YOU'RE SUCH A GOOD ARTIST!
THE JOSH PIT

SO WE ARE GOING TO HANG THIS UP IN THE COURTYARD AND RUN RIGHT BACK?
NO. WE'RE GOING TO TAKE THE FLAGPOLE AND PUT IT UP IN FRONT OF REHOVOT.
WHAT?
THERE USED TO BE A FLAGPOLE OUT FRONT. THE HOLE IS STILL THERE.
EILAT
YOU'RE GOING TO CARRY A METAL FLAGPOLE DURING AN ELECTRICAL STORM?
IT'LL BE FINE! WE'RE NOT GOING TO BE CARRYING IT STRAIGHT UP.

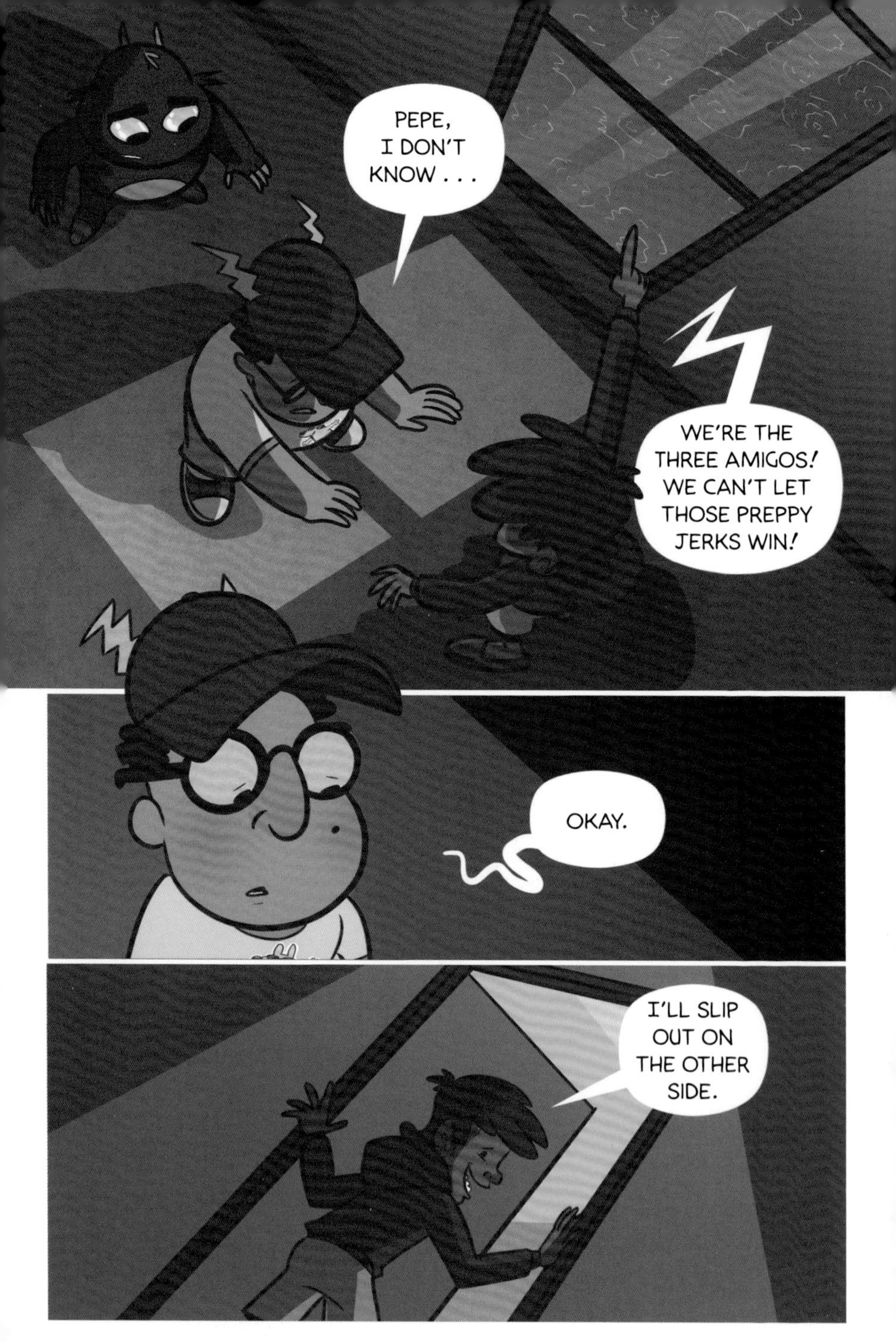
PEPE, I DON'T KNOW . . .
WE'RE THE THREE AMIGOS! WE CAN'T LET THOSE PREPPY JERKS WIN!
OKAY.
I'LL SLIP OUT ON THE OTHER SIDE.

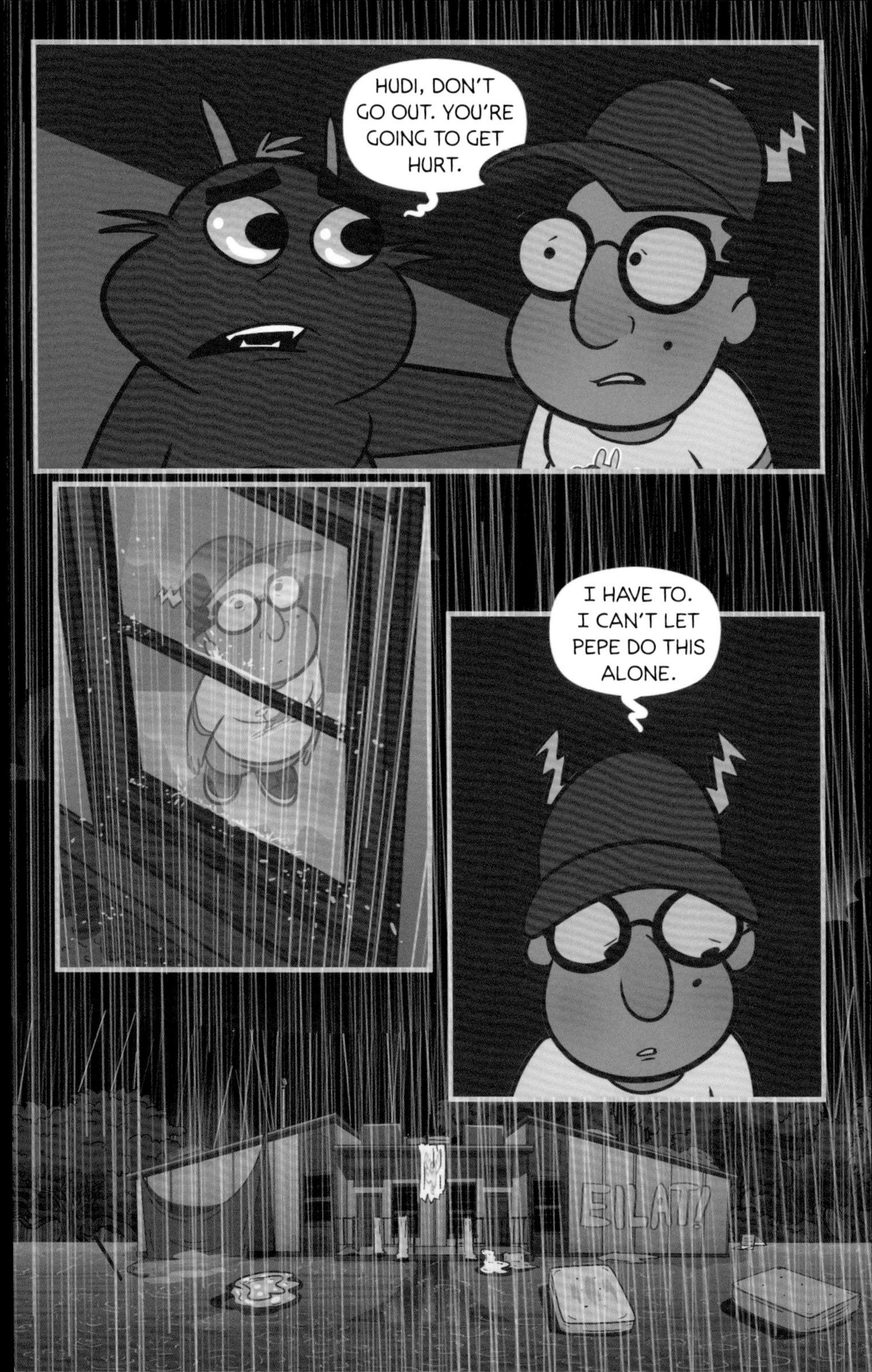
HUDI, DON'T GO OUT. YOU'RE GOING TO GET HURT.
I HAVE TO. I CAN'T LET PEPE DO THIS ALONE.

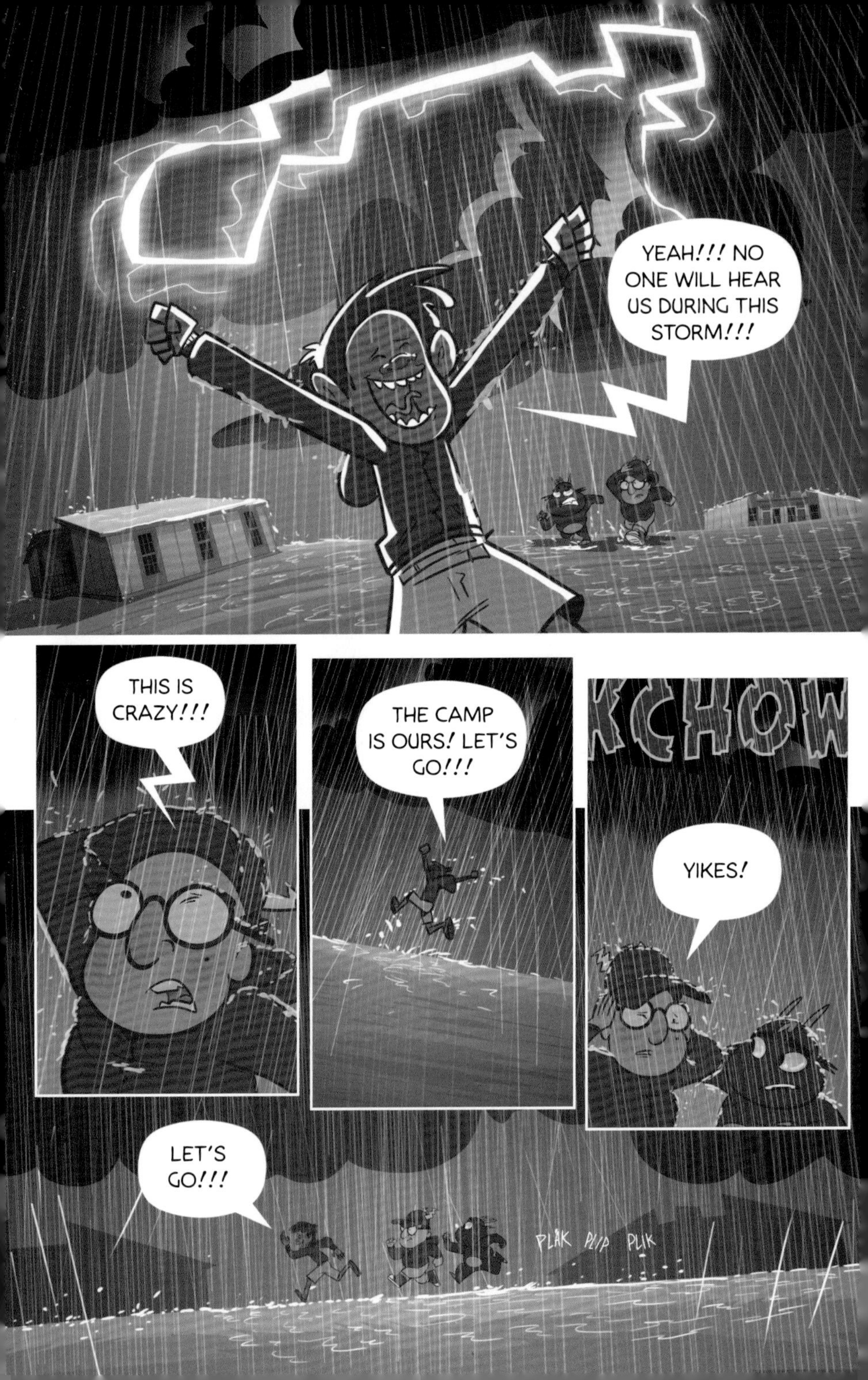
YEAH!!! NO ONE WILL HEAR US DURING THIS STORM!!!
THIS IS CRAZY!!!
THE CAMP IS OURS! LET'S GO!!!
KCHOW
YIKES!
LET'S GO!!!
PLAK PLIP PLIK

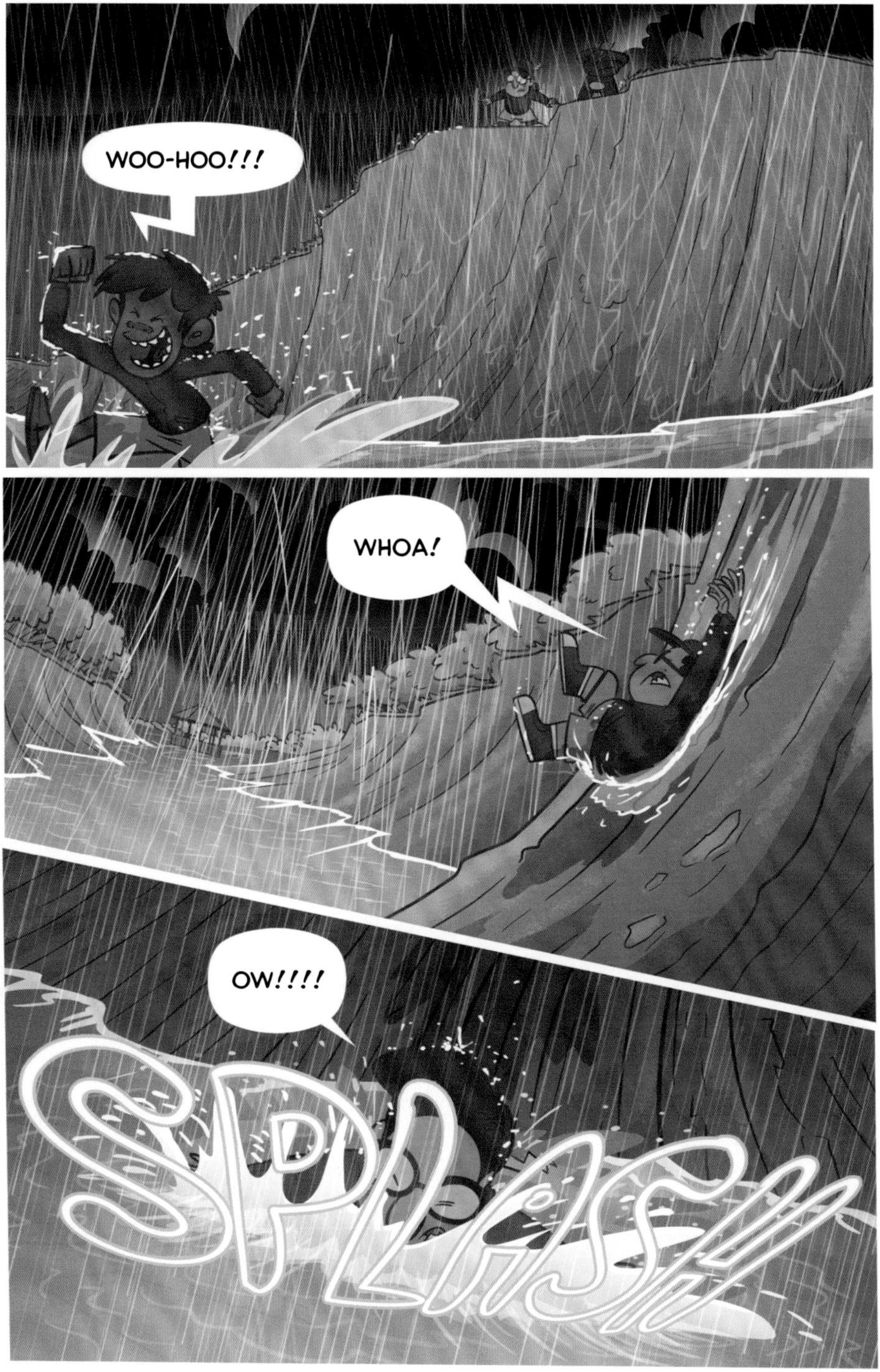
WOO-HOO!!!
WHOA!
OW!!!!
SPLASH

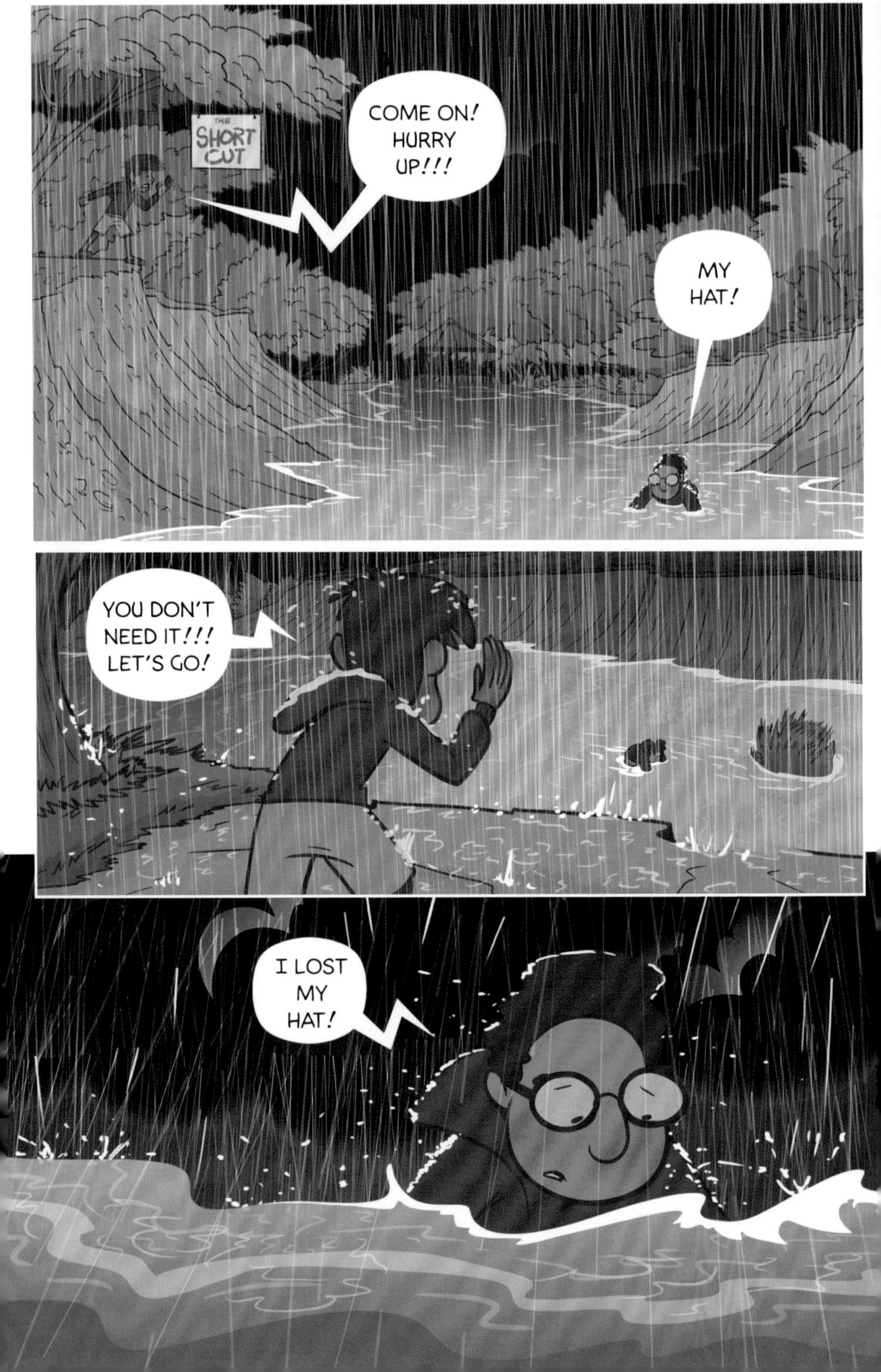
THE SHORT CUT
COME ON! HURRY UP!!!
MY HAT!
YOU DON'T NEED IT!!! LET'S GO!
I LOST MY HAT!

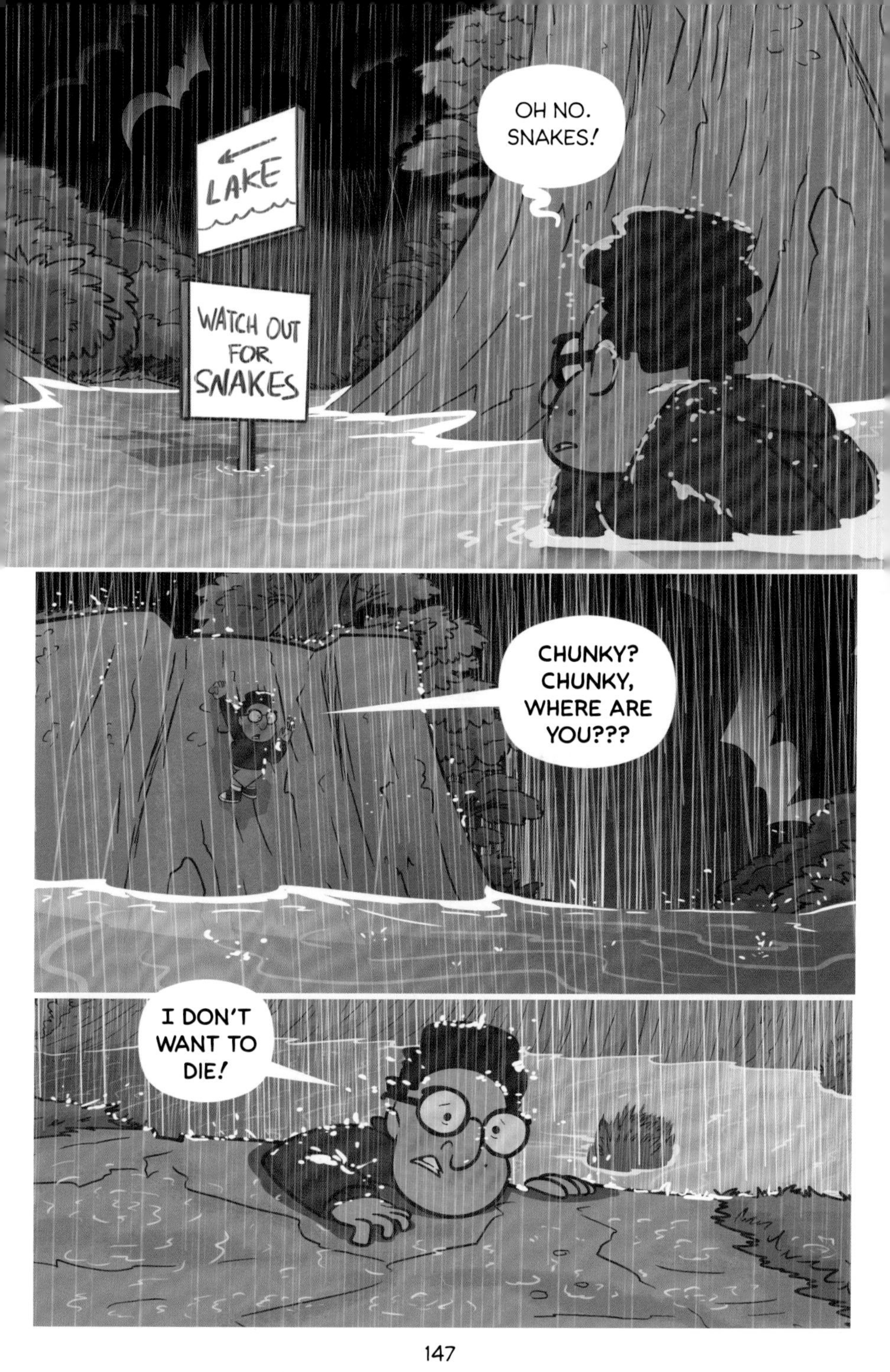
LAKE
WATCH OUT FOR SNAKES
OH NO. SNAKES!
CHUNKY? CHUNKY, WHERE ARE YOU???
I DON'T WANT TO DIE!

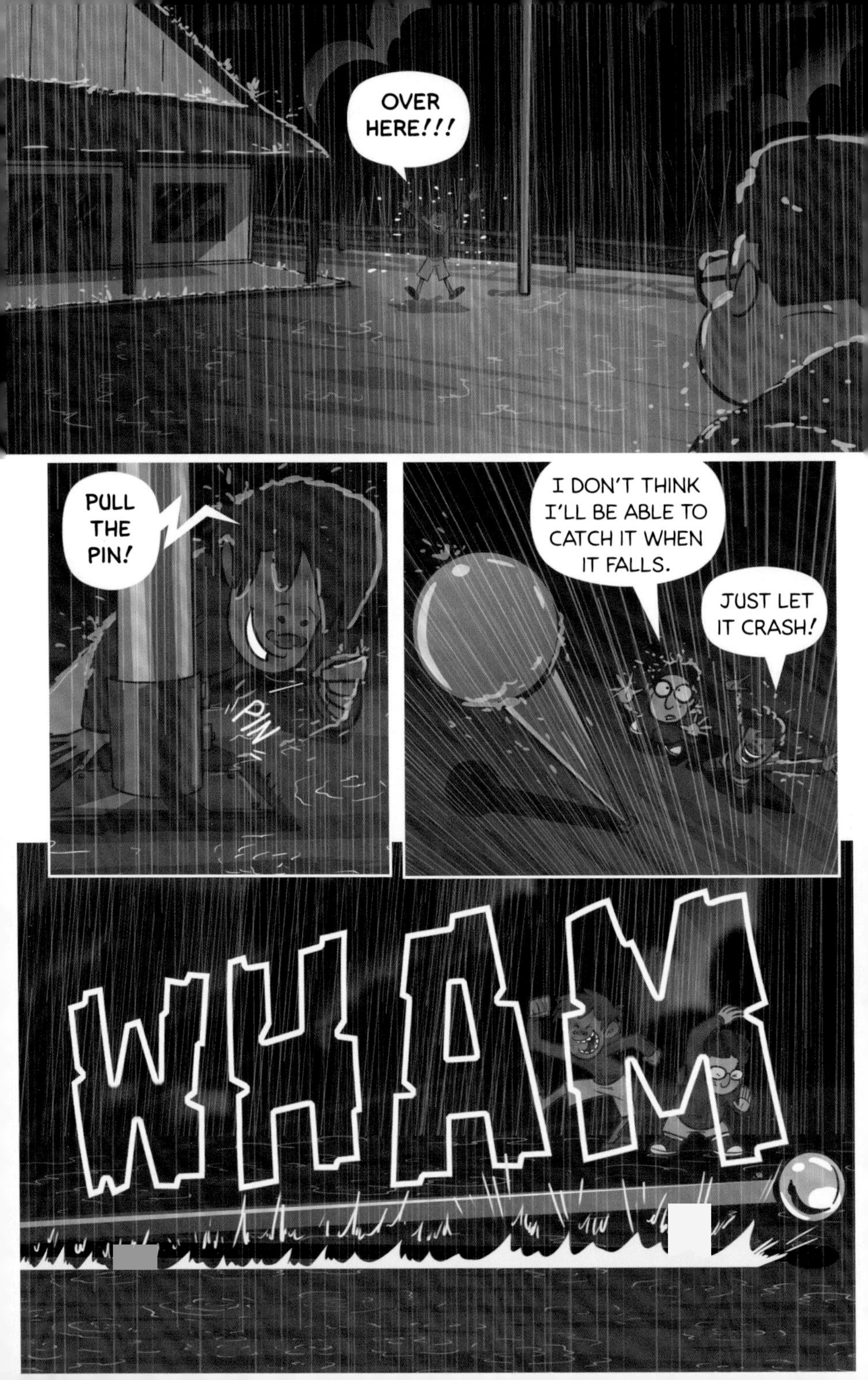
OVER HERE!!!
PULL THE PIN!
PIN
I DON'T THINK I'LL BE ABLE TO CATCH IT WHEN IT FALLS.
JUST LET IT CRASH!
WHAM

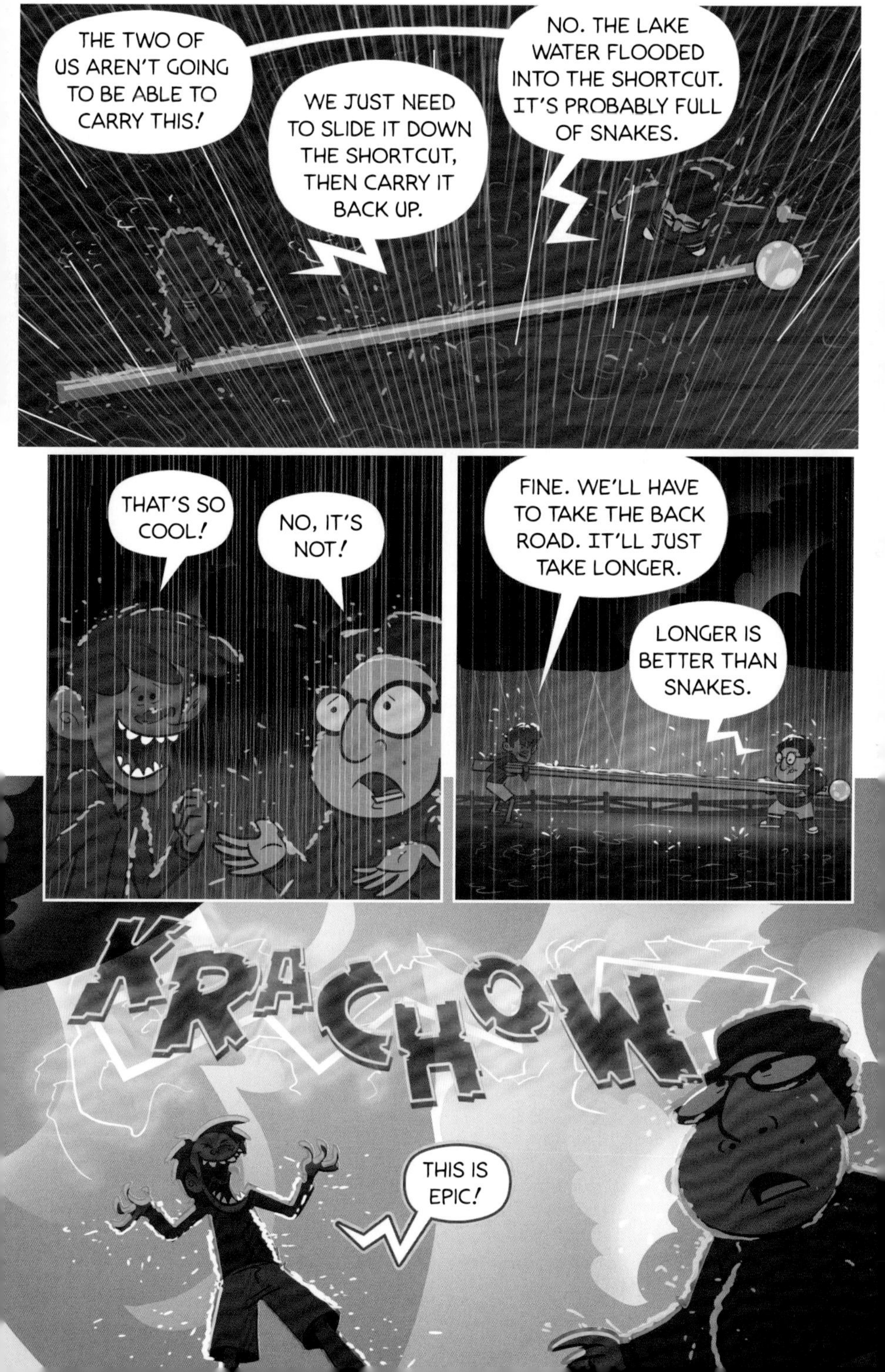
THE TWO OF US AREN'T GOING TO BE ABLE TO CARRY THIS!
WE JUST NEED TO SLIDE IT DOWN THE SHORTCUT, THEN CARRY IT BACK UP.
NO. THE LAKE WATER FLOODED INTO THE SHORTCUT. IT'S PROBABLY FULL OF SNAKES.
THAT'S SO COOL!
NO, IT'S NOT!
FINE. WE'LL HAVE TO TAKE THE BACK ROAD. IT'LL JUST TAKE LONGER.
LONGER IS BETTER THAN SNAKES.
KRACHOW
THIS IS EPIC!

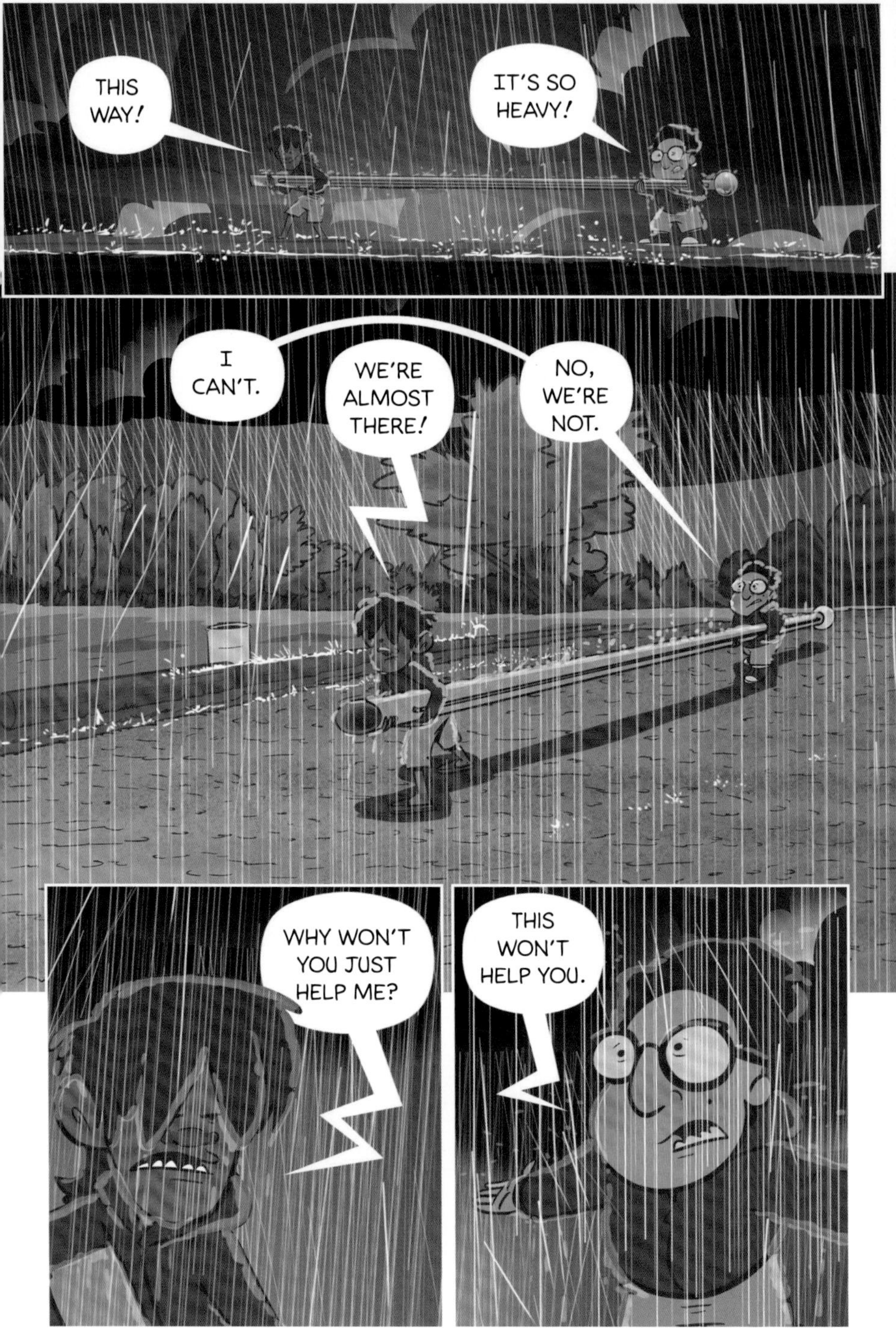
THIS WAY!
IT'S SO HEAVY!
I CAN'T.
WE'RE ALMOST THERE!
NO, WE'RE NOT.
WHY WON'T YOU JUST HELP ME?
THIS WON'T HELP YOU.

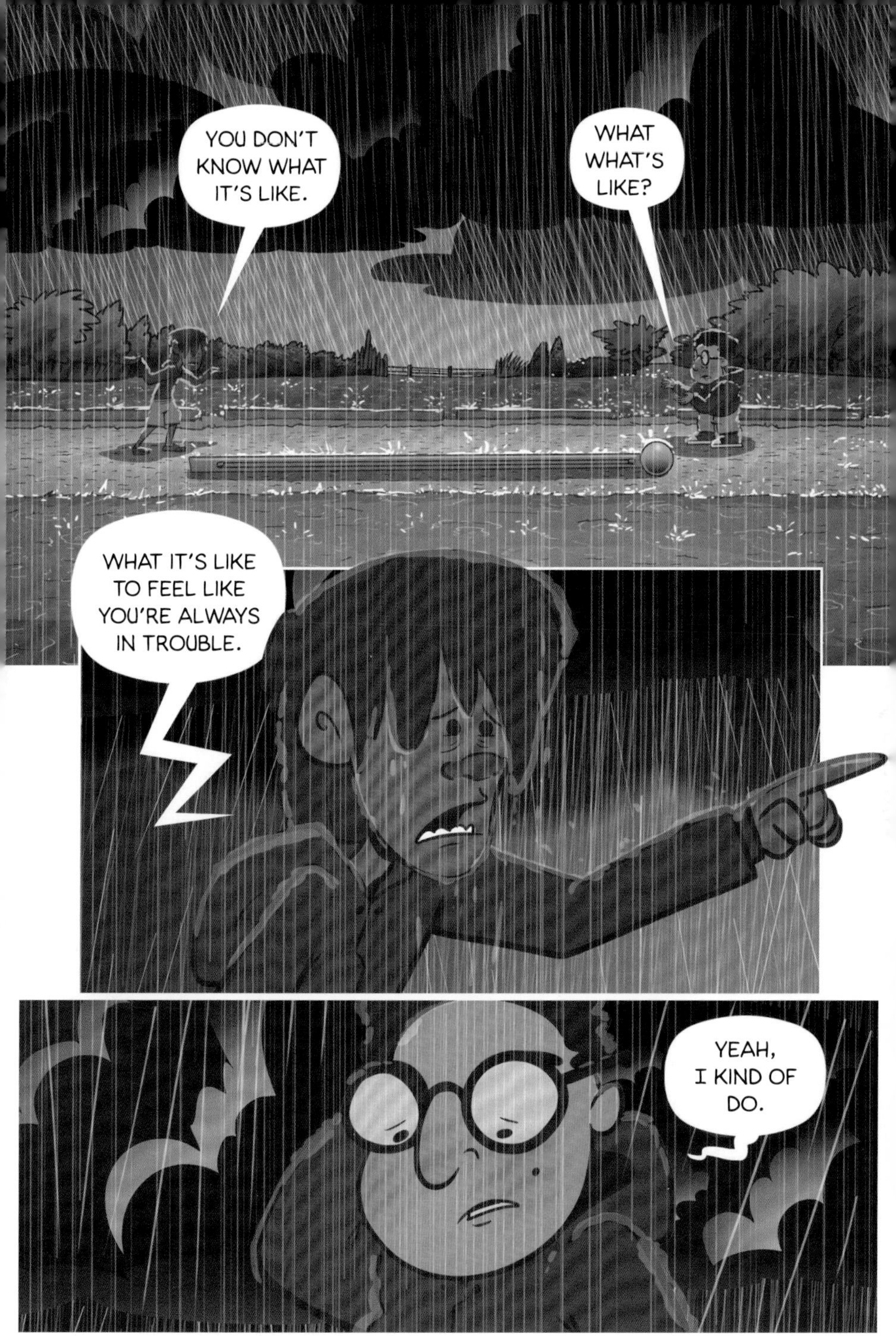
YOU DON'T KNOW WHAT IT'S LIKE.
WHAT WHAT'S LIKE?
WHAT IT'S LIKE TO FEEL LIKE YOU'RE ALWAYS IN TROUBLE.
YEAH, I KIND OF DO.

BUT WHEN YOU GET IN TROUBLE, **YOUR** PARENTS DON'T SEND YOU AWAY.
THEY DON'T ABANDON YOU TO ANY STUPID BOARDING SCHOOL THAT WILL CASH THEIR CHECKS.
THEY DON'T MAKE YOU SPEND YOUR ENTIRE SUMMER AT CAMP. I'M THE **ONLY** CAMPER WHO STAYS IN AN EMPTY CABIN BETWEEN SESSIONS.
DO YOU KNOW HOW DEPRESSING THAT IS? I ONLY SPENT TWO WEEKS IN MY OWN BED LAST YEAR. DO YOU KNOW WHAT THAT'S LIKE?
NO. BUT I'M SURE IT WOULD MAKE ME MAD.

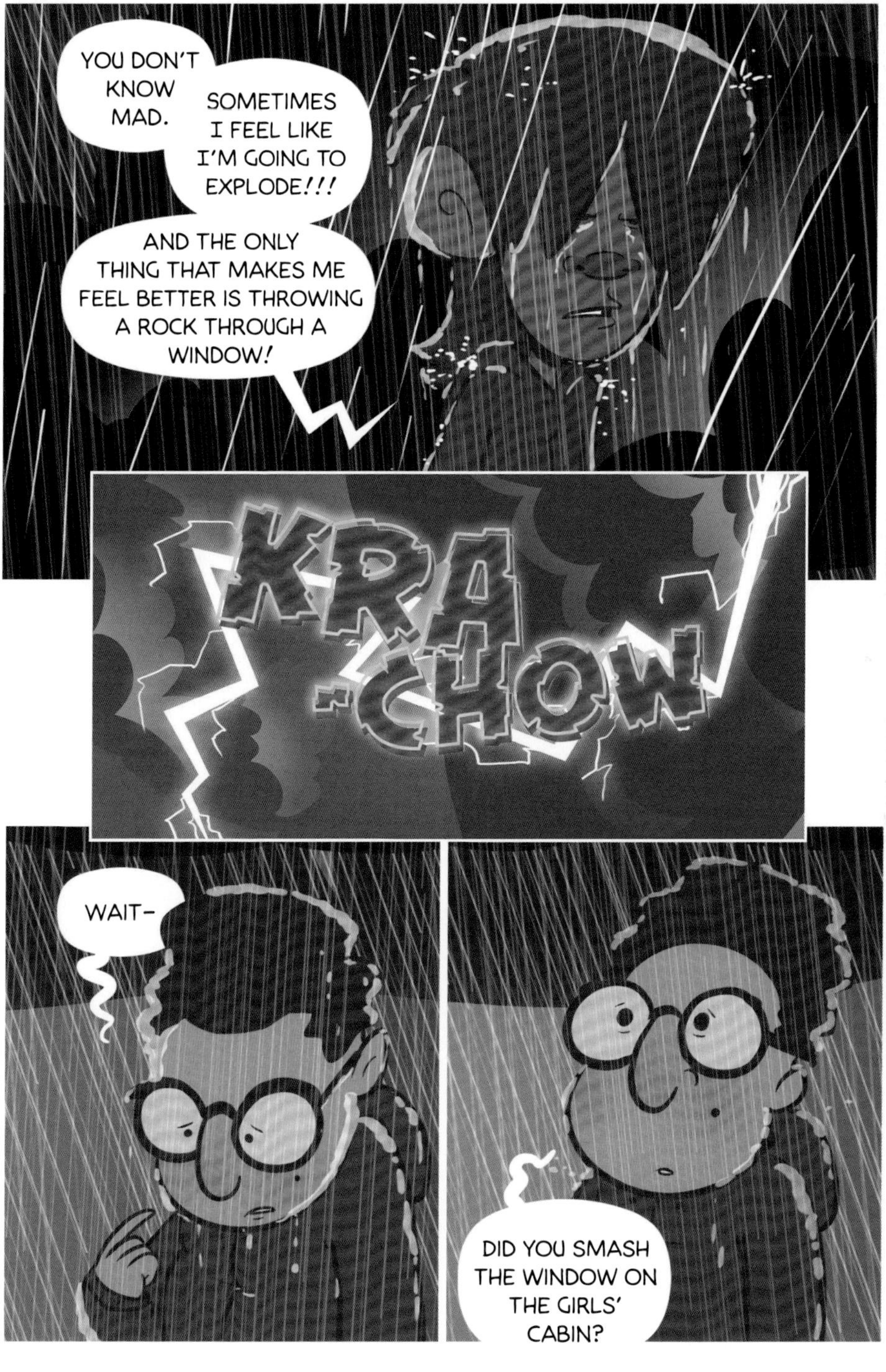
YOU DON'T KNOW MAD.
SOMETIMES I FEEL LIKE I'M GOING TO EXPLODE!!!
AND THE ONLY THING THAT MAKES ME FEEL BETTER IS THROWING A ROCK THROUGH A WINDOW!
KRA-CHOW
WAIT-
DID YOU SMASH THE WINDOW ON THE GIRLS' CABIN?

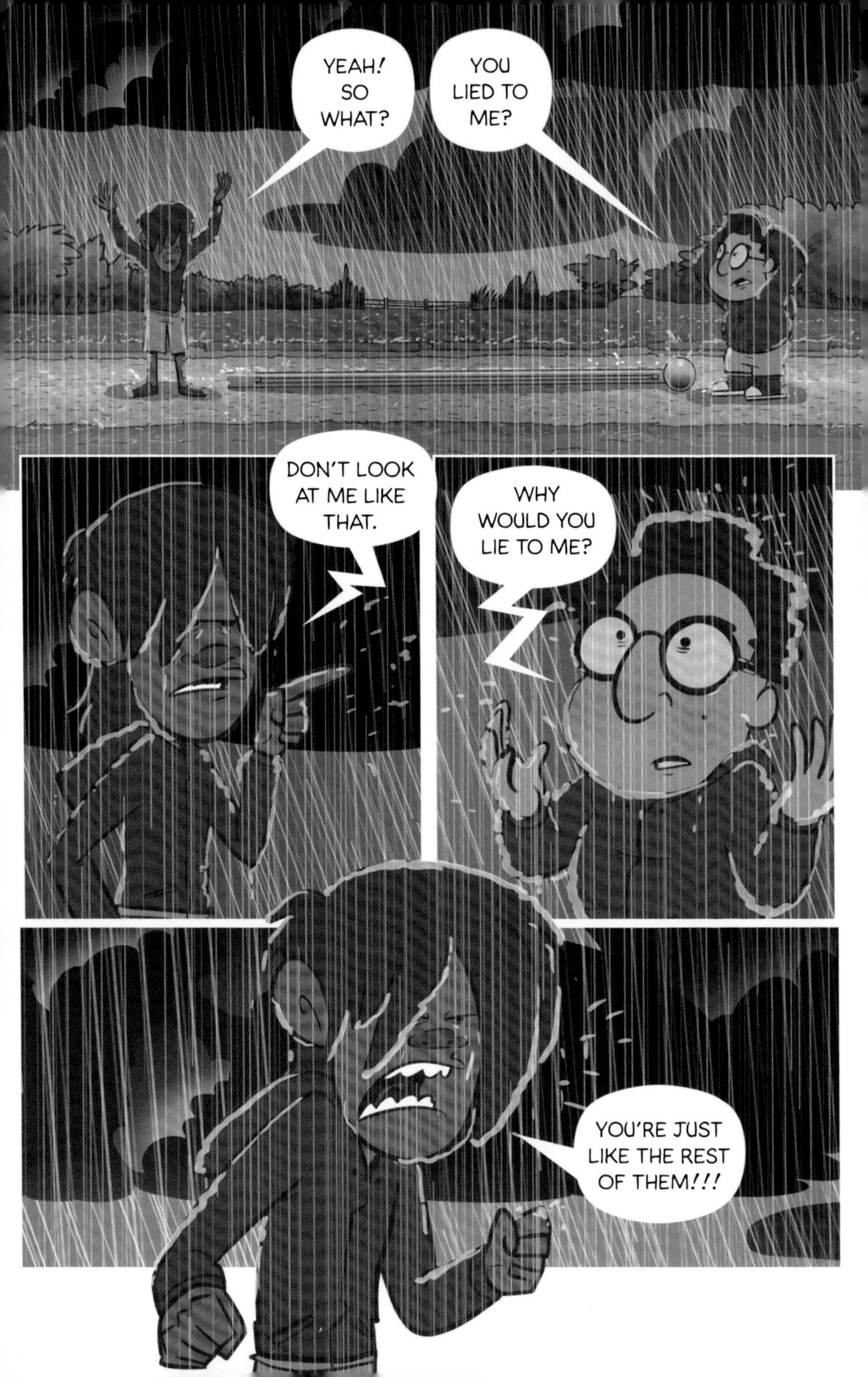
YEAH! SO WHAT?
YOU LIED TO ME?
DON'T LOOK AT ME LIKE THAT.
WHY WOULD YOU LIE TO ME?
YOU'RE JUST LIKE THE REST OF THEM!!!

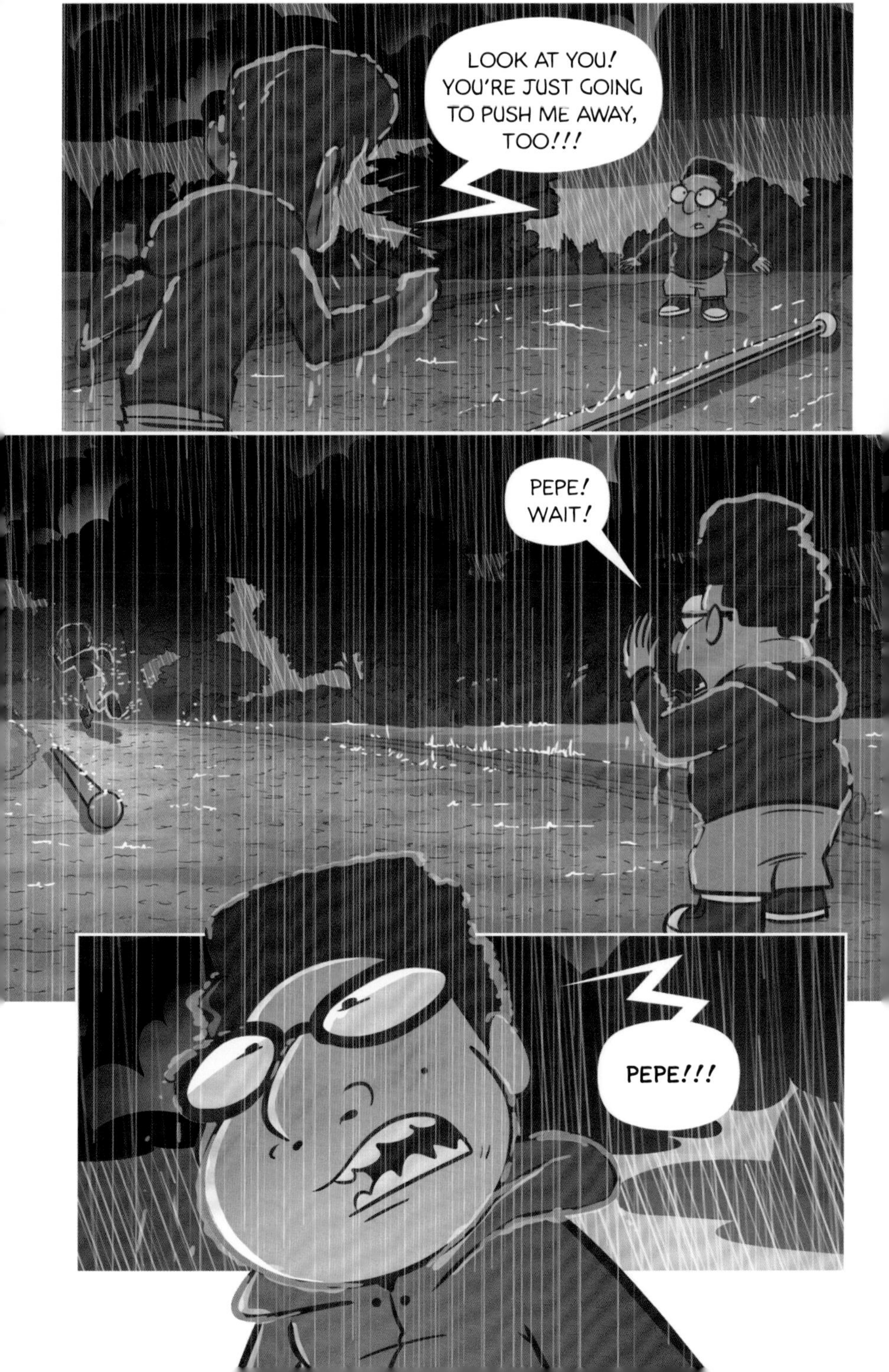
LOOK AT YOU! YOU'RE JUST GOING TO PUSH ME AWAY, TOO!!!
PEPE! WAIT!
PEPE!!!

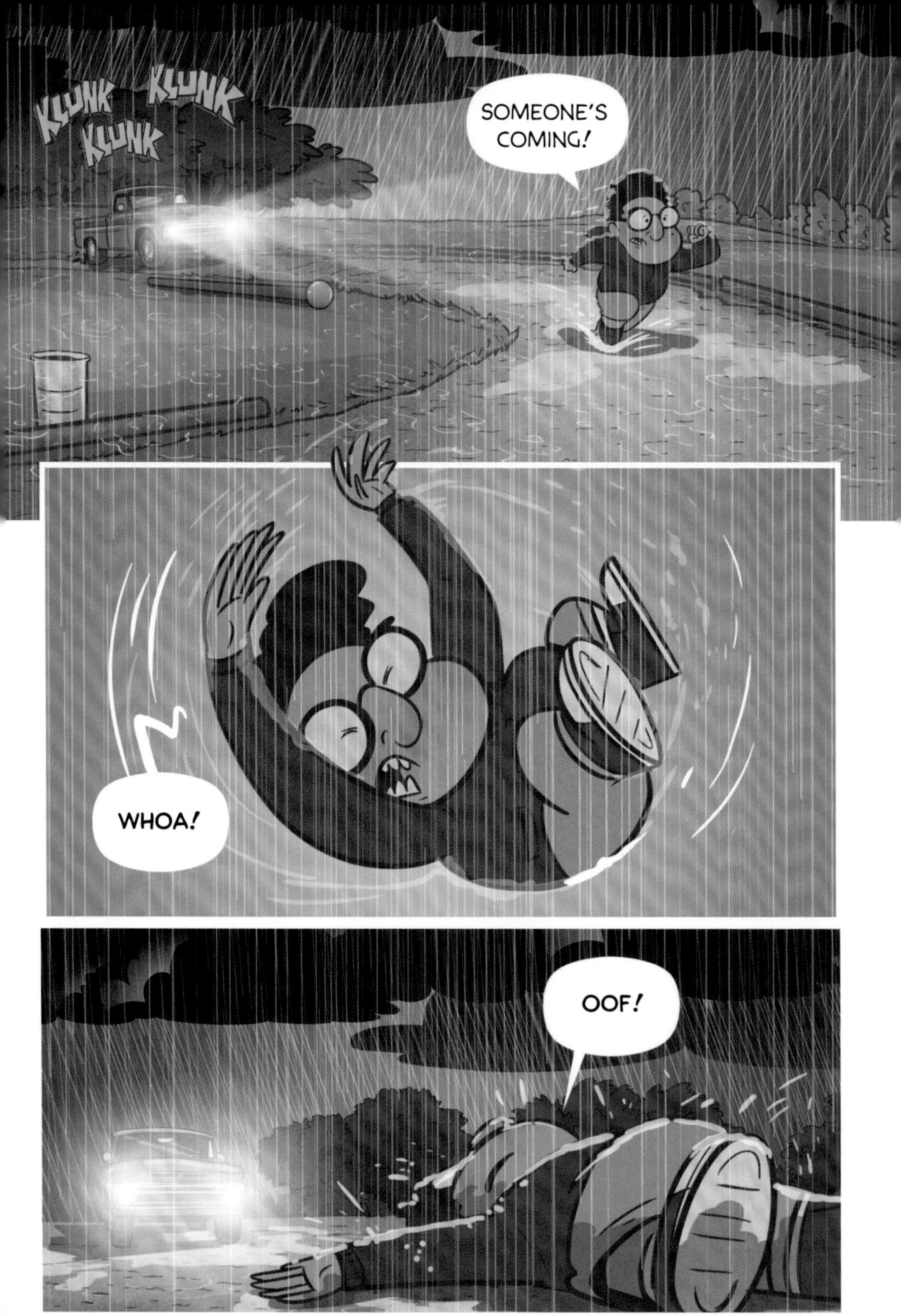
KLUNK KLUNK
KLUNK
SOMEONE'S COMING!
WHOA!
OOF!

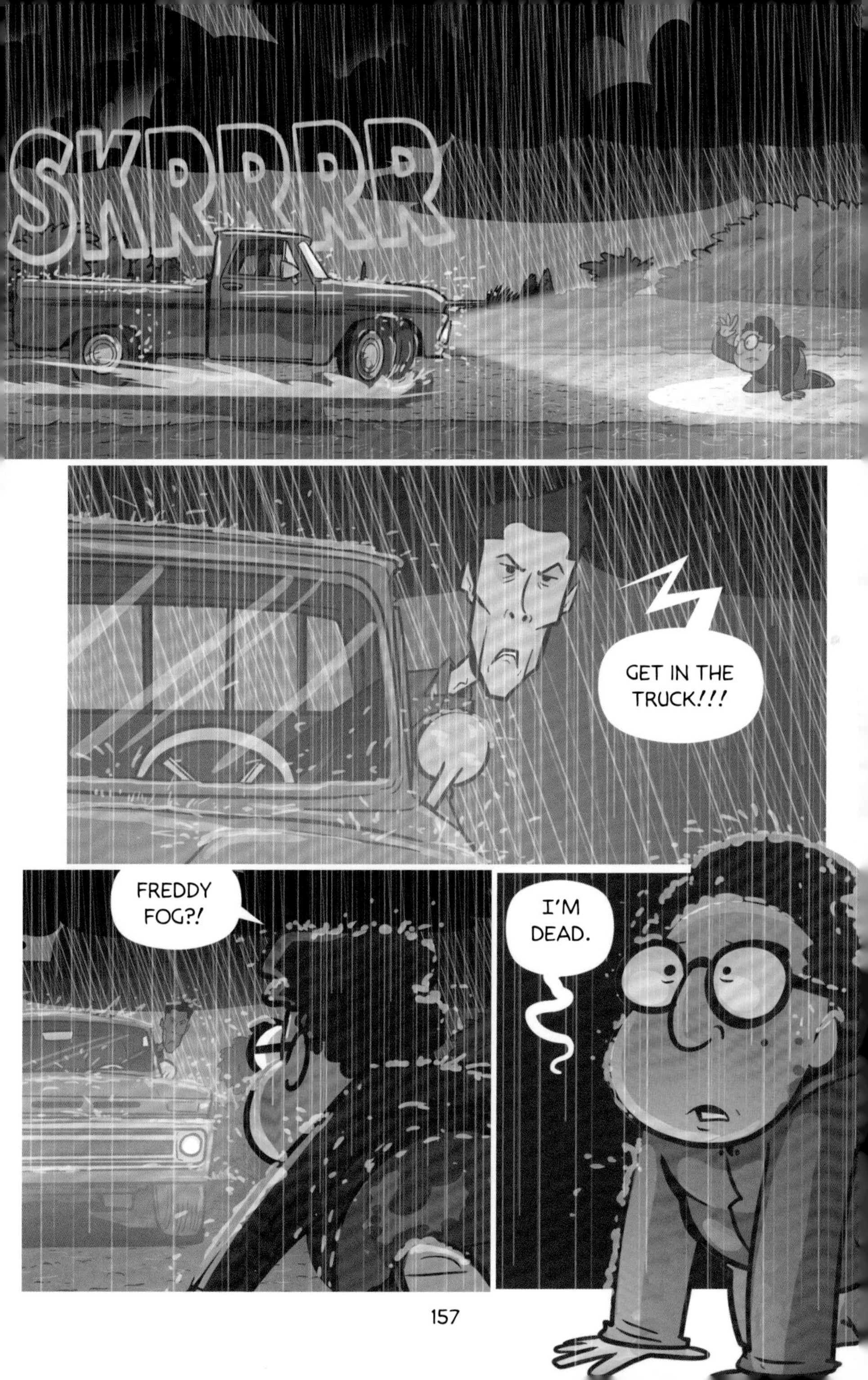
SKRRRR
GET IN THE TRUCK!!!
FREDDY FOG?!
I'M DEAD.

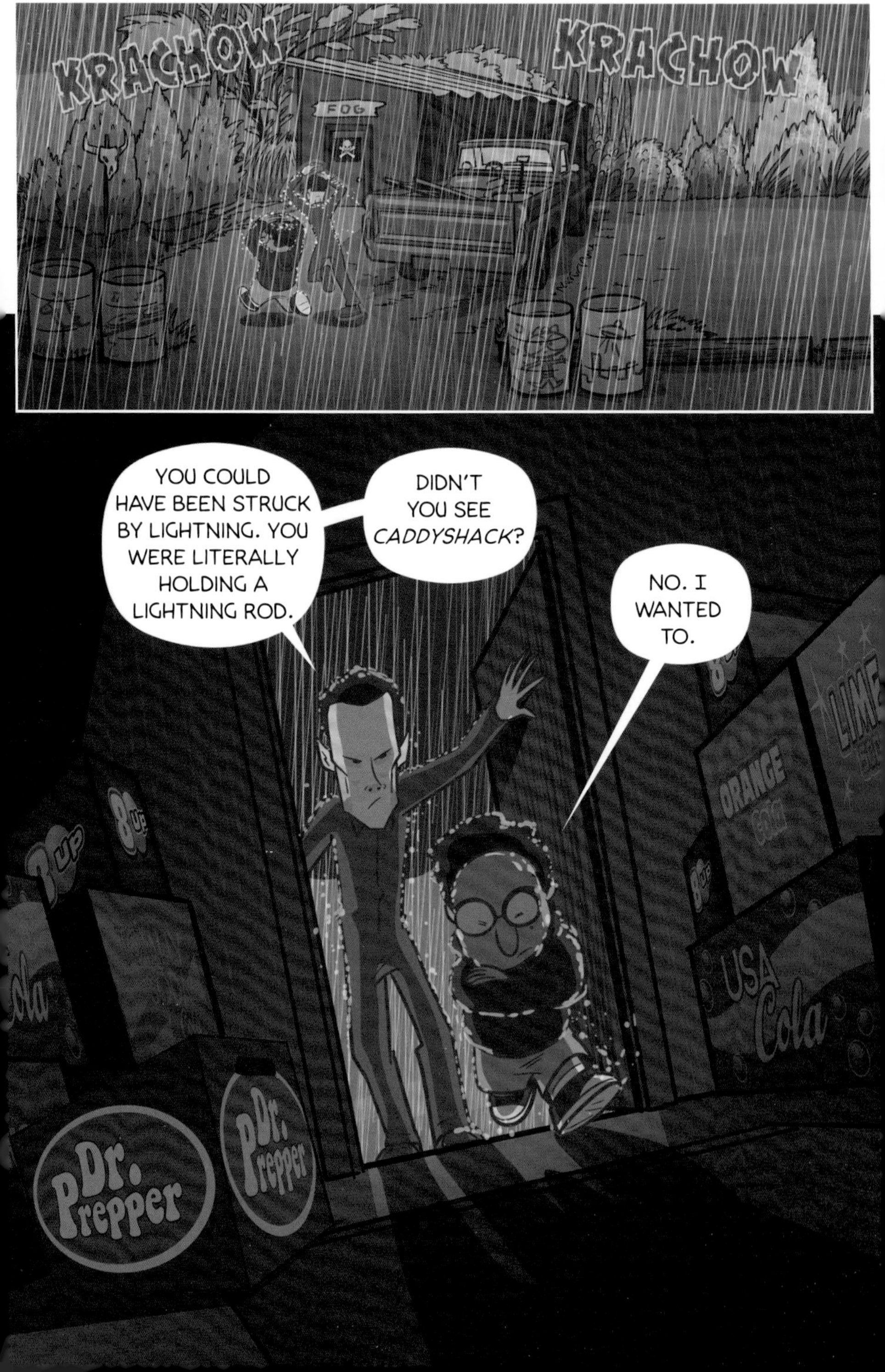
KRACHOW
KRACHOW
FOG
YOU COULD HAVE BEEN STRUCK BY LIGHTNING. YOU WERE LITERALLY HOLDING A LIGHTNING ROD.
DIDN'T YOU SEE *CADDYSHACK*?
NO. I WANTED TO.
8up
ORANGE
USA Cola
Dr. Prepper
Dr. Prepper

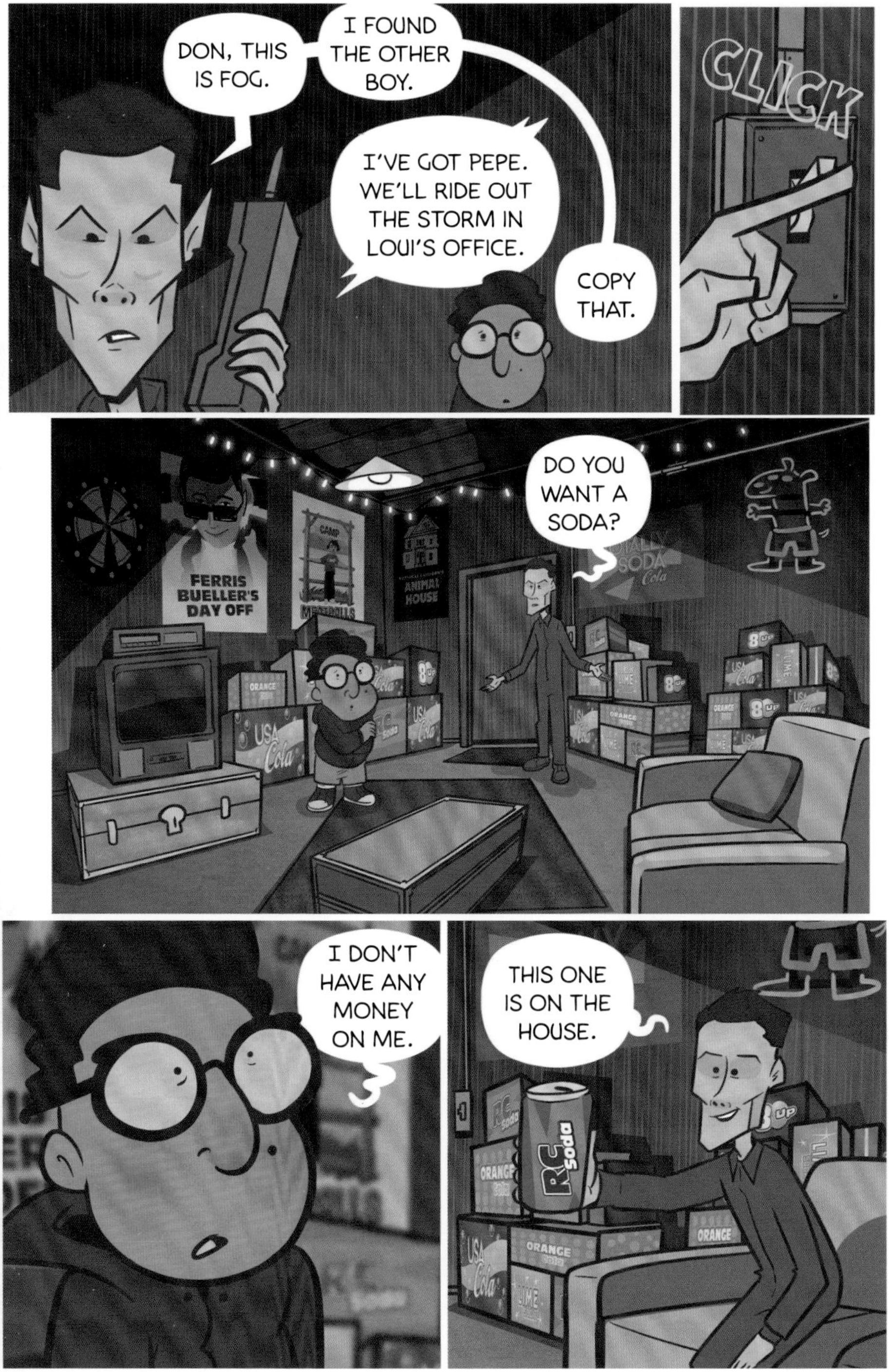
DON, THIS IS FOG.
I FOUND THE OTHER BOY.
I'VE GOT PEPE. WE'LL RIDE OUT THE STORM IN LOUI'S OFFICE.
COPY THAT.
CLICK
FERRIS BUELLER'S DAY OFF
ANIMAL HOUSE
DO YOU WANT A SODA?
I DON'T HAVE ANY MONEY ON ME.
THIS ONE IS ON THE HOUSE.

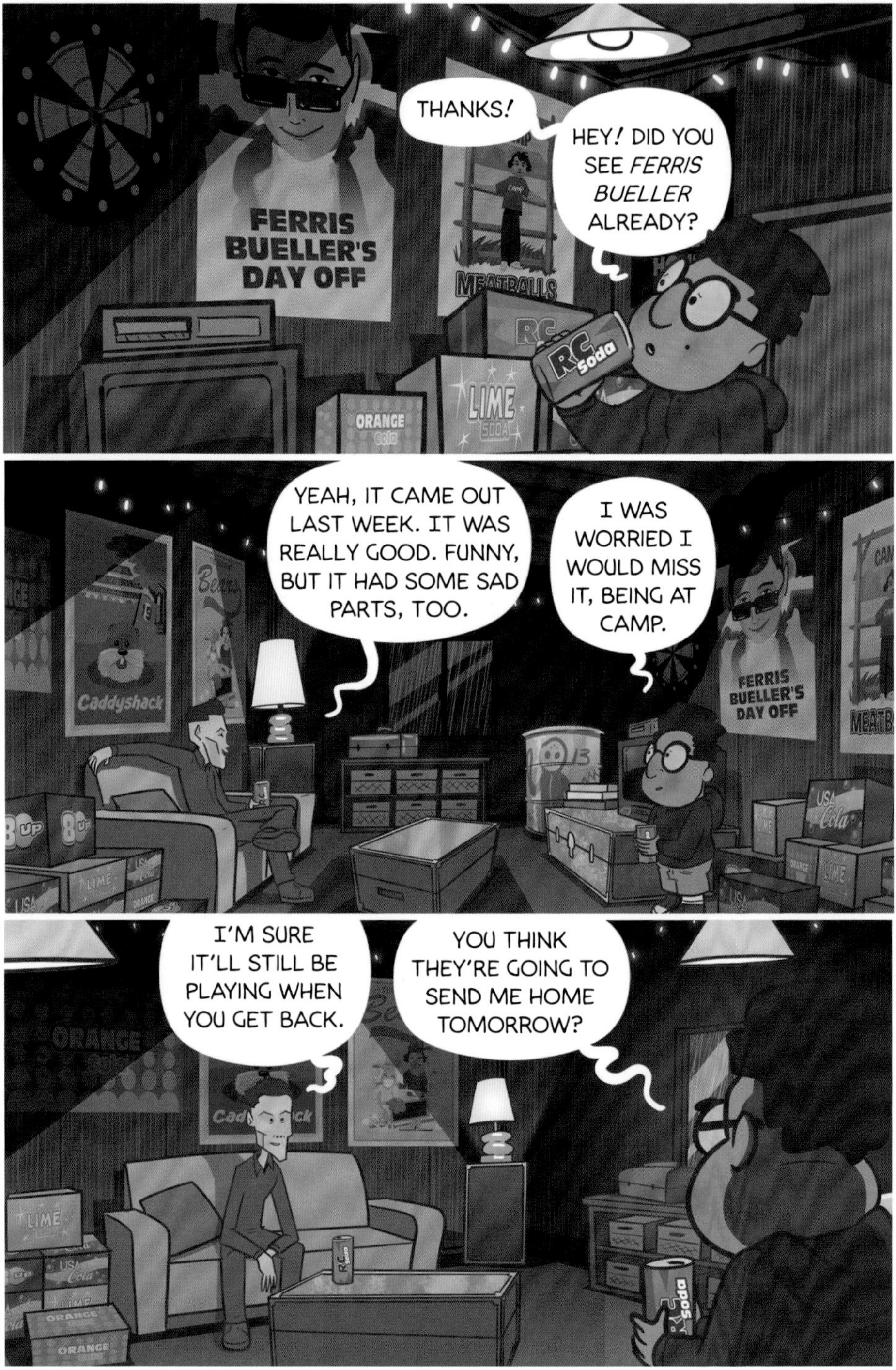
FERRIS BUELLER'S DAY OFF
MEATBALLS
THANKS!
HEY! DID YOU SEE *FERRIS BUELLER* ALREADY?
YEAH, IT CAME OUT LAST WEEK. IT WAS REALLY GOOD. FUNNY, BUT IT HAD SOME SAD PARTS, TOO.
I WAS WORRIED I WOULD MISS IT, BEING AT CAMP.
Caddyshack
I'M SURE IT'LL STILL BE PLAYING WHEN YOU GET BACK.
YOU THINK THEY'RE GOING TO SEND ME HOME TOMORROW?

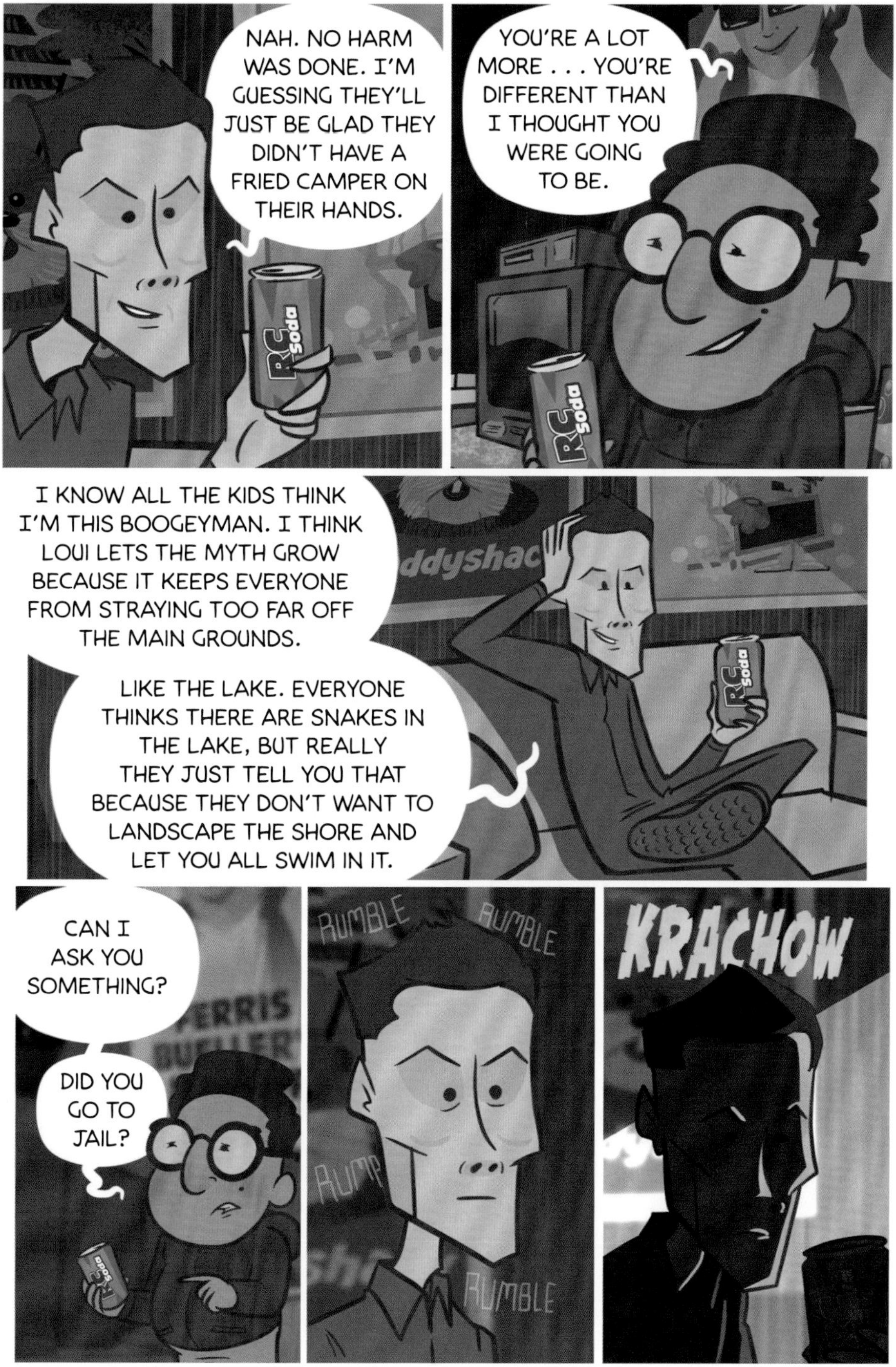
NAH. NO HARM WAS DONE. I'M GUESSING THEY'LL JUST BE GLAD THEY DIDN'T HAVE A FRIED CAMPER ON THEIR HANDS.
YOU'RE A LOT MORE . . . YOU'RE DIFFERENT THAN I THOUGHT YOU WERE GOING TO BE.
I KNOW ALL THE KIDS THINK I'M THIS BOOGEYMAN. I THINK LOUI LETS THE MYTH GROW BECAUSE IT KEEPS EVERYONE FROM STRAYING TOO FAR OFF THE MAIN GROUNDS.
LIKE THE LAKE. EVERYONE THINKS THERE ARE SNAKES IN THE LAKE, BUT REALLY THEY JUST TELL YOU THAT BECAUSE THEY DON'T WANT TO LANDSCAPE THE SHORE AND LET YOU ALL SWIM IN IT.
CAN I ASK YOU SOMETHING?
DID YOU GO TO JAIL?
RUMBLE
RUMBLE
RUMP
RUMBLE
KRACHOW

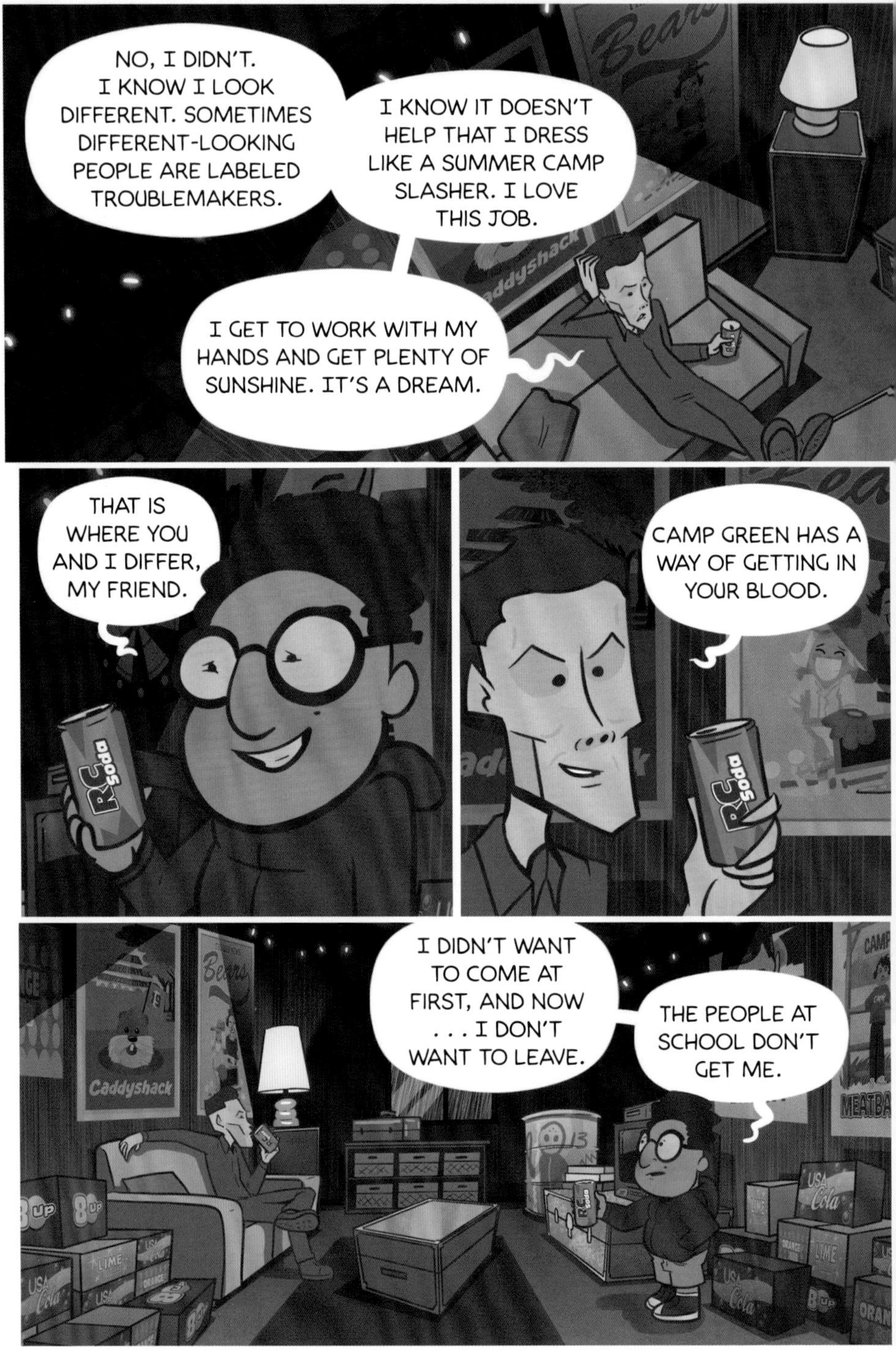
NO, I DIDN'T. I KNOW I LOOK DIFFERENT. SOMETIMES DIFFERENT-LOOKING PEOPLE ARE LABELED TROUBLEMAKERS.
I KNOW IT DOESN'T HELP THAT I DRESS LIKE A SUMMER CAMP SLASHER. I LOVE THIS JOB.
I GET TO WORK WITH MY HANDS AND GET PLENTY OF SUNSHINE. IT'S A DREAM.
Caddyshack
THAT IS WHERE YOU AND I DIFFER, MY FRIEND.
RC Soda
CAMP GREEN HAS A WAY OF GETTING IN YOUR BLOOD.
RC Soda
I DIDN'T WANT TO COME AT FIRST, AND NOW . . . I DON'T WANT TO LEAVE.
THE PEOPLE AT SCHOOL DON'T GET ME.
Caddyshack
USA Cola
LIME
ORANGE

I KNOW WHAT IT'S LIKE TO BE TREATED LIKE A CRIMINAL.
SOMETIMES YOU GET TO A PLACE WHERE YOU THINK, HEY, THEY ALREADY THINK I'M A CRIMINAL, SO WHY NOT JUST BREAK THE LAW ANYWAY?
THE SNEAKING OUT AND PRANKS ARE ONE THING, BUT YOU DON'T EVER WANT TO GET TO A PLACE WHERE YOU'RE CAUSING REAL DAMAGE, BECAUSE THEN IT'S NOT FUNNY.
BUELLE
UNDERSTOOD.

HUDI on TRIAL

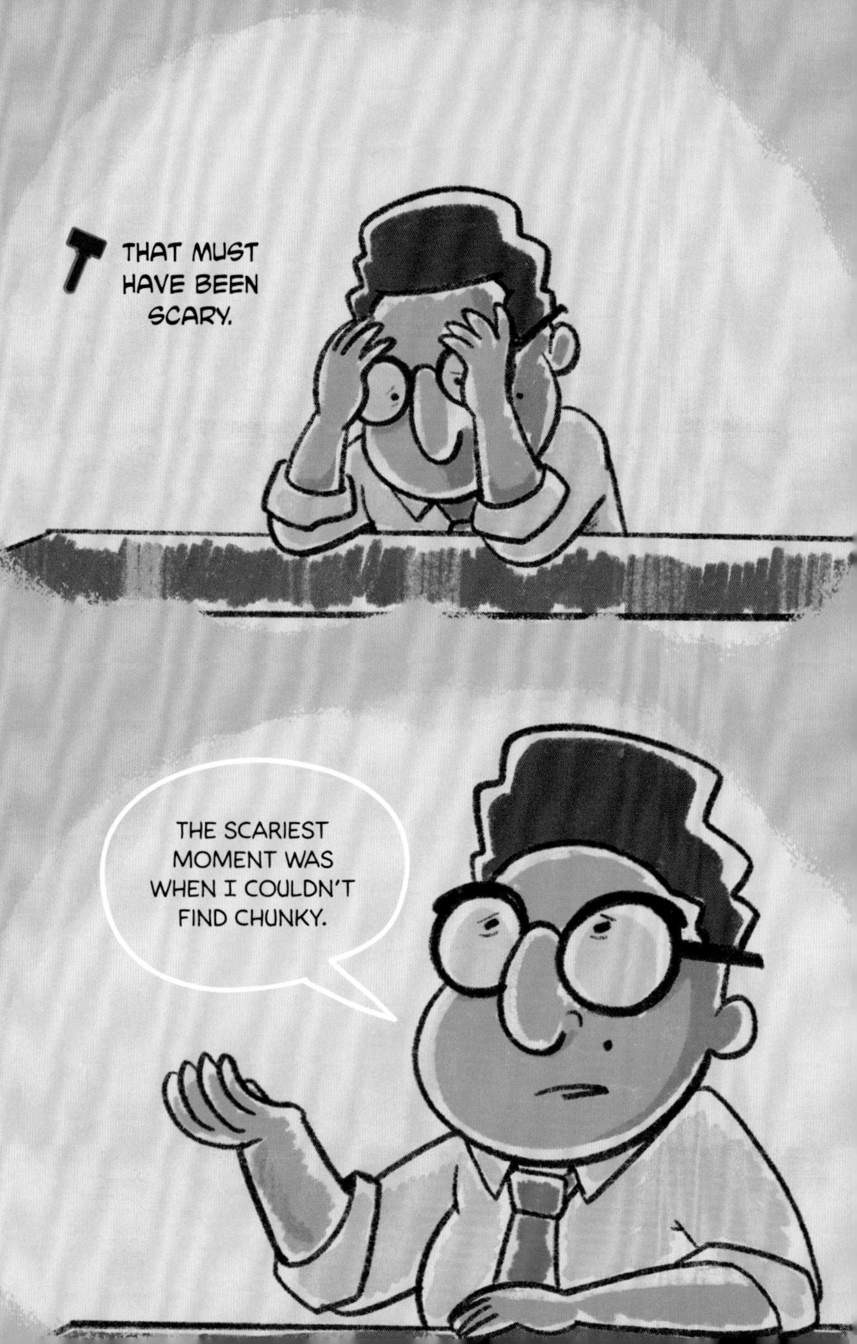
THAT MUST HAVE BEEN SCARY.
THE SCARIEST MOMENT WAS WHEN I COULDN'T FIND CHUNKY.

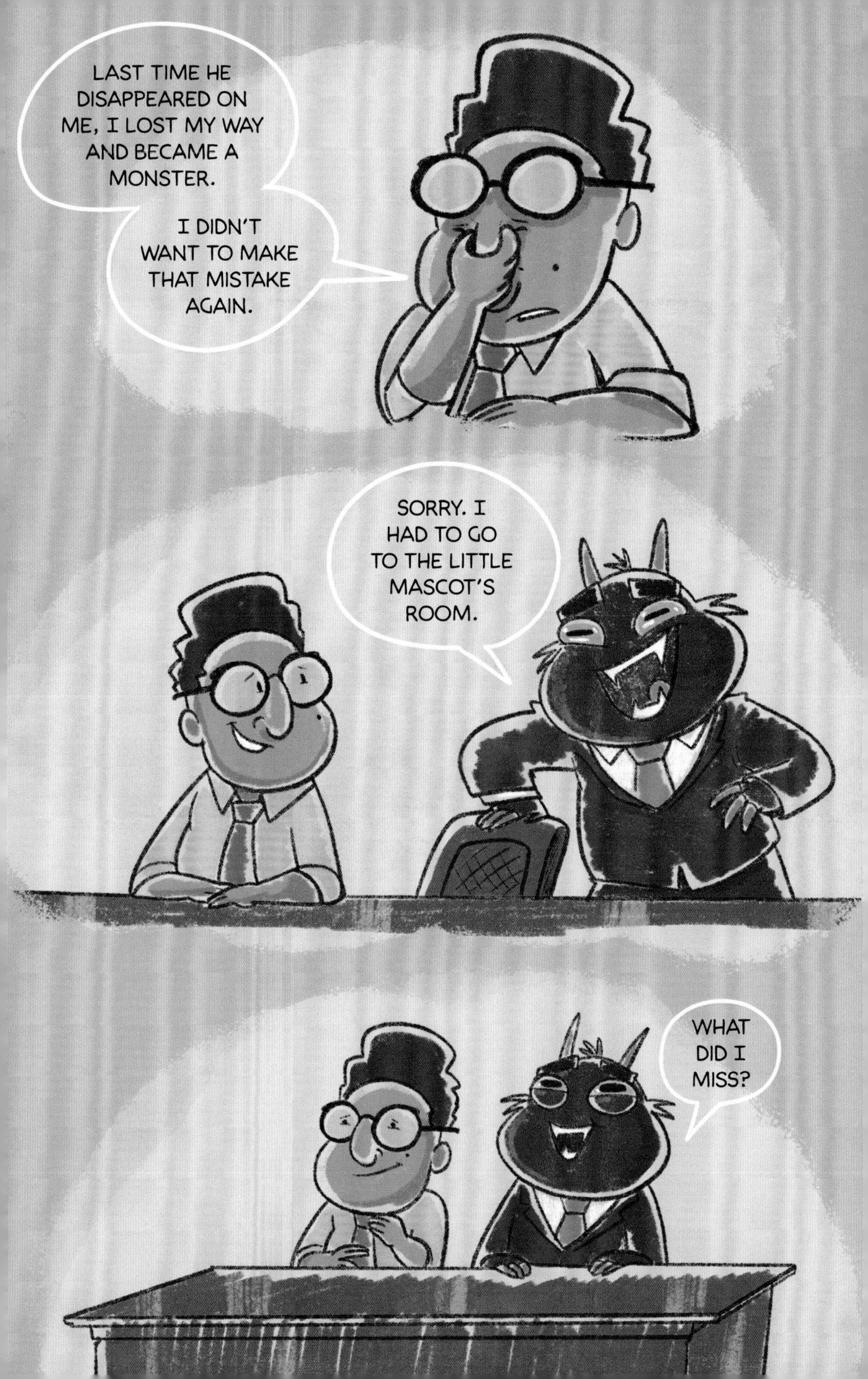
LAST TIME HE DISAPPEARED ON ME, I LOST MY WAY AND BECAME A MONSTER.
I DIDN'T WANT TO MAKE THAT MISTAKE AGAIN.
SORRY. I HAD TO GO TO THE LITTLE MASCOT'S ROOM.
WHAT DID I MISS?

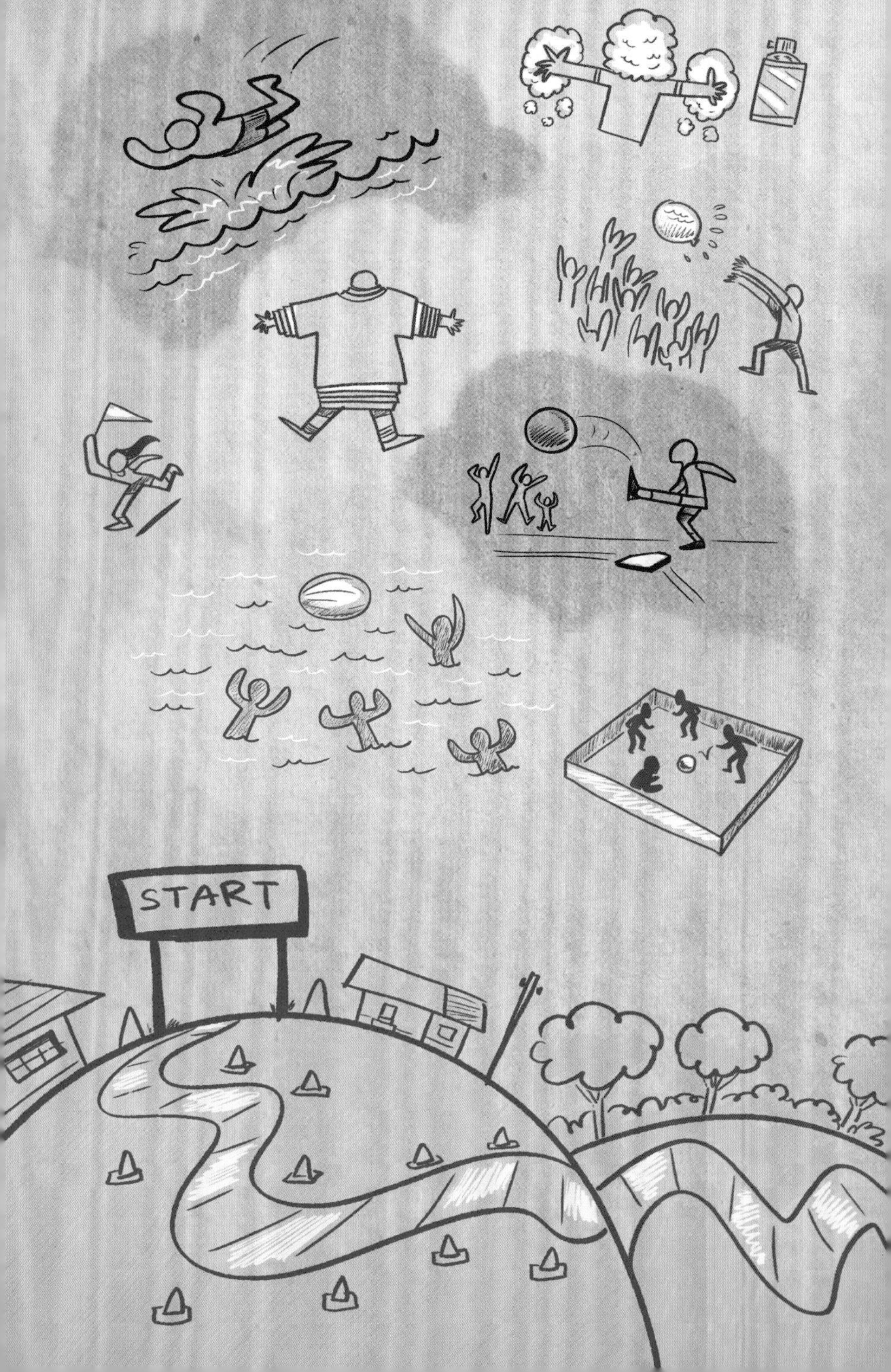
START

CHAPTER SIX
MACCABIAH

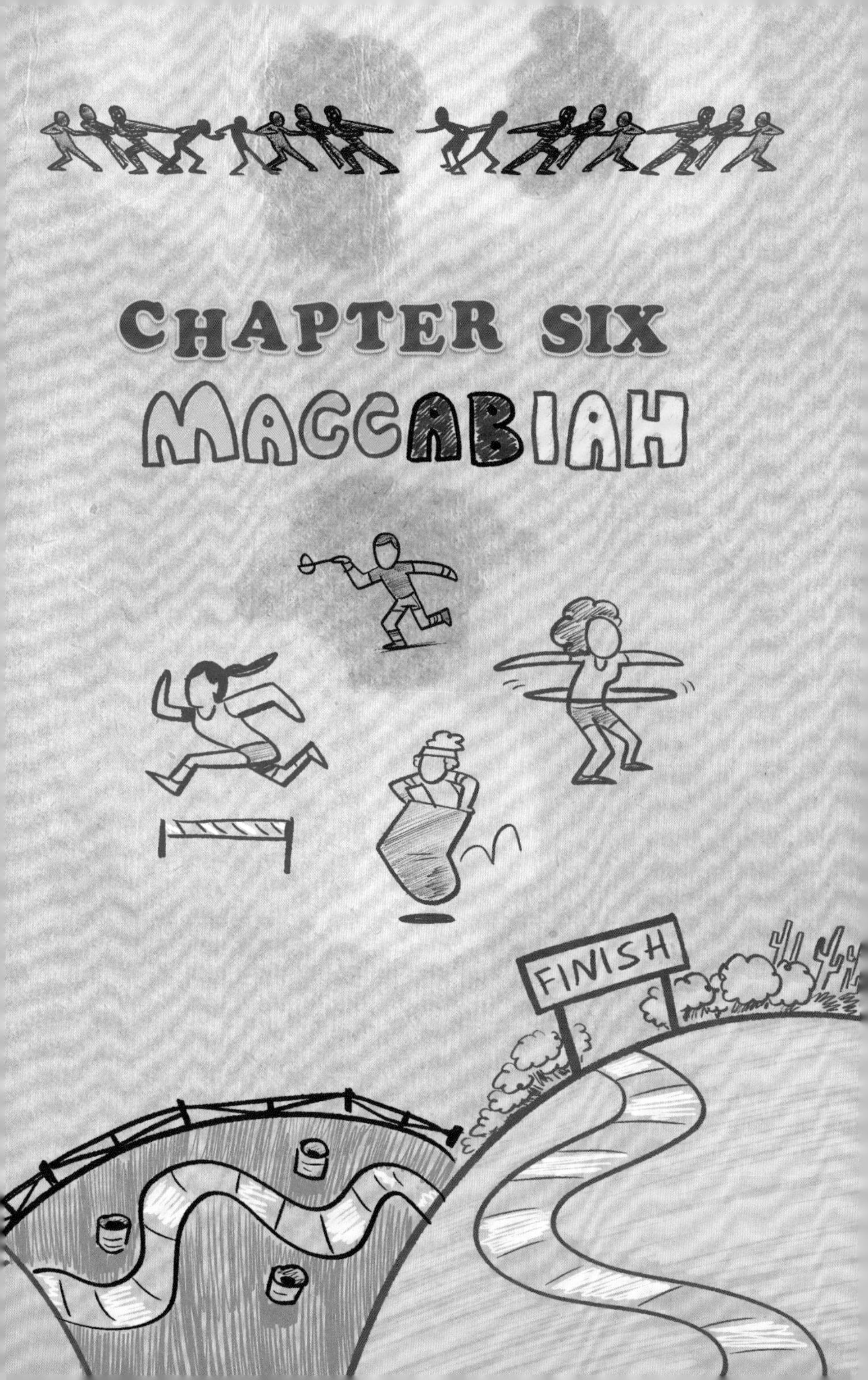
FINISH

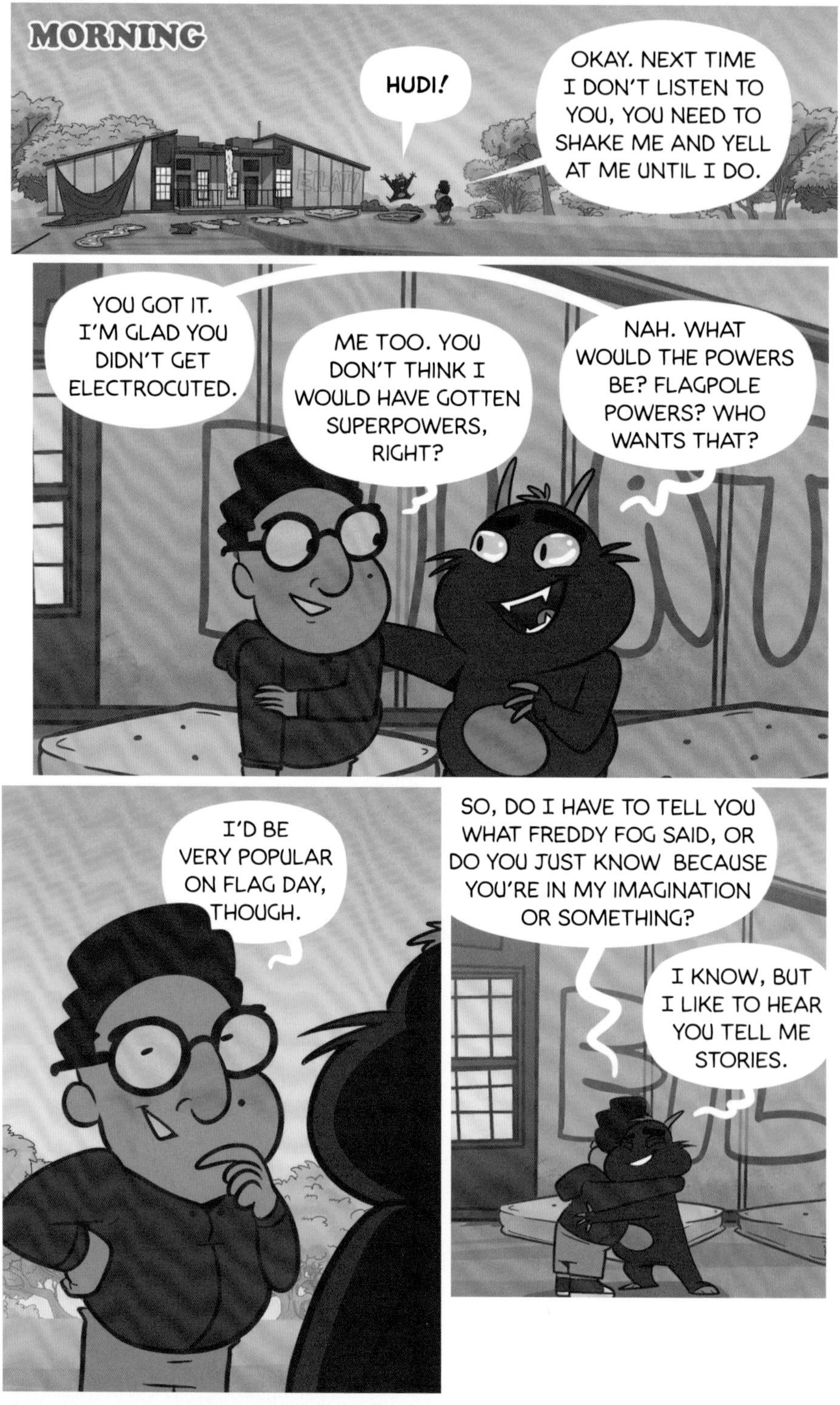
MORNING
HUDI!
OKAY. NEXT TIME I DON'T LISTEN TO YOU, YOU NEED TO SHAKE ME AND YELL AT ME UNTIL I DO.
YOU GOT IT. I'M GLAD YOU DIDN'T GET ELECTROCUTED.
ME TOO. YOU DON'T THINK I WOULD HAVE GOTTEN SUPERPOWERS, RIGHT?
NAH. WHAT WOULD THE POWERS BE? FLAGPOLE POWERS? WHO WANTS THAT?
I'D BE VERY POPULAR ON FLAG DAY, THOUGH.
SO, DO I HAVE TO TELL YOU WHAT FREDDY FOG SAID, OR DO YOU JUST KNOW BECAUSE YOU'RE IN MY IMAGINATION OR SOMETHING?
I KNOW, BUT I LIKE TO HEAR YOU TELL ME STORIES.

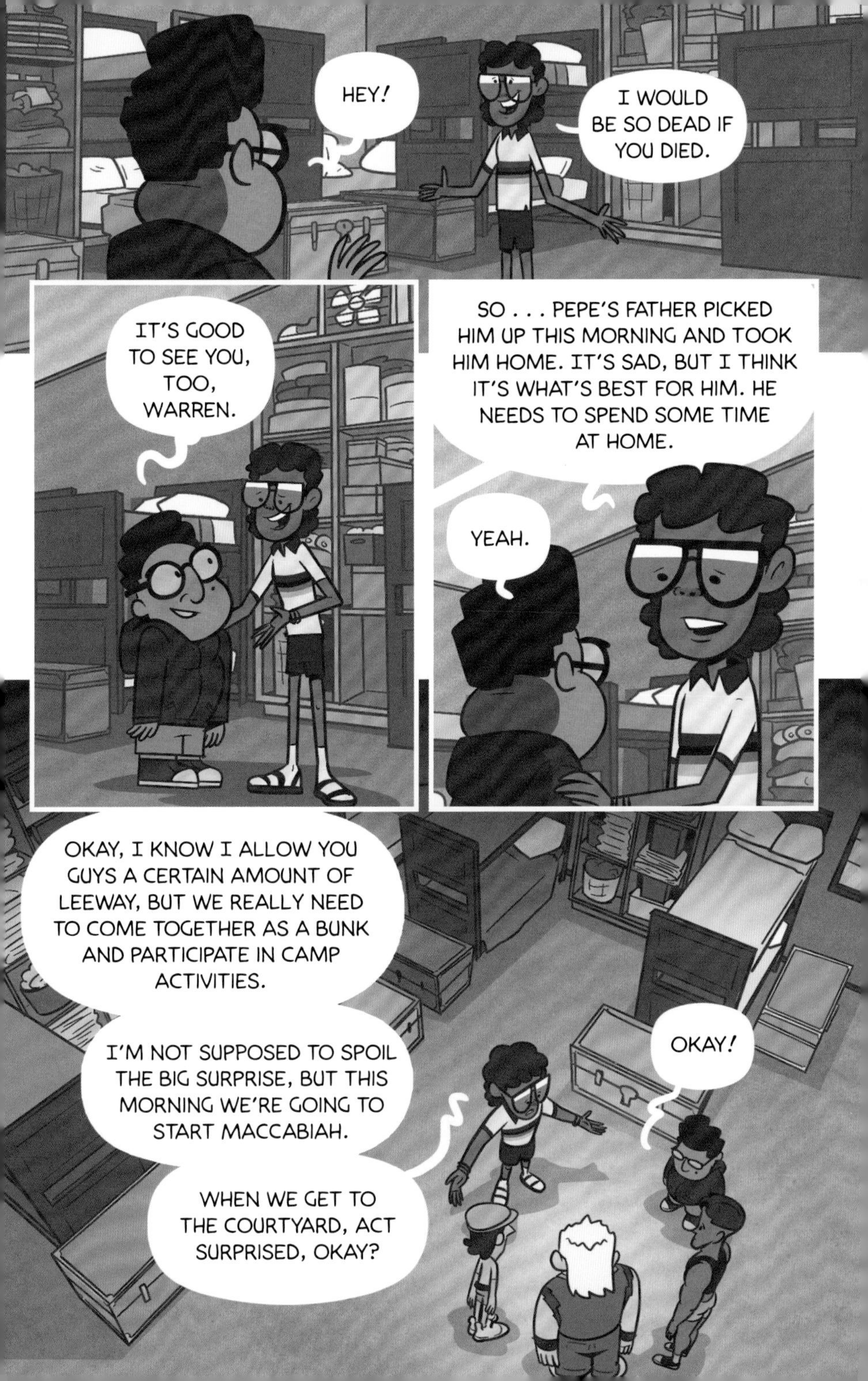
HEY!
I WOULD BE SO DEAD IF YOU DIED.
IT'S GOOD TO SEE YOU, TOO, WARREN.
SO . . . PEPE'S FATHER PICKED HIM UP THIS MORNING AND TOOK HIM HOME. IT'S SAD, BUT I THINK IT'S WHAT'S BEST FOR HIM. HE NEEDS TO SPEND SOME TIME AT HOME.
YEAH.
OKAY, I KNOW I ALLOW YOU GUYS A CERTAIN AMOUNT OF LEEWAY, BUT WE REALLY NEED TO COME TOGETHER AS A BUNK AND PARTICIPATE IN CAMP ACTIVITIES.
I'M NOT SUPPOSED TO SPOIL THE BIG SURPRISE, BUT THIS MORNING WE'RE GOING TO START MACCABIAH.
WHEN WE GET TO THE COURTYARD, ACT SURPRISED, OKAY?
OKAY!

MACCABIAH!
MACCABIAH
RED TEAM
BLUE TEAM
GREEN TEAM
ALL RIGHT, CAMPERS! GATHER ROUND! MACCABIAH IS LIKE THE OLYMPICS OR LIKE FIELD DAY AT SCHOOL BUT WAY MORE FUN!
WE'RE GOING TO DIVIDE YOU ALL INTO FOUR TEAMS. RED, BLUE, YELLOW, AND GREEN! WITH A TEAM CAPTAIN, OR ALUFIM.
BUT THIS IS ALL FOR FUN, SO LET'S NOT GET TOO CRAZY.
MACCABIAH
EACH EVENT WILL GIVE POINTS, AND THE EVENTS RANGE FROM SWIMMING RACES TO WATER BALLOON TOSSING.
THE TEAM WITH THE MOST POINTS ON DAY THREE WILL WIN!

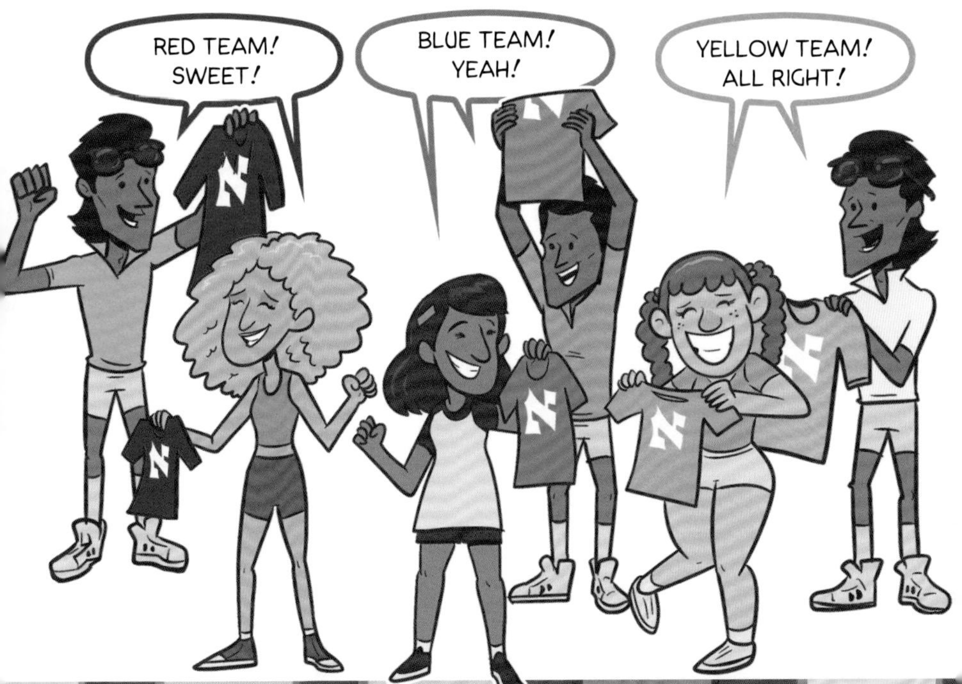
RED TEAM! SWEET!
BLUE TEAM! YEAH!
YELLOW TEAM! ALL RIGHT!

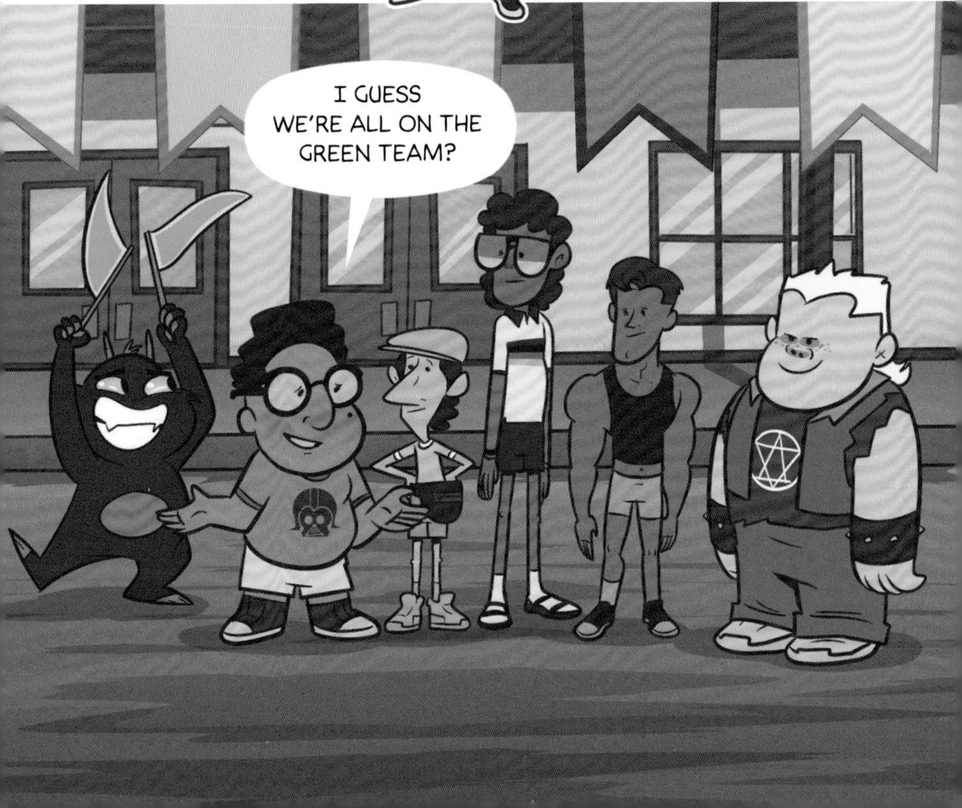
I GUESS WE'RE ALL ON THE GREEN TEAM?

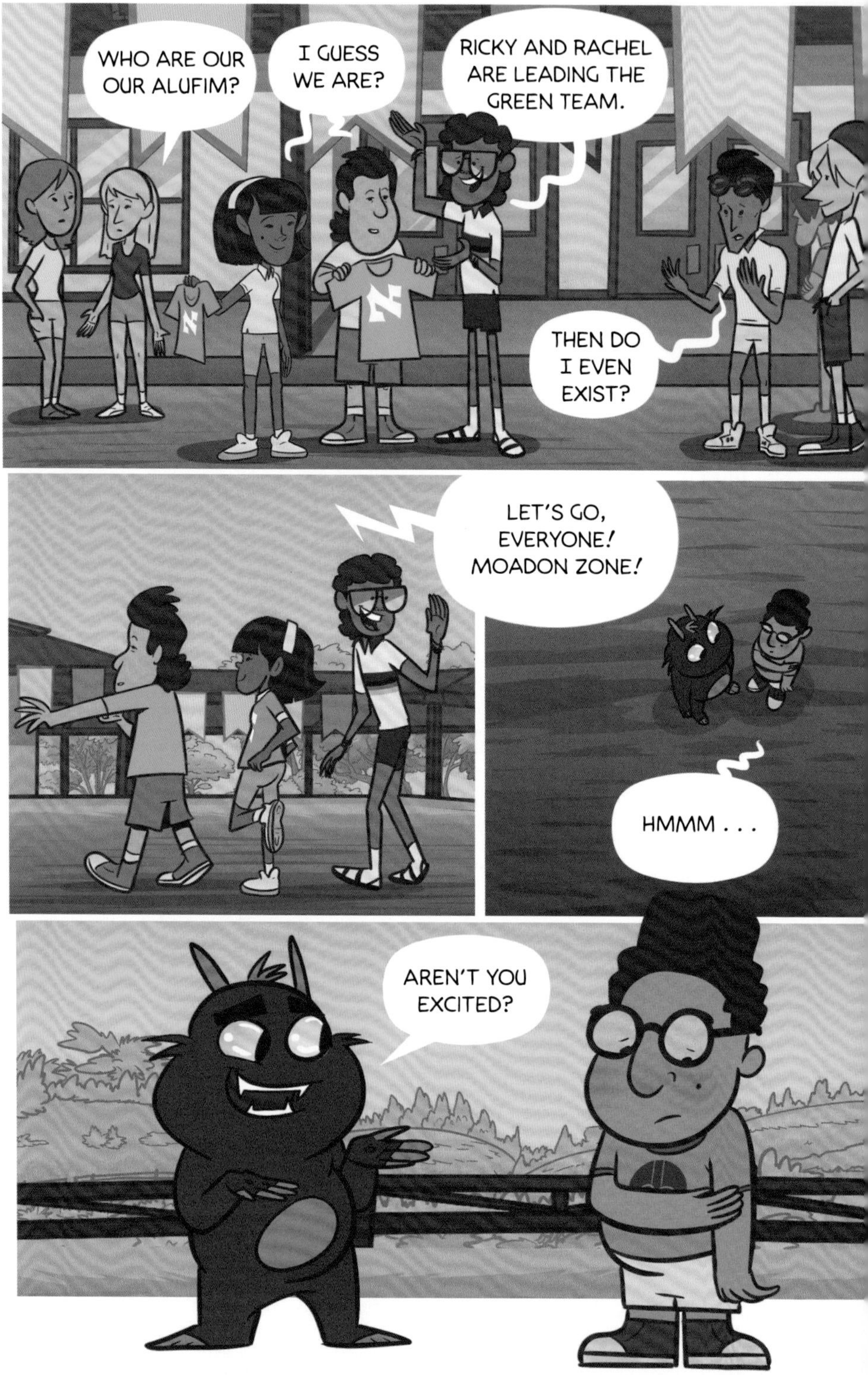
WHO ARE OUR OUR ALUFIM?
I GUESS WE ARE?
RICKY AND RACHEL ARE LEADING THE GREEN TEAM.
THEN DO I EVEN EXIST?
LET'S GO, EVERYONE! MOADON ZONE!
HMMM . . .
AREN'T YOU EXCITED?

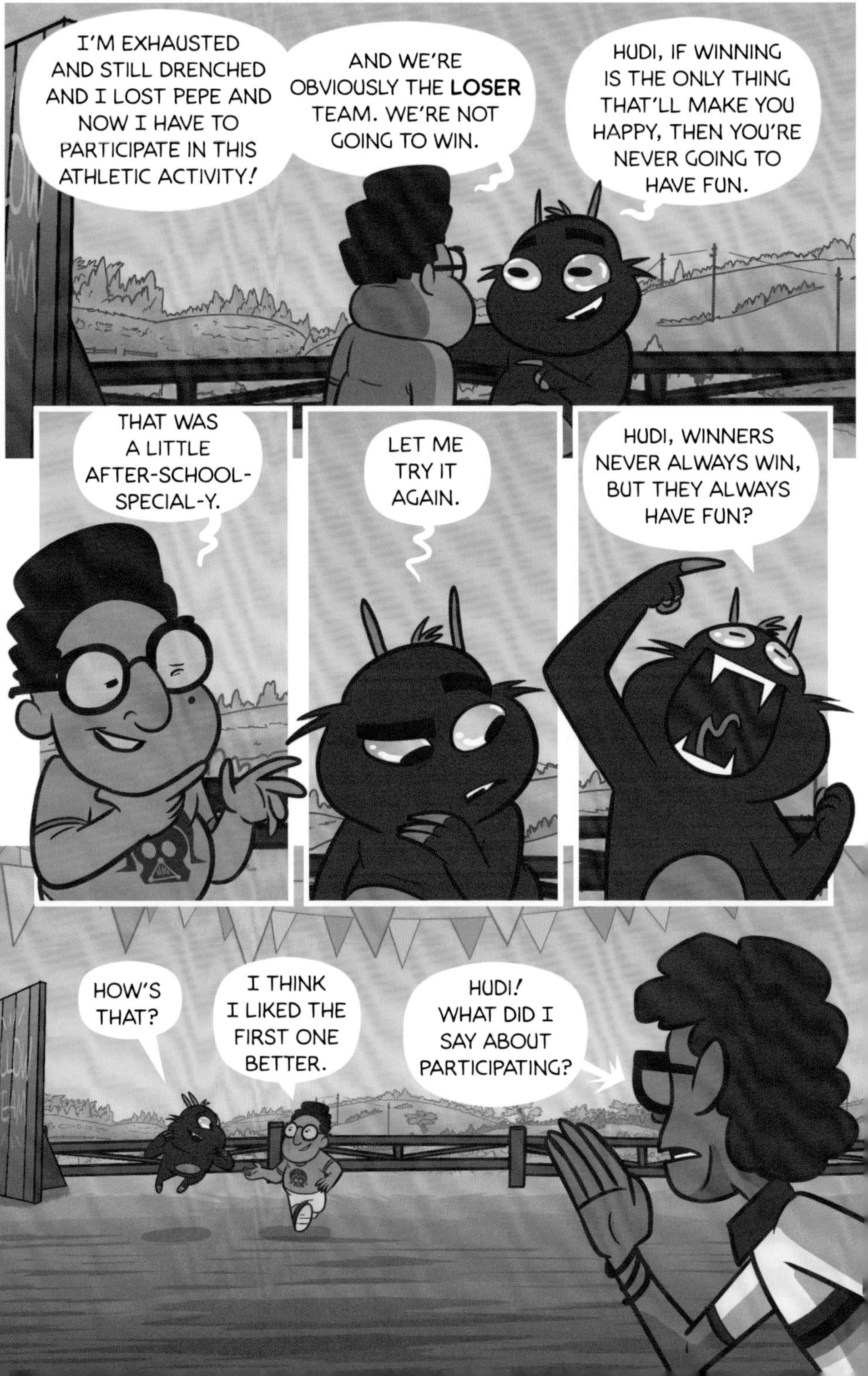
I'M EXHAUSTED AND STILL DRENCHED AND I LOST PEPE AND NOW I HAVE TO PARTICIPATE IN THIS ATHLETIC ACTIVITY!
AND WE'RE OBVIOUSLY THE **LOSER** TEAM. WE'RE NOT GOING TO WIN.
HUDI, IF WINNING IS THE ONLY THING THAT'LL MAKE YOU HAPPY, THEN YOU'RE NEVER GOING TO HAVE FUN.
THAT WAS A LITTLE AFTER-SCHOOL-SPECIAL-Y.
LET ME TRY IT AGAIN.
HUDI, WINNERS NEVER ALWAYS WIN, BUT THEY ALWAYS HAVE FUN?
HOW'S THAT?
I THINK I LIKED THE FIRST ONE BETTER.
HUDI! WHAT DID I SAY ABOUT PARTICIPATING?

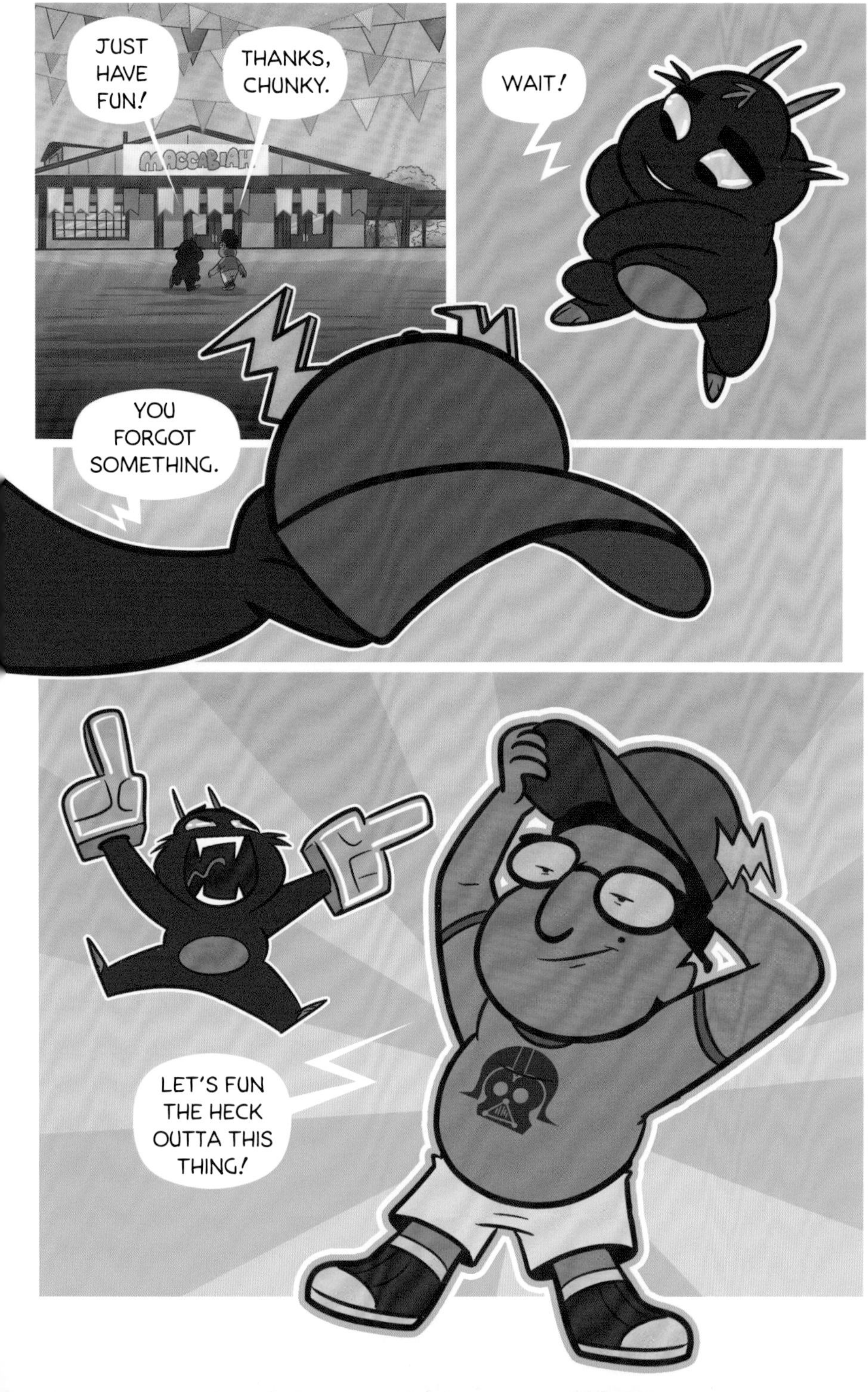

JUST HAVE FUN!
THANKS, CHUNKY.
MACCABIAH
WAIT!
YOU FORGOT SOMETHING.
LET'S FUN THE HECK OUTTA THIS THING!

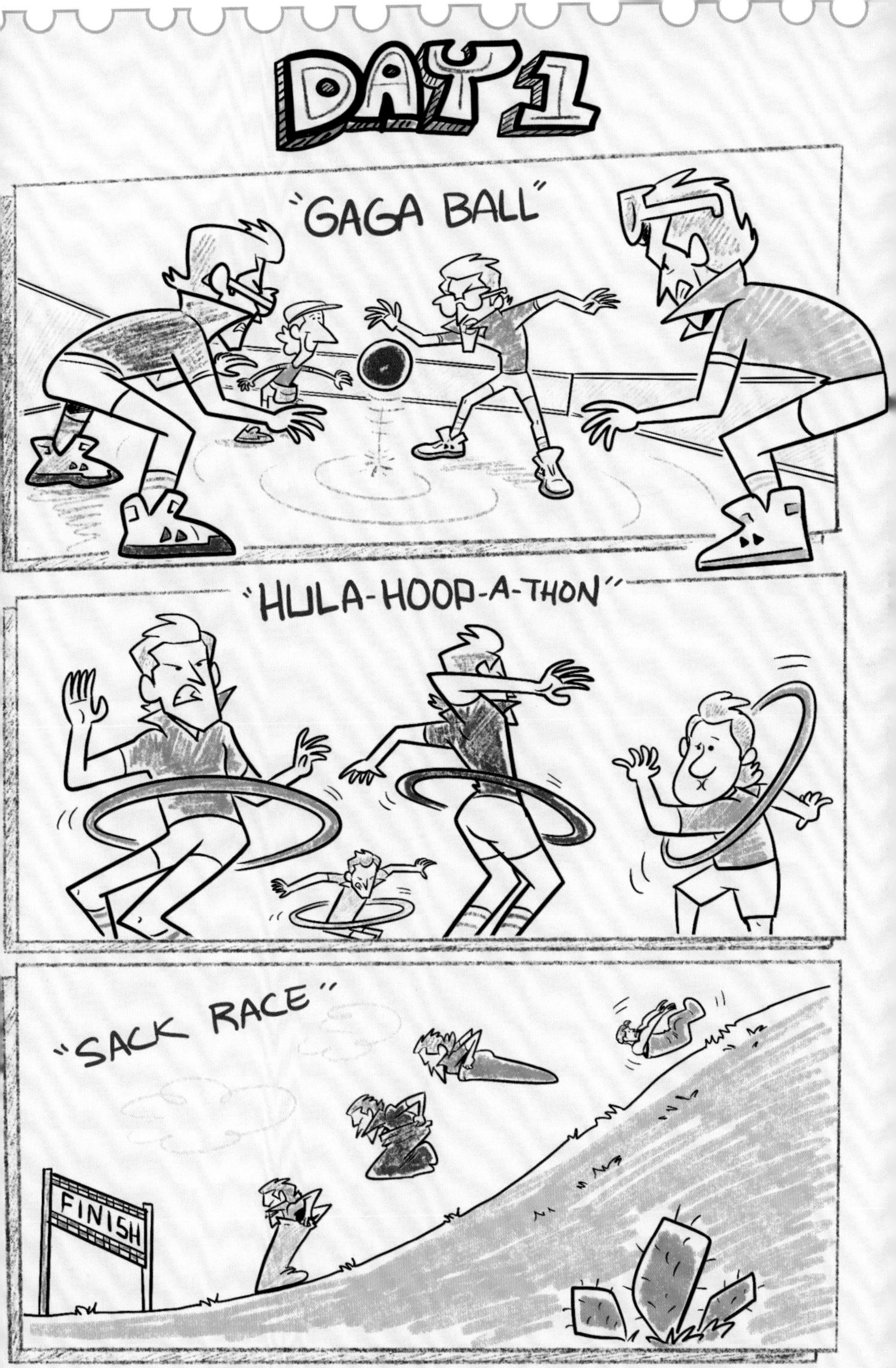
DAY 1
"GAGA BALL"
"HULA-HOOP-A-THON"
"SACK RACE"
FINISH

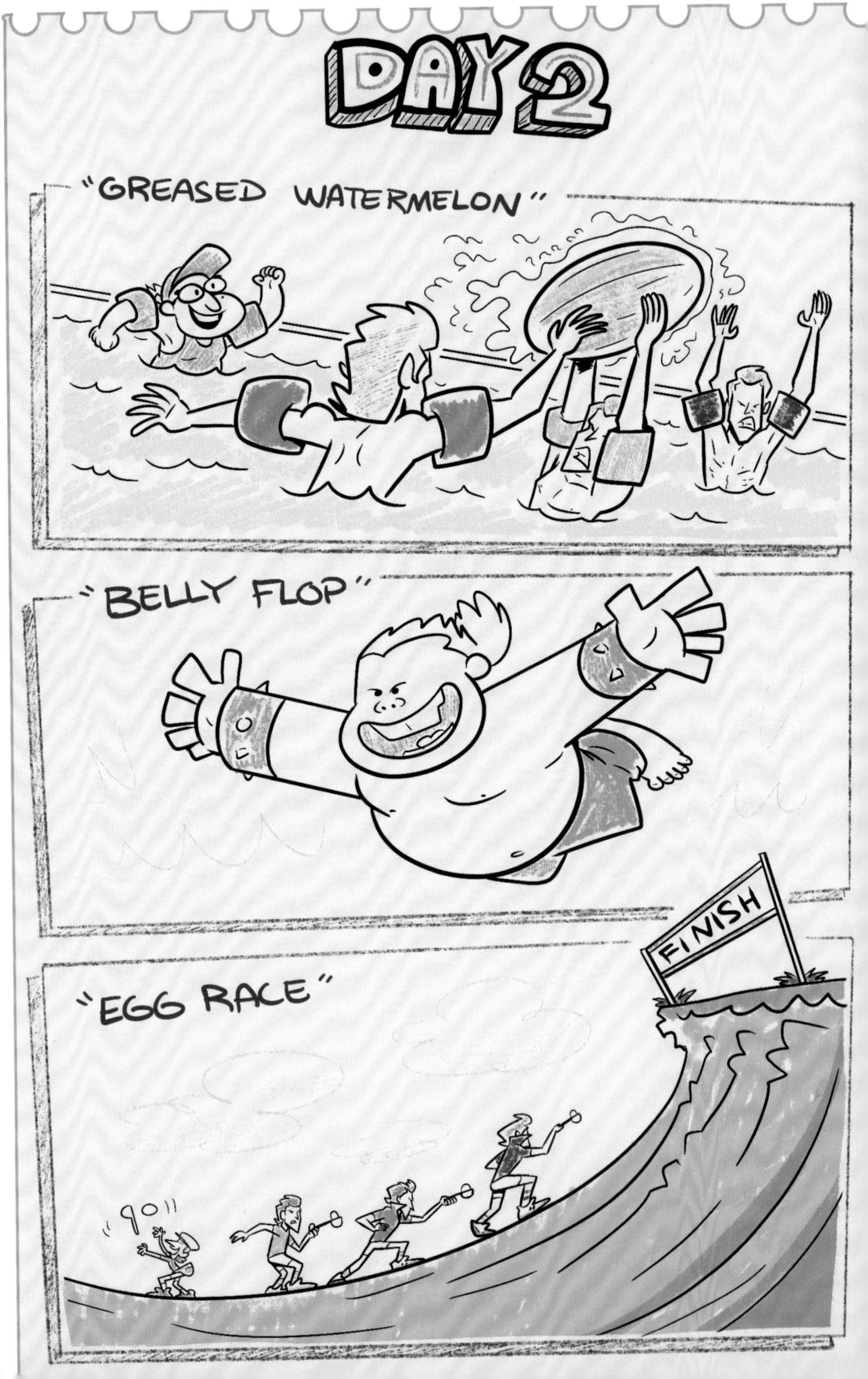
DAY 2
"GREASED WATERMELON"
"BELLY FLOP"
"EGG RACE"
FINISH
GO!!

SUPER DAY 3 RELAY

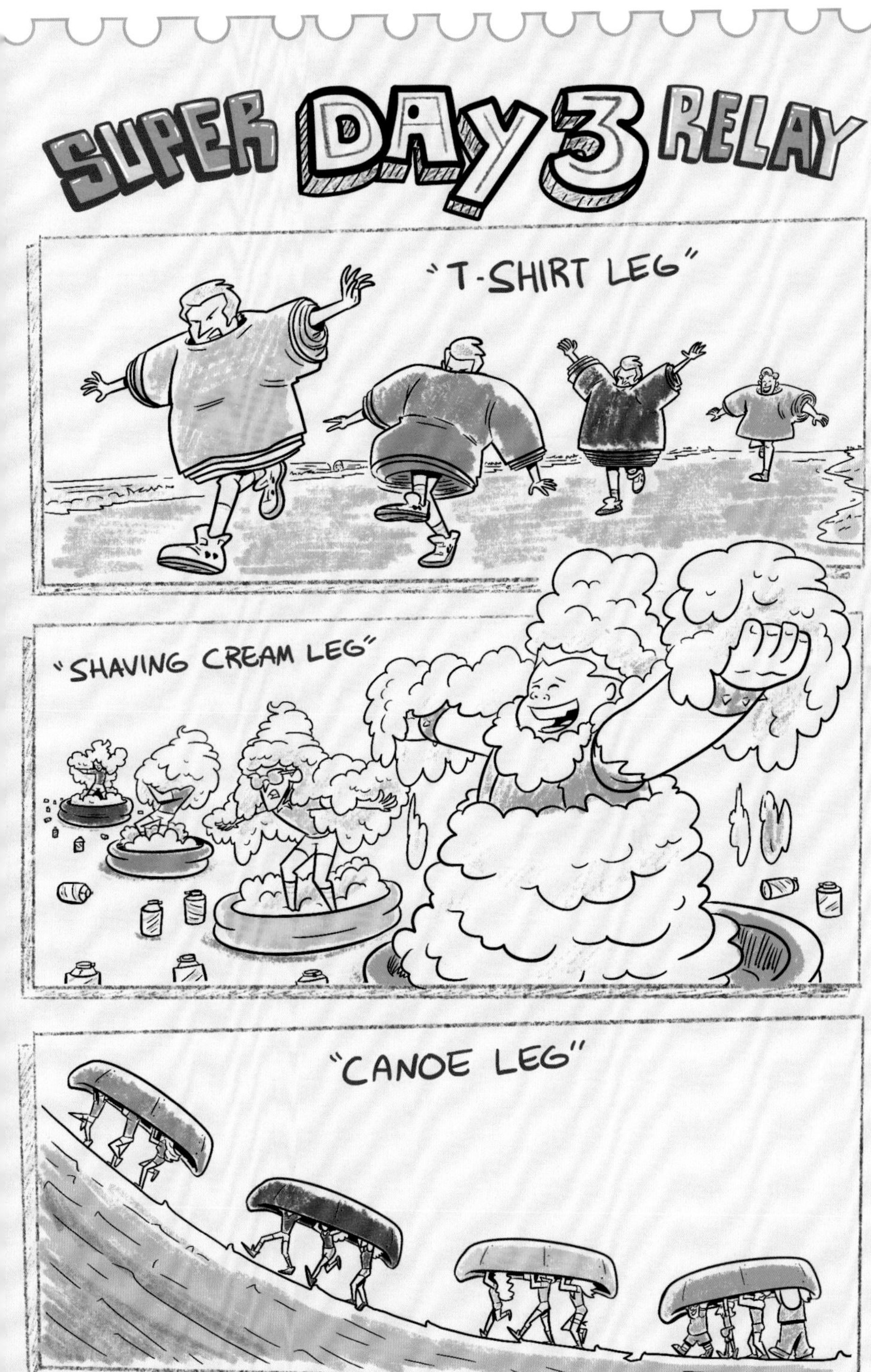
"T-SHIRT LEG"
"SHAVING CREAM LEG"
"CANOE LEG"

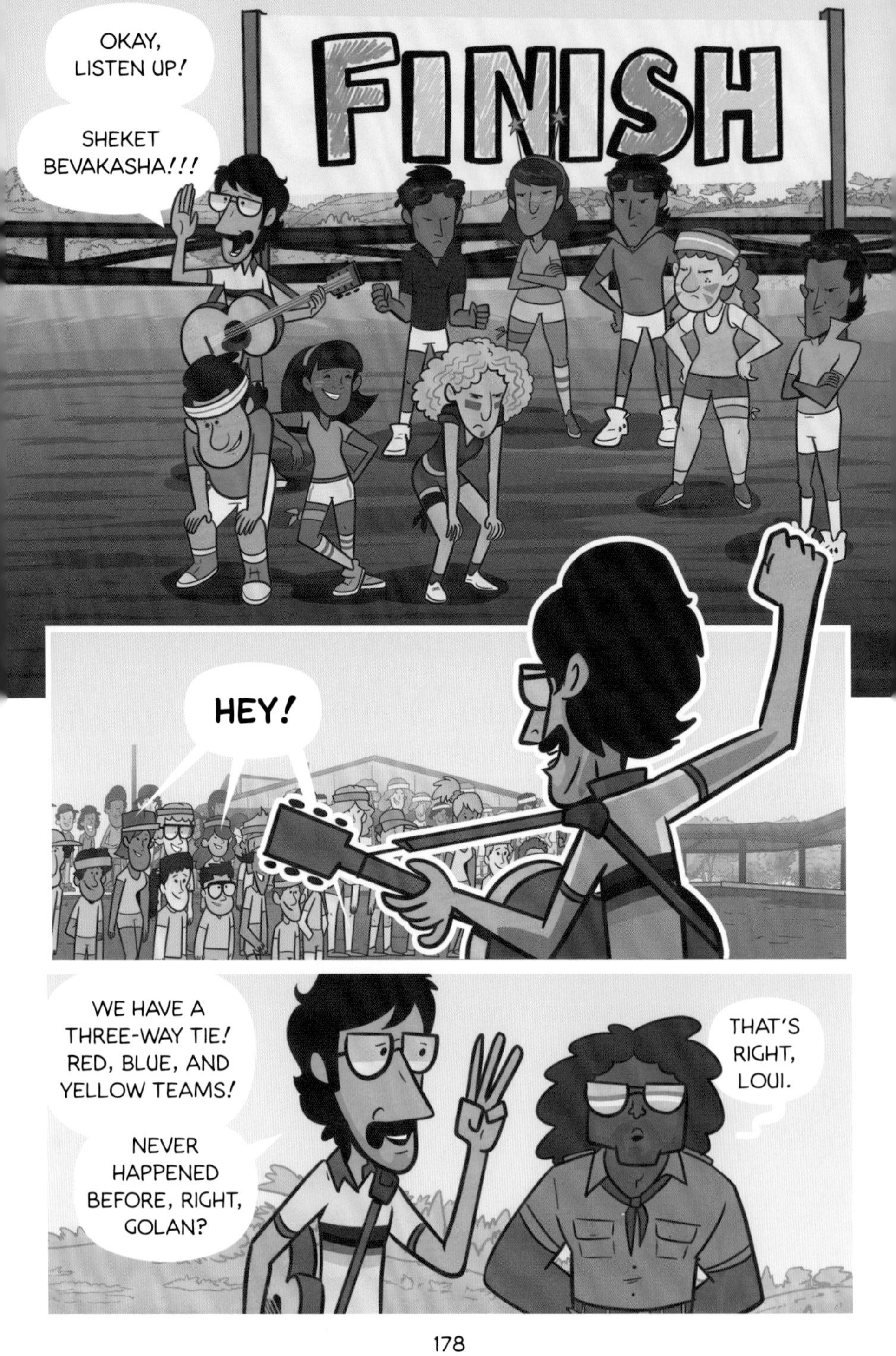
OKAY, LISTEN UP!
SHEKET BEVAKASHA!!!
FINISH
HEY!
WE HAVE A THREE-WAY TIE! RED, BLUE, AND YELLOW TEAMS!
NEVER HAPPENED BEFORE, RIGHT, GOLAN?
THAT'S RIGHT, LOUI.

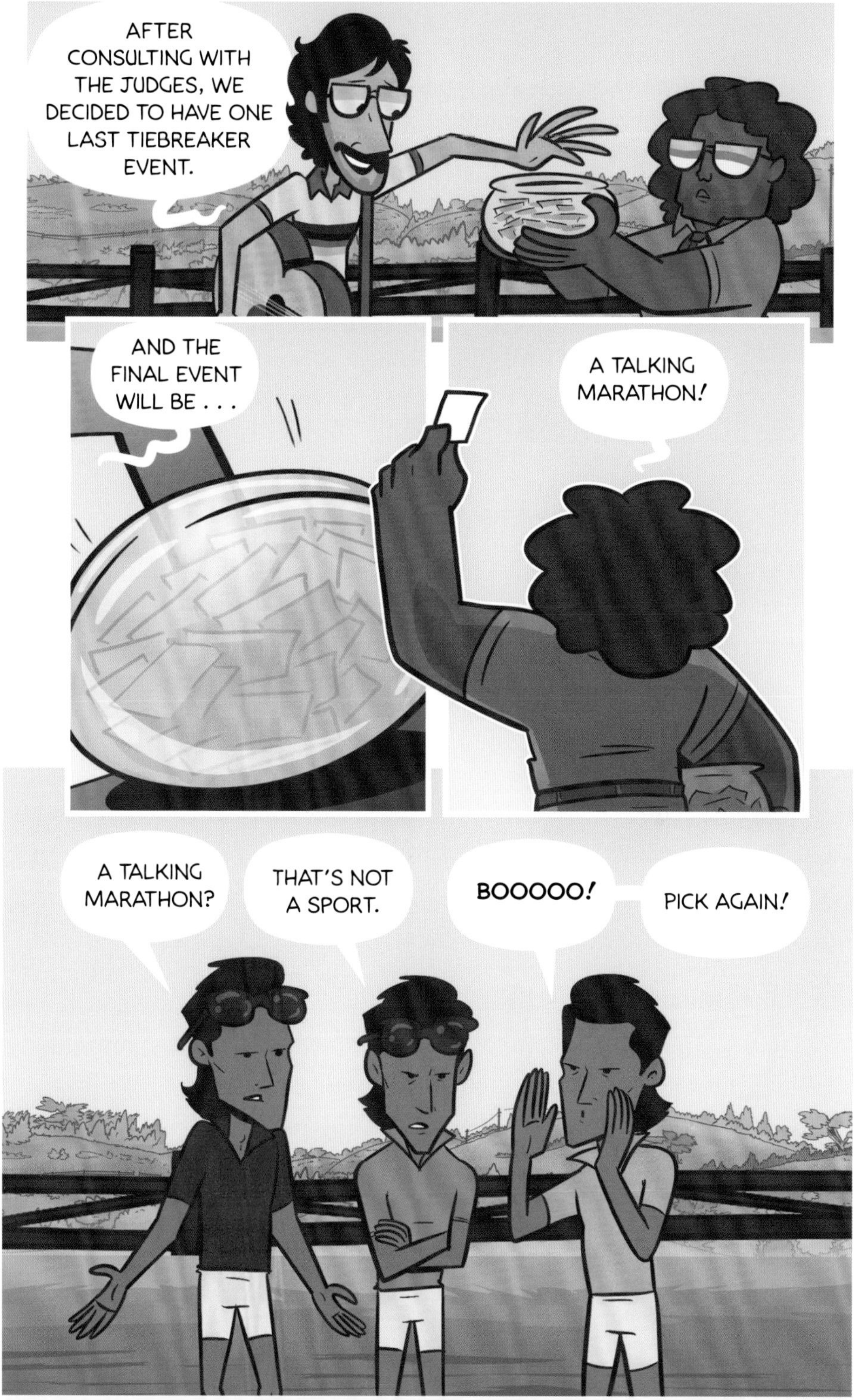
AFTER CONSULTING WITH THE JUDGES, WE DECIDED TO HAVE ONE LAST TIEBREAKER EVENT.
AND THE FINAL EVENT WILL BE . . .
A TALKING MARATHON!
A TALKING MARATHON?
THAT'S NOT A SPORT.
BOOOOO!
PICK AGAIN!

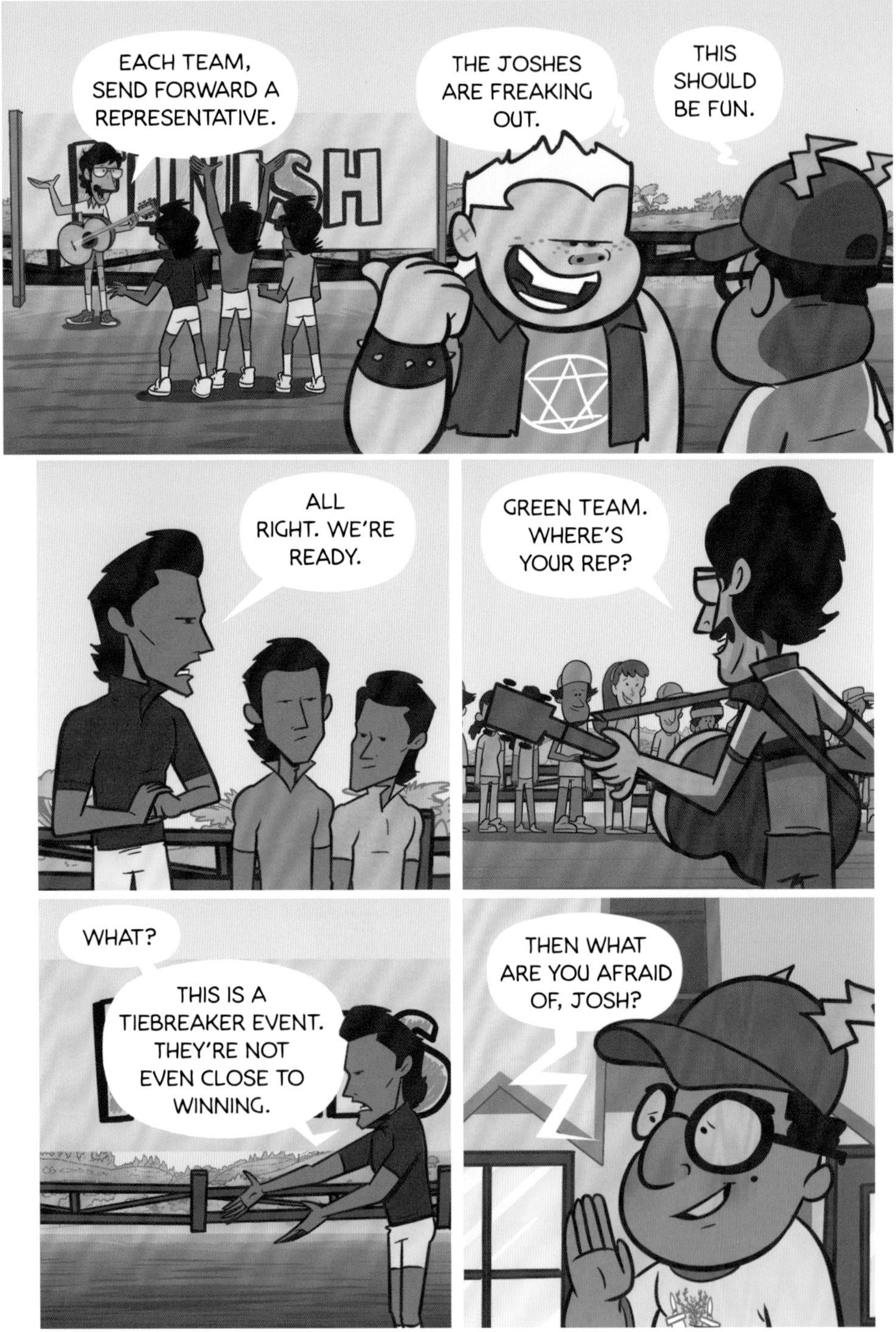
EACH TEAM, SEND FORWARD A REPRESENTATIVE.
THE JOSHES ARE FREAKING OUT.
THIS SHOULD BE FUN.
ALL RIGHT. WE'RE READY.
GREEN TEAM. WHERE'S YOUR REP?
WHAT?
THIS IS A TIEBREAKER EVENT. THEY'RE NOT EVEN CLOSE TO WINNING.
THEN WHAT ARE YOU AFRAID OF, JOSH?

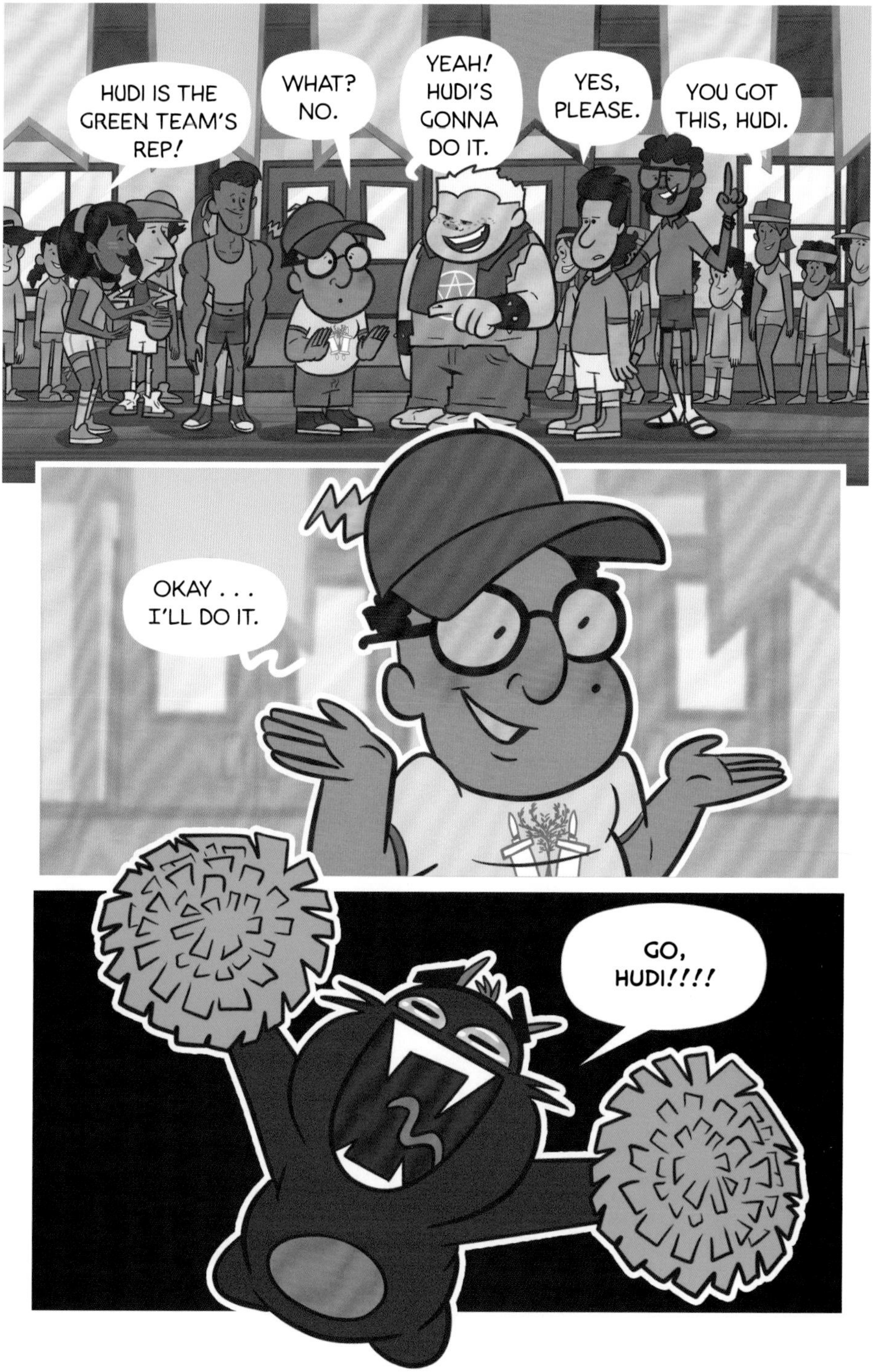
HUDI IS THE GREEN TEAM'S REP!
WHAT? NO.
YEAH! HUDI'S GONNA DO IT.
YES, PLEASE.
YOU GOT THIS, HUDI.
OKAY . . . I'LL DO IT.
GO, HUDI!!!!

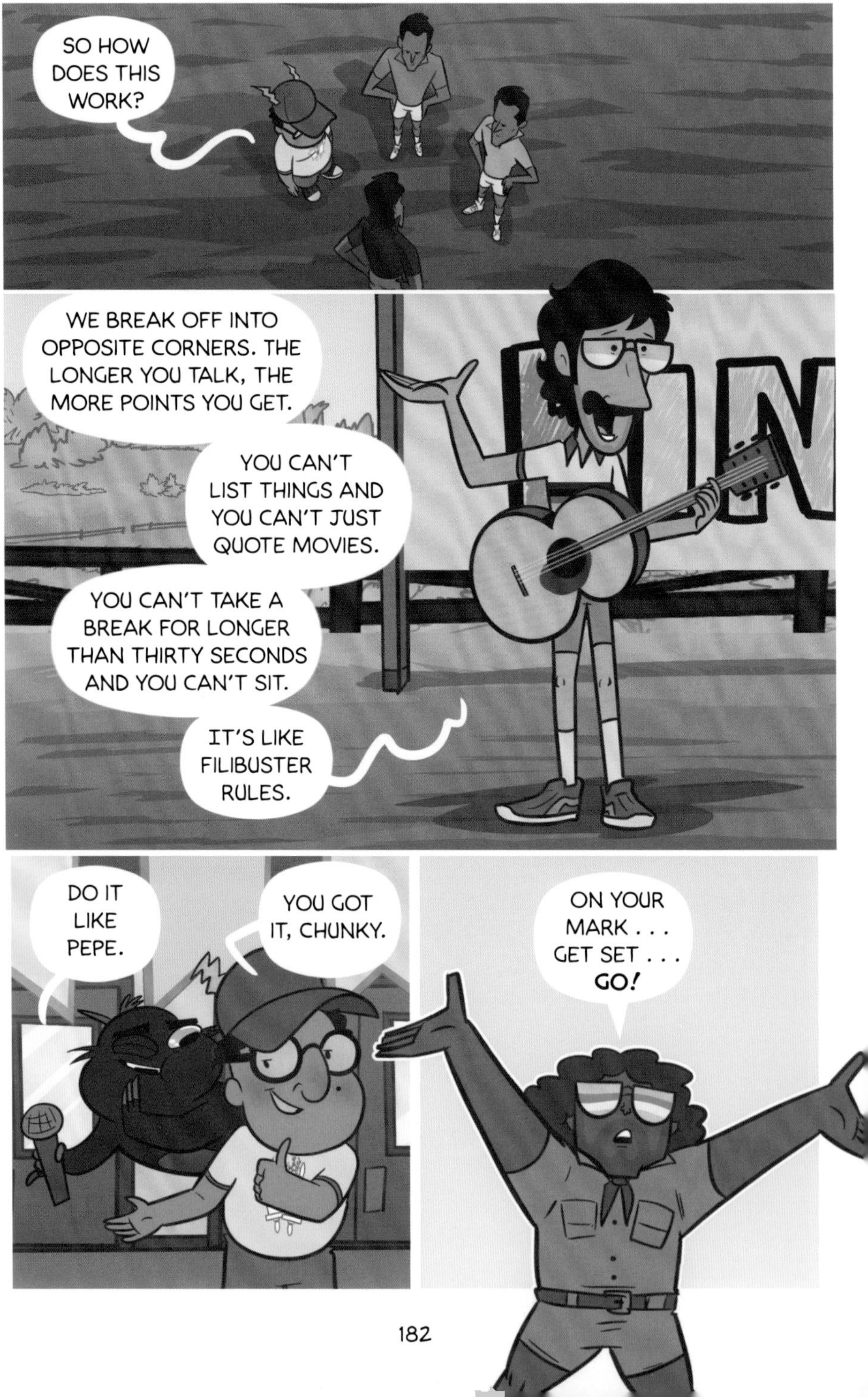
SO HOW DOES THIS WORK?
WE BREAK OFF INTO OPPOSITE CORNERS. THE LONGER YOU TALK, THE MORE POINTS YOU GET.
YOU CAN'T LIST THINGS AND YOU CAN'T JUST QUOTE MOVIES.
YOU CAN'T TAKE A BREAK FOR LONGER THAN THIRTY SECONDS AND YOU CAN'T SIT.
IT'S LIKE FILIBUSTER RULES.
DO IT LIKE PEPE.
YOU GOT IT, CHUNKY.
ON YOUR MARK . . . GET SET . . . **GO!**

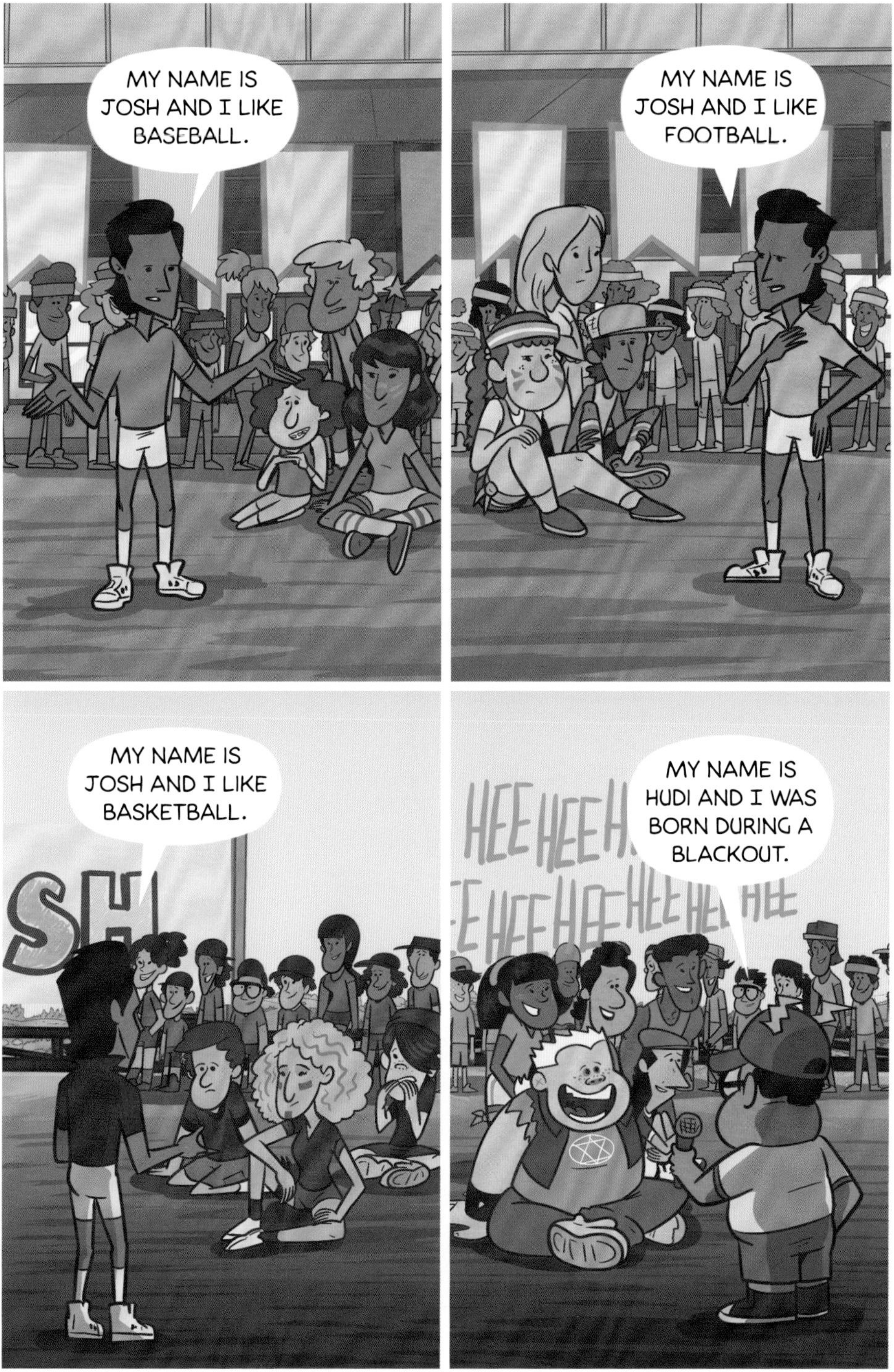
MY NAME IS JOSH AND I LIKE BASEBALL.
MY NAME IS JOSH AND I LIKE FOOTBALL.
MY NAME IS JOSH AND I LIKE BASKETBALL.
SH
HEE HEE
MY NAME IS HUDI AND I WAS BORN DURING A BLACKOUT.
HEE HEE

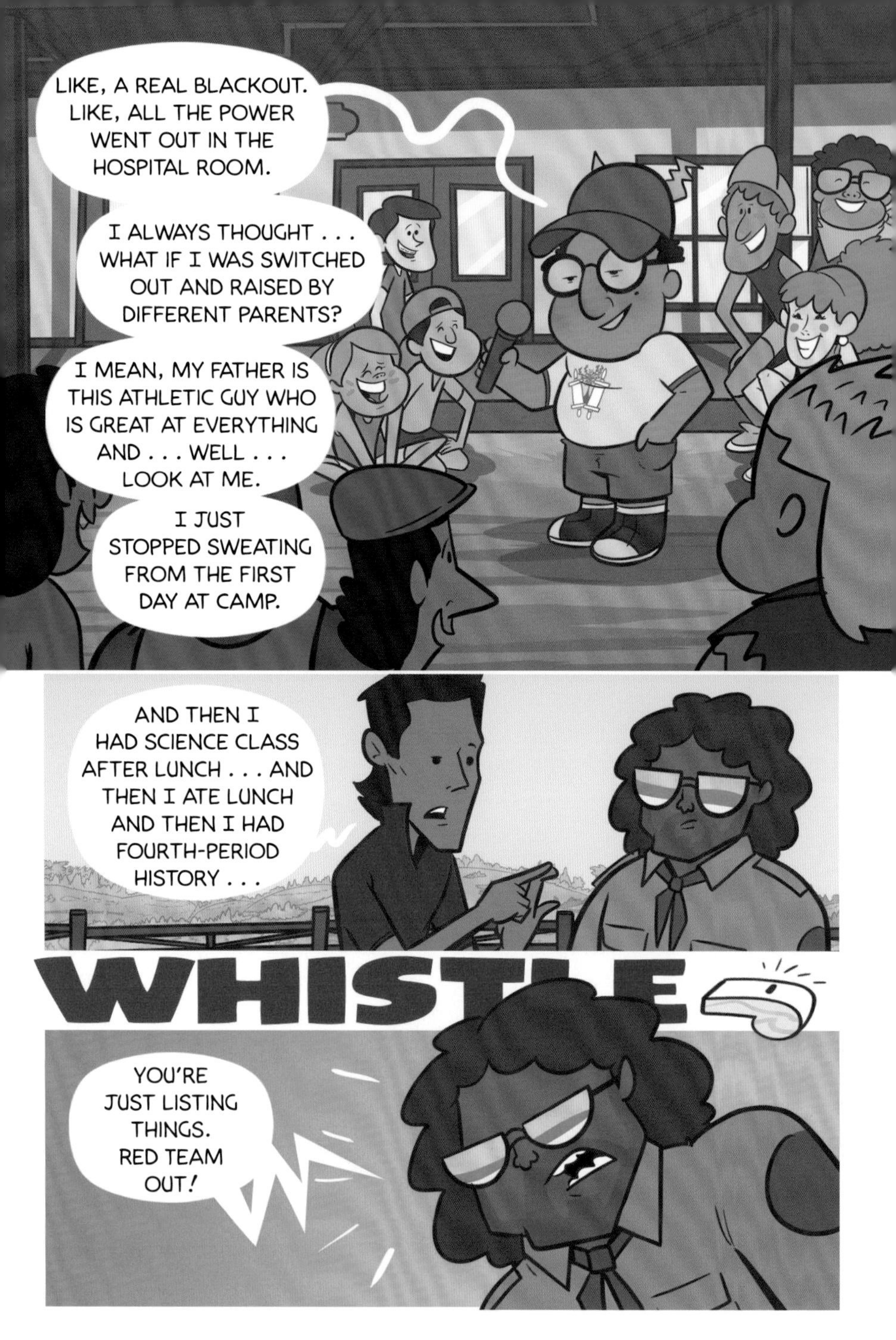
LIKE, A REAL BLACKOUT. LIKE, ALL THE POWER WENT OUT IN THE HOSPITAL ROOM.
I ALWAYS THOUGHT . . . WHAT IF I WAS SWITCHED OUT AND RAISED BY DIFFERENT PARENTS?
I MEAN, MY FATHER IS THIS ATHLETIC GUY WHO IS GREAT AT EVERYTHING AND . . . WELL . . . LOOK AT ME.
I JUST STOPPED SWEATING FROM THE FIRST DAY AT CAMP.
AND THEN I HAD SCIENCE CLASS AFTER LUNCH . . . AND THEN I ATE LUNCH AND THEN I HAD FOURTH-PERIOD HISTORY . . .
WHISTLE
YOU'RE JUST LISTING THINGS. RED TEAM OUT!

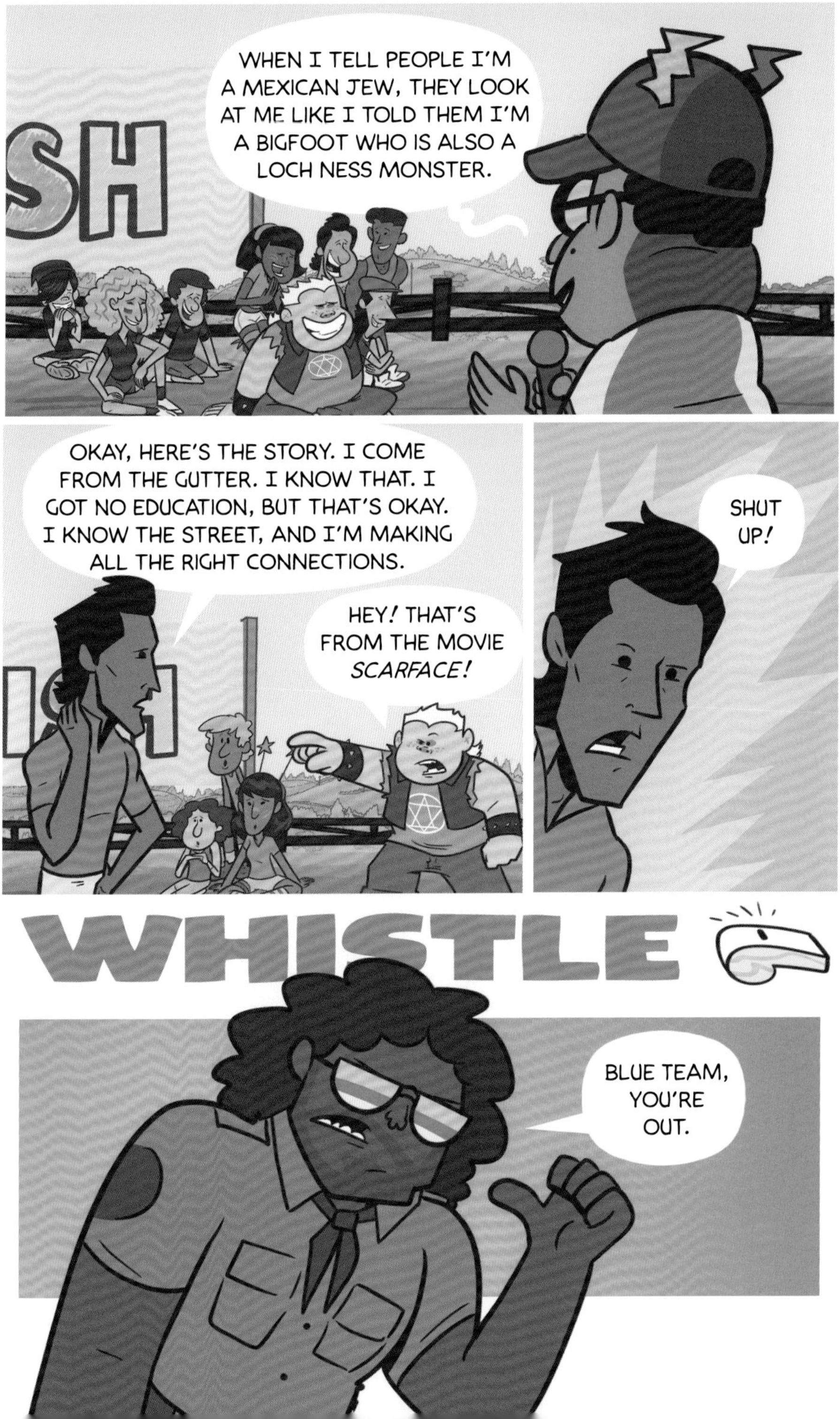

WHEN I TELL PEOPLE I'M A MEXICAN JEW, THEY LOOK AT ME LIKE I TOLD THEM I'M A BIGFOOT WHO IS ALSO A LOCH NESS MONSTER.
OKAY, HERE'S THE STORY. I COME FROM THE GUTTER. I KNOW THAT. I GOT NO EDUCATION, BUT THAT'S OKAY. I KNOW THE STREET, AND I'M MAKING ALL THE RIGHT CONNECTIONS.
HEY! THAT'S FROM THE MOVIE *SCARFACE!*
SHUT UP!
WHISTLE
BLUE TEAM, YOU'RE OUT.

SPEAKING OF BIGFOOTS. IS IT BIGFEETS? OR BIGSFOOT? CAN WE TALK ABOUT FREDDY FOG FOR A SECOND?
DID . . . I MENTION . . . I LIKE BASKETBALL?
HA HA HA
I'M NOT SAYING FREDDY FOG IS THE SCARIEST HUMAN ALIVE . . . BECAUSE HE'S PROBABLY STANDING RIGHT BEHIND ME.
I'M KIDDING. I KID, FREDDY FOG. HE'S A GOOD GUY. HE'LL GET YOU A GREAT DEAL ON OVERPRICED GENERIC SODA. SERIOUSLY, WHERE DO YOU FIND DR. PREPPER COLA?
HA HAHA HAHA
I MEAN, I GUESS IT MAKES SENSE. HIS SHED LOOKS LIKE IT'S FROM THE DOOMSDAY PREPPER COLLECTION AT MACY'S.
HAHAHA HAHAHA HAHAHA HAHAHA
IT'S TRUE!

BUT FREDDY FOG IS LIKE A PERFECT BALANCE TO LOUI.
OH NO! HERE WE GO.
LOUI, I LOVE YOU, BUT YOU KIND OF LOOK LIKE IF THEY SHAVED BIG BIRD AND GAVE HIM A GUITAR.
BUT I CAN'T NOT TALK ABOUT MY BOYS. THE EILAT CREW. I MEAN, LOOK AT US. I'D SAY WE LOOK LIKE THE SWEATHOGS, BUT IT'S PROBABLY NOT KOSHER.
YOU GOT LEWIS, WHO, I'M SORRY, BUT YOU LOOK LIKE YOU'RE THIRTY YEARS OLD. ARE YOU, LIKE, AN UNDERCOVER HEAVY METAL COP OR SOMETHING?
AND LONNIE. LONNIE IS AS TINY AS LEWIS IS LARGE. YOU'RE LIKE LAUREL AND HARDY BUT SOMEHOW MORE PALE. AND THAT OLD-TIMEY NEWSIE CAP ISN'T HELPING. I GOT NEWS FOR YOU: THOSE HATS WENT OUT OF STYLE WITH POLIO.

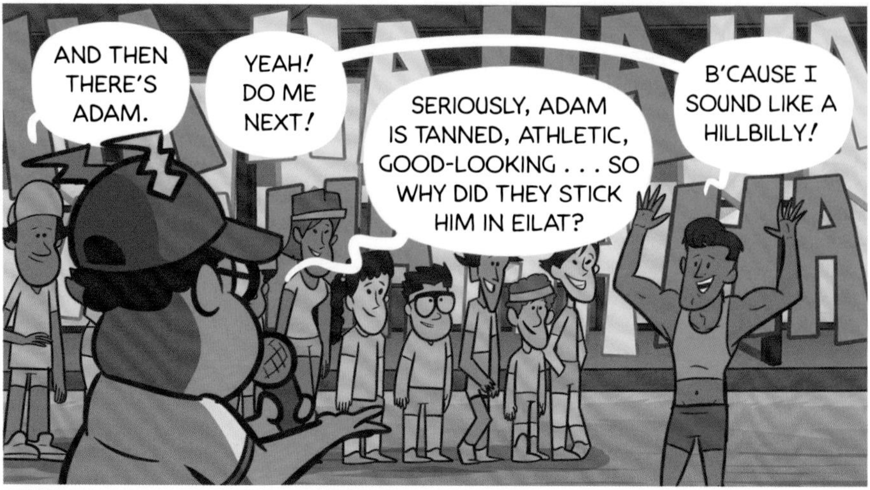
AND THEN THERE'S ADAM.
YEAH! DO ME NEXT!
SERIOUSLY, ADAM IS TANNED, ATHLETIC, GOOD-LOOKING . . . SO WHY DID THEY STICK HIM IN EILAT?
B'CAUSE I SOUND LIKE A HILLBILLY!

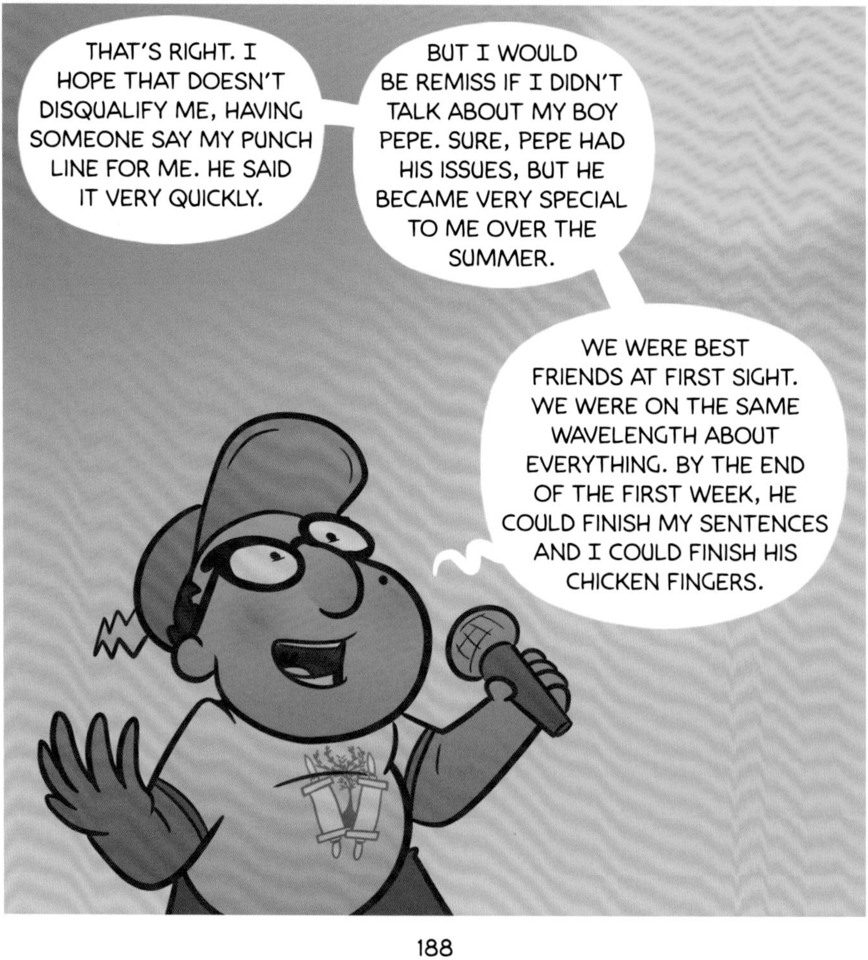
THAT'S RIGHT. I HOPE THAT DOESN'T DISQUALIFY ME, HAVING SOMEONE SAY MY PUNCH LINE FOR ME. HE SAID IT VERY QUICKLY.
BUT I WOULD BE REMISS IF I DIDN'T TALK ABOUT MY BOY PEPE. SURE, PEPE HAD HIS ISSUES, BUT HE BECAME VERY SPECIAL TO ME OVER THE SUMMER.
WE WERE BEST FRIENDS AT FIRST SIGHT. WE WERE ON THE SAME WAVELENGTH ABOUT EVERYTHING. BY THE END OF THE FIRST WEEK, HE COULD FINISH MY SENTENCES AND I COULD FINISH HIS CHICKEN FINGERS.

BUT CAN WE TALK ABOUT THE SOCKS THING? WAS PEPE ALLERGIC TO SOCKS? DID HE FORGET TO PACK SOCKS? I THINK WARREN GAVE HIM **HIS** SOCKS, BUT PEPE DID NOT TAKE THE HINT.
WE ALL BECAME IMMUNE TO THE SMELL AFTER A WHILE. YOU KNOW HOW LOUD NOISES CAN DAMAGE YOUR HEARING? I'M PRETTY SURE NONE OF US WILL BE ABLE TO SMELL FRESHLY BAKED PIE EVER AGAIN.

BUT I THINK THE "NO SOCKS" THING WAS MORE ABOUT REBELLING AGAINST CONFORMITY THAN IT WAS ABOUT ANYTHING ELSE.
THE GUY HAD TO WEAR A UNIFORM ALL YEAR AT BOARDING SCHOOL, SO WHEN HE GETS TO CAMP GREEN, IT'S HIS CHANCE TO GO AGAINST THE GRAIN. TO BE AN INDIVIDUAL. TO STAND OUT.

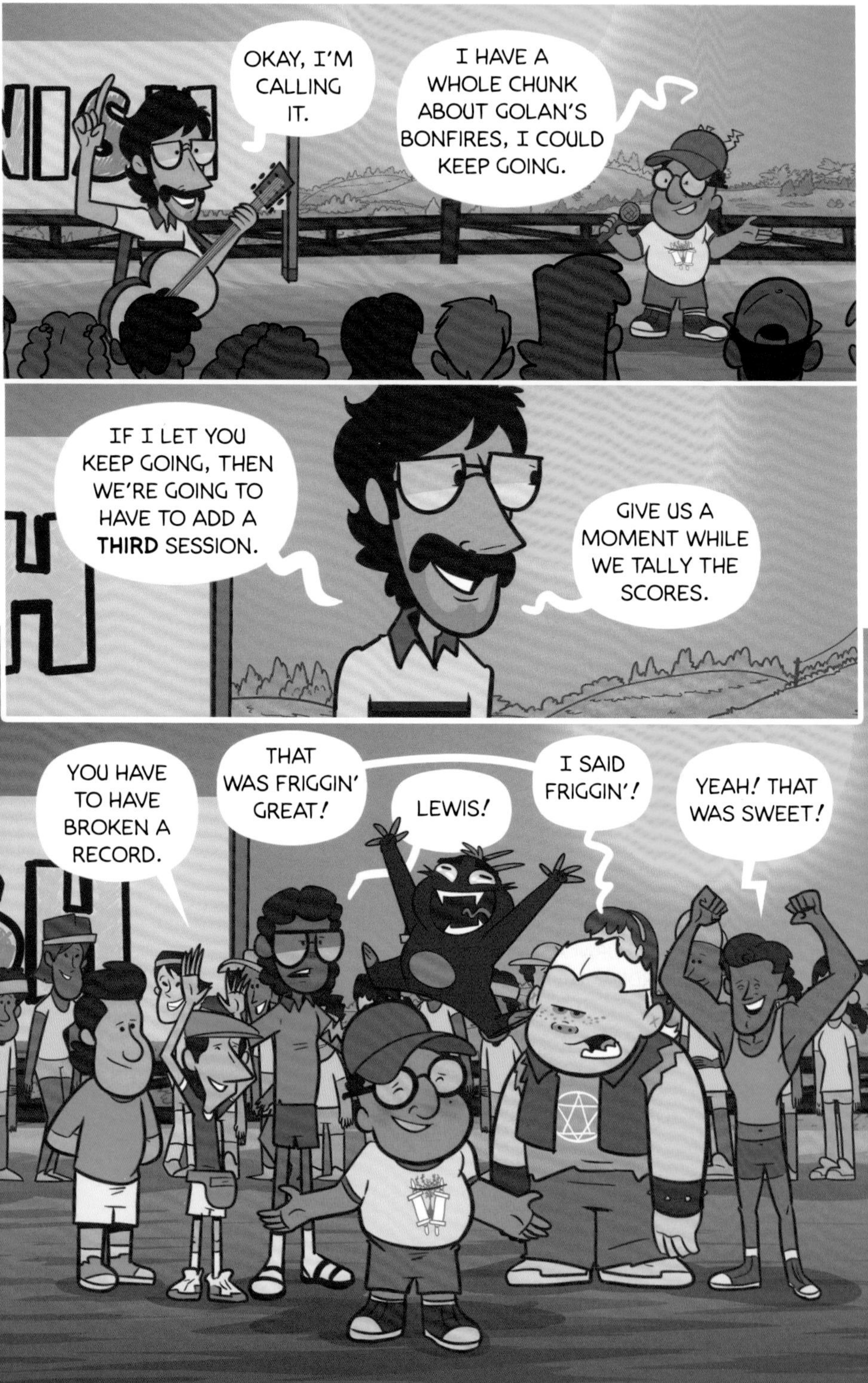
OKAY, I'M CALLING IT.
I HAVE A WHOLE CHUNK ABOUT GOLAN'S BONFIRES, I COULD KEEP GOING.
IF I LET YOU KEEP GOING, THEN WE'RE GOING TO HAVE TO ADD A **THIRD** SESSION.
GIVE US A MOMENT WHILE WE TALLY THE SCORES.
YOU HAVE TO HAVE BROKEN A RECORD.
THAT WAS FRIGGIN' GREAT!
LEWIS!
I SAID FRIGGIN'!
YEAH! THAT WAS SWEET!

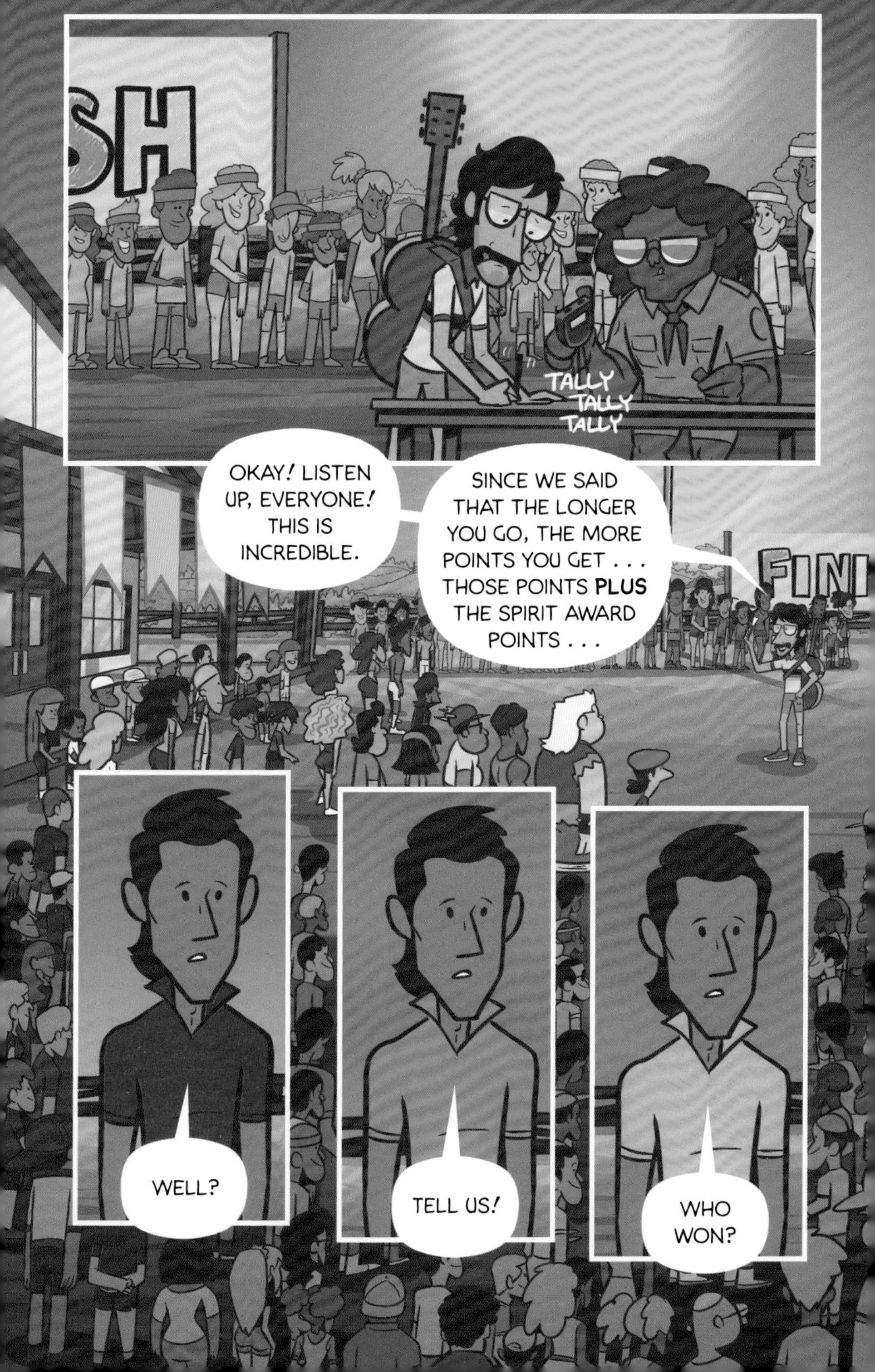
TALLY
TALLY
TALLY
OKAY! LISTEN UP, EVERYONE! THIS IS INCREDIBLE.
SINCE WE SAID THAT THE LONGER YOU GO, THE MORE POINTS YOU GET . . . THOSE POINTS **PLUS** THE SPIRIT AWARD POINTS . . .
FINI
WELL?
TELL US!
WHO WON?

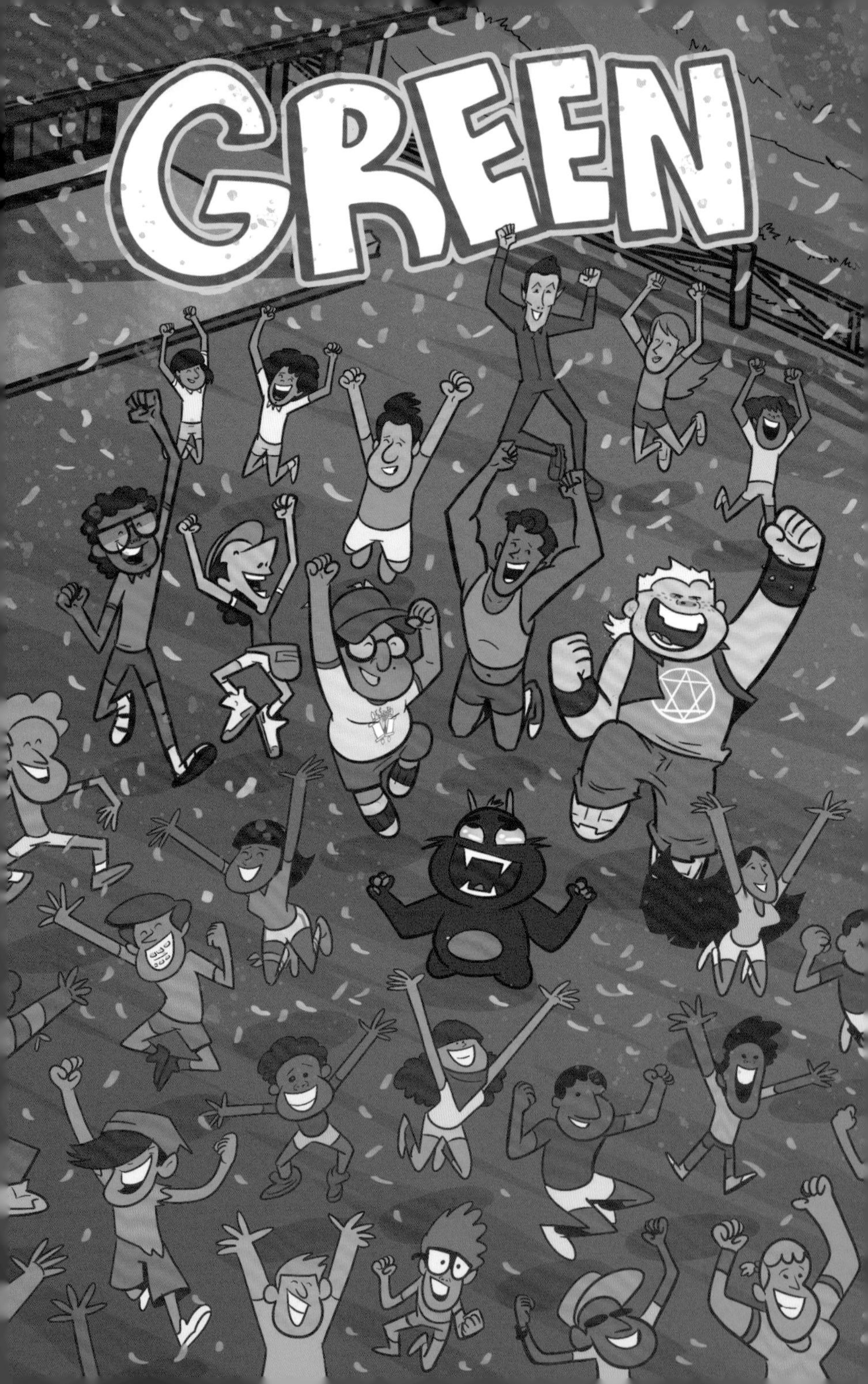
GREEN

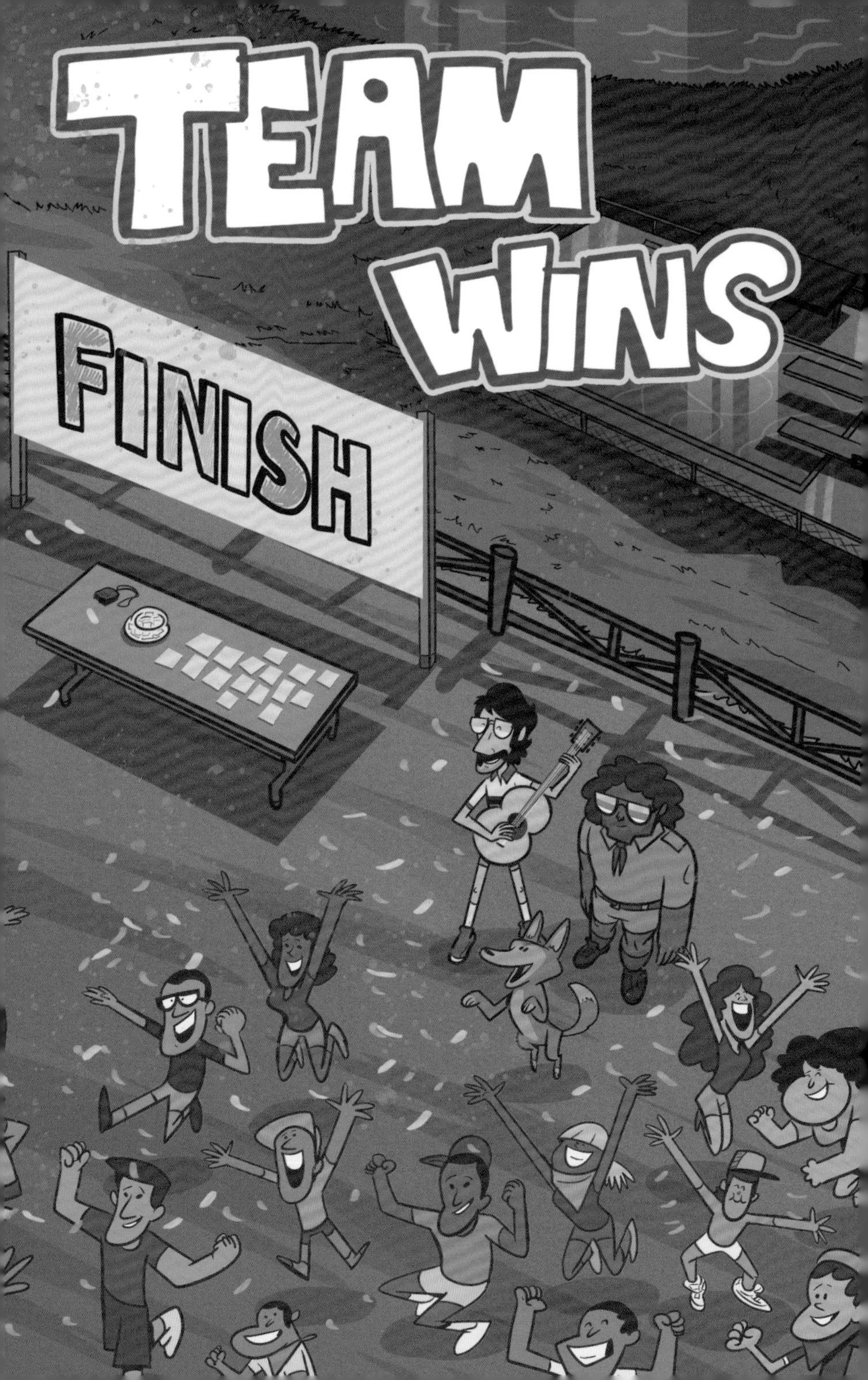
TEAM WINS
FINISH

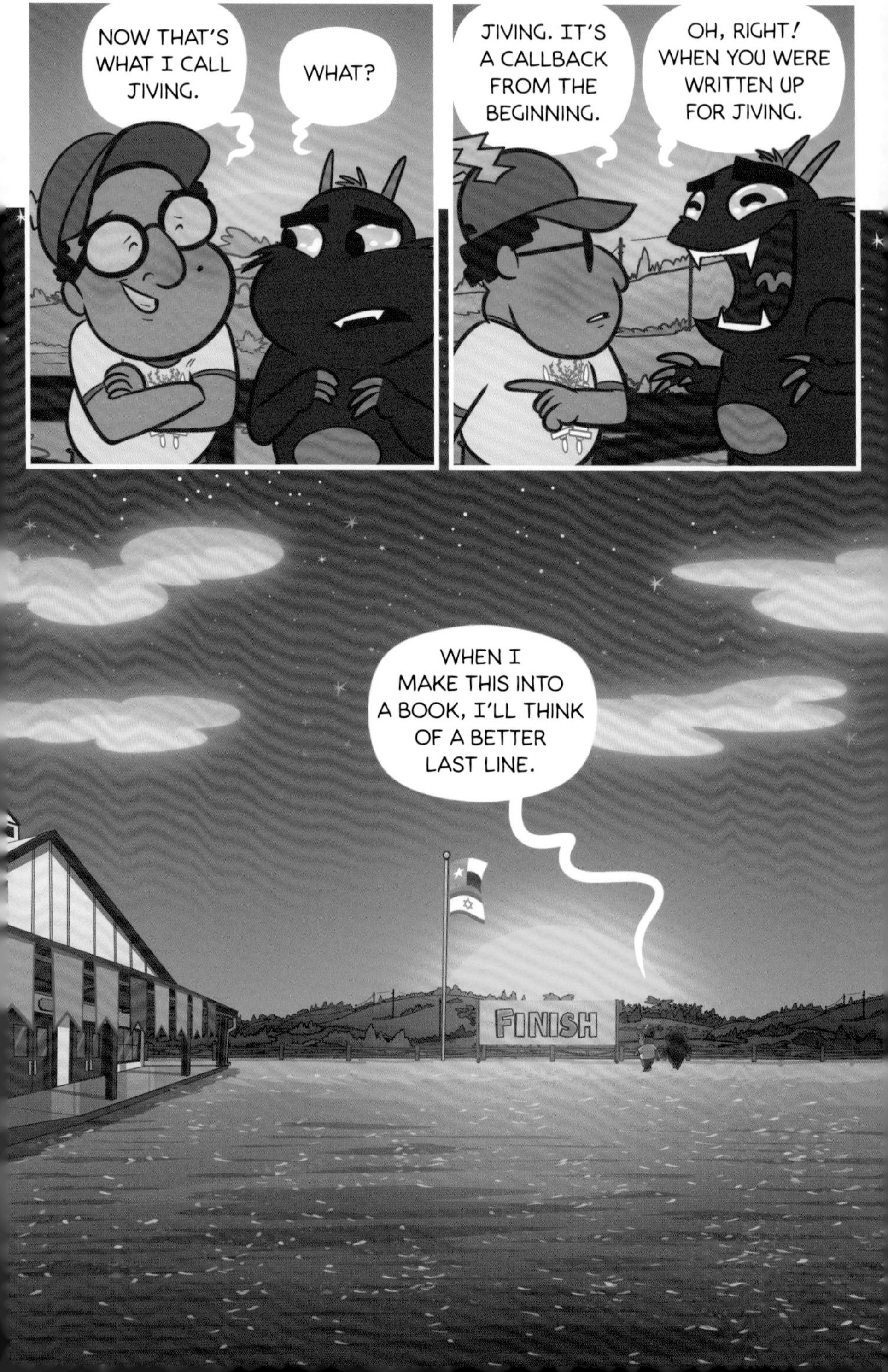
NOW THAT'S WHAT I CALL JIVING.
WHAT?
JIVING. IT'S A CALLBACK FROM THE BEGINNING.
OH, RIGHT! WHEN YOU WERE WRITTEN UP FOR JIVING.
WHEN I MAKE THIS INTO A BOOK, I'LL THINK OF A BETTER LAST LINE.
FINISH

THE LAST DAYS OF CAMP KIND OF BLENDED TOGETHER.
I MADE LIFELONG FRIENDS IN ONLY FOUR WEEKS.
AND I NEVER HAD TO GO TO THE INFIRMARY.
BEST TIME OF MY LIFE.

HUDI on TRIAL

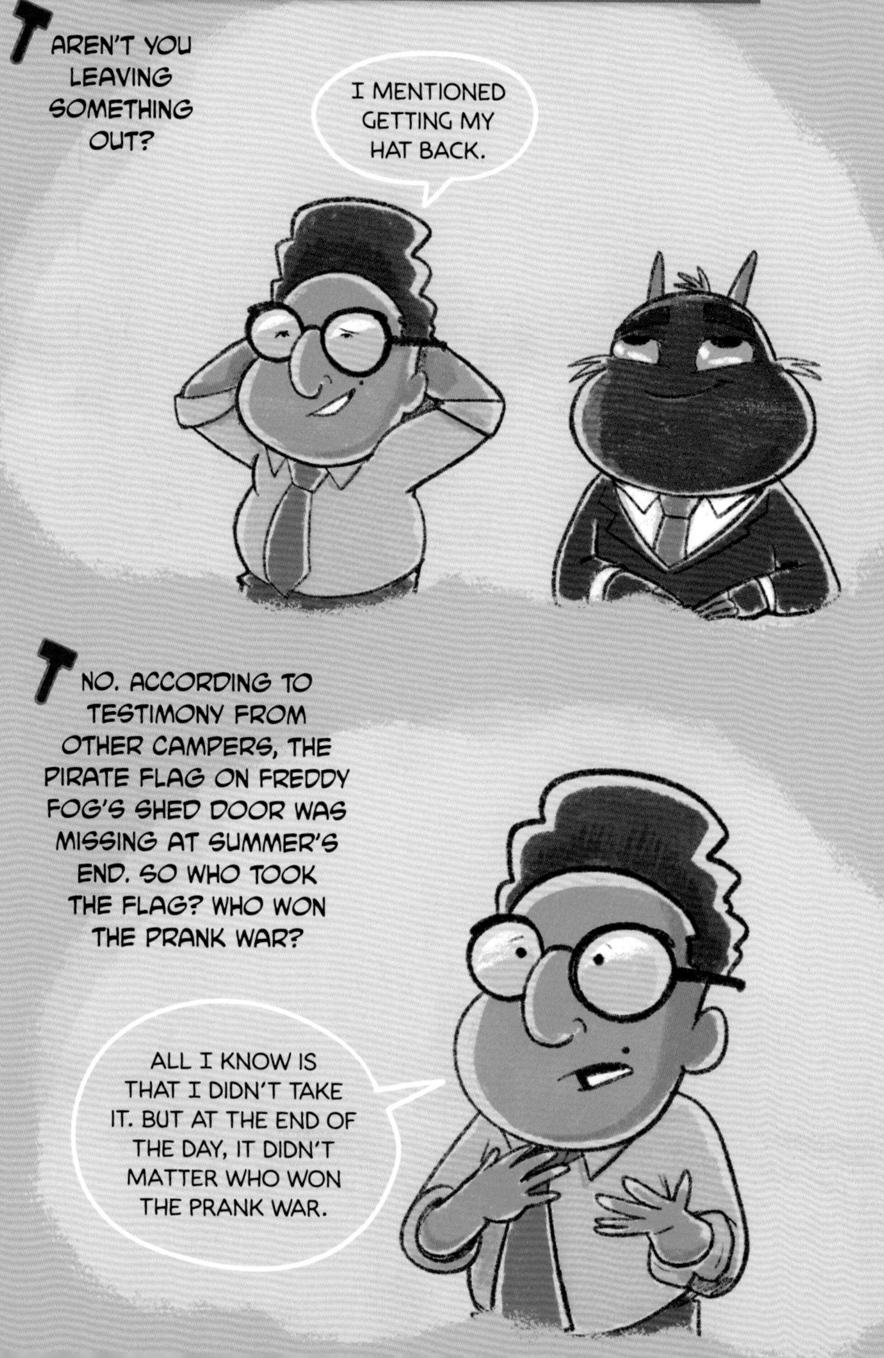
AREN'T YOU LEAVING SOMETHING OUT?
I MENTIONED GETTING MY HAT BACK.
NO. ACCORDING TO TESTIMONY FROM OTHER CAMPERS, THE PIRATE FLAG ON FREDDY FOG'S SHED DOOR WAS MISSING AT SUMMER'S END. SO WHO TOOK THE FLAG? WHO WON THE PRANK WAR?
ALL I KNOW IS THAT I DIDN'T TAKE IT. BUT AT THE END OF THE DAY, IT DIDN'T MATTER WHO WON THE PRANK WAR.

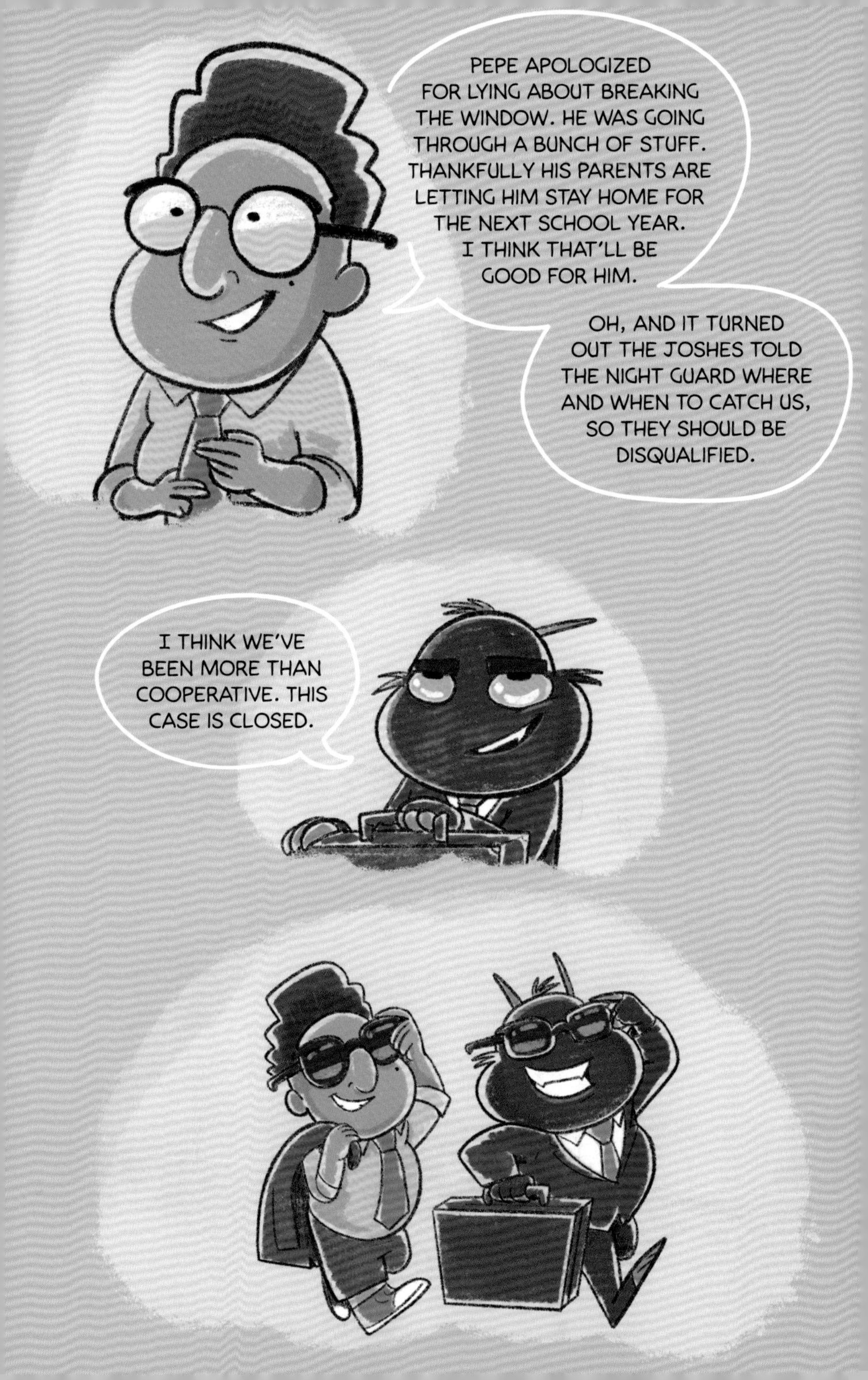
PEPE APOLOGIZED FOR LYING ABOUT BREAKING THE WINDOW. HE WAS GOING THROUGH A BUNCH OF STUFF. THANKFULLY HIS PARENTS ARE LETTING HIM STAY HOME FOR THE NEXT SCHOOL YEAR. I THINK THAT'LL BE GOOD FOR HIM.
OH, AND IT TURNED OUT THE JOSHES TOLD THE NIGHT GUARD WHERE AND WHEN TO CATCH US, SO THEY SHOULD BE DISQUALIFIED.
I THINK WE'VE BEEN MORE THAN COOPERATIVE. THIS CASE IS CLOSED.

CHAPTER SEVEN
BACK TO SCHOOL

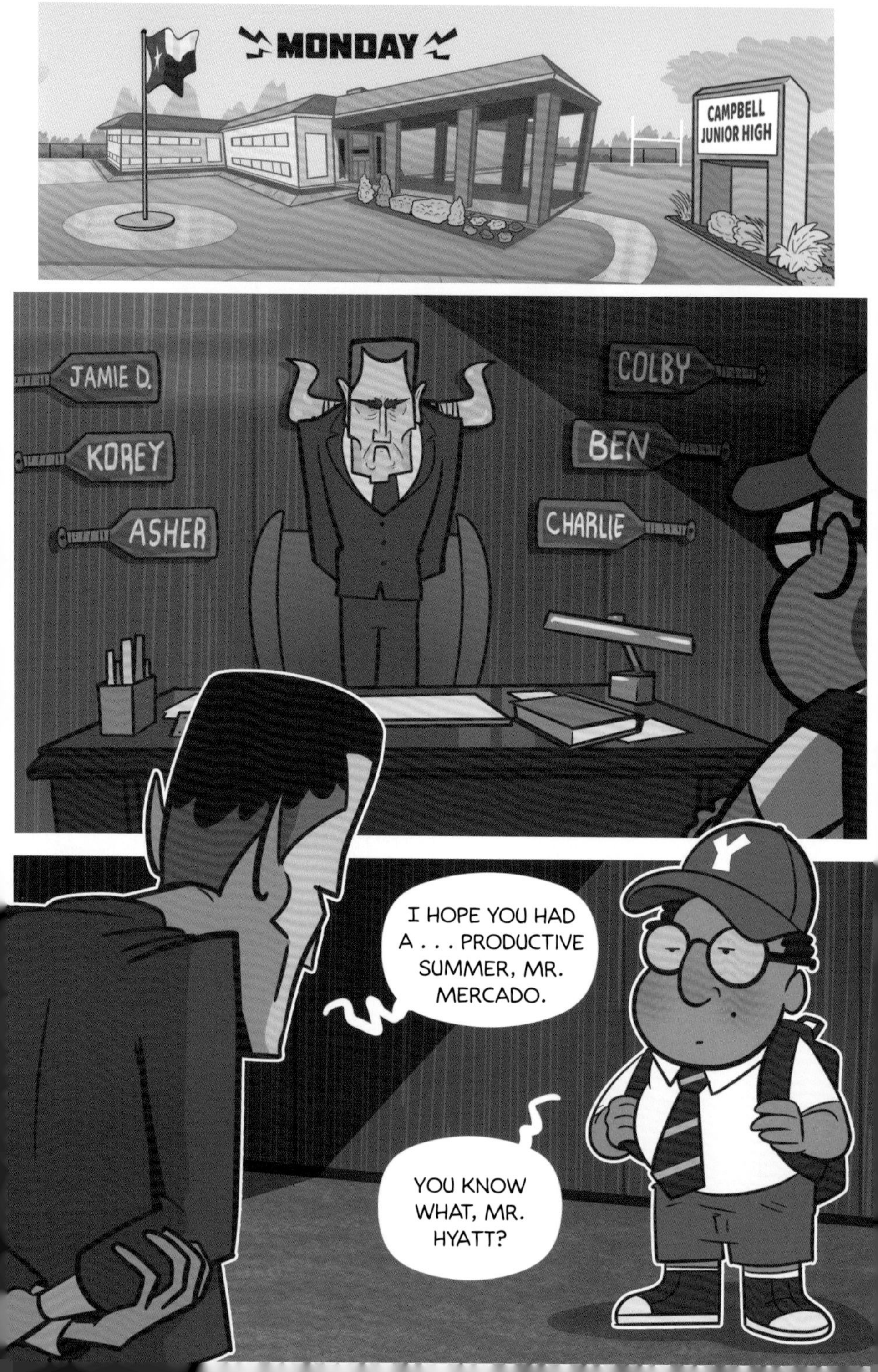
MONDAY
CAMPBELL JUNIOR HIGH
JAMIE D.
KOREY
ASHER
COLBY
BEN
CHARLIE
I HOPE YOU HAD A . . . PRODUCTIVE SUMMER, MR. MERCADO.
YOU KNOW WHAT, MR. HYATT?

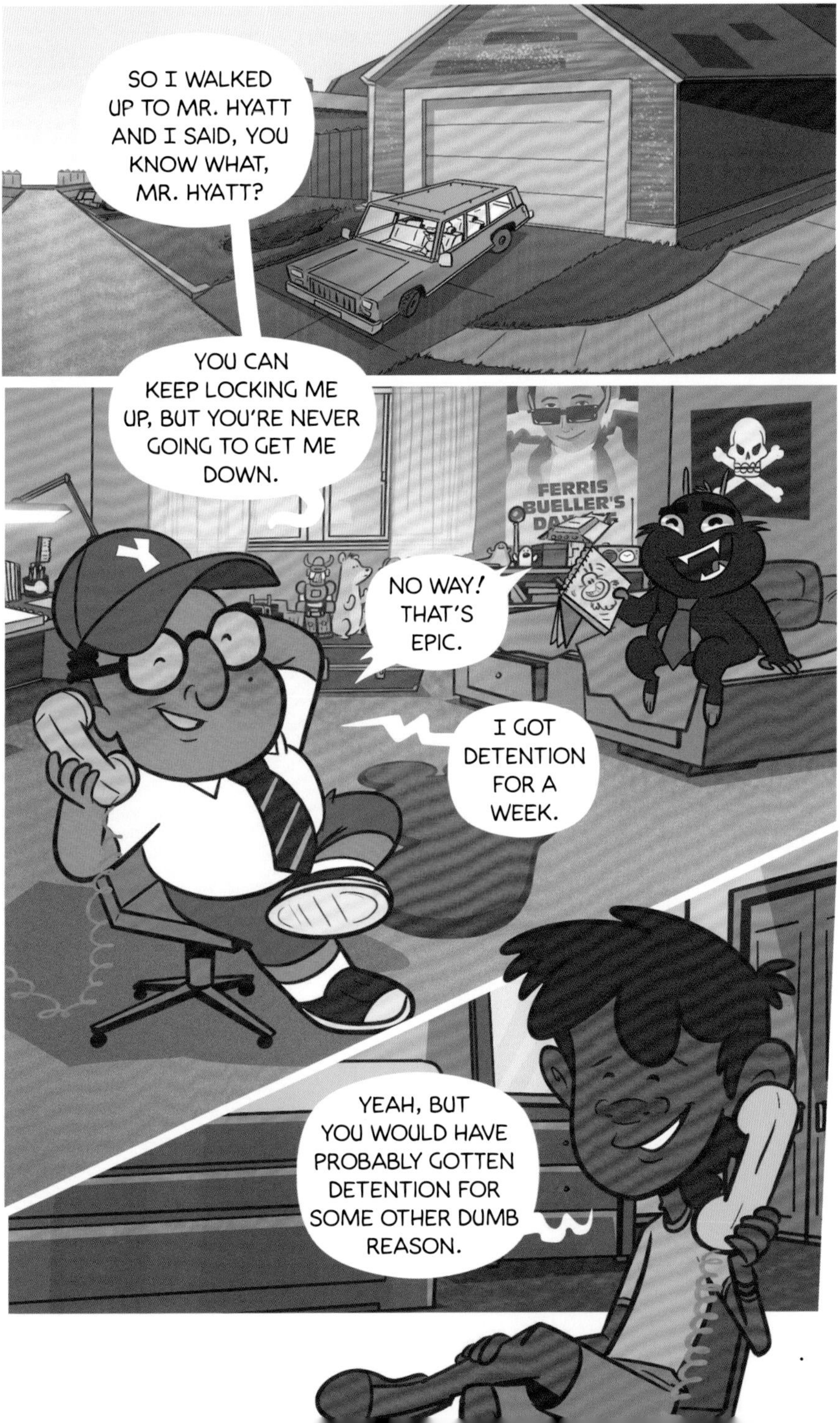
SO I WALKED UP TO MR. HYATT AND I SAID, YOU KNOW WHAT, MR. HYATT?
YOU CAN KEEP LOCKING ME UP, BUT YOU'RE NEVER GOING TO GET ME DOWN.
FERRIS BUELLER'S
NO WAY! THAT'S EPIC.
I GOT DETENTION FOR A WEEK.
YEAH, BUT YOU WOULD HAVE PROBABLY GOTTEN DETENTION FOR SOME OTHER DUMB REASON.

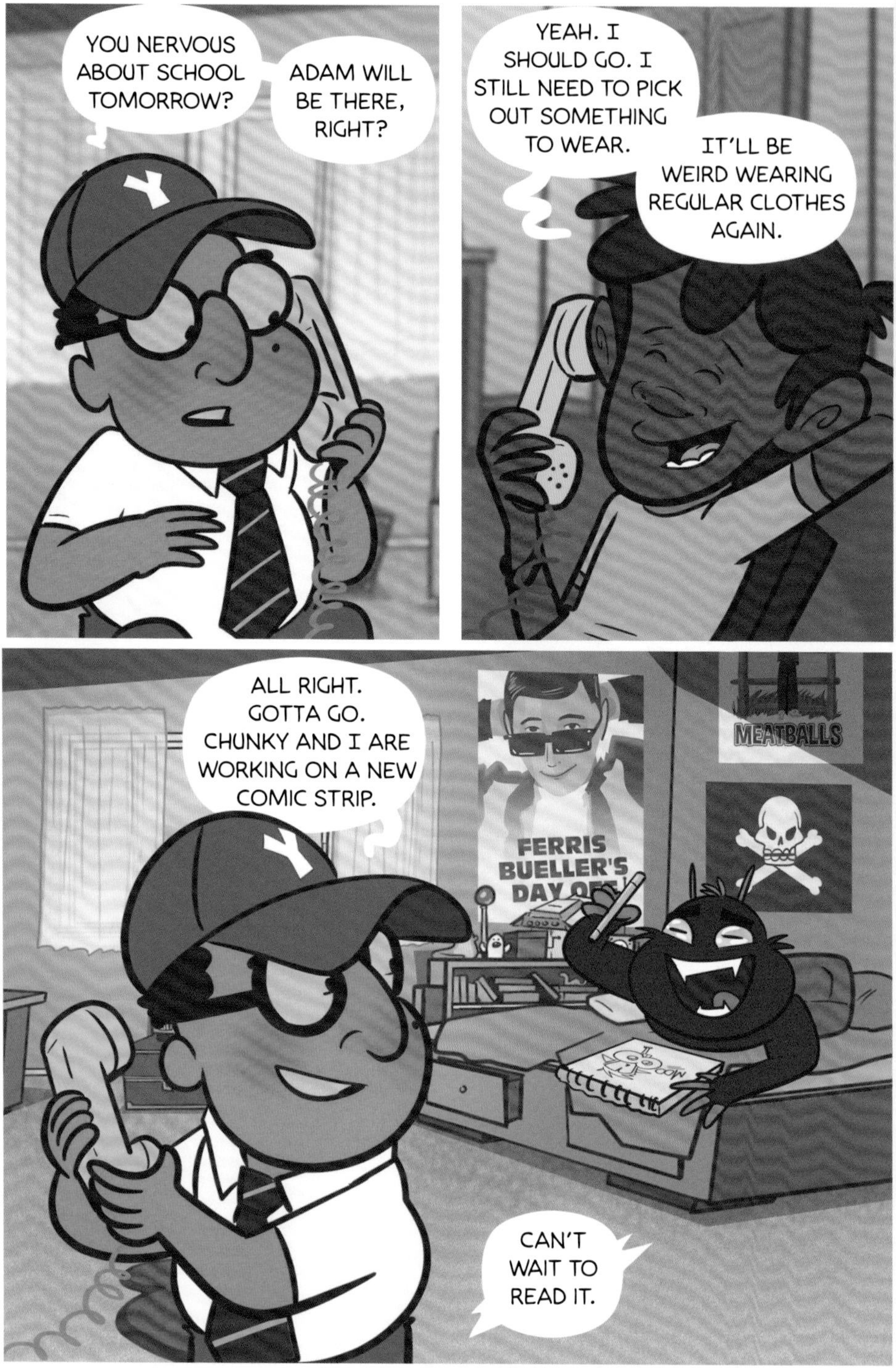
YOU NERVOUS ABOUT SCHOOL TOMORROW?
ADAM WILL BE THERE, RIGHT?
YEAH. I SHOULD GO. I STILL NEED TO PICK OUT SOMETHING TO WEAR.
IT'LL BE WEIRD WEARING REGULAR CLOTHES AGAIN.
ALL RIGHT. GOTTA GO. CHUNKY AND I ARE WORKING ON A NEW COMIC STRIP.
FERRIS BUELLER'S DAY OFF
MEATBALLS
CAN'T WAIT TO READ IT.

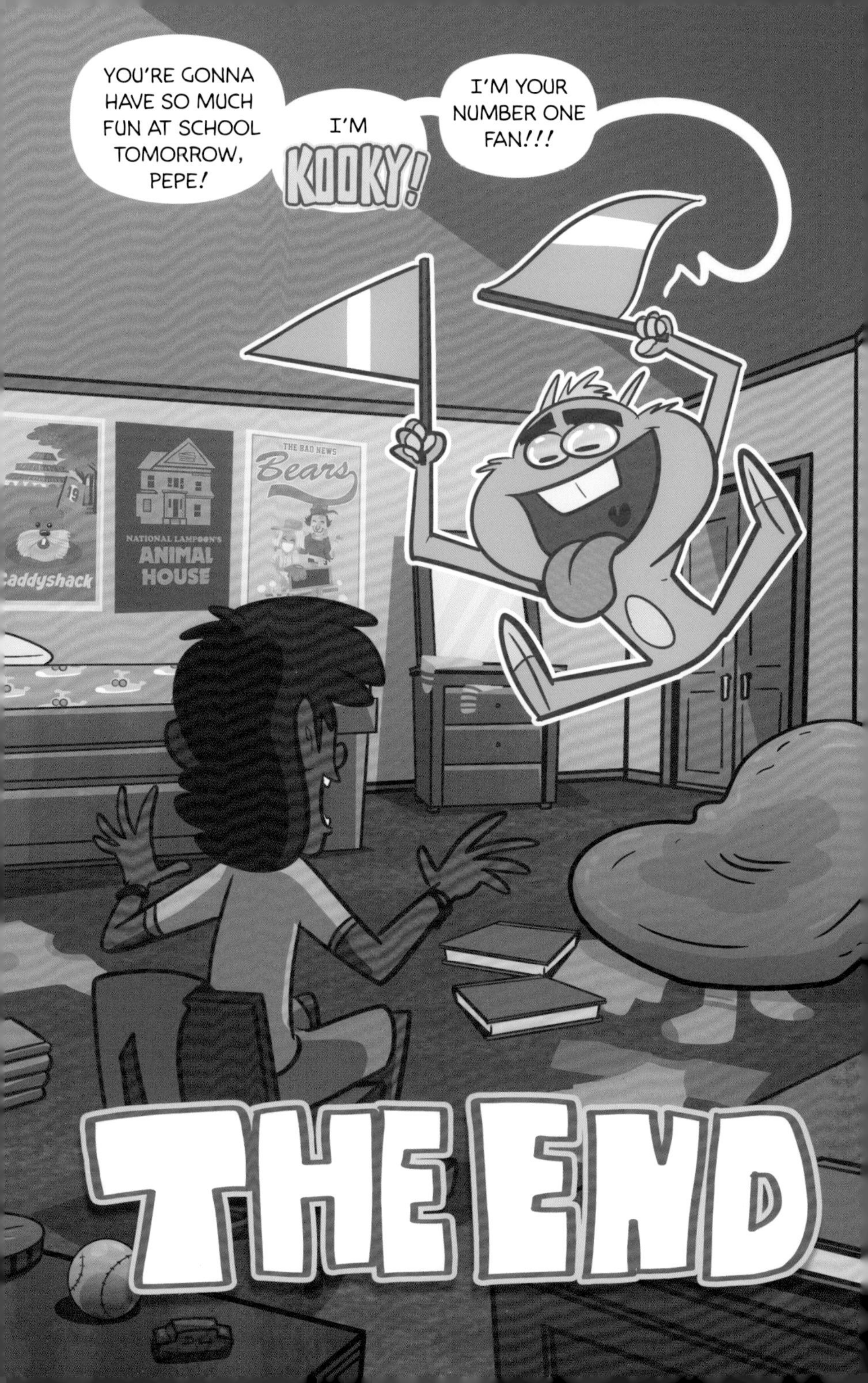
YOU'RE GONNA HAVE SO MUCH FUN AT SCHOOL TOMORROW, PEPE!
I'M KOOKY!
I'M YOUR NUMBER ONE FAN!!!
THE BAD NEWS Bears
NATIONAL LAMPOON'S ANIMAL HOUSE
addyshack
THE END

A NOTE FROM PEPE GUZMAN

I am so honored to play such a prominent role in this highly entertaining book. As this story contains many true events, I just wish to point out that my bad behavior was all my own and not due to any indifference by my parents. I am one of those lucky people who knew that my parents loved me dearly.

I would also like to point out that if you asked a hundred of our fellow campers who was funnier, me or Yehudi, all of them would have said Yehudi. The part where people lined up to have Yehudi make fun of them happened daily. Never did someone speak to Yehudi and not smile. To put it simply, he brightened everyone's day with laughter and is the most popular person I have ever met. To be Robin to his Batman was the absolute pinnacle of camp life for me and something I treasure to this day.

This book and its predecessor (and all Yehudi's books!) not only show his great talent and humor but also his gift of making one smile, laugh, and just feel good.

−Pepe Guzman

A NOTE FROM YEHUDI

The real-life Chunky in my camp experience was my lifelong friend Lonnie Levitan. He was actually the third amigo and was the one on the shabbat stage with Pepe and me during the infamous Stars and Clouds Incident. It's still our inside joke that cracks us up to this day. While we did carry a flagpole during a lightning storm, I invented the scene in Freddy Fog's shed. There was a real-life groundskeeper for the camp, and I did buy a six-pack of RC Cola from him for twenty dollars, but his persona and his backstory were fictionalized for this book. To me he represents the misunderstood boogeyman, which ties into the way I felt I was treated in school.

If *Chunky* was about my journey as a middle grader finding my funny, then *Chunky Goes to Camp* is about finding my people. Meeting Pepe Guzman at the Jewish summer camp was like meeting an imaginary friend in real life. It's a miracle to meet someone and instantly be on the same wavelength, especially when it comes to comedy. Being a funny kid was great, but it also put a target on my back when it came to teachers who didn't get me.

For some reason I spent a lot of time in detention as a kid. I was not a bad kid, but the faculty of my school seemed to want to convince me I was. In fact, I was sent to detention for "jiving," and I was given the choice of being paddled by my vice principal or given more detention. I'm pretty sure they don't paddle kids anymore in public school, and it seemed barbaric at the time. I do have to say that I did have a handful of teachers who did get me and appreciated my humor.

Greene Family Camp was such a formative time in my life. My fellow bunkmates were all such oddballs, just like me. We were all weirdos. We didn't feel like we fit in with the other bunks, and I loved that about us. If any of you reading this book feel like you don't belong, I promise that you have a special tribe of people waiting for you somewhere, ready to cheer you on. Find your Chunky.

Special thanks to:

Ben Rosenthal
Amy Ryan
Laura Mock
Caitlin Lonning
Kristen Eckhardt
Alexandra Rakaczki
Charlie Olsen
Loui Dobin
Ludmilla and Gerardo
The Hoodis family
The Warfields
The Pueblitz Boys
Raina Telgemeier
Dave, Scoot & Brandon
Colby Sharp

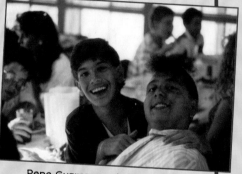

Pepe Guzman and Yehudi Mercado

Wynnie, Yehudi, Gerardo (father), and Yoni Mercado